REAP THE WHIRLWIND

BY

BILLY BENNETT

Saber Books

BILLY BENNETT

Published by Saber Books

BOOKS BY BILLY BENNETT

BY FORCE OF ARMS
REBEL EMPIRE
REAPING THE WHIRLWIND
STARSTORM
BATTLE LINE

FORTHCOMING BOOKS BY BILLY BENNETT

THE LAST HURRAH
BARBAROSSA
FLAGS AND GLORY

Dedicated to my beloved Grandfather,
Billy Bennett

***

Thank you Granddaddy for always believing in me and for so many wonderful memories. I have no doubt that it is from you that I get much of my strength, creativity, and independent spirit.

BILLY BENNETT

I

The CSS Texas crashed through a large wave that hit the massive battleship head on. At her bow, the Confederate Battle Flag fluttered with such intensity in the howling wind, that it seemed on the verge of being torn from its mast head. The pride of the Confederate States Navy was one of the heaviest battleships afloat, but the raging storm around them was strong enough to rock them back and forth like a row boat.

"You alright in there, Jeb?"

From inside the head (as sailors called the latrine) Captain Blake Ramsey could hear his young Yeoman Jeb Ferguson puking his guts out.

"Yeah...Cap..." his sentence was cut short by the renewed sound of Navy chow erupting out of him like a putrid volcano. In seas as rough as what they were enduring, even lifelong sailors could get sea sick. For a young pup like Yeoman Ferguson on one of his first voyages...

The sound of more violent heaves came from behind the door. Shaking his head, Ramsey turned away and headed down the narrow corridor that let him back onto the bridge. Through the view ports, Ramsey watched a massive bolt of lightning flash across the sky. A large muscular sailor was manning the wheel. The ship lurched as another large wave crashed into them. Ramsey braced himself in the door way. Several of the officers and crew weren't as quick, and they toppled off to the starboard. The helmsman remained rooted at his post, latched onto the wheel with all of his strength.

"Leave it to the politicians to fight a war in the middle of hurricane season," said Commander Ray Brisk as he pulled himself back to his feet. He rubbed his head where he'd smashed into the wall, then made his way back over to the navigation table.

Ramsey nodded. The tropical storm they were passing through wasn't actually a hurricane, but it was close enough. The chronometer read 1300 hours, but the sky was dark with thick black clouds. Ramsey pulled a cigar from his gray uniform coat, struck a match and got it going. He then made his way over to the maps.

"Assuming we come through this storm intact, we should make the coast of Spanish Sahara in about two more days," said Brisk.

Ramsey nodded and exhaled a large cloud of smoke as he examined the chart. His eyes came to rest on the small port of Villa Cisneros.

"I wonder why we're being sent all the way over here when all the fighting is back in Cuba?" asked Brisk.

"I think Richmond is trying to send a couple of messages to the Spanish. First we're showing them that our forces have reach. If we can hit the Spanish Sahara we can hit Spain itself. Second, we're trying to remind the Spanish that they have other possessions to worry about. Maybe they'll come to their senses and call it quits before they lose more than just Cuba."

Brisk swore derisively. "Why would we want a useless stretch of sand on the African coast like the Spanish Sahara?"

Ramsey took a long, contemplative drag on his Cuban cigar, then exhaled a large cloud of smoke. "Because there's a lot of people who want to have a place to ship all the niggers if slavery ever does end. I've heard talk for years about the Confederacy obtaining a possession in Africa."

"Sounds like a good idea to me," replied Brisk. "We can start shipping all the free-niggers back right away as far as I'm concerned. The South is a white man's country, nothing else but…"

Suddenly, the ship lurched again. Ramsey and Brisk both grabbed onto the map table which was bolted to the floor. A few moments later, the ship righted herself.

"It's a good thing you ordered us to take on extra ballast."

Ramsey nodded. All the extra weight was killing their fuel efficiency, but only a fool would risk capsizing to save a few tons of coal.

"Sending all the negroes to Africa is unfeasible if you ask me," said Ramsey. "There's not enough boats and ships in the Confederacy to do it. They'd breed faster than we could ship them back." *And besides, who'd do all the back breaking, dirty, or servile work like digging ditches, hauling garbage, serving tables, and cutting hair and all the other stuff that people like you disdain to do.* Ramsey had grown up on a farm before joining the navy. His family had owned a couple of slaves but his father had worked him and his brothers just as hard. He knew and appreciated hard work. But there were a lot of white people in the South who'd become so accustomed to letting blacks do the dirty work that they thought it beneath themselves to do the things that had come to be called "nigger-work." "In any event, I think all we're doing right now is giving the Spanish another jab in the eye. We want them to give up Cuba, so we're showing them that if they continue this war they stand to lose more territory—especially if it gets to the point that France jumps in."

Brisk nodded.

"If France jumps in, Spain can kiss whatever of its empire is left goodbye." He swore derisively then continued. "They can probably kiss Spain itself goodbye. France occupied Spain under Napoleon I. I'm sure Napoleon IV would love to do the same."

Ramsey exhaled cigar smoke, took a breath then sighed. His first officer had a habit of seeing things the way he wanted to see them. Ramsey, however, couldn't help but think of all the unpleasant variables.

The best part about being a pessimist is that you are either constantly being proven right or you are pleasantly surprised. He knew things weren't as simple as Brisk saw them. Spain was outmatched for sure, but far from beaten. As for France...

"Don't forget that the King of Spain is related to the King of Prussia. If the French jump in, they may find themselves fighting a two front war."

"That's true, sir. But if Prussia goes to war against France, then they also go to war with ourselves, Mexico, and Austria Hungary. The Prussians may be tough and they may not like France going to war with Spain, but I doubt they'd risk those odds."

Yeoman Ferguson then reentered the bridge. He looked slightly less green than he had a few minutes before, when he had abruptly abandoned his post holding his hand to his mouth.

"Request permission to return to my station, sir."

"Granted," said Ramsey without a hint of disdain or mockery. He knew the boy would soon get his sea legs.

Suddenly, the telephone connecting the bridge to the crow's nest rang. Ramsey picked up the earpiece, brought it up to the side of his head, and then shouted into the receiver.

"Bridge!"

"Captain! Off to the port, sir!" shouted the lookout in a panic. The sailor's voice had been so excited with sheer terror that Ramsey had barely understood him through the crackly connection.

"What is it, sailor?"

"A wave, sir! An enormous wave! Headed right for us."

Ramsey dropped the receiver without bothering to hang it up. He grabbed his binoculars and rushed to the port side of the bridge.

"What is it?" asked Brisk.

Ramsey had no time to answer. He raised his binoculars to his eyes and looked north. At first he could see little but rain and dark gray sky. Then he saw it. It was an enormous wave more than sixty feet tall. The massive wall of water was raging towards them at great speed and tremendous force.

"My God…" It was not a blasphemy. It was the shortest prayer he could pray before shouting "Hard to port! Engines full ahead!" The helmsman immediately began to turn the great wheel to the left as quickly as possible. Brisk and the others, however, seemed paralyzed with fear. They too had seen the wave. Now they stood like stone statues, frozen with terror, transfixed upon the watery titan that was poised to come crashing over them. Ramsey rushed to the engine telegraph and personally pushed it to "full ahead."

Down in the engine room the telegraph bell rang loudly three times.

"Full ahead, boys!" cried the chief engineer. The coal heavers—the only black men on the boat—hurriedly began shoving more coal into the furnaces of the ship's boilers, while the engineers worked the valves that would force more steam to the propeller shafts.

Back on the bridge, the telegraph bell rang three times in reply, as the engine room acknowledged receipt of the order. A moment later the ship lurched forward. She had already begun to turn into the oncoming wave. Now with the added power to her engines she began to turn faster, but to Ramsey she still turned agonizingly slow.

"Come on! Turn!" said Ramsey. As the Texas finally came about, the forward viewports were filled with the view of the oncoming tidal wave. Impact was only moments away.

"Sound collision!" ordered Ramsey. Angry klaxons sounded throughout the ship. The bow of the battleship began to slide down into the trough that was just ahead of the approaching wave. *We're hitting it head on. At least we've got a chance.* Had they taken the wave on the ship's flank, they would almost certainly have capsized.

The ship began to climb the wave. For a brief moment, Ramsey thought they might just make it over the top but it was too high. The top thirty feet of the wave came crashing down onto the ship with tremendous force. One of the viewports shattered with the impact and water came flooding in. The ship lurched to the port, harder and farther than it ever had before. Inside the battleship the crew toppled like rag dolls as what were once floors became walls and what were walls became floors.

Dear heaven, we've capsized! The thought brought to mind nightmare stories, told by that small handful of sailors who had actually experienced and survived a capsizing. They were stories that conjured to mind pictures of hell itself.

God please save us! The ship slowly began to right itself. Ramsey tried to make his way towards the wheel, but the bridge was half flooded with sea water. As the ship struggled to continue to right itself, Ramsey turned to look out of the forward viewports. They were now atop the giant wave. The battleship was perched atop a massive hill of water and they were about to plunge down the other side. He had to make sure the rudder was amidships. He lunged for the wheel, just barely catching it. He then pulled himself to the helmsman's position. With all of his strength he started to turn the wheel to get the rudder into position. The ship lurched forward and down. Throughout the ship, men toppled forward and the CSS Texas descended the backside of the wave. Brisk and the other members of the bridge crew also slid forward. Much of the water that had flooded the bridge had already drained down to the lower decks, however, what remained also rushed forward and started to pour out of the broken viewport that it had come in through in the first place.

The Texas slid down the watery embankment. It reached the bottom just in time to begin to crest another, but mercifully much smaller, wave. Ramsey let out a long exhale. His fists were clenched so tightly onto the spokes of the wheel that his fists were white as snow. He released his iron grip and with a gesture of his arm he ordered the helmsman to resume his post.

He took a moment to survey the carnage that was his bridge, knowing that the same state of disorder and chaos probably pervaded every deck of his ship.

"Mr. Brisk, have the engineer sound the ship from bow to stern. I want a full damage report! Have him get the bilge pumps working to get rid of any water we've taken on. I also want a head count of the whole crew and a report of all injuries."

Brisk saluted, and then rushed below to carry out his Captain's orders. Ramsey reached into the pocket of his soaked uniform coat and pulled what turned out to be a ruined Cuban cigar from his pocket. He threw it in disgust over into a pool of water that had largely gathered on the port side of the bridge.

We're still listing, he suddenly realized. *We must have taken on more water than I thought...* Suddenly the ship lurched again with the impact of yet another rave. *We're not out of the storm yet...*

II

The sound of a steam whistle shrieked through the air as a passenger train chugged its way through the cotton fields of southern Georgia. Negro slaves lifted their heads to stare at the passing locomotive, many of them taking the opportunity to wipe sweat from their black skinned faces, before being prompted back to work by white overseers sitting on horseback.

On board the train, Cole Allens stared at the passing cotton fields with an almost comatose look. It seemed as if they'd been passing through Georgian cotton fields forever and before that it had seemed like they had been passing through South Carolina cotton fields forever.

And before that it was the tobacco fields of Virginia and North Carolina. The trip from Richmond down to Florida was turning out to be long and arduous. The stifling heat was worse than anything he'd ever experienced in Kentucky.

It's the blasted humidity! The window to his right was open. In fact, just about every window on the train was open. It helped a little—but only a little. To his left, his young wife Helen was asleep against his shoulder. He envied her ability to sleep on a jouncing train. Across from Cole and his wife, Lieutenants Winston Churchill and Reginald Barnes sat. They looked even more miserable in the heat than Cole. The two fresh faced British officers had been their travelling companions ever since leaving Richmond. For the first half of the trip, the two young men had pressed him for every detail of his experiences as a war correspondent during the Second War of Rebellion. He'd reluctantly done so. He ordinarily talked very little of his experiences during the war. But since the two British officers were about to get their own first-hand experience at being war correspondents, he decided to open up to them and to attempt to dispel them from any of the fanciful notions of glory and excitement that young men so often associated with war. They were just about the same age he had been when he went off to follow an army to war, and they reminded him much of himself.

But they've not yet come under fire. Cole shifted uncomfortably in his seat, being careful not to wake his wife. He desperately wanted a cigar, but didn't want to disturb Helen. He knew she didn't like the smell of his tobacco smoke—though she'd never complained. He picked the newspaper back up that he'd purchased at their last stop. The headline screamed in massive capital letters that Havana had fallen to Confederate forces.

"It does perplex me," said Churchill suddenly. The British officer was staring out of the train at the swarms of negro slaves working in the seemingly endless cotton fields.

"What is that, Lieutenant?"

Churchill leaned forward and spoke softly. They were on a train filled with Southerners and he had no desire to offend any of them.

"How a nation as seemingly civilized and advanced as the South, could cling to such a primitive and backwards institution as slavery."

Cole understood the young soldier's confusion. The vast majority of Southerners he'd met had been kind, polite, and refined people.

"They pride themselves on their independence and freedom and yet they deny that very freedom to over a third of their population," continued Churchill.

Cole nodded. Most of Confederate culture seemed almost elegant. But like a black stain on a silky white cloth, slavery seemed to overshadow any other positive and appealing values that seemed to be held by the people of the Confederate States—and yet…

He opened up the newspaper to the third page and held it up to Churchill. The title to the article read: STONEWALL ADDRESSES CROWD OF 1000 IN CHARLESTON.

"Former Confederate President Thomas Jackson seems to be gathering a growing audience for his abolitionist views."

Churchill nodded.

"So it would seem. But do you actually suppose that he and his followers will ever be able to bring about the end of slavery?"

"I honestly don't know," said Cole. "But of one thing I'm sure. Slavery in the CSA will eventually end—one way or the other."

Suddenly, the train began to screech to a halt. Helen woke suddenly. She let out a loud yawn and asked, "Where are we?"

"We're not in Jacksonville yet," said Cole.

"No," said Churchill, "…but wherever we are now, we're not scheduled for a stop."

A few moments later a gray uniformed train attendant entered their car.

"Sorry for the delay ya'll. We've been asked by the army to take some of their railcars south. It shouldn't take more than an hour or so to get them hooked up. We're in the town of Tebeauville Georgia if anyone would like to stretch their legs."

"I certainly do," said Helen. A few moments later when they had stepped off of the train she said, "Uhhg… what is that smell?" It was a strong musky aroma that smelled of dying plants and other vegetation.

"There are swamps not far from here," said another passenger who had also disembarked.

Helen held up her hands to shield her eyes from the sun that was glaring down on them. As far as Cole could tell, there was not a cloud in the sky. The humidity was almost unbearable. Everyone was drenched with perspiration. It was almost like being in a pressure cooker. A large fly buzzed past Helen and a moment later she swatted a mosquito that had landed on her arm.

"That's it!" she said. "I'm getting back on the train." Without another word, she did an about face and marched back to their railcar. Cole took that opportunity to pull a cigar out of his pocket and light it. He pleasurably exhaled the smoke, grateful for that one small luxury. After smoking the cigar down, he tossed the butt away. He was about to turn and join his wife back on the train when he noticed that something had drawn the eyes of the two young British officers. A moment later he caught sight of it himself. It was a column of five horseless carriages, each driven by a gray uniformed Confederate soldier. Each horseless carriage also looked to be armed with a tripod mounted machine gun.

"Take a good look, Winston," said Barnes. "That is the future of cavalry."

"It should be interesting to see how they perform," replied Churchill.

"Are those British maxim's they are armed with?" asked Cole.

13

Churchill shook his head.

"Some foreign variant. Probably French or Swiss."

Behind the horseless carriages came an equally surprising sight. A column of gray clad negro soldiers marched in column formation down the main street of the town. The Confederate Battle Flag was held aloft above them, though there was no breeze to stir the military banner. Cole noticed that there were no cheering crowds like what he'd seen in other Southern towns where local men had set off to war. Cole knew there were a lot of white people in the South who were vehemently opposed to negroes carrying guns. Nonetheless a whole company of them stood before their eyes, armed with rifles and about to head south to join the CSA's war with Spain.

An hour later, the train was once again underway. To Cole's dismay the train's speed was down, due no doubt to the extra cars. It took another three agonizing days before the southbound train finally reached the end of the line at Key West Florida.

After getting his wife settled in at the town's only hotel, Cole joined Churchill and Barnes for the walk to the nearby coast and Fort Zachary Taylor. He found it difficult to keep up with the two young British officers. It reminded him in a not to subtle way that he was twice their age. There was a cool ocean breeze blowing from the west that smelled of seawater. It wasn't long before they came in sight of Fort Zachary Taylor. It was a massive trapezoid shaped fortress built of both stone and masonry. It bristled with modern artillery pieces, the vast majority of which pointed out to sea. A massive Blood Stained Banner floated above the fort. A large moat had been dug on the side of the fortress which faced the land. The entire fort was, therefore, completely surrounded by water. A small wooden bridge connected it with the mainland.

The three men walked nervously across the bridge. They were confronted at the far end by a pair of gray clad sentries who looked suspiciously at the two foreign soldiers who were dressed in their khaki colored British uniforms. Churchill and Barnes held out the military passes they had been issued in Richmond by the Confederate War Department.

"We are war correspondents with the British Army," explained Churchill as a Confederate sergeant scrutinized the passes. "We were instructed to report here, by General Patton." The Sergeant sent word to his superiors and a few minutes later an officer emerged from within the Fort.

"Gentlemen, I am Captain Mercer T. Chadwick. On behalf of General Wheeler, it is my pleasure to welcome you to Fort Zachary Taylor. The General sends his apologies but he is indisposed today with preparations. The war department sent us a wire to expect you." After shaking hands with Churchill and Barnes, the Confederate captain turned to Cole.

"And you must be Mr. Allens. You're probably anxious to know sir, that General Wheeler has approved your military press pass and you may accompany these gentlemen to Havana."

"Thank you, sir," said Cole, with great relief. He'd feared he may well have come all that way for nothing. Now he came to the more awkward subject of his wife. When Helen had surprised him by joining him on the train, he'd not had the heart to make her return to Louisville.

I'm a fool for not sending her back. Ever so casually he asked, "Will we be landing in Havana?"

"Yes," replied Captain Chadwick.

"And what is the present condition of the city? Is it safe?"

The Confederate Captain now looked at him with a perplexed look on his face.

He thinks I'm a coward who's overly worried about my own safety...

"Havana is secure and by all reports in good order," said the Captain. "The vast majority of Cubans have welcomed us as liberators."

For his wife's sake, Cole hoped that last part was more than just Confederate propaganda.

"As long as you stay in the city, you should be relatively safe. Of course, in a warzone, there are no guarantees."

"I understand," replied Cole. "I wasn't asking for myself. My wife decided to accompany me, and chose not to let me know until we were on the train together."

The Confederate's expression changed from one of barely concealed contempt to one of surprise and amusement.

"Your wife must be quite a woman."

"She most certainly is, sir. She is young and adventurous and quite stubborn when she sets her mind on something."

The Captain, smiled.

"I'll have to clear it with the General but I don't think it will be a problem. Unless of course you want the answer to be no?"

Cole was almost willing to say yes to the Captain's offer.

I can't. This means too much to her…

"That won't be necessary, sir," said Cole. "We understand the risks."

The Captain nodded.

"Well then gentlemen, the rest of our forces are expected in three more days. We'll then head for Havana."

The Captain then offered to give them a tour of the fort, an invitation to which the two young British officers readily agreed. Cole, however, excused himself. The thought of spending three days and nights with his wife in south Florida had sent him heading back to the hotel with a spring in his step that hadn't been there just a few minutes before. He'd regretted not being able to take her to a beach for their honeymoon. With the loss of the entire South and California to secession, the United States was sadly lacking warm beaches.

At least now I can make it up to her!

"Well?" she asked him when he returned to their room.

"My military pass has been approved, and the officer with whom I spoke was fairly certain that you'd be allowed to accompany me to Havana. In the meantime we've got three days to spend here…"

He'd barely finished his sentence when she screamed with delight and excitement. She ran to him and embraced him so rapidly it took his arms a moment to catch up with his brain. He took her tightly in his arms and their lips met passionately. For the next three days at least, the honeymoon was back on.

III

Nathan Audrey sat atop his horse watching as a column of green clad soldiers tramped through the dust of western Nevada. At the head of the column, the Californian flag fluttered in the light breeze. It was a small mercy in the sweltering heat. Overhead the sun was glaring and hot. The whole scene reminded Audrey of his Foreign Legion days down in Mexico, twenty-six years earlier, when he also had pounded the ground as an infantryman in the blazing heat of the desert. As he watched them tramp across the harsh terrain he nodded in approval. They may have been hot and miserable, but they had plenty of water. Audrey had made certain of that.

He knew the terrain well. He'd tracked outlaws in the area for years. It had always been dangerous. Now that the long volatile tensions between California and Deseret had erupted into open war over the bleak but mineral rich territory of Nevada, it was about to become deadly.

It had been two days since they had left Fort Truckee in eastern California and begun their march towards Carson City. Audrey eyed the Krag Jorgensen 1892 rifles that over half his force was armed with and again nodded in approval. When they'd arrived at Fort Truckee four days earlier, over half his men had been unarmed. He'd been worried that the Mormons might cross the border into California and seize Truckee and the rifles before they could arrive.

Audrey pulled a metal canteen from his saddle bag and brought it to his lips. He sighed with pleasure then returned the canteen to the bag.

Goldwyn was right.

Suddenly, off to the northeast Audrey heard the familiar sound of gunfire. He brought his horse around and urged him forward using the pressure of his legs and a flick of the reins. Up ahead he spotted General Goldwyn and his aid galloping towards him on horseback. He had an almost gleeful smile on his face.

"Good afternoon, Colonel Johnson," said Goldwyn. He used Audrey's longtime alias naturally and without a trace of irony. Audrey didn't like having anyone know who

17

he really was, but so far Goldwyn had given no indication that he'd ever betray him.

If he wanted to betray me he could easily have done so already, Audrey reminded himself for about the thousandth time. Far from turning him in, Goldwyn had given Nathan "Johnson" a commission in the Army of the Republic of California. Audrey supposed he'd have to learn to live with it. At the moment, all General William Goldwyn seemed concerned with was the brewing battle up ahead.

"A force of Mormons has taken up position on a hill half a mile north of here. They ambushed a few of our scouts. I'm sending the cavalry around the flanks I don't want them getting away."

"Do you want me to deploy the men and assault the hill?" asked Audrey.

"Not yet. Unlimber the cannons and put some fire on that hill!"

Audrey brought his hand up in salute. Goldwyn returned it then galloped back towards the hill's right flank.

"Sergeant Jones! Unlimber the guns!" barked Audrey. While the artillerymen started deploying the gun batteries, Audrey brought his binoculars up to his eyes and surveyed the hill. Like most of the surrounding desert it had scarcely any vegetation at all. The Mormons were taking cover behind rocks and boulders. Off to the left and the right of the hill, the gunfire was growing in intensity. The Californian cavalry had dismounted and was fighting on foot. With all the rough terrain it was hard to make out what kind of progress they were making.

A short while later the air resounded with the thunderous noise of artillery fire. The sound took him back to the many battles of his past, though in comparison, this was little more than a skirmish. Atop the hill, iron cannon balls and explosive shells crashed down on the Mormon defenders. The Californian artillerymen worked furiously to reload their guns and keep up a steady flow of fire. To the left and right of the hill the gunfire finally reached a climax then started to decrease in intensity. Through his binoculars, Audrey could see the dismounted Californian cavalry pulling back. He was pleased to see that it was more of a fighting withdrawal than it was a retreat. A short while later Goldwyn came riding up again.

"They had a reserve force positioned behind the hill but without infantry we have them completely outnumbered. Keep up the barrage another ten minutes or so and try to land some shells behind the hill. At my signal we'll launch a coordinated attack. The cavalry will hit both flanks simultaneously and you'll lead the infantry up the hill."

"Surely they can see we have them outnumbered," replied Audrey. "If they're holding their ground then they must be expecting reinforcements."

"Possibly," said Goldwyn.

By his tone, Audrey could tell that Goldwyn found the idea unpleasant.

"Don't forget that these Mormons are religious fanatics," said Goldwyn. "They could very well decide to die on that hill rather than yield it to us."

"You may be right, sir," said Audrey. "But if there are enemy reinforcements on the way, then we don't want to be taken by surprise."

Goldwyn looked towards the northeast and bit his lip. He swore under his breath and then looked back at Audrey.

"Alright, Colonel. I'll detach some more scouts. If the Mormons do have more troops on approach we'll know. In the meantime, prepare the infantry to attack immediately. If enemy reinforcements are nearby then it's imperative we take that hill as quickly as possible. If this turns in to a full scale battle I want to make blasted sure we hold the high ground!"

Audrey saluted and then started barking orders at his men. While Goldwyn regrouped the cavalry for another assault on the flanks, Audrey deployed the infantry into a wide skirmish line. As he awaited the General's signal to begin the attack, Audrey pulled a rifle stock from his saddlebag. He then pulled a barrel which he attached to the stock. Finally, he pulled out a small scope and fixed it on top of the rifle. The custom made sharpshooter rifle had served him well as a bounty hunter and as a lawman. He loaded three bullets and worked the lever.

Suddenly, a trumpet blast signaled the order to begin the attack. Audrey pulled the small silver crucifix from underneath his shirt and kissed it. He then ordered his men forward. He kept close behind his men. Being one of the only mounted men in a formation of foot soldiers was dangerous in that it made him a tempting target, but for what he had in mind he needed the extra height that he gained from staying mounted. Large volumes of rifle fire erupted to the left and right as the Californian cavalry reengaged the Mormon flanks. A few moments later, bullets starting shrieking through the air and whirring past Audrey as the Mormons atop the hill also opened fire. The Californians returned the rifle fire in kind, sending a torrent of lead up the hill. Though the Californians had the Mormons outnumbered, the latter had the benefit of fighting from behind rocky cover. Several of Audrey's men were killed or wounded in the first couple of minutes of the advance.

Though he'd grown older, Audrey still had the eyes of a hawk. He raised his scoped rifle and took aim at a half concealed blue-uniformed Mormon who was shooting at his men. Audrey squeezed the trigger and the rifle barked. He watched through the scope as a fountain of blood erupted out of the Mormon's neck. Audrey worked the lever on his rifle then took aim at another distant Mormon. The rifle cracked again and another Mormon fell dead—this one with a bullet hole right between his eyes. Audrey worked the lever again and searched for another target.

Suddenly his horse took a hit. The bay reared violently then collapsed underneath him. Audrey hit the rocky ground hard. He tried to haul himself to his feet but his right leg was trapped underneath his fallen mount. Ignoring the pain, and hoping nothing was broken, Audrey strained and pulled until he freed his leg from beneath the dead animal. He staggered to his feet then looked around for his rifle. Several bullets kicked up dirt around him. He grabbed his rifled and then hurriedly made his way further up the slope to rejoin his men. On the way he passed several more Californians who'd been killed or wounded. He hurriedly reloaded his rifle.

Audrey was both surprised and pleased that the men were doing as well as they were. For most of them, this was their first time under fire. At the head of the advancing troops, the Bear Flag fluttered determinedly. About mid-way up the hill, the flag bearer went down. Another soldier caught the banner before it could fall and pressed forward, holding it aloft.

Audrey feared that they'd have to route the Mormons out of the rocks above on top of the hill, but to his surprise the soldiers from Deseret came out on their own. They came charging down the hill, brandishing bayoneted rifles and screaming like wild beasts. It was an impressive display of courage and battlefield ferocity but Audrey also noticed that the Mormons were no longer shooting at them.

They're out of ammo! Audrey raised his rifle and dropped one of the oncoming Mormons. A few moments later he shot another and then another a few moments after that. He had no time to reload his rifle, so he let it fall to the ground and pulled his revolver. The advancing Californians met the charging Mormons head on. Audrey hung back. He wasn't afraid, but he also knew that he was a little old for close quarters fighting. He held his pistol at the ready. The Californians had the Mormons heavily outnumbered, so almost none of the charging enemy troops made it through the Californian line. Audrey dropped the few that did with expert shots from his revolver.

A few of the Mormon survivors attempted to flee back up the hill. Most of those were gunned down by the oncoming Californians.

"Move forward, men! Don't let them get away."

The Californians let out a cry that reminded Audrey of the Rebel Yell. They then surged up the hill with renewed determination. Audrey continued to follow close behind. Bloody blue-clad Mormons littered the top of the hill. As they reached the crest of the hill the Californians began to hoop and holler in victory. The Sergeants quickly brought them back under control. Audrey could remember more than one occasion where the tide of a battle had turned simply because the side that was winning became drunk with victory and lost discipline.

After reaching the crest of the hill, Audrey paused to catch his breath. To the north east he saw he the remnants of the Mormon force in full retreat. Below on the far side of the hill, General Goldwyn and the cavalry had captured several enemy soldiers who hadn't managed to get away in time. Goldwyn seemed to be conversing with a captured enemy officer. From what he'd seen the Mormon Army had based their uniforms and ranks of off the U.S. Army. From the bronze oak leafs on the officer's shoulder straps, Audrey could tell that he was a Major. Off to the right one of Goldwyn's troopers was examining a captured Mormon flag—a horizon blue banner emblazoned with a beehive.

"Colonel, may I present to you Major Amos Caine of the Army of Deseret."

Audrey nodded briskly at the downtrodden enemy officer.

"Your men fought well, Major."

"The fight isn't over, Colonel."

"I'm afraid it is for you, Major," said Goldwyn. "Colonel, see that the prisoners are secured and sent to the rear."

Audrey, detailed several soldiers to take charge of the Mormons and escort them to the rear. He also detailed men to gather the enemy rifles and ammunition. The Mormons were all armed with U.S. 1892 Springfield Rifles and old 1869 C.S. Richmond rifles. With the captured enemy weapons, the vast majority of the Californian infantry were now adequately equipped.

Less than an hour later they were again on the move. *That Mormon was right. This is just beginning...*

IV

Thomas Jonathan "Stonewall" Jackson stared grimly at the column of ragged negro slaves being marched up the dirt road towards the auction as he rode past them in his carriage. Sandie Pendleton maneuvered Jackson's carriage off to the side so that they could get past the marching group of miserable humanity. The black men, women, and even children were chained one to another and herded along like cattle by whip bearing white men on horseback. The slaves all walked with their faces towards the ground. None dared meet the gaze of the overseers.

"Pick up the pace, niggers!" shouted the horseman at the head of the column. A couple of the others cracked their whips menacingly. They didn't actually strike any of the slaves, but the sound of the whip was enough to get them moving faster.

Jackson's face hardened further. The head taskmaster turned his cruel gaze towards the former Confederate President. Jackson met it without flinching. He stared at the man on horseback with a glare as menacing as any he'd ever given the Union troops he'd defeated in not one but two wars. The taskmaster looked away and went back to berating the negroes.

Jackson lifted his eyes to the sky.

This must end, Lord. This must end. He'd helped lead the Confederacy to victory in both the War of Confederate Independence and the War of 1869. For him, the conflict had never been about slavery, but about honor, independence, and defending his home from an aggressive military invader. As he'd told countless crowds across the CSA, they'd fought for the right to decide for themselves what their destiny and course of action would be in the matter of slavery—and all other things. They'd won that right on the battlefield by force of arms.

Now it's time for us to decide to bring this injustice to an end.

"Are you alright, sir?" asked Pendleton. He'd served Jackson for nearly thirty-five years, first as his adjutant during the War of Confederate Independence and then later as his aid during the ten years of his Presidency. When he'd first started serving Jackson he'd been a fair faced young boy barely out of his teens. Now he was a fifty-five year old man whose mostly gray hair looked more like that of the elderly former President he'd served for so long.

"I'm fine Sandie," replied Jackson.

They were about twenty miles north of Memphis Tennessee.

"We should be at the auction in about ten more minutes, sir."

Jackson nodded. He then reached down and felt the heavy bag of gold coins he had secured to his belt, reassuring himself that it was still there. He let out a sigh and then fought the urge to lean back in the carriage and go to sleep. A few minutes later he was startled to full consciousness by a loud noise behind them like the sound of a miniature train engine. Jackson turned to see a horseless carriage making its way down the dusty dirt road. No matter how many of the contraptions he saw, he would never get used to them. His mind went to the last chapter of Daniel where the scriptures stated that at the time of the end "knowledge would be greatly increased." Jackson watched as the horseless carriage went around his own carriage and passed he and Pendleton as quickly as they'd passed the column of marching negro slaves. The driver gave he and Sandie a friendly wave has he went by.

"I find myself wondering, sir, if there is a military application for those machines."

"There are indeed," said Jackson. "My contacts in the war department have informed me that several horseless carriages armed with machine guns are being deployed to Cuba."

"Horseless cavalry?"

It sounded like an oxymoron, but Jackson nodded.

"It makes me wonder what else man will invent in the next few years."

Thinking on his contacts in the War Department in Richmond, reminded Jackson of an article he'd yet to finish reading. He pulled out a copy of the Chattanooga Times that he'd picked up during their last train layover in Tennessee. Like virtually all papers in the Confederate States, its front page was still trumpeting the Confederate capture of Havana. Jackson had to go to the third page of the paper and look in the lower corner to find the article he was looking for.

FIELD COMMANDERS REPORT NEGRO PERFORMANCE IN BATTLE EXCEEDS EXPECTATIONS.

While certainly, not equaling the skill and bravery of soldiers of the Anglo-Celtic race, the negro conscripts sent to fight in Cuba have proven themselves in battle against the Spanish oppressors of Cuba. Both Army and Marine Corps commanders report that black troops played a small but positive role in the capture of Havana, and that while the Spanish forces they faced were not the best the enemy had to offer, the negroes facing them showed a level of manliness and courage hitherto unseen and unexpected amongst their

*race. Despite opposition and protests from numerous groups
in the Confederate States, President Stone and the War
Department continue to tout the advantages of using negro
troops in the liberation of Cuba. While the primary reason
given is that the negro, by virtue of his tropical heritage—
having come from the jungles of Africa—is more suited to the
hot and humid conditions and more immune to tropical
diseases such as malaria; it is very clear to this paper that
Richmond is using this program to indicate to hostile foreign
markets that the first steps towards abolishing the institution
of slavery in the Confederacy is underway.*

Jackson folded the paper up and put it under his seat.
According to telegrams received from his contacts in the War
Department, the negroes fighting for the Confederate Army
in Cuba had played more than a small part in the capture of
Havana. In fact they had probably been the deciding factor in
the capture of the eastern beaches.

Jackson suddenly felt an overwhelming sense of
satisfaction. He'd championed the negro conscription act as
President back in the 1870s. It had nearly cost him his
presidency. He was convinced that one day the Confederacy
would once again be fighting for its survival against the
tyrannical bankers and industrialists of the North. Twice he'd
seen the South nearly crushed by the North's superiority in
numbers. Thanks to the negro conscription act, if another full
scale war erupted between the Confederate States and United
States, the Confederacy would be able to make full use of its
available manpower. He also had the bittersweet thought that
if such a war ever came, it would certainly spell the final
doom of slavery in the CSA, if he and his coalition failed in
their efforts.

"We're here, sir."

Ahead, Jackson could see a large crowd gathered in a
field off of the main road. A large sign read: SLAVE
AUCTION. Pendleton parked the carriage and then hurried
to help Jackson down from it. Leaning on his cane far more
than he cared to, the former Confederate President made his
way towards the auction. Ordinarily, men who recognized
him would at least tip their hats to him. Ladies would give
him curtsies. Contrary to common belief outside the CSA,

most Confederates did not own slaves. When it came to Jackson, large numbers of Confederate citizens were willing to ignore the "eccentricity of his old age" and treat him like the man who more than anyone—save Robert E. Lee himself—had helped win the Confederacy its independence and who, in 1869, had led the military campaign that expanded Confederate territory to the shores of the Pacific Ocean.

That was not the kind of reception he received at the slave auction. A couple of men—obviously veterans—removed their hats as he walked by, but most of those who recognized him, glared at him. Jackson could sense their malice and their hatred.

The people at this auction represent those who most vehemently wish to keep slavery in tact in the CSA. With no small amount of spite he looked forward to their reactions when he started purchasing slaves at the auction for the explicit purpose of setting them free. His hand reached down and patted the bag of gold coins tied securely to his belt. The money donated by the British Anti-Slavery Society—half of which had been donated by Queen Victoria herself—was about to be put to good use. Only Jackson and Pendleton new of the money's origin. Using money obtained from foreign sources to purchase and free negro slaves was illegal in the Confederate States. Jackson let it bother him little. Instinctively he quoted the book of Acts in his mind.

We ought to obey God rather than men… The British Society representatives had scrupulously exchanged the British Sovereigns for Confederate coins to prevent the money being traced back to them.

Jackson made his way towards the front of the crowd to take his place amongst the men who would be doing the bidding. A finely dressed, planter, with white handle bar mustaches turned to face Jackson. From his gold rings and ivory trimmed boots Jackson could tell that he was exceedingly wealthy. The man took a long drag on his long, thin cigar and blew out a cloud of smoke in Jackson's face.

"Well if it isn't Abraham Lincoln!" he said.

Jackson was used to coldness from such people, but seldom had he been so openly and rudely mocked. His grip tightened on his cane until his knuckles were white. Had

Pendleton been standing there, he would probably have struck the man with the back of his hand. Dueling was officially illegal in all thirteen Confederate States plus its three—soon to be four—territories. Nonetheless, planters and men who had served as officers during the War of Confederate Independence enjoyed a certain amount of immunity. Jackson hadn't ever heard of anyone being prosecuted for dueling, but all the same he was glad his long time friend and aid had not witnessed the insult.

A moment later, the auctioneer climbed the stage and addressed the crowd.

"Ladies and gentlemen, it's my pleasure to welcome you to today's auction. Be assured we have the finest niggers this side of the Mississippi to offer you today—slaves to serve in both the field and the home. I would also like to assure you that all negroes sold at this auction come with certificates of national origin so that there can be no future question on the ownership of your property. Also all purchasers today will be supplied with complementary chains and shackles provided by Henderson Brothers Steel in Memphis, to insure that your merchandise does not wander off. And, of course, as always, all sales are final. Now ladies and gentlemen if you would look at the stage."

A young black teenager climbed up onto the stage. He stared at the assembled crowd with terror on his face. Behind the stage, an older negro woman was crying uncontrollably, comforted by a large black man about the same age.

"Our first offer of the day is this strong young boy from Clement Plantation near Huntsville Alabama. He's fourteen years old, strong, healthy and obedient. This boy's been picking cotton since he was a two year old pickaninny. He's a hard worker and he'll be an asset to his new master. We'll start the bidding at five-hundred dollars."

"Five-hundred!" cried the planter who had insulted Jackson.

"Five-hundred dollar bid from Mr. Johnny Dupree! Do I hear six-hundred?"

"Six-hundred!" cried another Planter from Texas.

The bidding rose rapidly to one-thousand-five-hundred dollars.

"Fifteen hundred dollar bid, from Mr. Dupree. Fifteen hundred once! Fifteen hundred twice!..."

"Sixteen hundred dollars!" cried Jackson as if yelling an order to a regiment.

Dupree looked at Jackson in disgust and then said "Seventeen-hundred."

"Eighteen-hundred," said Jackson.

Dupree again looked at Jackson with disgust. He then turned to the auctioneer.

"Do you know, sir, that this nigger loving black republican is only purchasing slaves so that he can set them loose? Loose to commit crime. Loose to steal paying work from descent hard working white folks? I think it only right and proper that he be excluded from this auction."

There was a gasp from the crowd and not a small number of shouts of consent—all of them from among the prospective buyers. The auctioneer looked confused and indecisive—completely unsure of what to do or how to respond. At last he hopped down from the stage to consult with the sellers. A few moments later he climbed back onto the stage.

"I'm sorry Mr. Dupree, but President Jackson's money is as good as anyone else's. What he does with his property after he buys them is his own business. The bidding stands at eighteen hundred dollars."

Dupree's face turned several shades of red. He turned and addressed his fellow planters who had come to buy.

"I don't know about you, gentleman. But I'm not going to buy from anyone who's willing to take this nigger lover's money and help him ruin the South by turning slaves loose." With that he stormed off. A couple of others joined him, but the vast majority remained.

"Eighteen-hundred going once! Eighteen-hundred going twice! Sold to President Jackson for Eighteen hundred dollars!" The auctioneer held up the shackles and addressed Jackson.

"I assume, Mr. President that he will not be needing these?"

"He will not."

As the auction proceeded, Jackson bought the boy's father, mother, sister, and twelve other negroes, using ever last dime that the British had donated—over fifteen thousand dollars in total. With Pendleton's help he filled out the paper work that certified their freedom. He also gave each one five dollars in gray-backs. Most of the slaves were overwhelmed with gratitude.

"Thank you Massa Jackson! Thank you suh!"

A few seemed absolutely terrified. They had spent their entire lives doing as they were told and having all things provided and managed for them. Now they were about to enter the world outside slavery where they would have to fend for themselves and Jackson knew that it was going to be a hard and unfriendly place for them. There were those in the CSA who objected to freeing slaves on the basis that they weren't capable of providing for themselves.

The transition will be long, hard, and painful, but it MUST be made!

The last negro to receive his small stipend of cash was the teenage boy who'd been first on the auction block. He stared at Jackson with something not unlike religious awe.

"Yous is jus' like Moses suh!"

Jackson knew the comparison had more to do with the fact that he set slaves free than with the large gray and white beard that he wore. Being compared to such a biblical character was at the same time gratifying troublesome. Jackson himself was far to humble to see himself as any sort of deliverer.

"You know your Bible?"

"Oh yes suh! I knows all da' stories! An Massa Jackson! I'd like to be like da slave's in da ole testament dat' stayed wit der' Massa's cause dey love dem."

"You want to stay with your old master, even though he was ready to sell you?"

"Not wit Massa Evers, suh. With you suh. I wants to serve you! I wants to hep' you set others free."

Jackson smiled at the boy's sincerity and a tear welled up in the stern General's eye.

"Your desire is admirable. But I have no slaves, voluntary or otherwise."

"Den suh, I's like to serve you as a free man suh! I do anything to hep' you suh!"

"Perhaps someday you will. For now your family will need you. Be strong for them. Now, what is your name, young man?"

"Calvin, suh."

"A fitting name for one who knows the Bible so well. And what do you want your last name to be Calvin? Your Father has chosen the name of your former master: Evers."

"Den suh, dat be my name too. I is Calvin Evers from now on."

V

"I thought that we were sailing from Boston and New York," said John Pershing.

Captain Dominic Malcom looked up from cleaning the pieces of his disassembled Enfield. The pieces were strewed about the floor of the train box car that they and about forty other members of Whitmore's Legion were riding in. It was the second time on that particular trip that Malcom had completely broken down the weapon. The Englishman was an obsessive soldier by even Pershing's standards. He was glad that Whitmore had made him company commander and Malcom his second in command. The Englishman—a former Royal Marine—had already earned a reputation for sternness with the troops. Pershing didn't think he would have enjoyed taking orders from him. He had already had to rein him in a little.

"Why would you think we aren't, Major?" replied Malcom with a heavy English accent. He then began hurriedly and expertly reassembling his rifle. Pershing reached up and felt the eight pointed gold star on his shoulder strap. He was still trying to get used to his new rank—and to wearing Spanish rank insignia instead of U.S.

Suddenly, the jouncing train caused one of the last pieces of Malcom's rifle to slide across the floor. Pershing grabbed it and tossed it back at Malcom who plucked it from the air. He then proceeded to answer the Englishman's question.

"Well for one thing about three hours after we left Massena there was that little incident where we stopped on a remote stretch of track, disembarked in a wooden area and force marched about ten miles to another train on another set of tracks."

"The old man was probably just giving the men a good work out." The ex-British Marine smiled savagely. "We used to do much worse to our own recruits. From the look of many of our men they could use a lot more working out. Heaven knows it won't be easy once we're trouncing through the jungles and hills of Cuba."

"There's also the fact that we've been on this train several hours more than what it would take if we were going to either Boston or New York," said Pershing, returning to the subject at hand.

"I'm afraid I'm not well studied on my North American geography, so I hadn't noticed."

He slid the last piece of his rifle into place with a loud click and then worked the bolt. He smiled with satisfaction at the smooth movement of the bolt action. The way he held the Enfield, Pershing thought he couldn't have been happier had it been a beautiful woman and not a piece of iron and wood. Pershing also took note of the fact that while most of the men had been equipped with Whitmore Rifles, Dominic Malcom had elected to retain his own nation's weapon. Pershing shrugged. The British Enfield used the same caliber ammunition as the weapon that had been manufactured by Joseph Whitmore's company.

"What exactly are you driving at, Major?" said Malcom.

"I think Whitmore is cleverer than a lot of people give him credit for. I don't think we're going to either Boston or New York. I think we're leaving from a different port."

Malcom shrugged his shoulders as though indifferent.

"Just as long as we get there."

Pershing studied the hard bitten British marine.

"If you don't mind my asking, Captain, what are you doing here?"

"I'm not some anti-slavery crusader if that's what you mean."

"Why are you here then?"

31

"In a word, Major,—money! The British Anti-Slavery Society offered me a large sum of money to sign up and serve."

Pershing was momentarily taken aback.

"You're a true mercenary then."

"Don't sound so condescending, Major. I admit that I couldn't care less about negro slaves in the South, but neither am I driven by greed and personal gain. My Father passed away three years ago. He left my mother heavily in debt. Whether I live or die in this endeavor, the money will settle her debts."

"I doubt she thought it's worth you going off to war."

"I've already fought in Afghanistan and India. I doubt Cuba will be any more dangerous."

Pershing nodded.

"And why are you here, Major?" asked Malcom.

Revenge. The cold and bitter thought came instantly along with the memory of a burning Missouri farm. Thinking about the Confederate guerrillas that had killed his entire family save his mother flooded him with hatred. Jennifer Harper had warned him that such hatred would eventually consume him. The woman with whom he knew he was falling in love, had begged him to let it go. Thinking of her beautiful face and smile dispelled the darkness and returned peace to his soul. He looked at Dominic Malcom who was still awaiting an answer.

"Among other things, the United States wants to get some of its younger officers combat experience. Our army really hasn't seen much action since 1869 other than against Indians and outlaws."

"Yes, the USA has been militarily desultory on the world stage for the past twenty-five years." Malcom looked at Pershing with his hawk like eyes and gave a sardonic grin. "So you're here in an unofficial official capacity." The British marine swore blasphemously then said, "I hate politics."

The rest of the trip proceeded in near silence. When it became increasingly clear that they weren't stopping anytime soon, Pershing leaned his head back and tried to get some sleep. It wasn't easy with the noise and motion of the train and the stench of the bucket latrines at the other end of the boxcar. He found his mind drifting uncontrollably to Jennifer Harper. The woman from Missouri was undoubtedly on one of the train cars. She'd warned him not to be burned up by a desire for revenge. She'd also shown not so unsubtly that she was attracted to him as much as he was to her. For the first time in his life, he'd met a woman he thought he could spend the rest of his life with.

And I'm taking her to war with me... Jennifer had volunteered and been accepted as a nurse. She'd serve well behind the lines, but in a warzone no one was free from danger.

Hours later the train screeched to a halt. As he climbed down from the boxcar, Pershing was taken by the chilliness of the air and by the rural scenery. Off to his right was a large forested area of fur trees. To the left was a field of tall and luscious green grass. Behind the train were two large wooded hills. Pershing also smelled the salty aroma of the sea. He knew that the ocean couldn't be far away.

"I've never been to New York or Boston," said Malcom. "But I'm pretty certain that this is neither. It looks like you were right, Major."

As the men of Pershing's company disembarked from the train, along with the troops of several other companies, Malcom and the Sergeants began to take charge of them and to get them into formation to march wherever they were going. Pershing had been given command of a company. One of his two platoons was composed almost entirely of negroes. Only the officers and non-coms were white. Officially they all had origins in the United States, though Pershing had seen that a few of them had lash marks on their backs. None of them would admit to being runaways. The United States had very few negroes and wasn't interested in gaining more. Any slaves trying to enter the United States from the CSA at official crossings were turned away as illegal immigrants. Many of those caught in the USA were returned to the Confederacy. The Underground Railroad, however, was still in operation, and many of them were given sanctuary in British Canada.

A few minutes later, General Whitmore's aid-de-camp, Lt. Colonel David Lovejoy came walking down the length of the train and shouting. His voice sounded less like the authoritative speech of a military man and more like the annoyed droning of a civilian trying to fill the role.

"All company commanders are to report to Mr—ere *General* Whitmore immediately!"

Leaving the company in Malcom's capable hands, Pershing made his way down the train towards the rear and Whitmore's personal Pullman. He kept his eyes peeled for any sign of Jennifer. He knew she was with the rest of the medical staff but was unsure in which car she'd ridden. He was unable to spot her before reaching Whitmore's train car.

The old millionaire was standing on the rear platform preparing to address the officers that were assembling around it. He was quite a sight in his fancy General's uniform. Pershing admired the old man for his audaciousness and patriotism in raising a mercenary force to fight the Confederates—even if they were doing so in the guise of the Spanish Foreign Legion. But Pershing also knew, that Whitmore was not a professional soldier. He was thankful, from what he had seen thus far, that Whitmore had recruited many professional soldiers to serve in his mercenary force. The old man held his cane like a sword and all but brandished it at his men as he addressed them.

"Welcome to New Brunswick Canada!" There was a slightly audible murmur from the assembled officers. Most of them had no doubt discerned for themselves that they were not in either New York or Boston.

"The blasted Rebels have spies everywhere! They no doubt have prepared a naval task force to intercept us. Since the Spanish navy is unable to protect us, it was necessary to out fox them! I have arranged for several of my ships to leave both Boston and New York to serve as decoys. In the meantime, three large British transport ships await us two miles from here in Maces Bay. We're sailing to Cuba under the Union Jack of the British Empire!"

A long loud cry erupted from about half the assembled men. About half of Whitmore's men were either from Britain or Canada. Though many were men who despised slavery enough to take up rifles and fight against the CSA, Pershing wondered how many of them were like Malcom and only in it for the money. After being dismissed by Whitmore, the officers all moved to return to their companies. Pershing himself had turned to leave, when he heard the General call his name.

"Major Pershing!"

Pershing did an about face, and approached Whitmore. Qualified or not, Pershing treated him as a real General. He came to rigid attention and gave Whitmore a precise and crisp West Point salute.

"At ease, at ease," he said. "I just wanted to say how pleased I am that you decided to accept a commission in the Legion. I wish more of my countryman had availed themselves of this opportunity."

"It is an honor, General."

"How have you found your command?"

"Most of my men are very eager to fight the Confederates."

"No doubt. As negroes, they undoubtedly have as much desire to give the Rebels a good thrashing as you do— which is why I placed you in command of them."

Pershing was unsure how to take Whitmore's remarks. When he'd first arrived in Massena New York Whitmore had asked him why he wanted to serve. He'd told him the same thing he'd told Malcom. Somehow the eccentric old man had decided his desire for vengeance made him perfect to command the Legion's company of negroes.

If anyone has motive to fight the Confederates they do.

After taking his leave of Whitmore, Pershing made his way back up the train, once again keeping his eyes out for Jennifer. Though he was still unable to spot her, he did spot Joshua, the negro doctor they had met on their train trip to New York from Iowa. The tall young black man was hard to miss. He was the only educated negro that Pershing had ever met, was undoubtedly one of only a handful on the continent to be educated enough to be a surgeon. Whitmore had accepted him into the medical staff gladly. From the uniform he was wearing, it looked as if Joshua had been made a senior field medic.

"Hello, Joshua! Have you seen Jennifer?"

Joshua was busy unloading a crate of medical supplies from the train. He set it down on top of a stack of others before turning to face Pershing and give him a friendly smile. He pointed to the car in front of the one he was presently unloading.

"The nurses were transported in that car. I don't believe they've disembarked as yet."

Pershing nodded his thanks. He was fascinated by Joshua's educated speech, which contained only a slight trace of the intonations of slavery. By contrast he could barely understand most of the negro soldiers in his company. The South had spent the past 400 years keeping black people as uneducated as possible.

And the states of the United States haven't exactly taken positive steps to improve the educational situation of its own negroes. Pershing wondered how Joshua Winslow had ever been able to afford his education.

No sooner had he approached the train car than several nurses began to climb down from it. It was a passenger Pullman.

At least the ladies didn't have to travel in a boxcar. The second woman out of the door was Jennifer. Her face lit up at the sight of Pershing.

"John!"

"I don't have long. We're about to march out by company."

She gazed deeply into his eyes.

"I'm sure I'll see you aboard the ship…"

"Miss Harper!" A grizzled old doctor had emerged from the car. "This is no time to be fraternizing with soldiers, you have work to do. There are medical supplies to be unloaded and transported   !"

"Yes, doctor." She gave Pershing a quick kiss on the cheek and then whispered in his ear.

"I'll see you on board…"

"Miss Harper!"

"Coming, Doctor."

Pershing walked back to his company with an uncharacteristic smile on his face.

"Are we ready to move out, Malcom?"

"Yes sir, but I'm afraid we have a slight problem. I've done a head count and we seem to be missing a man..."

VI

Roger Connery rushed up the grassy hill with determined resolve. Below him and behind him was the train that had brought him and Whitmore's mercenary force to wherever it was that they were. He'd managed to infiltrate Whitmore's Legion and had planned on sailing with them to Cuba, but now there had been a major complication.

I should have known that they'd be leaving from a different port! I must learn where we are! In fact, he had already sent coded messages to Richmond informing them that Whitmore's force would be leaving from Boston and New York. It was far too late to recall the ships that had been dispatched to intercept Whitmore's convoy. *But if I can get a message through in time, perhaps the navy can dispatch additional ships to the proper area.*

The hill was not well suited to climbing. At one point it became so steep that he literally had to claw his way up by digging his fingers into the soft muddy soil. By the time he reached the top of the hill his uniform was dirty, muddy, and wet. The air was far colder than anything Connery was used to. Having a soaked uniform only made him feel colder.

Fighting off a shiver he pulled his binoculars from his field pack and started surveying the area. Off to the east he could see a large bay where three large freighters were anchored. In a small way, he could admire Whitmore's deceitful cunning in arranging such a covert departure. He went over the ships with his binoculars. He could make out only one of the ship's names.

The Capricorn. He also noticed something else—something that would greatly complicate the Confederacy's ability to intercept them. Each of the three ships was flying the Union Jack of the British Empire. He'd expected Whitmore to sail under the US Flag, or possibly the Spanish flag to spare his own country diplomatic troubles. But sailing under the British flag was totally unexpected.

Either he's doing this on his own in which case the British will not be happy with him or... he's doing this with the blessings of the British government. Connery didn't like the implications of that second thought. Either way, the CSA would be in a bind. Seizing British ships could easily lead to war.

It's Richmond's problem, not mine. He swung his binoculars away from the bay and began to survey the area around him. Down below the Legion had nearly disembarked and looked to be preparing to march towards the bay. To the north he saw an empty shore, patches of wood and fields of grass. To the south he saw…

It looks like a small town. Stowing his binoculars, he then started down the south slope of the hill. It wasn't as steep as the east slope had been, but it was much thicker with brush and grass. After reaching the bottom, he stayed off the main road because it ran parallel to the railroad tracks. He didn't want to take a chance on being spotted by any of Whitmore's men. His platoon would almost certainly realize that he was missing.

Perhaps they'll think that I got mixed up with one of the other platoons during that last march. Not until he had nearly reached the town did he allow himself onto the main road. The sign outside of the small town gave him his first clue as to where he was. It was written in both French and English. The English lettering read: ST ANDREWS. As he made his way into the hamlet he began to take in the small town. The flag flying from the small post office confirmed his suspicion. It was a large red flag which used the British Union Jack as its canton. A golden coat of arms was emblazed on the banner's red field.

I'm in Canada. That undoubtedly means that the British are in on this scheme. He swore angrily under his breath and began to look for a telegraph office. He spotted it two buildings down from the post office. He went to open the door, but found that it was locked. It was still fairly early in the morning and the telegraph office was not yet opened. Connery swore again. He then fumbled in one of his pouches for a lock pick.

"Can I help you, sir?" Connery spun to see a short plump young man who looked as if he'd had far too many sweets growing up. To Connery's surprise he was wearing short sleeves and short pants despite the cold weather. The young man had spoken so slowly that Connery had almost had difficulty understanding him.

"I just needed to send an urgent telegram. My ship will be leaving soon and I'm afraid I'm in a hurry."

"Just let me open up, eh?" he replied in that same slow deliberate speech. He pulled a set of keys from his pocket and unlocked the office door. "Now then…" he said as he went behind the counter and pulled out a piece of paper. "Just write your message out here and I'll send it off quick as a fiddle."

Connery accepted the proffered paper, took a pencil from the small holder atop the counter and started to write.

Dear Dad. Big change of plans. My ship is about to leave… He looked up and addressed the clerk again.

"I know I'm in St. Andrews but what is the name of this state…err…province?"

"You're in Maces Bay, New Brunswick, my friend."

Connery nodded and resumed his message.

My ship is about to leave Maces Bay, New Brunswick Canada. I'm travelling aboard the British freighter Capricorn along with two other British ships. Boston and New York were big disappointments. Tell Johnny the combination to grandpa's old safe is 7381. Love, Frank.

Connery then addressed the message to the address of one of his operatives in Maryland, just over the river from Confederate Virginia. With any luck, Richmond would have the message by the end of the day. Connery handed the message to the Canadian clerk who took it, counted the lines and said: that'll be ten cents to go out immediately. Connery pulled out a US dime and slapped it down on the counter. Apparently they weren't too far from the US border. The clerk snatched up the US coin and deposited it in his drawer.

"Will you be needing a receipt sir?"

"No, but do you have a place I can change."

"The clerk motioned to a small restroom only slightly bigger than a closet. Connery went in, pulled his spare uniform tunic from his bag and then changed as quickly as possible. When he left, he saw that the clerk had manned the telegraph and was already taping out his message in Morse code. He exited the telegraph office and then double timed it for the train. His mind raced with possible excuses as to where he'd been. He thought of a few, some more plausible than others. Which excuse he used would depend upon if, when, where, and how he was discovered.

When he first spotted the end of the train, he feared he might have been too late. Whitmore's personal Pullman car and the cars immediately behind it looked completely deserted. But as he followed the train around a bend he noticed that a large number of troops were still unloading crates of supplies. Ever so casually he joined in the work. The crates were exceedingly heavy. Something metallic rattled inside. He set his first crate down hard on a stack of similar crates. Each crate had an Eagle stenciled on it along with the words US Army.

"Careful their soldier. Those are artillery shells. It's not a good idea to set them down so hard."

"Sorry, Sergeant," said Connery. He treated the next load with a good deal more respect—and care. After three more trips his back was killing him, but he was keeping up with the others—and building an alibi.

To his great relief the next car did not contain crates of artillery shells. They contained artillery pieces themselves. These, however, were on wheels. Connery helped three other soldiers wheel one of the howitzers down the ramp of the box car. He took careful note of the weapon. It was breech loaded. The narrow barrel showed that it was certainly a rifled cannon. It was stamped with a Seal that said "Whitmore Ironworks."

So this is one of Whitmore's cannons. Connery made certain to get an exact count on the artillery pieces (there were ten), though he was unsure when he'd get another chance to send another report to his superiors in the Confederacy.

After unloading the cannons they moved onto the next car and began to unload crates of gunpowder. They treated these with the same respect that they had treated the crates of explosive artillery shells.

Just as they finished unloading the last few crates, a loud angry voice cried out.

"Murphey!" Connery spun around and came to attention trying to look innocent and nervous at the same time. It was Captain Malcom. The former Royal Marine swore angrily.

"Where the blazes have you been?"

"I'm sorry, sir. I'm afraid I'm a rather heavy sleeper. When I woke up I found the train car empty."

"Sergeant Gilman told me he checked the car and you weren't in it."

"The thing is sir, I'm honestly not sure I was in the right car. I got separated when we changed trains. I'm not good at memorizing faces and haven't been with the platoon long. In any event I was sleeping under two or three old blankets, Sergeant Gilman might have missed me. I'm very sorry."

Malcom sighed heavily.

"Well you obviously haven't deserted and it looks like you haven't exactly been lolly gagging. Let's get to the boats. Major Pershing will decide what to do with you."

Connery followed Captain Malcom in silence. They marched along the train, passed the locomotive, and then turned east and headed for the shore. Several long boats were making trips back and forth between the shore and the waiting ships, ferrying Whitmore's troops. Large pontoon rafts were being loaded down with crates. Sailors with long poles would then push out the boats to where the cargo would be loaded on the freighters by way of ship board cranes.

Pershing's company was sitting quietly on the beach, awaiting their turn to board the ships. Malcom looked disapprovingly at them. He'd have insisted that they stand at attention the entire time. Pershing himself was talking with an attractive young woman that appeared to be a nurse. Malcom marched up to them with Connery in tow and came to rigid attention. When Pershing failed to notice his presence he cleared his throat loudly.

"I have found our missing man, Major."

Pershing turned, obviously displeased at being distracted from his beautiful company, and addressed Connery sternly.

"Where have you been, soldier?"

Connery gave Pershing the exact same story he'd given Malcom.

"I found him helping unload supplies near the rear of the train," added Malcom.

"Well at least you made yourself useful. Don't let this happen again, or you'll be very sorry. Now go have a seat."

With that Pershing turned back to the beautiful young woman. Malcom looked incredulous at best and scandalized at worst. Connery could tell he'd expected the company commander to dispense some form of punishment. It seemed Pershing was too enamored with the young lady to care.

Connery took a seat with the other soldiers, making sure to sit with the white platoon. To his disgust two of this companies three platoons were composed of negroes. He wanted to curse Whitmore for arming blacks but found himself unable to.

How can I when we're arming niggers too?

A short while later their turn finally came. Malcom ordered them to their feet and then to board the long boats. The water in the bay was very calm as they rowed out to the ships. As the longboat came alongside of the *Capricorn* Connery noticed that large nets had been thrown over the side of the ship. At Malcom's orders they began to climb. Connery slung his rifle over his shoulder and started up. Even at that moment he was plotting what he would do next…

VII

"Welcome aboard the Capricorn, General Whitmore."

Whitmore looked the British Merchant Marine Captain in the eye.

"You may dispense with the pleasantries, Captain. Are we ready to get underway?"

"We are indeed, sir. Just as soon as we have finished loading your men and supplies. We have prepared a cabin for you, however, there is an important gentleman on board, a representative from Her Majesty's Government. He's waiting for you in the ward room and wishes to speak to you alone."

Whitmore turned to David Lovejoy.

"See that the men are properly settled in for the voyage."

"Yes, sir. I'll also see to your things."

The Captain led Whitmore through a hatch in the superstructure.

"This is a fine vessel," said Whitmore. "It's the finest freighter I've ever been on, and that's a fact."

"You'll find that the Capricorn and her sister ships are far more than they appear. On the outside they are designed to look like top of the line freighters, nothing more. Their engines, however, are far more powerful than those of a normal cargo vessel. The tarp covered crates on the bow conceal a three-inch deck gun, and the accommodations inside are especially suited to transporting troops and special persons such as yourself."

"Exactly who is this gentleman that I am meeting?" asked Whitmore as they stepped through yet another hatch.

"Charles Landon, Mr. Whitmore," said a deep booming voice.

Whitmore suddenly realized that they had now stepped into a luxuriously decorated and furnished wardroom.

"I am pleased to meet you, sir," said Whitmore extending his hand. Landon was also an elderly man, whose years easily matched Whitmore's own. Whitmore had grown used to being the oldest person in almost any situation. It felt strange and yet somehow comforting to meet a man of his own generation who was apparently still as active as he himself.

Landon shook Whitmore's proffered hand. He was a heavy set clean shaven man with a full head of closely cut, solid white hair. With his finely tailored black suit, Landon looked like he belonged more on the dance floor of a London ball or on the floor of Parliament rather than on a merchant vessel at sea.

"I'm afraid, Mr. Landon, that you have me at a bit of a disadvantage. If you'll pardon my being blunt, what exactly are you here to tell me."

"I represent the British Admiralty—specifically Naval Intelligence. London thought it necessary that you be brought up to speed on events happening abroad or rather on things that are about to happen."

"I'll assume whatever information you've brought me is of imminent importance," replied Whitmore.

"You are very astute, sir."

At that moment a steward entered carrying a tray with a pot of tea and two cups. After the tea had been poured and the sailor had withdrawn, Landon continued.

"Our intelligence sections in Paris have learned that the French are planning on entering the war against Spain."

Whitmore very nearly choked on his tea. He recovered quickly.

"They have declared war on Spain then?"

"Not yet. But our information indicated that it will only be a matter of days before Emperor Napoleon IV issues the declaration."

"Won't this provoke a war with Prussia? King Leopold is related to King Wilhelm."

"It's possible, but unlikely. The French Empire has strong allies in the west German states of the Rhineland and in Bavaria and in the Austro-Hungarian Empire not to mention their alliance with the CSA and the Empire of Mexico. If Prussia goes to war with France it will find itself fighting multiple enemies on two fronts—I doubt even the Prussians will take those odds."

"I thought that a convenient rebellion was being instigated in Algeria to keep the French busy."

"It is. But it has not yet come to fruition. In the meantime we've learned that French forces are on the move elsewhere."

"They're sending troops to Cuba?" Whitmore managed to sound at the same time both agitated and concerned. Fighting the Confederates was going to be tough enough. Fighting both the Confederates and the French would be nigh impossible. But Landon shook his head.

"The French are content to leave Cuba to the Confederacy. By all reports the Confederate States campaign in Cuba is going far better than anyone expected but we'll come to that matter in a moment. France is out to seize other Spanish territories that are ripe for conquest. Specifically we've learned that a large force will be sailing from Saigon in French Indo-China to launch an invasion of the Philippines."

Whitmore allowed himself a brief sigh of relief. France's imminent entry into the war was not good news, but a conflict on the other side of the world would affect his plans in Cuba very little.

"French forces are also planning an operation in this hemisphere. According to our sources French troops in Mexico are being prepared for deployment somewhere in the Caribbean."

"You just told me the French were leaving Cuba to the Rebels!"

"They are. As far as we can tell, these troops are going to be sent to capture the island of Puerto Rico—either for themselves or to help the Confederates obtain it."

"I've never heard anything about the Confederates being interested in Puerto Rico," said Whitmore.

"Regardless, it is of vital importance that we keep Puerto Rico out of the hands of both the CSA and the French Empire."

"Why?"

Landon unrolled a map and pointed at the small Spanish possession east of Cuba and Hispaniola.

"Because Puerto Rico commands the sea lanes between North America, South America, Europe, Africa, and the rest of the world for that matter. Most importantly it commands the sea routes to the canal that the French and Confederates are building in Panama. In the hands of the Spanish it is little more than an undeveloped island but in the hands of a more ambitious and aggressive power it would make a powerful naval base. One far more advantageous then the one your government has been seeking from Spain by obtaining or leasing Guantanamo Bay in Cuba."

Whitmore stared grimly at the island.

"Then why was Washington trying to buy Cuba and failing that trying to lease a naval base at Guantanamo?"

"At the risk of offending you, I believe it is because your government is more interested in thumbing its nose at your former compatriots in the Confederacy than with seizing strategic spots."

Whitmore leapt to his feet and let out a growl. Not at Landon, but at the aforementioned Confederates. He swore profanely then slammed his fist down on the map atop the Confederate States of America.

"Yes, we do want to deal those filthy traitors a proper punch in the eye. They ripped our nation in two, caused two wars that cost the lives of hundreds of thousands of Americans—they humiliated us not once but twice!"

Whitmore stopped suddenly. He had worked himself up until he was literally red in the face. Both his heart and his head were pounding. He was nearly hyperventilating.

"Please calm down, Mr. Whitmore," said Landon. "You'll do neither your country any good, nor your enemies any harm if you give yourself a heart attack or a stroke here today."

Whitmore took a deep breath as he returned to his chair.

"If Napoleon wants Puerto Rico he can have it!" he said obstinately. "The Confederates want Cuba and by Jove I will stop them from getting it."

"Even if you succeed in keeping the Confederates from taking Cuba—a feat I believe highly unlikely or more plausibly you manage to hold on to Guantanamo until our two governments can convince Spain to sell or lease it to the Unites States it will largely be for naught if the Confederacy or France obtain Puerto Rico. Any US base in Cuba would be heavily isolated. Resupplying and protecting it would be difficult just because of its proximity to the Confederate States. If either the CSA or France controls Puerto Rico, however, it would be all but impossible. Confederate-French control of that island would also threaten our own naval bases in Jamaica and British Honduras, something we cannot allow."

As was his habit, when he was excited or annoyed, Whitmore rose from his feet and began to pace the floor, holding up his cane like a sword.

Landon was content to remain seated. At that moment he was slightly jealous of his fellow elder, who despite his age, seemed to still posses great vigor and strength—even if he did walk with a cane.

These Americans are passionate, thought Landon. *Passion can be a source of great strength. It can also be a hindrance, especially when it crosses the line into pride.*

Whitmore continued to pace the wardroom, muttering to himself. As much as he hated to admit it, Landon had a point.

He should know, thought Whitmore. *The British have made a habit of controlling important strategic points around the world.* His mind drifted to the Suez, the Straight of Gibraltar, and the attempted British capture of New Orleans during the long ago War of 1812 where a still united America had successfully defended the port that controlled the mouth of the mighty Mississippi. He once again turned to face Landon.

"You said a few moments ago that the Rebel campaign in Cuba was going far better for them than expected, and a few moments ago you expressed doubt that my forces will be able to make a difference in Cuba. I'd appreciate it if you'd elaborate further."

Landon poured himself another cup of tea. He also refilled Whitmore's half empty cup and gestured for him to have a seat. The agitated millionaire let out a sigh but once again took a seat across from the representative of the British Admiralty.

"The Confederates have completely secured Havana, and their forces are pushing rapidly across the island."

"How are they moving so quickly?"

"Because they have attacked with a massive invasion force and because they are meeting so little resistance. Most of the island has risen up in rebellion against the Spanish. For the most part the Confederates are being treated as liberators. The Spanish garrison is under attack from all directions. The Confederate navy has successfully blockaded every major port on the island."

Landon unrolled another map on top of the first, this one of Cuba and its coastal waters.

"These ships will not be able to just sail into Santiago de Cuba. We'll have to put you ashore several miles up shore from the port. Even that will be risky. The area will likely be crawling with Confederate ships."

"We're flying the British flag. The Confederates wouldn't dare attack us."

"If they catch us offloading hostile troops in a warzone I doubt they'd hesitate at all regardless of the consequences. You Americans—both Northern and Southern—all have much in common, including a propensity to act on passion and in the heat of the moment without a forethought for the consequences."

"Perhaps you could put us ashore at night."

"That is a possibility. But that would entail dangers and difficulties of its own."

Whitmore grunted.

"Are you trying to tell me that we should go to Puerto Rico instead?"

Landon nodded his head.

"That would be the most prudent course of action. As we discussed, the news of the French threat to Puerto Rico has greatly altered the dynamics of this situation. My counterpart in New York is trying to convince your government to change its focus from Guantanamo to Puerto Rico. If a combined US / British fleet is to confront the Confederates and French it would be far more advantageous to do so over Puerto Rico rather than a small Cuban port that will be completely surrounded by Confederate forces. If your government agrees then hopefully we can convince Spain to sell the United States Puerto Rico before the French attack. But if our negotiations with Spain fail then it would be far more advantageous to have you and your forces on Puerto Rico, rather than being trapped in Cuba."

Whitmore did not like what he was hearing at all. Almost uncontrollably he rose to his feet again.

"If Puerto Rico is as important as you say it is, then why don't you British take it for yourselves! You've got the military muscle to do it."

"Yes, we do. But there are a number of reasons why we'd prefer not to. In the first place, by the time we assembled an expedition it would most likely be too late, on the other hand your country has a garrison prepared and ready to set sail to take possession of Guantanamo. It could just easily sail for Puerto Rico instead. As I've tried to convince you, you and your men could go there and help secure it now. If Britain tries to take the island after French forces have taken possession of it then that will mean war.

Neither of our countries is prepared for full scale war right now. I fear the day is coming and is probably inevitable that a great intercontinental war will be fought but now is not the time. In the second place, Britain does not want to take Puerto Rico because we are committed to helping the United States regain a position of power in the western hemisphere. A US controlled Puerto Rico would go a long way towards strengthening the strategic situation of the United States. France has helped develop the CSA into a formidable ally, it's in our best interests to do the same with the United States."

"Is that how you British see us? As a pawn against the French?"

"Personally, I think Britain sees the United States as younger brothers. We have much in common, your country and mine. These commonalities go far beyond the mere philosophy of 'the enemy of my enemy is my friend'. The United States is a great nation, Britain can help you regain your rightful place as the dominant power of the western hemisphere. Now will you please consider our proposition?"

"I've already told the Spanish, the United States and the world that I would keep the Confederates from capturing Cuba."

"Mr. Whitmore, if you are unsuccessful, it is very unlikely that either the Spanish or your force will be able to escape Cuba to reinforce Puerto Rico."

"You are that certain that our defense of Cuba will fail?"

"I'm afraid I am."

"Well right or wrong, Joseph Whitmore does not go back on his word. I will hold Cuba against the Rebels, or die trying."

Now it was Landon's turn to sigh. He shook his head admitting defeat.

"Mr. Whitmore, I wish you all the luck in the world..."

VIII

"Keep your heads down!" cried Corporal Jefferson Case to his squad of Confederate Marines. At the moment, bullets were flying through the air just above them, and though they could not see their attackers who were taking refuge in the tree line up ahead, Case's squad was, unfortunately, out in the open.

I knew we shouldn't have tried to cross this field. Case and his men had come to respect the deadly accuracy of the Mauser rifles being carried by the Spanish troops. Case was thankful that the grass of the field they'd chosen to cross was relatively tall. It provided them a small amount of cover but no protection at all.

They'd been in hot pursuit of the shattered remnants of the Spanish force that had defended Havana but despite what the papers were saying back in the CSA, the Spanish troops were not in full retreat. Instead they were engaged in a "fighting retreat." They would make the Confederates fight tooth and claw for a position, fall back, and then make another stand. The Confederates were winning, but only just.

Not far from Case a marine started cursing louding, swearing profanely, and uttering blasphemies. Such language was common in the Confederate Marine Corps, but there was a distinct sense of urgency and panic in the man's tirade.

"I'm shot!" he cried, clarifying the obvious.

Case rolled over to the wounded Marine. He'd taken a bullet in his upper thigh. There was a lot of blood, but fortunately there was no crimson fountain spraying from it.

"It looks like it didn't hit any major arteries. As long as it didn't hit the bone you should be fine. Just keep pressure on it until they can get a tourniquet on it!" While staying on the ground Case looked back towards the direction they'd been coming from and shouted over the sound of the gunfire.

"Medics!" He then addressed his men.

"Stay low and move forward!"

With Case in the lead, the squad began to crawl towards the tree line. A while later, from the opposite end of the field, two Confederate medics with conspicuous white arm bands and vests emblazoned with red crosses entered the field carrying a stretcher. So far the Spanish had apparently kept to the so-called rules of war. Case hadn't heard of any medics being shot, though the campaign was only a couple of weeks old. He hadn't seen any Spanish medics. If he did he wouldn't shoot them, though bullets often didn't care who they maimed and killed.

Suddenly, thunder boomed overhead. They sky was dark with thick gray rainclouds. Case had already felt a few drops of rain hit him. A few moments later it was pouring. If it hadn't been for the tension of being in battle, he might have found the overcast a welcome relief from the glaring tropical sun and the cool rain a comfort from the sweltering heat.

But when the sun comes back out it will all turn to steam and we'll be in a pressure cooker. A moment later a bullet hit the ground near him, bringing his mind back to more pressing matters. He was pretty sure the tropical heat would only make him feel like he was going to die. Getting shot was sure to do the trick.

They were now less than twenty yards from the enemy held tree line. Case could see the fiery muzzle flashes of the Spanish rifles and could just make out the silhouettes of a number of enemy soldiers. The sky blue uniforms worn by the Spanish weren't really suited to the environment.

Of course, reflected Case, *gray isn't the best color either.* In point of fact, however, it was so stained with mud that it looked more like a mottled uniform of brown-gray, which made it a virtual camouflaged uniform. He worked the bolt on his 1892 CS Richmond Rifle, aimed at one of the muzzle flashes and pulled the trigger. His squad mates also opened fire. The gray-uniformed Confederate marines sent a torrent of fiery hot led towards the tree line—far more than they had been receiving. Case worked the bolt-action lever and fired again.

We must have them outnumbered! The marine next to Case took a bullet in the head. Blood and brains sprayed everywhere. Ignoring it, Case kept up his fire. There was nothing that could be done for him and ever since landing on Cuba, he had been hardened to such sights. After firing his last round he rolled over and laid flat on his back. He pulled the bolt on his rifle all the way back and locked it into place. He then reached into his black leather ammo bag and pulled a brass cartridge which he pushed down into the rifle. He loaded six more then chambered the first found by working the bolt again. He hoped the falling torrent of rain wouldn't interfere with the firing mechanism. So far Case had found the Richmond Rifle extremely reliable. He'd heard some Marines say that you could drag it through the mud or carry it through a creek and it would still fire. He didn't care to put such notions to the test.

Case rolled back onto his belly and again took aim at the tree line. He spotted a muzzle flash and afterward was just able to make out the form of a sky-blue clad Spaniard. Case took aim. His rifle barked and the enemy soldier crumpled to the ground. He emptied his rifle a second time and then after reloading yet again he called out to his men.

"Fix bayonets and make sure you're fully loaded!" The storm of bullets coming from the Confederates ceased momentarily as each man stopped to reload his magazine and fix his bayonet. Case pulled his own bayonet from its scabbard and affixed it to the end of his rifle. He'd personally notched the blade making it an even more gruesome weapon.

Case took a couple of deep breaths and then roared the order to charge. The Confederate marines leapt to their feet and charged with a fury. They let loose the high pitched cry of the Rebel Yell which pierced through the air like the screams of a thousand banshees let loose from the pit of hell. Case fired a couple of times as he charged for no other reason than to try to keep the Spaniards' heads down. Running at break neck speed it was impossible to aim. He fired no additional shots because he wanted to have plenty of bullets in his rifle when he was finally face to face with the enemy. Other Marines weren't so reserved. Several completely emptied their rifles in their dash towards the tree line.

A few of the Spaniards were so startled by the sudden Confederate charge that they turned and ran rather than fight the gray-clad grunts man to man. Others stayed at their posts and fired at the oncoming Confederates. Four more marines went down clutching bloody wounds. A couple of others slipped in the massive mud puddles caused by the falling rain. The rest surged into the tree line.

A bullet cracked past Case's head, impossibly close. Another inch and he'd have been dead. A second later a second bullet whirred past him, not as close as the first but still dangerously near the mark. Case raised his rifle and fired at the Spaniard that had been trying to kill him. The enemy soldier's head exploded like a ripe melon. Case next took aim at another Spaniard taking cover behind a tree and apparently trying to reload his Mauser. He squeezed the trigger and a fountain of blood erupted out of the sky-blue clad soldier's neck. He then fell over sideways and hit the muddy ground, never to rise again.

He charged forward again. Seemingly out of nowhere the wooden end of a rifle came swinging towards his face. A Spaniard had swung it like a club from behind a tree. It struck Case in the face like a baseball bat, busting his nose and sending him reeling back. Case fell backwards and landed on his back in the mud. In addition to the intense pain, he felt a warm-wet sensation on his face that had nothing to do with the rain fall that was seeping its way through the tree tops. In his mouth, Case tasted the iron flavor of his own blood. His vision was so blurred by a face filled with blood and mud that he couldn't see. It would only be a second before the Spaniard would be on him to finish the job. Instinctively he raised his rifle and started pulling the trigger. He fired off his last three shots and over the sound of the other rifle shots being fired around the wood, Case heard an angry pain filled voice cry out in Spanish.

Case felt a sudden surge of adrenaline. He leapt to his feet and wiped the blood and mud out of his eyes with his dirty uniform sleeve. One of his shots had indeed wounded the Spaniard in the side. But the enemy was not down. Both men let loose with fierce battle cries and charged one another with empty but bayoneted rifles. The Spaniard lunged at Case violently trying to impale him with the end of his bayonet. Case dodged expertly, finally thankful for the grueling bayonet training his instructors had so violently instilled in him. He'd hated them back then, but not now. He put their vicious instruction to use. He brought up his rifle butt and struck the Spanish soldier in the face, paying the Spaniard back for his own busted nose. He followed the blow up with another, this one to the Spaniards solar plexus, then with all of his strength and a howling cry Case reared back and plunged his bayonet into the man's ribs. The Spaniard let out a pain filled cry, dropping his rifle and then falling to his knees. His eyes locked momentarily with those of his killer. Case kept tight hold of his rifle. With his bayonet's notched blade it wouldn't just come out. It was, in fact, securely lodged between two of the Spaniard's ribs. Case brutally kicked the enemy soldier in the chest with his booted foot and simultaneously ripped his bayonet out of him. The notched blade ripped bits of flesh, muscle, guts, and bone out of the man so that a massive jagged hole was left in his side. There was a sudden spray of warm blood that hit Case in the face. The Spaniard fell backwards onto the muddy ground. Blood poured from his nose, his mouth and above all from the massive wound in his side. He tried to speak but all that came out was the bubbly garble of a man dying in total agony.

Taking a deep breath, Case looked around to assess the situation. The Confederate marines had cleared the wooded area of Spanish troops. All the members of the enemy force had either fled or were lying dead in the mud. He took a moment to reload his rifle, then yelled for his squad to rally around him. They then pressed forward as a group. Here and there they passed the bodies of fallen soldiers and marines. The sound of rifle fire had largely ceased, replaced by the droning cries of wounded and suffering men. Some of the cries were in English, others in Spanish. Case sent a runner back towards the rear to tell the medics to come forward and deal with the wounded. They then took a few minutes to give their wounded comrades what aid they could while they waited for the medics to arrive.

Case stooped over a wounded marine. The man's gray uniform was stained with blood where the sleeve met the tunic. He'd taken a bullet in the arm pit. On further inspection Case also noticed that the man had been shot in the knee cap. Case loosed the man's canteen from his belt and gave him a drink of water. After making him as comfortable as possible (not that that was at all possible) he rose to his feet. Suddenly, off to the right, Case heard a desperate frantic voice calling out in Spanish. He spun around and saw a young Spanish soldier lying against a tree. He couldn't have been any older than eighteen—possibly younger. His sky-blue uniform was soaked with blood. He'd taken two bullets in the chest, though they had apparently missed his heart. He stooped down beside the Spaniard. He looked even younger up close.

"Madre! Madre!" he cried with tear filled eyes. He didn't seem to realize that Case was there. Case took his own canteen and lifted it to the boy's lips. The boy was suddenly startled. His gaze locked with that of Case then he took a sip from the canteen. He said a few more words of Spanish, none of which Case understood. The boy took his hand. Case let him. A few moments later the boys grip loosened and Case let his lifeless hand fall to the ground. He reached out and closed the boy's eyes then forced himself to his feet. He felt more than tired. He felt hollowed out, as if he had no soul.

When the medics finally came on the scene, Case's shouted to his squad and they pushed forward yet again. As they neared the other end of the wood, the sound of rifle fire picked up again. It was accompanied by another sound. At first Case thought it was more thunder but the falling rain had lessened considerably. Then he heard it again.

Artillery...He was unsure to which side it belonged, but he had no doubt as to what it was. From behind, he caught the sound of a horse whinny. He turned and saw three gray uniformed mounted officers riding towards he and his squad. They were accompanied by another rider that held aloft the Blood Stained Banner. The only one of the men that Case recognized was Captain Fordice. Though he didn't know who the officer in the lead was, he recognized from the three gold wreathed stars on the man's uniform that he was a General. He had a salt and pepper mustache and chin beard that made him look like a Frenchman. There was, however, something familiar about the man. Case called out to his squad.

"Attention!"

The officers reined in and Case brought his arm up in salute.

"Report Corporal!" said Captain Fordice.

"We've just about cleared the woods, sir."

"From what I saw back there, it seems that you men had quite a scrap with the enemy," said the General.

"We had a little run in, yes sir."

"From what the Colonel commanding this section told me, your squad practically carried the positon by yourselves," said the General.

Case was unsure what to say. They'd simply done their job and given the Spaniards a good kick in the teeth.

"You've done well, Corporal. With men such as yours we'll soon have this whole island in our pocket! Keep up the good work. Good day, *Sergeant!* With that the General spurred his horse and continued on. The others followed after him. Captain Fordice hung back briefly.

"Keep moving forward till you reach the end of this wood. It should be just ahead. When you get there hold your position until you receive further orders."

"Yes sir. Sir, if ya don't mind me asking, who was that General?"

"That, Sergeant, was General Fitzhugh Lee."

IX

Ebenezer swung his hammer with all the fury that burned within him, driving an iron nail through two pieces of wood. He drew another and repeated the process. He then made sure that the wooden stud was firmly attached to the plate attached to the top board. He'd nailed over a dozen such studs, but he had over a dozen to go. He rose to his feet, took a deep breath, then wiped dirty sweat from the brow of his black skinned face. Building Mansel Dumas' newest storage shed was hard enough in the simmering heat—there wasn't so much as a wisp of cloud in the sky. Doing it by himself, however, was sheer agony.

A few yards away there was an old tin pale that he used to hold his water. He kept it under the shade of a tree so that it wouldn't become hot in the blazing sun. Nothing made him sicker to his stomach than drinking hot well water. He walked over, lifted the pale to his lips and drank straight from the bucket. After taking a refreshing drink, he dipped his hands in the remainder of the water and splashed his face to cool his burning cheeks and forehead. He took another handful of water, leaned his head down and let it pour down the back of his neck and down his back. He then turned to regard his work in progress.

The skeletal wooden frame was coming together slowly but surely. His master, Mansel Dumas, had given him one week to finish the frame and no help whatsoever. He was on day three. He'd have to work from dawn till dusk for the next two days to make sure he finished on time. Ebenezer wondered if it was Dumas' way of letting him share in Cap's punishment for running away. Cap had been given only a short while to recover from his flogging. Cap was hard at work in the fields, and from what Ebenezer had been told the overseers weren't giving him an easy time. He'd had all privileges revoked for the indefinite future and Dumas had brought his days of working alongside Ebenezer to a permanent end. Still, it could have been worse.

If this were Sharpstone Plantation, Cap would have been killed and every last slave given a beating. He'd received more beatings in his life at the hands of his former master than he could count. Still, just thinking about it made him feel the fiery burning of the lash upon his back. He'd thought Dumas was different and in a way he was. Whereas Fitch Haley would whip his slaves brutally on a whim, Ebenezer hadn't seen a single slave on Twin Harbours Plantation whipped until Cap ran away. What more, Ebenezer had seen genuine remorse on Duma's face when he'd had Cap flogged.

Not dat it made a bit o' diff'ence fo' Cap. All he wanted was his woman and his youngin'! Gritting his teeth, Ebenezer left the shade of the tree to return to his work.

Massa Mansel is less cruel than Massa Fitch, but he still cruel. Suddenly, Ebenezer wondered if the other slaves on Twin Harbors saw it that way. The vast majority of them had spent their entire lives on the plantation, never knowing anything else. Back on Sharpstone all the slaves had feared Fitch Haley and rightfully so. They had also quietly hated him with a deep simmering hatred that raged like a small but intensely hot fire within the soul. But many of the slaves on Twin Harbours seemed to genuinely respect and even love the Dumas family. He wondered how they would react when the soon coming revolt began. Uncontrollably his gaze shifted to the thick wooded area down by the river bank. Ebenezer knew that there were dozens of rifles hidden there.

He'd held one with his own hands. Caesar had made it clear that it would only be a matter of weeks.

Then da day o' judgment and jubilee finally be here! Caesar had tasked him with carefully recruiting slaves for the coming revolt. So far he'd only informed a few—all of them former slaves of Sharpstone. He was too worried that one of the Twin Harbour negroes might get word to the Dumas. He still hadn't told Cap. That would happen that coming night, when Caesar was supposed to return after nightfall to get a report.

He set about his work again with a fury. The excitement of the soon coming revolt flooding him with adrenaline. The hard labor at least gave him an outlet for the tempest brewing within him. He'd finished nailing another half dozen studs when he caught sight of Rosy. The house slave had been giving him not to subtle signs that she liked him. She seemed to keep finding little excuses to come and see him during the day and evening. Today she was carrying a basket which was emitting a very pleasant and appetizing aroma.

"Hello, Ebe'nezza!" she said. "Miss Flossy, she tell me ta bring you some of des' fresh butter'd biscuits, since you workin so hard." She stopped and starred at his hard muscular body. He'd been working with his shirt off. Though he was filthy and drenched in sweat her heart pounded in her chest.

He turned momentarily to set down his hammer and then she caught sight of his back. It was a labyrinth of scar tissue. Her face went from one of feminine desire, to one of shock and near horror.

"O' you po' man! Dat mean ole' Fitch is a devil jus' like dey say!" Ebenezer looked around quickly to make sure no white folks were around. Most whites in the Natchez area despised Fitch Haley and would have agreed whole heartedly with her statement. Even so, it was extremely dangerous for any black to ever say anything bad about a white man, no matter how true it may have been.

Dat will change soon!

He took the basket from Rosy and practically stuffed one of the delicious biscuits into his mouth.

"You as bad as da youngins' you know dat?"

He smiled then responded by scarfing down another.

"I's hungry," he said as he regarded her with his eyes, suddenly realizing he was hungry for more than just biscuits.

"Well tonight, how bout' I come by yo' cabin and bring you a special suppa. I think I can git' us some fried chicken."

Ebenezer's mouth suddenly started watering. He'd only had fried chicken once in his life.

"Won't you git in trouble fo' swipin' food from de kitchen?"

She shook her head and smiled.

"Miss Flossy say it okay, jus dis once. And afterward... we's can have...dessert."

The way she looked at him left little doubt as to what she had in mind for 'dessert.' His heart started pounding in his chest and he suddenly felt extremely invigorated. Then, like a hundred ton of bricks it hit him.

Caesar! Caesar be here tonight! He looked at her.

"Rosey I'd love to be wit you tonight, I's truly would. But I cain't... not tonight..."

In an instant her face went from romantic enchantment to a pain filled face as though he had slapped her. He saw her eyes swell with tears.

"Why not?" she said in a voice like ashes.

"I cain't explain right now I jus' cain't"

The tears started to flow down her face and she turned to leave.

He grabbed her, by the arms and pulled her back to him, firmly but without malice or hurting her.

"Rosy, I likes you a lot, I really do. And I do want to be wit you! You come to me tomorrow night and I promise I tell you everything! I gots business tonight that I cain't put off. It's important."

"What is it?"

"I tol' you I cain't say, not here not now." He looked around quickly to once again make sure no one was within listening range. He looked back at her, and then— impulsively—he wrapped his arms around her and kissed her—long and passionately. At first she tensed, but then she yielded and wrapped her own arms around him and pressed her lips even more firmly against his.

Meanwhile, Mansel Dumas, the master of Twin Harbours Plantation was directing his negroes on the river docks as they loaded bales of cotton onto a waiting river barge. At one time the cash crop had been known as "white gold." For generations of Southerners it had been "King Cotton," and the lifeblood of the Southern economy. For hundreds of years negro slavery had been the heart that kept that life blood pumping.

Long lines of strong and muscular black slaves made their way from the storehouses. Each one carried a large bale of cotton his back. Once they reached the docks they set down their burden then returned to get another. On the docks other burly negroes man handled the bales onto the waiting barge while the white men—both Mansel's hired overseers and the bargemen stood around and watched. One bargeman and one of Mansel's men each counted the bales as they were loaded and together composed two copies of the manifest.

Twin Harbours was doing far better than most of the other plantations in Mississippi and the Confederacy at large, but Mansel knew it was not nearly as profitable as it had been in his father's day. By God's grace, his plantation had been spared the boll weevil infestation that had swept much of the CSA and with a lot of hard work and good management he'd made it as productive as possible. But decreased cotton demand and hostile foreign markets were impossible to avoid.

When the last bale had finally been loaded, Mansel examined both copies of the manifest, then he and the barge captain each signed them. Mansel kept one for his own records and the other went with the barge. Not long afterward, the barge got under way, pulled by a steam powered tug boat that would take it all the way to the markets of New Orleans. From there it would be exported to the world. The next day, another barge would arrive that would take another load of cotton up river to the markets of Memphis and St. Louis. Ironically most of that cotton would be sold to textile companies in the United States. Mansel didn't send any more cotton north than he had to.

Confederate excise taxes and U.S. trade tariffs cut deeply into the profits from such sales.

After the barge had departed, Mansel made his way back towards the mansion. As he walked along the stone path, he noticed his two young daughters—Nancy and Connie—playing in the garden. They got excited when they saw him, and the two little girls came skipping hand in hand towards him. Nancy was nine and Connie was seven, but the years just seemed to be flying by. Seeing the two girls made Dumas think of his son Mitchell, now eighteen years old and off serving in the militia. Mitchell hadn't been home from the militia in weeks.

"Hi Daddy!" chorused the little girls.

"Hello, my little songbirds. What have you been up to this fine afternoon?"

"We've been picking flowers in the garden," said Nancy.

"And playing with rollie pollies," said Connie.

"Why are your hands so dirty?" asked Mansel.

"We've been making mud pies," replied Nancy. Mansel smiled.

"Well you two had best get washed up before your Mammy sees you."

As if on cue, a large, rotund black woman appeared brandishing a wooden spoon like a weapon.

"Nancy! Connie! Where you girls at? Oh hello Massa Mansel!" She then noticed the girls muddy hands. "Look at yo' hands! You two git up to da house and wash up! Suppa' gone be ready soon, now git!"

Mansel smiled in spite of himself, watching the fussy mammy all but chase the children back to the mansion. He followed along at a leisurely pace, taking the time to enjoy the fresh air and the beauty of the plantation. Two or three slaves walked past busy with their chores. They tipped their hats and greeted him with smiles. When he finally made it to the mansion he found his wife, Florence waiting on him. Crippled by a stroke years earlier she stood with one arm hanging limp, yet at heart she was the strongest woman he had ever known. He kissed her on the cheek.

"Did everything go well at the docks, my dear?"

He nodded.

"As well as possible I suppose. If cotton prices drop any more I'm not sure what we're going to do."

"This plantation has been in your family for over one-hundred years. With the good Lord's help we have always prospered. That is not about to change." He nodded and kissed her again. With her good hand she took hold of her husband's arm and the two of them began to slowly make their way towards the front door. A finely dressed slave named Berry was already holding it open.

"Do you think that Mitchell will be home soon?"

"He's mad at me for having Cap whipped," said Dumas.

"I do wish that hadn't been necessary. If anything for Mitchell's sake. He's always been such a sensitive boy."

"Flossy, he's going to have to learn that order must be maintained on a plantation. If he's going to be the master of this plantation one day he's going to have to learn to be firm."

"Still, you could have shown Cap some leniency, considering the circumstances. That's the first time we've had to whip a slave in years."

"If I'd let Cap go unpunished it would only have encouraged other runaways."

Suddenly, they heard a strange noise, like a miniature train engine. Dumas turned to see a horseless carriage coming up the drive of the plantation.

"Good heavens!" said Flossy, "that must be one of those contraptions that Mitchell was making such a fuss about!"

Mansel nodded.

"I'll see what this gentleman wants. Why don't you go on into the house, my dear. Berry see that Mrs. Dumas gets in safely."

"Yes, suh!" said Berry and offered his mistress his arm.

Mansel walked down the front steps just as the horseless carriage came to a halt in front of the mansion. The driver, a finely dressed young man in his late twenties or early thirties turned off the engine and spryly jumped down from his contraption. Though it had been nearly three months, Dumas recognized him as the same man he and Mitchell had met at the auction where he'd purchased Ebenezer, Cap, and the other slaves he'd obtained from Fitch Haley.

"Good day to you, sir," said the man and lifted his top hat to Dumas.

"Good day to you. What can I do for you today?"

"Mr. Dumas, my name is Lester Jones, I own Turtle Creek plantation about twenty miles north of here. I doubt you remember but I met you and your son at a slave auction not far from here."

"I do indeed remember you, Mr. Jones. It was hard to forget you. Your contraption is all my son spoke of for weeks."

Lester smiled.

"Indeed. And where is the young master?"

"He is serving in the county militia."

Lester smiled again.

"I'm sure you are very proud of him."

"We certainly are. So what can I do for you today?"

"I have come to invite you and your family to a small get together at my home. I have a very special guest coming that I would like all of my fellow planters in this area to get to meet."

"And just who would that be?"

"Former President Thomas Jonathan Jackson, himself."

"Stonewall?"

Lester smiled and nodded.

"In the flesh." He handed Dumas a small ornate envelope containing an official invitation. "I do hope you will come and hear what he has to say."

"If he's coming to Mississippi to convince us to free our slaves, he's wasting his breath and his time."

"I can see you're going to be a challenge, Mr. Dumas. If I may say, you remind me much of my late father. I would like to personally assure you, that Mr. Jackson's view and my own has nothing to do bringing about nigger equality with the white man or of bringing about anarchy by cutting the negroes loose without any constraints or controls. He is not the black republican he is so often portrayed as in the papers. What we are talking about, sir, is adapting to the changing circumstances of the world." He motioned to the horseless carriage behind him. "The future belongs to the wonders of technology. What we are seeing now is only the tip of the iceberg of what is to come. Mr. Jackson has a plan that will greatly expand, improve and industrialize the economy of the entire Confederacy."

"You mean make us more like the Yankees," said Dumas coldly.

Lester smiled disarmingly.

"Just think, sir. If Mr. Jackson's plan comes to fruition the government will pay you a fortune to emancipate your slaves and the best part is most of them will stay on with you anyway and work for a pittance. At the same time you get to invest that money in an industrial venture. Just imagine sir. A cotton mill and textile factory right here beside your plantation. Just think of the profits to be reaped! Confederate textiles will be able to undercut all the other textiles in the world because we'll be able to manufacture right here where the cotton is grown, while the rest of the world has to pay to import! What cotton we do still export to the outside world will go up in value!"

"You have a vivid imagination, sir."

Lester smiled again.

"Well I hope, sir, that you will at least think about it."

He extended his hand. Dumas shook it. Lester went to the front of the horseless carriage and turned the crank that started the engine. He then climbed aboard, gave Dumas a wave, and was off.

Dumas starred after him, shaking his head.

Down at the slave cabins later that night, as most of the blacks sat around fires eating cornmeal and singing spirituals, Ebenezer made his way over to Cap.

"I needs you to come to da cabin wit me."

"I turn in soon enough," he replied. "Dey's work me harder den all da rest all day long and I's jus wants some time to wind down fo' I goes to bed."

"I needs you to come to da cabin wit me right now," re-iterated Ebenezer.

"What fo'?"

"I canst say here. You jus' has to trust me."

Sighing loudly Cap rose to his feet, wincing slightly as he did so. His back was still in a lot of pain. Cap followed Ebenezer through the miniature shanty town to a dimly lit cabin. Once they had entered, Cap saw that there were about fifteen other black men crammed inside, all of them sitting on the dirt floor. They all turned to look at Cap and Ebenezer as they entered. Cap quickly realized that they were all former slaves of Sharpstone—all except one. At the far end of the cabin sat an elderly negro. The old man seemed strangely familiar, then all of a sudden he realized who he was.

"Caesar!"

"Hello, Cap. It be a long time!"

Cap was stunned and confused.

"You get away a long time ago! What fo' you come back here?"

Caesar held up an object of iron and wood. Cap's eyes grew wide with shock and disbelief at what the old man lifted up to him. In his hands Caesar held an Enfield rifle.

"I have come back to set you free."

X

Major Antonio Vega was exhausted. His sky-blue uniform was torn, tattered and absolutely filthy. The men of his under-strength company that had been thrown together from surviving infantry elements that had survived the defense of Havana were in the same shape as himself. They trudged through heavy woods and over hills. They marched, single file to hide their numbers from the Confederates that were advancing behind them. For Antonio, each step was a chore. He wanted nothing more than to stop and rest.

What I would not give for a siesta! But he was the ranking officer, and he had to be a pillar of strength for his men. They had just barely escaped the flank attack that the Confederates had designed to cut off the retreat of the Spanish forces. Antonio and his men had made it. Many others had not. Now they had been driven almost entirely from the northern shore of Cuba to the southern. He had an important decision to make. He had hoped to make contact with other Spanish units and specifically with a higher ranking officer that could give him orders. Colonel Gonzales and Major Ortega had joked about him being on the general staff one day. Ortega had been mocking him. Colonel Gonzales had been half serious. Now both men were gone. Antonio hadn't seen the Colonel since the fall of the La Cabana. He didn't know if his commanding officer was alive or dead. He felt a surge of guilt for abandoning the fort without knowing what had become of his commander. As for Ortega, Antonio knew where he was.

Burning in the fires of infernio! He'd personally witnessed Ortega's demise. The man had escaped the La Cabana only to be cut down by the shrapnel from a shell fired by a Confederate armored gunboat. Antonio crossed himself. He took no pleasure in Ortega's death, but all the same he would not miss him.

An hour later, when he truly felt they could go no further, Antonio called his small company to a halt.

"Ten minute break! Sanchez! Julio! You're both on guard duty!" The looks on the faces of the two young soldiers were those of devastation. They didn't dare protest, but after such a long march they weren't happy about spending the first break in hours standing point for their resting comrades.

Someone has to do it. He hadn't chosen them for any particular reason other than that it was militarily prudent.

Besides, they aren't the only ones who will spend this time working.

"Perez, come here!"

Captain Perez came bounding up quickly. He was the only other officer in the group other than three fresh faced second lieutenants that were little more than boys. Antonio cared more for the opinion of the Sergeants than them.

Antonio pulled out a mud stained map and unfolded it.

"We have come almost as far south as we can. We soon must turn to the east or to the west."

"It would be far easier to go to the west," said Perez. "We will be much more likely to run into our own countrymen."

"But if we do that," replied Antonio "…we will be on the western tip of the island, cut off from the rest of Cuba and with our backs to the wall."

"Si, Major Vega. However, going east is fraught with dangers of its own. We have no idea how far the Confederados have managed to advance in that direction. We also know that the great bulk of the west has been given over to the rebels."

Antonio pointed at the western tip of Cuba.

"In my opinion the fall of the west is inevitable. The Confederados have us outnumbered and outgunned. Any reinforcements from Spain will come from the east, through Santiago de Cuba. It is from there that the holy crusade to drive the Confederados from Cuba and punish their rebel collaborators will be launched." *And if we are defeated, it will be the last Spanish stronghold on the island and perhaps our best chance to get back to Spain.*

He kept that last part to himself. He wasn't a coward, but he was certainly a pragmatist and fast becoming a pessimist.

"You are in command," said Perez. "We will follow you. You are right that Santiago would be the ideal place to be. But the journey there will be long and dangerous. How do you suggest we proceed senor?"

Antonio took a deep breath and then sighed. He examined the map closely.

"We'll keep heading south for now. It can't be that much farther to the coast. Then we'll strike out east along the beach and follow it along the entire southern coast until we reach Santiago. That should keep us well ahead of the Confederados' advance and allow us to avoid the bulk of the rebel strongholds."

"Si, Colonel Vega. It is a good plan but there is one additional difficulty." He pointed at the southern coast of Cuba well to the east of their present position. "This area is thick with swamps. Going through it will be far harder than you think and going around it will send us through an area swarming with rebel guerillas."

"We will deal with that when we come to it."

Antonio then instructed Perez to order two other soldiers to relieve Julio and Sanchez so that they too could get a much needed break. Antonio replaced the map, opened his canteen and took a long refreshing drink of water.

Suddenly several rifles barked and bullets cracked through the air—one of them dangerously close to his head! Antonio threw himself flat on the muddy grounds as did the rest of his men. One of them didn't get down in time and was shot in the chest. The soldier fell to the ground bleeding and dying.

"Return fire!" ordered Antonio bringing his own Mauser to bear in the direction of the incoming fire. He took about a half second to send a fraction of a Hail Mary towards heaven, and then started hunting for targets. He caught sight of a few muzzle flashes, but he could not see any of the attackers clearly enough to see who they were. Antonio and his men sent a hail of lead into the trees. As he slammed a fresh magazine into his rifle, Antonio muttered under his breath.

We don't have the ammo for this! About thirty seconds later the enemy fire seemed to stop.

"Cease fire!"

Antonio waited a couple of minutes.

"They may have gone off, senor," said Captain Perez who had crawled along the ground to Antonio's side.

"Or they are trying to draw us into the woods so they can get better shots at us," replied Antonio. He pointed to right.

"Send Julio and Sanchez around that way. Tell them to keep low. Send two others around to the left. Everyone else stay at the ready!"

Ordinarily he would have given the scouts covering fire as they moved forward. As low as they were on ammunition, he couldn't afford to. After a few tense minutes the four scouts reported back.

"Major Vega!" said Corporal Sanchez "There are two dead rebel escoria about fifteen meters inside the wood. It looks like a small group of others fled towards the south!"

Antonio followed them into the wood to see the dead rebels for himself. One was an older man with dark skin and a graying mustache. The other was a man who looked no older than twenty. Both had olive green bandanas tide to their arms.

"Must have had them greatly outnumbered, otherwise they would have made more of a fight of it," said Antonio.

"The rebel gilipollas were just taking pot shots at us!" replied Perez.

Antonio nodded and studied the dead bodies further. There were no ammo boxes or pouches on the bodies nor were their rifles anywhere to be seen.

"The rebels must have carried them off," said Antonio. Surveying the ground, Antonio spotted a trail of boot prints that led in a southerly direction.

"There is a village not far from here, Major Vega. It is on our path to the coast. Perhaps they came from there. Should we try to go around?"

"No," said Antonio. "Let's pay them a visit."

They returned to the main road. He went to check on his wounded soldier only to find that the man had died moments before. They had no medic among them, nor did they have any medical supplies. There was simply nothing they could have done for him.

Antonio crossed himself and said a prayer for the man, but it brought him no peace. A sudden burning rage began to grow inside of him and he began to understand why General Weyler had instituted his policy of placing Cuban peasants in *reconcentraci'on* camps. Rebel's had been attacking them during their entire flight from Havana.

Fighting the Confederados is hard enough without having to deal with these filthy traitors. This was the seventh man he'd lost to rebel ambushes. *If they are going to fight dishonorably, then there is nothing dishonorable about doing whatever is necessary to defeat them.* His mind went back to the camp that he had visited not long before. He remembered the thousands of rotting dead bodies piled up outside and the birds that feasted on their putrid flesh. He remembered the men, women, and children inside who were so starved that they were mere walking skeletons—the inhabitants of the closest thing to hell on earth. Above all he remembered the smell, the awful, nauseating, stench of the dead and dying. His conscience had tormented him for weeks. He'd had nightmares about it nearly every night. No amount of prayer and confession had been able to alleviate his guilt. Now all of a sudden his sense of guilt was all but gone, and though he finally felt the certitude and confidence he had once enjoyed, he also felt his heart growing harder and colder.

They headed south at the double quick. The men were no longer lagging from their long journey. Getting shot at had a way of getting the adrenaline flowing. They were on high alert and marched with their rifles at the ready. If the villagers gave them trouble they wanted to be prepared.

If the escoria give us trouble, we'll make them sorry. His trigger finger suddenly started to itch. Though he had fought for Spain, he'd never had the desire to kill before. But he did now.

Heaven help me, I do now!

The Cuban village was not very large. A small stone church stood at the front of a small central square. Muddy dirt roads extended from that square to the north, south, east and west. Each road was lined on both sides by small wooden houses. The east road led to nearby tobacco fields. There were many Cubans on the sides of the streets as the column of Spanish troops marched into their village with weapons at the ready. Only a few of the inhabitants looked scared—mostly the women and children. The vast majority of the villagers stared at the Spaniards with looks of hatred and contempt. Antonio kept his eyes on the houses, wary of an ambush.

If they attack us I swear I will burn this entire village to the ground! When they reached the center square, Antonio saw that the villagers had erected a flag pole, but it was not the la Rojigualda which flew from it. Instead it flew the flag that had been used by Cuban revolutionaries and separatists for nearly half a century—a flag with three blue stripes on a field of white, with a triangular red canton emblazoned with a single white star.

"Who's in charge here! Who's responsible for this...this...BLASPHEMY!" To Antonio, Leopold ruled by divine right—no less than God's appointed King over Holy Spain and its possessions. Blasphemy was therefore the only word he thought appropriate for such treason.

"I said, who's responsible for this!"

No one came forward, and to his annoyance most of the villagers did not look afraid.

That's about to change…

He pointed to a random man in the crowd.

"You. Get over here."

At first the man stood there defiantly. But when a couple of Antonio's men leveled their Mausers at him he moved to obey so quickly it was as if he were walking barefoot on hot coals.

"Take down that mierda rag!"

Hesitantly the man obeyed. He untied the rope, lowered the flag, and then unfastened the flag from the clamps.

"Now set it on fire."

Again the man hesitated, longer this time. He then obstinately crossed his arms, still keeping tight hold of the banner. Antonio drew his bayonet and then leveled it at the man's throat.

"I said burn it."

The man turned red in the face, but he started fumbling for some matches. One of the Spanish soldiers kicked in the door of a small house and stormed inside. He emerged a moment later with a small kerosene lamp. He poured kerosene on the Cuban flag and then tossed the man a pack of matches. The man held the kerosene soaked banner at arm's length, struck a match and then touched the flame to the bottom of the cloth. The fire spread quickly. He released the burning flag and let it fall to the ground where the flames consumed it to ash.

"Major!" cried one of the nearby soldiers. A rifle shot suddenly rang out. Antonio turned just in time to see one of his soldiers less than a foot from him fall to the ground, a pool of blood rapidly pooling around him. There was a cry of panic and surprise from the crowd. The soldier had thrown himself in front of Antonio and taken the bullet. Another gunshot rang out. This one passed inches from Antonio's arm. At last he spotted the shooter standing between two shabby houses. To both his rage and horror it was a boy, no more than twelve years of age with a green bandana tied around his arm. The boy was struggling to reload the rifle. Spanish soldiers converged on him quickly. He turned to run but it was too late. One of the Spaniards grabbed him and pulled the rifle from his small hands, tossing it aside. The Spaniard then back fisted the boy knocking him to the ground. He then grabbed the Cuban boy by the hair of his head, dragged him along the ground and then threw him at Antonio's feet.

The boy looked up at Antonio with hatred in his eyes. Blood poured from the side of his mouth. Antonio felt a battle being waged within him, possibly for his soul, between the light and the growing darkness that was beginning to consume him. The fire raging within him was overwhelming. Part of him wanted to take the boy in his hands and personally squeeze the life out of him. Another part wanted to stab him in the gut with his bayonet and let him die a slow and painful death.

But to kill a child...to kill one so young.... Such an idea would once have been unthinkable to him. Even now something inexplicable held him back.

Suppressing his conscience with all his might, Antonio forced himself to chamber a round and level his rifle at the boy's head.

"Please!" came a desperate tear filled cry from the crowd. A middle age man came charging out of the crowd. Antonio's men brandished their rifles at him but he ignored them. He stumbled forward and fell to his knees before Antonio.

"Please, Senor! Please do not kill my son! He is my only son! Please have mercy! Please!" Tears of terror and desperation poured from the man's eyes who held his hands folded together as if he were kneeling in prayer. "His brother was killed earlier today fighting your men in the forest. I told my older son not to go but he did not listen he went and now he is dead, but please have mercy on my youngest child, he's only a boy, do what you want with me, punish me, only let my son live! Please!" At that point the man totally broke down and buried his face in the dirt at Antonio's feet and grasped his boots with his hands.

Antonio's heart was pounding. His adrenaline rich blood surged through his veins. There were tears in his eyes as well. Tears of rage and intense hatred. He still had his rifle leveled at the boy. Antonio's eyes grew hard and his entire body tensed as he started to pull the trigger. At the last possible instance he stopped. He exhaled hard and then took a deep breath of fresh air. He turned away from the boy and looked at Captain Perez.

"Release, the boy."

"Si, Major Vega."

"Shoot the father…"

XI

Richmond, Virginia, the capital City of the Confederate States of America was winding down for the day. The sun was getting low in the sky, and the Blood Stained Banner would soon be lowered from the Capitol and other government buildings for the night. There were still a good number of horses, coaches, pedestrians and even horseless carriages on the streets, but the trolleys had made their last rounds for the day and would soon return to the depot outside the central station for the night.

John Wilkes Booth, the Director of the Confederate States Secret Service, exited the Richmond Theater, placed his top hat on his head and made his way down the front steps of the building and onto the side walk. He carried a black cane with a gold handle. At fifty-seven years old Booth had begun to feel aches and pains that hadn't been there a few years earlier but even so the cane was more of an accessory than a necessity, (though like Booth, there was more to it than met the eye).

The theater had transported Booth's mind back to a much earlier period of his life. He'd actually played the character of Horatio, in Hamlet, in that very theater back in 1858. His older brother had played the title character. Booth walked away from the theater, down North Belvedere Street, reciting his favorite lines from Hamlet under his breath. A few passersby looked at him as though he were an eccentric crackpot that talked to himself but he paid them no mind. He hadn't acted in years, though he'd always told himself he'd one day return to his favorite profession. Though this had been the first time he'd seen the play in over a quarter century, the lines had come back to him like he'd performed them only a day earlier. It had goaded Booth terribly to have to sit as a member of the audience but he was glad for the experience even if it did remind him of a long lost phase of his life and of his estranged and late brothers who had passed away years earlier even though Booth hadn't actually seen or spoken to either of them in more than twenty-five years. When Booth had been exposed in Washington as a

Confederate agent at the height of the War of 1869, his brothers Junius and Edwin had been arrested on suspicion of espionage and high treason. When John Wilkes Booth had eluded capture and subsequently carried out a successful kidnapping of then US President Sherman and other high ranking US government officials it hadn't helped his brothers' cases. The two siblings had languished in the Old Capitol Prison for months before finally being released. The family scandal had nearly ruined their acting careers and they had never forgiven John for any of it. Now they were gone.

Booth sighed at the bitter memories.

My country and race came first! For them, no sacrifice is too high! He'd been justifying his actions with those thoughts for a quarter century. They mostly worked. Nonetheless a single minor tear welled up in his left eye.

As was his custom when walking in the city, Booth discretely looked behind himself periodically to make certain he wasn't being followed. As the director of his country's intelligence service for the past quarter-century, he knew he had a lot of enemies in the world. A man who regularly sent assassins, spies, provocateurs, and saboteurs to plague and manipulate other nations didn't sleep well at night. He knew nations hostile to the Confederacy such as the Union to the north and Great Britain across the Atlantic had agents of their own. But Booth refused to hide in in under-ground sanctum beneath the treasury or in his fortified house at all times. There were times he just needed out for a walk and a breath of fresh air.

Or a trip to the theater.

Booth then turned right down East Broad Street. Many of those still on the street at that late hour were negroes. In the years since the Confederacy won its independence, Richmond's population had exploded to nearly a quarter of a million people, and nearly a quarter of those were black. About half were slaves and half free, but regardless they were moving with much more urgency than their white counterparts. In most cases negroes could not legally be out on the streets of the city after sun down unless accompanied by an owner or employer. An entire division of the Richmond police department was dedicated to slave patrol and curfew enforcement. Booth nodded in satisfaction to see that they were already out in force.

All unaccompanied negroes had to carry papers. Slaves needed passes from their masters, and freedmen needed a passbook issued by the Department of Servitude. Those papers could be demanded by any white person at any time and all negroes were legally required to produce them. A negro without his paperwork became sorry very fast. Because all routes out of the city were patrolled, it was virtually impossible for a negro to enter or leave the city without getting his papers checked. The same system was used throughout the Confederate States with great effectiveness.

Most negroes were eager to obey the curfew. The owner of an unescorted slave caught outside after dark—even with a pass from his master—would be cited and fined. Unaccompanied Freedmen caught out after curfew would spend a very unpleasant time in the city jail. There were of course a few exceptions. Negroes whose primary duty was the care of their elderly or infirm masters / employers, were permitted to break curfew for certain acceptable reasons (though their paperwork had better be in perfect order). Those in the service of government or military officials likewise had certain exceptions (once again with the proper paperwork). But the majority of blacks wanted to be certain to be at home when night fell. It was made difficult by the fact that in Richmond (as well as most of the cities in the Confederate States) it was not permissible for negroes to go shopping until later in the day after all the whites had had time to do their own. As such, blacks had to hurry to get the things they needed and get home. They had no time to dawdle, and even then they often found themselves rushing to make certain they got home in time.

Nine minutes after leaving the theatre on foot Booth entered Capitol Square. He had plenty of carriages, horses, and drivers available, but he enjoyed taking a good constitutional a couple of times per week, though he did so as randomly as possible. He walked between the two magnificent equestrian statues of George Washington and Robert E Lee and past the Confederate Capitol itself. He was just in time to see the Blood Stained Banner lowered for the night and reverently folded by the Capitol color guard. After crossing Capitol Square Booth turned right onto East Cary Street and then left onto ninth-street and followed it past the large Confederate Treasury Building.

Booth owned a large home just behind the treasury. It was as luxurious as any owned by a planter. It was surrounded by a large wrought-iron fence. Most days he didn't depart or return to his home by its main entrance. A secret tunnel system ran from his home's basement to the basement of the Treasury building (where his true sanctum was located) and from there on to the War Department and the Department of Servitude. It had taken a select team from the army corps of engineers two years to excavate the tunnels in secret. Only a select few people knew of their existence. One day Booth hoped to have every major government building connected to the system. He used it to insure that foreign agents couldn't follow his movements along with various other means. But every so often he'd come and go from his home by the front door. He didn't want foreign agents to suspect that something like the secret tunnel system existed.

After walking through the front door of the house, his personal slave Martin came down the stairs and took Booth's coat and hat.

"Master John, I hope you had a pleasant evening at the theater."

"It was thoroughly enjoyable," said Booth. "Though it makes me want to take up acting again. I do love it so."

"Your supper is ready and waiting for you in the dining room, sir. It is baked chicken as you requested."

"Very good."

"Shall I draw you a bath after supper, sir?"

"No, I've got too much work to take care of. After supper you may retire for the night at your leisure."

"Thank you, sir."

The long oak table in the dining room was large enough to seat a dozen people. Booth sat at its head alone. Martin served as Booth's butler, house keeper, and cook all in one. While Booth ate, Martin acted like a waiter, keeping his master's glass of iced tea full and bringing him anything he needed. When he'd finished wolfing down his supper, Booth wiped his face with a napkin, then rose to his feet and went upstairs for the evening leaving everything for Martin to clean. Booth entered his office and closed the door behind him. Like the rest of the house it was lit by electric lights. Martin had laid out the day's mail on the desk. One of the letters was from Virginia Military Institute where Booth's son was a fourth year student. John Wilkes Booth Jr. and his father had never really gotten along. Booth's wife Abigale had died in child birth and Booth, both unable and unwilling to be a single parent, had paid for the boy to be raised first by his late wife's sister and then later to attend a boarding school. Booth had used his influence to get his son an appointment at VMI. He'd met his son only a handful of times.

The letter was brief, and to the point. It was an invitation to the upcoming graduation. Booth checked his calendar and wrote a quick reply.

Will be there if not hindered by other duties.

Booth sealed the brief message in an envelope and then placed it in a basket for Martin to post in the morning.

Suddenly the candlestick telephone in the office rang. Booth picked up the earpiece with one hand brought it to his ear and then picked up the stick mounted receiver with the other hand and brought it up close to his mouth.

"This is Booth."

"It's Simmons, sir,"

"What could you possibly need at this hour, Simmons?"

"We've received two communique's sir. They came in one right after the other. I'm certain that they are far too important to wait until morning."

Booth sighed heavily.

"I'll meet you in my office in ten minutes. Don't be late, and this had better be as important as you say."

With that Booth hung up. He looked at the grandfather clock standing in the corner of the room. It was nine O'clock PM. Through the windows he could see that it had gotten dark. Without further ado he rose to his feet and headed for the basement. It was a brief walk through the tunnel that connected his home with the massive basement of the Treasury Building. Simmons was already waiting for him at the reinforced steel door that led to Booth's personal sanctum. He unlocked the three massive bolt locks with his key. Only when they were securely inside the sanctum did Booth finally ask:

"What's so important?"

Simmons nervously fumbled inside his leather satchel, pulled out the first communique and handed it to Booth who proceeded to take a seat behind his desk.

"Agent Connery has reported that the convoys leaving Boston and New York are decoys. Whitmore and his men are actually sailing out of Canada and not only that but the British are giving him passage on their own merchant ships."

Booth hurriedly scanned the details of the communique for himself. As he did so his face became flushed.

So, the British are granting our enemies passage. I swear I will make them pay for this. Years earlier with the help of agents in Britain Booth had begun to compile a list of British politicians and other influential people hostile to the Confederacy. Every so often one of the persons on the list would abruptly change his views. All men have secrets they'd rather not come to light, and Booth's men worked hard to find those things. Sometimes they even helped arrange them. Female agents were particularly good at such things, particularly when another agent happened to be nearby. Modern cameras were amazing things. But every so often one of the names would come off because the person suffered a sudden and tragic accident. That didn't happen very often, but when Booth felt it necessary (or when he was out for some cold blooded revenge) he didn't hesitate. Of course such operations weren't confined to Britain. He had similar operations in the US and other countries. He even had a similar operation in the Confederacy itself (which gave him quite a bit of influence and power). There were some members of the Confederate congress and not a small number of other officials that had no choice but to dance to his tune.

"When I find out who is responsible for this…"
Booth didn't finish the sentence. Simmons didn't need to know (not that the intelligence analyst had any trouble filling in the blanks). Booth got to his feet and walked over to the far left wall where there hung large maps of North America, South America, and Europe. Booth used pins to show the locations of his different agents around the world. The color of the pin determined the type of agent. Black was for assassins, green for provocateurs, red for saboteurs, brown for spies, and gold for the handful of the Confederacy's most elite agents.

Booth pulled the gold pin that represented Connery and moved it from New York to Canada.

"What are we going to do, sir?"

"None of your concern. What's the other matter?"

Simmons once again fumbled with his satchel pulling out another communique.

"This is from one of our agents in the underground rail road. A group of radical abolitionists based in Canada with ties to both Britain and the US is trying to incite a slave revolt somewhere in the Confederacy."

Whereas before Booth's blood had become heated, now it boiled. He literally snatched the communique from Simmons.

"Does it say where?"

"Not specifically, but our source is certain that it will be somewhere along the Mississippi river."

Booth grunted.

"Great. That only narrows it down to Missouri, Arkansas, Tennessee, Mississippi, or Louisiana."

"I'm not sure, how serious we should take this second report sir. It says that thousands of military grade rifles have been smuggled into the Confederacy. I just don't see how that's possible."

"Stop and think for a moment, Simmons. As part of the final treaty of peace between the United States and the Confederate States, signed in 1870 both sides agreed that all civilian and commercial vessels would have free passage of the river, without interference from one another's river navies. A thousand Yankee boats and barges come down the

Mississippi every day and no one checks them. Would it be that hard for them to put guns ashore at remote river shore points at night?"

The light of understanding suddenly dawned on the analyst.

Booth's mind, however, was growing darker. Not darker in a sense of ignorance, but his deviousness was beginning to formulate not just a plan, but a way to turn the situation to his advantage.

"You are not to breathe a word of this to anyone. You hear me? I mean no one. If you do, you better believe it'll be the last thing you ever do."

The analyst gulped.

"Don't worry, sir. I won't say anything to anybody."

"Good boy. You know the way out, and close the door behind you."

As Simmons hastily retreated from Booth's chamber, the director of the Confederate Secret Service pulled out a large map of the Confederacy, unrolled it on his desk, and began to contemplate.

This is perfect. If anything will drive a stake through the heart of all this nonsense about freeing the niggers a good slave uprising is it. I just have to make sure that the fire can be contained. I want it to do enough damage so that no white person ever considers freeing the niggers again, but at the same time I don't want it so large it endangers the nation. Fire can be a useful tool but it must be contained. We've got to figure out where this is going to happen so we can have the appropriate forces on hand to deal with it.

Booth's eyes fell on Missouri. It shared a long river border with the US and there were still plenty of people both white and black there that would support a Unionist uprising.

But that's some of the most fortified and patrolled sections of river bank on our entire frontier.

Booth's eyes followed the Mississippi south.

Arkansas would be more likely than Missouri but there's not near as many slaves there as further south. Same goes for the part of Tennessee that touches the Mississippi. It has to be Mississippi or Louisiana. Maybe both.

Booth's eyes fell on Vicksburg. It was one of the major bases for the Confederacy's river navy. *If we put together a decent force of ironclads, troop barges, and marines at Vicksburg they should be able to respond in a matter of hours to any trouble off the Mississippi within a hundred miles. I've just got to get the Secretary of the Navy to help me do it without alerting the President.* Booth didn't know much about Hilary A. Herbert, but the Secretary of the Confederate Navy agreeing to concentrate marines, gunboats, and transports at Vicksburg would be a major part of Booth's new scheme. The Secretary would want to know why, and asking him not to inform the President would look highly suspicious. Booth's mind went through the usual options.

Blackmail...no dirt and no time to manufacture any. Direct threat...likely to have the opposite effect on a man like Herbert. Bribery...same as direct threat.

A smile spread across Booth's face as the solution presented itself. He didn't have to keep the concentration of marines, gunboats, and transports secret from the President, he simply had to come up with another viable reason to concentrate them at Vicksburg.

And I've got it.

XII

Captain Blake Ramsey took a deep breath of fresh sea air as he stood at the bow of the *CSS Texas* surveying the African shoreline before him. The region around the small port of Villa Cisneros was a mostly desert region. Only a few splotches of green stood out against the sandy brown of the shoreline. Had it not been for a small plateau behind the small port, it would have been nearly impossible to tell where the beach ended and the land proper began.

"It looks like its all sand," said Brisk as he came along side Ramsey. "You'll be happy to know that the last of the repairs are complete."

Ramsey nodded. They'd come out of the tropical storm that had nearly capsized them in far better condition than he could have hoped.

Brisk turned to regard Villa Cisneros for himself.

"I wonder how they ever grow enough food to survive here?" asked Brisk.

Ramsey pointed at the docks, where a veritable fleet of fishing boats were tied to the wooden moorings.

"The Azores are just east of here. This port is of vital importance to Spain's fishing industry."

"Well I sure don't see much to protect it," said Brisk.

Ramsey nodded. A large antiquated fort flying the red and gold Spanish flag stood on the shoreline like a massive stone sentinel. But it seemed even more ancient than the forts that had defended Havana—more suited to combating the sixteenth century galleons from the bygone days of the Armada, than contending with a modern late-nineteenth century battleship. Its obsolete cannons were no threat to the CSS Texas.

Ramsey continued to regard the small port city through his binoculars. A massive Roman Catholic Cathedral rose far above the mud brick huts and small stone structures that made up the majority of the city. Ramsey regarded its beautiful architecture and ornate spires, but thought the immense and extravagant church looked out of place when compared with the poverty stricken city around it. The massive bells atop the Cathedral's tower were sounding the alarm. The small port had seemingly gone into panic at the appearance of the Confederate warship. As he zoomed in closer with his binoculars, he could see that large numbers of people had begun to flee to the high flat land just behind the city.

"What is that funny looking building?" asked Brisk as he pointed at the northern shore of the port. He was pointing at the only other large building in the city other than the fort and the cathedral. "Another church?"

Ramsey shook his head.

"That's a Mosque, Ray," said Ramsey. "It's where the Mohammedans worship."

Brisk nodded, but Ramsey doubted his first-mate had any real idea what he was talking about. The Confederate Naval Academy spent very little of its time teaching its officer candidates about world history and religion.

And Ray didn't exactly graduate at the top of his class.

Ramsey pulled a cigar from the inside of his gray uniform coat and stuck it in his mouth. He then struck a match, held the flame up to the cigar and started to puff until the Cuban was fully ignited. He tossed the match overboard and then took a good long drag on the cigar, savoring the strong rich taste of the tobacco smoke. He was about to order Brisk to sound general quarters and prepare for the bombardment of the Spanish city when suddenly Yeoman Jeb Ferguson came running up to him at breakneck speed. He came to a halt just in front of Ramsey and brought his arm up in salute.

"Beggin' your pardon, Captain, but the lookouts report a contact just north of us. From the size of it they say that it might be a battleship!"

"Get to the bridge!" said Ramsey at once. "Tell them to sound General Quarters, I'm on my way!"

The young sailor saluted and then dashed away at full speed. Ramsey and Brisk followed close behind him. They climbed down from the forecastle to the main deck, and made their way aft. They passed the large turret mounted twelve-inch gun and then headed for the side of the superstructure. Ramsey then made his way up a gangway to the second level. About that time klaxons started sounding throughout the ship and the crew began to rush to their battle stations. Ramsey entered the bridge and went straight to the telephone that connected the bridge with the crow's nest. Keeping his cigar tightly secure in his teeth, he lifted the earpiece from the receiver and then spun the crank on the side of the phone. He then removed the Cuban from his mouth and shouted into the wall mounted receiver.

"Crow's Nest," came the crackling static filled answer.

"This is the Captain. What do you see?"

"It's definitely a warship of some type, sir. Bearing 355. We can't make out any flags yet, but from the smoke coming out of her stacks she's heading this way at full steam."

"Let me know the instant that you make out her colors!"

"Aye, sir!"

Ramsey slammed the earpiece back into place.

"Bring us about! Engines full ahead! Make your course 355!" He then rushed to the viewports to scan the horizon with his binoculars. He could just make out the approaching smoke plume, but as yet he could not see any of the ship itself.

"Captain, all hands are at general quarters."

"Tell the gunners to keep a tight hold on those happy trigger fingers and to keep the guns in standard position," said Ramsey with the cigar still clenched in his teeth. "We don't fire till I give the order. We don't know if they're hostile yet."

"If it's not the Spanish then who is it?" asked Brisk.

"I'm not sure," said Ramsey, "but I'm not taking any chances." He then glared at his first officer with a look that said he would brook no further delay in the carrying out of his orders. Brisk got the message and rushed to inform the gunnery officers to hold their fire.

The deck began to vibrate as the Texas' steam engines roared to full power. As the ship came around, Ramsey changed his position to gaze out of the forward view ports. He could now make out the forward silhouette of the approaching ship. Ramsey slowly and surely smoked down his cigar as they made their way closer to the contact. After what seemed an eternity, but was in actuality only a few minutes, the telephone connecting the bridge with the crow's nest rang.

"Bridge!" said Ramsey.

"She's British, sir! We can make out the Royal Navy flag flying from her masthead as sure as day!"

"Are her guns trained on us?"

"Negative, sir."

Ramsey took a deep breath and then exhaled long and loud.

"Keep a close eye on her. Let me know if there's any change."

"Aye, sir!"

Ramsey then turned to Brisk.

"Slow to half speed. Come left four degrees, so we're not headed straight for them. I don't want to provoke them."

"I know most of the Brits don't like us," said Brisk "but I don't think they're here to cause trouble—not with only one ship."

"I don't think so either," said Ramsey. "But the Royal Navy's got the most powerful warships afloat, and that looks like one of them. She's Majestic class unless I miss my guess. She's over a hundred feet longer than we are."

"Her primary guns aren't any bigger than ours," said Brisk.

"That's true," said Ramsey, "but she's got twice as many. Four twelve-inch guns are nothing to shake a stick at. If they wanted to cause us trouble it wouldn't be a problem."

"I think the Imperial French Navy's got ships every bit as good as what the Brits have," said Brisk. "They've been building some pretty big monsters themselves. The French attaché in Mobile showed me some schematics for a battleship they've got in the works. The blasted thing looks like an iron castle meant to float on the water."

Ramsey nodded. He'd seen the same specs.

"If the arms race between Britain and France continues at this pace, I'm scared to know what the ships will be like in ten or twenty years."

The minutes slowly passed and the silhouette of the approaching warship grew, becoming clearer and more distinct as they drew nearer.

"Definitely Majestic class," said Ramsey. He then swore long and loud. "Look at all those guns."

The British warship slowed its approach and adjusted its course so that she would pass parallel to the *Texas'* starboard side. Ramsey made his way to the starboard side of the bridge so that he could get as clear a view as possible.

"She's running up signal flags, Captain," said Brisk.

Ramsey said nothing in reply. He could see them for himself. Forty-two separate flags on two different lines. He set to reading them immediately.

Parle requested. Request permission to send envoy.

"All stop," ordered Ramsey. "Run up the affirmative pendant."

"What's happening, Captain?"

"We're about to have guests, Mr. Brisk."

He turned back to the British battleship which had also disengaged its engines. The bow plate of the British vessel read: *HMS Magnificent.*

They made their way out of the bridge and down the side of the superstructure to the main deck. Through his binoculars, Ramsey watched as a longboat was lowered from the British battleship and began to row towards the *Texas*. It looked to only have five men aboard—four burly sailors to row and an officer.

"Get the pilot ladder ready," ordered Ramsey. Several Petty Officers rushed to obey. A few moments later, a sailor emerged from below deck with a rolled up pilot ladder. He firmly affixed it to the edge of the deck and then let the rope and wood ladder drop and unroll down the side of the ship. The longboat slowly maneuvered into position and a moment later a British officer in a dark blue uniform climbed the ladder. Ramsey went forward personally and extended his hand to the Royal Navy Man to help him aboard. The officer was in his late thirties—about Ramsey's age. His hair was auburn and he was clean shaven except for a well-trimmed and thin mustache.

"Welcome aboard, Lieutenant Commander," said Ramsey to the British officer as he regarded the gold braid on his sleeve—a gold stripe topped by a thinner gold stripe topped by another gold strip with a loop. The British officer momentarily raised an eyebrow in curiosity before noticing the braid on Ramsey's and the other Confederate officers' uniforms. They were almost identical to that used by the royal navy.

"Thank you, Captain," said the officer and raised his hand in salute. "Lieutenant Commander John Merrick, Captain, sir, of Her Majesty's Royal Navy. Request Permission to come aboard, sir."

"Permission granted. If you'll step this way, I'll escort you to our wardroom and we can talk about whatever it is you've come to talk about."

Ramsey then led Merrick through a hatch in the side of the superstructure and then down a narrow corridor to the wardroom.

"I'm sure it's not as fancy as what you're used to on board your own ship…"

"Nonsense," said Merrick, as polite as pie. "You have a splendid vessel."

"Would you care for some tea? I know you British fella's like tea." Without waiting for the British officer to respond Ramsey snapped his fingers and directed an orderly to fetch two cups of hot tea.

"Now have a seat, Commander, and tell me what's on your mind."

"First, Captain, may I ask if you have yet attacked Villa Cisneros?"

Ramsey shook his head.

"We were just about to leave our calling card with the Spanish when you arrived."

"In that case, Captain, I have been directed by my own Captain to request that you postpone any hostile action until we have had a chance to carry out our own mission here."

"Your mission?" asked Ramsey confused.

The steward suddenly entered carrying a tray on which sat two steaming cups of tea. The British officer accepted his with a nod of thanks to the steward, and then took a cautious sip before continuing.

"We have been dispatched to retrieve all British subjects from the ports of the Spanish Sahara and to insure that all British flagged vessels are allowed to safely depart. This is our last port of call."

Ramsey looked at the clock on the wall and then back at Merrick.

"That shouldn't be a problem as long as it doesn't take too long and as long as the Spanish don't try to take advantage of the situation and evacuate their fishing boats."

"Six hours is not a very long time," said Merrick. "But we are understandably pressed for time. Your friends are, after all, right behind us."

"Our friends?" asked Ramsey in a confused tone. As far as he knew the *Texas* was the only Confederate vessel operating in the area.

"Yes," said Merrick. "I must applaud the coordination between your two navies, your timing is exquisite."

"Commander, I'm afraid I have no idea what you are talking about."

"Good heavens," said Merrick. "You mean you really don't know that a fleet of French battleships and troop ships are en route here as we speak?"

"We've been at sea for weeks," said Ramsey. "I knew there had been talk about France joining the war, but had no idea it had actually happened."

Merrick nodded.

"Napoleon declared war on Leopold five days ago. From what we can tell French troops have already invaded the northern portion of the Spanish Sahara from Morocco and Algiers. We've also confirmed that a French fleet is moving along the coast seizing the various ports."

"They didn't waste any time," said Ramsey.

"Your friend Napoleon IV has been prepared for this for quite some time," said Merrick. "He's also demanded that Spain cede most of its other possessions to France including Puerto Rico and the Philippines. No offense intended, but your little spat with Spain is now threatening to engulf half of Europe in war. There is already open fighting along the Pyrenees, and King Leopold has formally asked his cousin King Wilhelm of Prussia to come to his aid. France and Austria Hungary have fully mobilized their armies and those of their western German allies."

"If you don't mind my asking, Commander, what's your own government saying?"

Merrick's face became suddenly hard and stern, as if powerful personal feelings had begun to seep out of his cool British exterior.

"There is a bitter divide in Parliament. Leopold is related to our own Queen Victoria, albeit distantly."

Ramsey wanted to roll his eyes. From what he knew there wasn't a crowned head in Europe that wasn't related to another. "While many fear the prospect of a massive European war and wish to avoid it at all costs, there are, thankfully, those who have seen that we cannot allow Napoleon to go unchecked. That madman's great uncle devastated the continent with his wars of conquest nearly century ago, we'd be fools to allow this latest Bonaparte to have his turn, even if it means war with France..." he turned suddenly to regard Ramsey with sad but serious eyes, "...and with all of its allies..."

Merrick paused, giving that last comment and its implications time to sink in. Ramsey understood what the British officer was saying.

Ramsey blasphemed silently in his mind.

He's talking about war... between the Confederacy and Britain...

"You and I are just sailors," said Ramsey taking a sip of his own tea. "But I know that my own country wishes yours no ill will."

"That may be so," said Merrick. "Personally, I've never harbored any ill will towards your Confederacy, even though I find your continued keeping of human slaves barbaric and disgusting."

I wonder what the people in India, and the aborigines in Australia and Tasmania would have to say about your enlightened empire, thought Ramsey. He could not stand to be lectured about the supposed moral lapses of his country from a man whose own country had its own list of crimes.

Far worse than any we've ever perpetrated. Nonetheless he held his tongue and allowed the British officer to continue.

"The way I've seen it," said Merrick "as long as you Confederates kept to yourselves and stayed out of our affairs we should respond in kind and stay out of yours. But you are allied with my country's greatest rival, and pleasant or not that means that our two nations are at odds with one another. If I were you, I should advise my superiors to break off their ties with Paris. You would find the British Empire a formidable opponent."

In spite of himself, Ramsey found himself smiling, much to the consternation of the British officer.

Who does this stiff necked little stuff shirt think he is?

Ramsey found himself wondering how many tense conversations just like that one were being played out on both sides of the Atlantic in Richmond, London and elsewhere. In any event he was about to let this particular British officer know where he stood.

Ramsey's face suddenly grew harsh and hard.

"As I said before, you and I are only sailors. I'm sure that you have no more influence with your own government than I have with mine. But you should inform your own superiors that the Confederate States of America are not easily intimidated nor will we be cowed by threat of force. We've taught the Yankees that lesson twice. If Britain would care to have a turn, we'll gladly teach it to you as well. Spain is getting what it deserves. I was on the Mississippi when she exploded, I saw the man responsible. Hundreds of my shipmates died! If Leopold had only been willing to admit responsibility and yield Cuba then none of the rest of this mess would have happened. He decided to fight and now he's paying the price. And if you decide to jump into a war to help a backstabbing country like Spain, then whatever happens will be on your own heads, not ours."

Without giving the British officer a chance to reply, Ramsey looked at the clock on the wall again and then back at the British officer.

"If there's nothing else then I suggest you return to your own ship and inform your Captain that you now have five hours and forty minutes to remove your people from Villa Cisneros. At exactly fifteen hundred hours the shells are going to start falling whether you're out of there or not."

He then turned to Brisk who had been standing silently off to the side listening to the whole exchange.

"Mr. Brisk, escort our guest back to his boat."

"With pleasure, sir."

XIII

The steam whistle on the *SS Harper*, sounded loudly as the transport made its approach towards Havana harbor. Cole and Helen Allens stood at the bow of the ship enjoying the sea breeze. Off to the west, the sun was getting low in the sky.

"This is so romantic. I feel like we're on a cruise," said Helen as she leaned her blond haired head against her husband's shoulder.

"I'm glad you came, darling," he said taking her more firmly into his arms.

She smiled, kissed him on the nose, and then buried her head against his chest.

"I'm glad I came too, but I'm afraid that the vacation part of our trip is about to end."

"Not for you," said Cole. "General Wheeler has assured me that Havana is perfectly safe. I'll be arranging for you to stay at the finest hotel in the city. You'll be able to relax, go down to the beach, work on your paintings..."

"How could I possibly relax with my husband being shot at?"

He looked at her closely and wondered if she'd really been asleep when he'd told the two young British Lieutenants about his experiences during the Second War of Rebellion.

Cole sighed.

"Darling, I'm a war correspondent, that's why I'm here."

"I know," she said bringing her finger up to his lips. "I didn't mean to restart the quarrel that we left back in Covington. I just want you to know that I'll be worried about you and that I love you."

He took a moment to just stare into her beautiful gray blue eyes. He then kissed her firmly and passionately. Afterwards he caressed the smooth skin of her face with the back of his hand.

"Just promise me you'll stay in Havana where it's safe. Promise you won't try to follow me again."

"I promise," she said.

He noticed a small tear make its way out of the corner of her eye and down her face.

"But you promise me you will come back to me."

Cole hesitated for only a moment. He planned on taking every precaution possible, but he also knew that there was no way in a battle field situation that he could guarantee her he would be okay. Nonetheless he looked her in the eye and promised. The lie seemed to reassure her. They then turned back to gazing at the Cuban coast.

Suddenly, Helen noticed a large black shape in the water. After she pointed it out to Cole, it took him a moment to realize that it was not one object but two and to recognize that they were the burnt and blackened hulls of two cruisers. The two burned out warships were anchored side by side in the shallows off the Cuban coast. In addition to the black scorched color, the superstructures of both ships seemed to have been wrecked by dozens of explosive shells. Cole tried to imagine the hellish fate of the sailors who had served aboard those two ships and then just as quickly he tried to push the thought out of his mind.

Confederate Battle flags were flying from makeshift flag poles atop both wrecks, but Cole was certain they had originally been Spanish warships. He was also certain that the Confederate Navy would get little use out of what remained of their captured prizes. Cole was surprised the heavily damaged hulks were still afloat.

As they neared the entrance to Havana harbor, they caught site of the remnants of Morro Castle, and the La Cabana. The La Cabana still resembled a fortress—albeit a heavily damaged one. The Confederate States national flag— the Blood Stained Banner—fluttered triumphantly above it. Below the La Cabana, however, there was virtually nothing left of Morro Castle other than a pile of rubble. The Confederate bombardment had done its job well.

The *Harper* made its way into the mouth of the channel and past several Confederate ironclads that were moored along its western bank. As Cole looked beyond them into the old city, he saw only a few signs of the recent military conflict. There were a few burned buildings and a few others that had obviously taken hits by explosive shells, but the vast majority of the city seemed to have escaped damage.

Havana Bay was divided into three natural harbors. Off to the right Cole caught site of the devastated, twisted, and half sunken remnants of the CSS Mississippi that still sat at her moorings. As he surveyed the wrecked battleship, Cole thought he finally understood how the Confederate people could be angry enough to go to war over it. He shook his head at the needless loss of life.

Confederate engineers had been hard at work upon the Mississippi ever since the CSA had taken Havana. Cole wasn't sure if the Confederates were trying to raise the wreck or dismantle it. In any event he pointed it out to his wife.

"There's what started this whole mess."

To his surprise, Helen pulled out a sketch pad and started to draw a picture of the wrecked Mississippi. To his greater surprise, she was actually able to produce a highly accurate illustration in the short time it took to pass the wrecked warship. Had Cole known that Helen would be joining him, he would have packed a camera so that she could go around Havana and take photographs that they could ship back to the Gazette.

The *Harper* turned to the left and made its way down the eastern most division of Havana bay. Cole and Helen quickly made their way back to the small stateroom they had been assigned for the voyage. The trip to Havana had only taken six hours but like a newly-wed couple they'd put it to good use. As always he was completely taken with his wife's youthful vivaciousness. He'd had a bout of serious depression four years earlier. He'd turned forty convinced he'd spend the rest of his life alone. He'd been married briefly when he was twenty-five, but his first wife had died in child birth a little over a year later. Afterward he'd spent nearly twenty years alone and buried in his work. But Helen had made him feel alive again. He loved her and everything about her—her personality, her beauty, her artistic creativity—even her stubborn independence. When they made love they did so with such life and exuberance that she made him feel twenty years younger. The love they'd experienced together for the seven months that they had been married seemed to make up for all his years of loneliness so that that long dark period of his life was nearly forgotten.

After returning to their stateroom they grabbed their bags and made their way back onto the deck just about the time that the sailors were throwing out the lines and securing the ship to the docks. They found Lieutenants Churchill and Barnes already waiting with their own duffle bags. The Captain had given orders that the special passengers be allowed to debark before the hundreds of troops below decks were mustered on deck and then disembarked themselves.

Cole, Helen and the two young Brits made their way down the gang plank and along the docks. A finely dressed Cuban in a gold embroidered black suit was waiting for them at the end of the dock. He had dark skin and slick black hair. He bowed and spoke in heavily accented English.

"Seniors, and Senora, I am Ricardo Aldama, with the Santa Isabel. We have a carriage waiting to take you to the hotel."

Ricardo clapped his hands and two young Cuban boys no older than thirteen sprang forward, took their luggage, and loaded it carefully onto the waiting landau. After the luggage was loaded, and Ricardo had personally helped Helen into the carriage, Cole and the others climbed aboard. The Hotel man climbed into the driver's seat, flicked the reigns and they were off through the streets of Havana.

It was one of the most beautiful cities that Cole had ever seen. The buildings were all built in baroque and neo classical designs that seemed to take him back to an older time. The streets were paved with beautiful lightly colored bricks and lined with gaslight lampposts that were already burning. Here and there palm trees also lined the streets.

Despite the setting sun, they saw no signs that the city would be winding down for the night any time soon. The streets were filled with people, and to the surprise of the four new arrivals, seemed happy. There was an almost celebratory atmosphere in Havana. Then for the first time, (though he could not figure out how he'd missed it until that point),Cole noticed the flags that seemed to be flying from nearly every other building. To his surprise they weren't Confederate flags. They were Cuban flags. Cole found himself wondering exactly what kind of status the Confederacy was planning on giving Cuba. He'd assumed they would just annex the island outright. Richmond had made it clear for decades that it wanted to do just that. Cole wondered whether the CSA's intentions had changed or if the Cuban celebrations were premature.

Either way, I'll find out soon enough.

The carriage pulled into a large colonial square—the Plaza de Armas. The center of the square was dominated by a massive ornate fountain which was itself surrounded by flowerbeds filled with tuberoses. The Santa Isabel was a massive and lavish building. It had originally been built in the seventeenth century as a mansion for Spanish nobility.

An enterprising Confederate businessman had purchased it thirty years earlier and turned it into a luxury hotel.

"The Confederacy is certainly seeing to it that we are comfortably taken care of," said Churchill. That the British officer was impressed, showed Cole just how opulent the Havana hotel was.

Cole noted that the hotel flew two flags—the Blood Stained Banner and the Cuban flag.

While Cuban bell boys handled their luggage, Cole and his wife followed Ricardo up the main steps and through an arched colonial façade and into an elegant lobby that was filled with beautiful antique furniture. Above them, crystal chandeliers hung from the ceiling. The Northern couple were followed closely by Churchill and Barnes. Helen was completely agape at the beauty of the hotel's interior.

Ricardo led them towards another well-dressed gentleman who was holding in his hand a half empty wine glass.

"Excuse me Senor Nelson, but you wanted to know when these guests arrived."

"Ah yes," said Nelson lighting up with a big smile and extending his hand—first to Cole and then to the two young British officers. When he noticed Helen he became almost reverent, and made a production of bending over her hand to kiss it.

"My name is James Nelson, I'm with the State Department. On behalf of the Confederate States government, it is my privilege to welcome you gentlemen and fine lady, to the city of Havana."

"We are very happy to be here, sir," said Churchill in his thick English accent. Cole and Helen felt absolutely surrounded. Everyone who spoke English spoke with either a Southern accent, a British accent, or a Spanish accent. That, perhaps as much as anything else, reminded them just how far away they were from their home on the Ohio River.

"I was about to take my dinner in the main dining hall. I do hope the four of you will join me. You'll find that Cuban food is fabulous and it will give me a chance to fill you in on things that have been happening here in Cuba!"

"We would be honored, sir," said Churchill.

Cole likewise nodded, though in reality he was extremely tired out from the trip. Helen, however, seemed very eager to hear all the Confederate bureaucrat had to say.

As Nelson had stated the food was exquisite. Cole had the boliche—a type of round roast stuffed with sausage—and a helping of white rice while Helen had the Arroz con pollo—a dish with baked chicken and yellow rice.

To Cole's surprise, and delight, Mr. Nelson's own wife, Kay, was waiting for them in the dining hall. The middle aged southern lady nearly burst in excitement when she saw Helen. Kay spoke with a very eloquent and soft Southern accent.

"My dear, it is such a delightful pleasure to have you with us. Now you must tell me all about your trip from up North…"

"My dear," said Nelson. "There shall be plenty of time for that later. Right now these gentlemen and I have important matters to discuss."

"Oh poo. You do fuss so, James. Surely after such a long journey they'd rather discuss something happier than politics and war."

Cole and the two young British officers smiled barely containing their laughter—Cole more in sympathy for Nelson than not. He wondered if perhaps he was looking at Helen in another fifteen or twenty years.

"Mr. Nelson…" asked Lieutenant Barnes, "if I may ask, sir, just what are the Confederacy's plans for Cuba?"

Nelson smiled as a waiter opened a bottle of white wine and filled his waiting glass. He then turned to regard his foreign guests and answer Barnes.

"An excellent, question Lieutenant. That answer depends on whether your question is meant in the political, military, or social sense."

"Are they not all three tied together?" asked Churchill.

"Not necessarily," said Nelson.

Cole noted from the bureaucrats answers that he sounded like several master politicians he'd had the displeasure to interview in the past—men who had fancy and eloquent ways of dancing around questions they didn't want to answer, but before Cole could ask a more pointed question of his own, Nelson went on.

"If you are talking about Cuba's future with regard to the institution of negro slavery then you can rest assured and you may report back to your nations, that the Confederate States has no intention of reinstituting slavery on this island."

"Then the Confederacy is not annexing Cuba?" asked Cole astonished. "You're granting Cuba its independence?"

"I didn't say that," said Nelson again sounding like a shifty politician.

"You'll forgive my confusion then, sir," said Cole as tactfully as possible. "But I fail to see how you can both annex the island and keep it free of slavery? If I understand your nation's constitution correctly, the institution of slavery is protected in all states and territories of the Confederate States."

"Yes, that is true," said Nelson. "In all states and territories. But President Stone has proposed to the Congress in Richmond that Cuba be made a 'commonwealth' of the Confederate States."

"What exactly does President Stone mean by 'commonwealth?'"

Nelson smiled.

"For all intents and purposes it means an unincorporated territory that *belongs* to the Confederate States but is not a *part* of the Confederate States. We have promised the Cubans self-government under a Constitution of their own, much as we have done for the Indians in Oklahoma, New Mexico, and Arizona territories. The Confederacy will maintain overall sovereignty over the island, and maintain a permanent military presence, but the Cubans will govern themselves with a minimum of interference from Richmond."

Mentally, Cole added Confederate President John Marshall Stone to his list of master politicians. The Southern Chief Executive had figuratively found a way to have his cake and eat it too. He got to fulfill the Confederate dream of acquiring Cuba, while at the same time seemingly avoiding the massive political damage on the world diplomatic front that would come with expanding slavery to the island.

Cole looked at Nelson.

"Would it be possible to get all the details of Cuba's new political status in writing so that I might be able to study it further and more accurately report it to my readers in the United States?"

"Yes," said Churchill. "That would be most helpful indeed."

"Well…" stuttered Nelson. He nervously drained his wine glass and then turned to again regard his foreign guests.

"I'm afraid that many of the finer details are still being worked out. But Secretary Holt himself will be arriving in Havana in a few days to personally carry out negotiations with Cuban leaders. Perhaps then I can supply you with more details. Now at this time I recommend that we all retire for the evening. In the morning I'll introduce you gentleman to an army officer who will take you to a site south of here where you can witness with your own eyes the horror and the brutality of the Spanish rule upon this island."

He then turned apologetically to Helen.

"I'm afraid my dear that it will be no place for a lady."

"That is quite alright, Mr. Nelson. My husband and I have already discussed it and I will be remaining in Havana for the duration of our stay."

Mrs. Nelson lit up like a candle at Christmas. James Nelson smiled.

"I'm sure my own lovely wife will be delighted to keep you company."

"I shall indeed," said Kay with an enormous smile on her face. "Now we shall have to visit…"

Cole smiled while Mrs. Nelson prattled on and on about how she and Helen had to visit the museums, and call on various other ladies, and visit all the dress stores in Havana. He smiled further as he watched his wife's stunned and dumbfounded look and he realized that he couldn't have asked for a better babysitter for his wife.

XIV

Some had said that the Capricorn was the most luxurious freighter they had ever been aboard. Laying in a make shift hammock, surrounded by over one hundred smelly infantrymen—half of whom were seasick—Roger Connery had a hard time thinking of the British transport as anything other than a hellhole. The air stank of vomit and body odor. Ordinarily Connery had a stomach of cast iron, even the waves of the sea could not shake him. His business as a Confederate agent meant that he had crossed the ocean several times. He had endured raging storms and sweltering seas. But the putrid stench of the air in the bowels of the freighter was enough to make even him feel queasy. The competing aroma of cigar and cigarette smoke helped to mask the stink, but only a little.

Connery also didn't care for the company he was forced to keep. Nearly half the men in the hold were negroes. Seeing them not only free, but armed and travelling as equals with white men on a journey to battle his own beloved country made Connery sick to his stomach where even the mighty North Atlantic had failed.

I hope that last communique reached Richmond. If so there should be warships on an intercept course.

Not for the first time he looked longingly at the gangway that led out of the hold and up towards the main deck. The desire to go topside was driven by more than the foul air. While he desperately wanted a breath of fresh oxygen, he also wanted to know if any Confederate ships were in the vicinity. They'd been out of port for two days. Assuming Confederate ships had left Norfolk the day they'd received his communique they should have been very close.

Unless of course we slipped past them. The ocean was a big place and the Confederate States Navy was not the largest on the waves. Complicating matters was the fact that the bulk of the Confederate fleet was engaged in the war with Spain and of those that remained available, the best ships had undoubtedly been dispatched to hunt down the decoys that Connery had discovered only too late. If Richmond had dispatched a force to intercept the real convoy, it was undoubtedly composed of a smaller number of second tier ships and crews. It was entirely possible that even though they knew the departure point and general course of Whitmore's convoy, they had failed to intercept it.

And even if they find this convoy, I wonder if they'll have the guts to stop it. The Capricorn and the other ships of the convoy were sailing under the Union Jack. As far as Connery knew there were no British warships escorting them. The British seemed complacent and confident that their flag alone would be all that was required to protect the small flotilla of transport ships.

The British have always been arrogantly overconfident about their power. Connery wondered what the Confederate ships would do if they actually managed to intercept the convoy. Firing on Spanish ships was easy. Firing on private US ships owned by a man the United States government had (at least officially) publically disavowed was equally risk free. The United States had walked on diplomatic egg shells as far as the Confederacy was concerned ever since they had been disastrously defeated in the War of 1869 by their estranged southern brothers. Like a castrated bull the US would make no undo fuss. Attacking ships sailing under the flag of one of the world's most powerful empires, however, was entirely different. The British would never take an attack on one of their transports lightly. If Confederate ships boarded or fired upon them, it would risk all-out war with Britain. Connery wasn't certain if it was worth the risk, though he knew for certain how his superior John Wilkes Booth would have had events unfold. The head of the Confederate secret service had not an ounce of give in him when it came to the enemies of the South or those that aided them. Connery had come to expect nothing less from a man that routinely ordered the assassination of foreign officials hostile to the Confederate States, and that had personally ordered the destruction of one of the Confederacy's own battleships to give the CSA a casus bell to declare war on Spain and invade Cuba. Connery was certain that Booth would have happily blown the British convoy out the water if they refused to surrender Whitmore and his men. Certain as he was, however, Connery doubted that John Marshal Stone would allow such an act. The Confederate President was so desperate to placate the British that he had activated the provisions of the negro conscription act.

And so now we've gone and armed niggers ourselves!
With a disheartened sigh, he glared around the hold at the
large numbers of colored mercenaries. In this latest war,
white men on both sides would be employing negroes as
weapons of war. *But Stone won't be on that ship. Maybe…
just maybe whoever's in charge will have the guts to do what
needs doing.*

Connery once again sent a longing glance towards the
exit from the hold. Officers had the privilege to go topside at
will. The enlisted men were going up in shifts and even then
only in small groups for short periods of time. Hoping to
distract himself while he waited for his turn, he spread a
khaki blanket on the deck beside his hammock and began to
break down and clean his rifle. The Whitmore was slightly
different from either an Enfield or a Richmond Rifle.
Connery had had extensive experience with the latter two and
so had taken well to the new Yankee Rifle. He found it
superior to the US Springfield, but no better than an Enfield
or a Richmond. He quickly cleaned it and then expertly
reassembled it.

"Well, Mr. Murphy you may sleep like the dead, but I
must say I'm pleased at your skill with a rifle."

Connery was momentarily startled by the sudden
British brogue. He looked up to see Captain Dominic
Malcolm staring down at him.

"Wouldn't want my rifle to fail me when I needed it
the most."

"Truer words have never been spoken," said Malcom
and nodded approvingly. He then looked questioningly at
Connery and asked: "Have you seen action before?"

"You could say that," said Connery. "When I was a
ten year old boy the Confederates invaded my home state of
Maryland at the start of the Second War of Rebellion. They
attacked the outskirts of Washington before falling back
across the Potomac." The story was entirely true, though
Connery failed to mention that his own family had welcomed
the Southern troops with open arms and that his father had
put on an old tattered gray uniform and gone out with a rifle
musket to help and not hinder the short-lived Confederate
invasion. A lot of Marylanders had wanted to secede with the

South. Daniel Connery's one regret in life was that Maryland had remained a US state.

"A young age to see war. Did you later serve in the US regular army?"

Connery shook his head.

"Just the militia."

"Is that where you got that nasty scar?" Malcom motioned to his own face. Connery feigned embarrassment.

"I'm afraid not, sir. I got this in a bar fight over a certain young lady."

Malcom's normally cold exterior melted for a moment and he allowed himself to laugh.

Suddenly four soldiers entered the hold. They looked none too pleased to be back in the hold. A non-com suddenly started shouting.

"Mason, Michaels, Murphey, Nichols—it's your turn to go topside. You've got fifteen minutes!"

A sea sick black soldier that was berthed a few feet from Connery suddenly began to throw up for what must have been the tenth time that hour. Captain Malcom walked over to him.

"You're dry heaving, soldier. Get yourself to the infirmary."

"Yassuh," he replied and then stumbled out of the hold and up the gangway that led to the sick bay.

Connery grabbed his binoculars and then proceeded up to the main deck. As soon as he emerged from below decks, he sucked in an invigorating breath of fresh sea air. It was icy cold but a welcome escape from the putrid stench below. All at once he felt better. He wasted no time, immediately walking to the side railing and bringing up his binoculars to scan the horizon. He spotted nothing off to the east. Undeterred he made his way forward. He passed the main mast which stood in front of the freighter's superstructure. The mast held a massive sail that remained almost permanently furled. The Capricorn was a steamship, and though she still carried sails they were only as a back up to her powerful steam engines.

After passing a couple of sailors who were busily swabbing the deck, Connery climbed up onto the forecastle and made his way towards the bow, stepping carefully to avoid tripping on the anchor chains.. Bringing up his binoculars for the second time he scanned the sea to the south but as before he spotted nothing. He made his way to the starboard side of the ship only to end up with the same results. Connery muttered a curse to himself. His fifteen minutes were running out quickly. Finally he made his way to the stern and ascended the aft deck by means of a steep set of stairs that more nearly approximated a ladder than a set of proper stairs. Connery quickly realized that the aft deck was not deserted. Major Pershing and the beautiful young nurse that Connery had seen him with earlier were standing together at the very rear of the ship beneath a large British merchant marine flag that was fluttering in the breeze. They were locked quite intimately in one another's arms—their lips pressed together in a passionate kiss. Connery was quite certain that Pershing would not take well to being interrupted and since he'd resolved to draw as little attention to himself as possible he decided simply to forgo scanning the northern horizon.

The North is the least likely direction they'd come from. The rest of the convoy is right behind us any way. I wouldn't be able to get a full view of the horizon. Deciding that the Confederate navy would either catch them or not and that there was nothing he could do about it, Connery loathingly headed back to the hatch that led back below decks. The time passed agonizingly slow as he laid in his hammock, waiting and hoping for some sign of his countrymen. But no alarm sounded through the ship. No soldiers or sailors spoke excitedly of warships flying the Blood Stained Banner. As afternoon gave way to evening, Connery came to the realization that the convoy would not be intercepted.

So be it. But I will still make certain that this boatload of niggers never reaches Cuba. In his mind he began to plot ways that he might sink the ship. When he had destroyed the CSS Mississippi in Havana harbor, he'd placed several explosive charges in the ships powder magazine. But Connery had used all of his explosive charges and had had neither the time nor the resources to construct more. He also reflected that the Capricorn was a freighter not a battleship. It had no gunpowder magazine. He toyed with the idea of commandeering the bridge and crashing the ship into one of the other ships in the convoy.

I could kill two birds with one stone. But he quickly dismissed the idea. For one thing he would have to kill or overcome the entire bridge crew. Not beyond his capability, but extremely risky nonetheless. He also knew there was a very good chance of him being spotted. Even if he concealed his face in some way, Whitmore would know in no uncertain terms that a Confederate operative was aboard.

It needs to look like an accident—at least plausibly. He grunted in aggravation. He was unused to uncertainty. He went back in his memory to when the ship was loaded. The rear hold was filled with men. The forward hold, however, had been loaded with artillery pieces and artillery shells.

Where there is artillery there is gunpowder. Everything I need to cause an explosion is there. All I need is time—time to find it and time to use it.

Connery waited until after night fall, lying in his hammock pretending to be asleep. He would have moved sooner, but a small group of non-coms had stayed up smoking and playing cards by the light of a small kerosene lamp. Even after they had finished and turned in, Connery waited patiently, wanting to make sure that everyone was asleep before he made his move.

When the darkness of the hold held nothing but the sound of breathing and snoring, Connery eased himself out of his hammock. His eyes had adjusted to the darkness as well as they could. The only illumination came from the starlight and moonlight that made its way through the rows of small portholes on both sides of the hold. He could just make out the path that led down the center of the hold towards the hatchway. He silently slung his haversack over his shoulder and made sure his knife was fastened securely to his belt where he could get at it. He then slowly but surely made his way past sleeping men and their gear and then down the path. Just before reaching the hatchway, he paused by the table where the non-coms had been playing cards. Connery grabbed the kerosene lamp and then quietly went through the hatchway and climbed up towards the upper decks. The corridor was dimly lit by small electric lights. The *Capricorn* was indeed a state of the art ship.

Connery made his way down the corridor and then passed up the gangway that led up to the main deck. Proceeding further forward he made his way past the infirmary and then went down a gangway that led deeper into the ship's bowels. His first two nights aboard the ship he'd made a point to venture out and explore the interior of the vessel, drawing a map within his mind.

A chronometer on the wall read 0130 hrs. So far he had encountered not a single soul. He'd been caught by a sailor his second night out but had simply explained he'd gone looking for the galley and had gotten himself lost. The sailor had accepted his story and nothing had come of it, but Connery didn't want to get caught again.

Not tonight. Connery's hand came to rest momentarily on the handle of the knife that he had secured to his belt. If he did encounter anyone that night, the unfortunate soul would never tell anyone about it. Connery made his way to the end of one last corridor where he finally reached the entrance to the forward cargo hold.

Then he opened the hatch with a loud clang. Hoping no one had heard it, he cautiously made his way inside. It was exceedingly dark and Connery could see nothing. Because of the electrical lights in the corridors his eyes were no longer adjusted to the darkness. Connery struck a match and then lit the kerosene lamp. Not wanting to make more noise, he eased the hatch to where it was just barely ajar. He then turned around and surveyed the massive forward hold. If it had electrical lights, Connery saw no switch for turning them on. The kerosene lamp would have to suffice.

The hold was stacked high with wooden crates. In addition to the artillery pieces and shells, the hold also contained crates of ammunition, extra-small arms, extra-uniforms and gear, food, medical supplies, and a whole host of materiel for use by Whitmore's Legion. Moving amongst the crates was almost like being in a small maze. He cautiously used the lantern to examine the crates. He remembered that the ones containing black powder or explosive shells had been stenciled with the image of an eagle and the words "US Army."

If I find the guns themselves, the powder and shells won't be far from them. His prediction proved correct. He found the rifled artillery pieces in the very front of the hold. Stacked not far away were the crates containing the shells and the black powder. Connery set the lantern on a crate several feet away and then pulled a small steel catspaw from his haversack. A proper crowbar would have been better but what he had sufficed. He pried open the first crate, pulled out a handful of straw that had been used as cushion filler and then pulled out a black powder charge. The charge was made of thick cotton twill and was cylindrical in shape. It was designed to be inserted into the breach of a rifled artillery piece. At nine inches long and three and a half inches wide it contained enough powder to hurl an explosive shell well over a mile away. Next he very carefully pulled out a 3.5 inch diameter artillery shell and set it aside. He continued to empty the crate. When the task was finished he had six shells and six charges. Wasting no time he hauled down another crate and pried it open, emptying its contents as he had the other. He opened another and another and another until he had thirty charges and thirty shells. He then took a moment to wipe sweat from his face and catch his breath.

This should be enough. If I'm lucky I'll cause a chain reaction of explosions that will cripple or even sink the ship. If not, I'll still do a lot of damage!

Next he set to work arranging the thirty artillery shells at the base of the crates containing the remaining shells and charges. He set the shells on their sides arranging them in three circles of ten shells each. He made certain that the rear of each shell which contained the fuse was pointed to the interior of the circle. He then grabbed the first black powder charge and cut into it with his knife. He emptied the black powder from nine of the charges into the first circle of artillery shells that he had made. He then did the same to the other two circles. In the end, he had three charges left. He cut a small opening in the first and laid down a thick trail of black powder that connected the three circles of shells and the powder within in them. He then used the other two charges to lay down a thinner but longer trail that led away from the circles, through the hold and close to the hatch that led to the rest of the ship. Whether from worry of getting caught or the excitement of what was about to happen, Connery felt a surge of adrenalin that helped him forget his exhaustion. He rushed back to the front of the hold. He then heaved another crate of explosive shells and set the whole crate atop one of the circles. He then place another crate atop the first. He repeated the process on the other two circles.

At last, he grabbed the lantern and made his way along the trail of black powder and back to the hatch that led out of the hold.

I need a time delay detonator. If he lit the gunpowder himself, he doubted he'd get far enough away to avoid risking serious injury. If the blast was large enough, the concussion alone could kill him. Fortunately, he was a resourceful man. Connery set down the lantern by the hatch. He then pulled out a cigarette and stuck it in his mouth. He removed his matches from his front pocket, struck one and then got the cigarette going. After one short drag, he placed the lit cigarette inside the book of matches with the lit end sticking out. He then very carefully set the book of matches at the end of the black powder trail that led back to the artillery shells he'd rigged to explode. The cigarette would act as a slow burning fuse. When the cigarette burned down, it would ignite the matches which in turn would ignite the gunpowder. And then...

Connery wasted no time. He made his way out of the forward cargo hold and back into the dimly lit corridor. He took the stairs of the gangway two at a time as he climbed to the next deck.

XV

In the infirmary of the Capricorn, Joshua Winslow and Dr. Willis Hylton sat huddled over an open textbook that sat on the ship's surgeon's desk. The medical text was open to a page that showed a detailed diagram of the human brain.

"So you actually opened his skull?" Joshua Winslow's voice radiated amazement as he asked the question. The ship's surgeon sitting across from him nodded assuredly.

"The blow he received to the head when the cargo crane collapsed had caused a massive amount of fluidic pressure on the right side of his brain." The British physician then pointed to the illustration to show Joshua the exact place of the injury he was describing. "I had to relieve the pressure, so I opened a small section of the cranium—about half an inch in diameter."

"Back in Chicago, Dr. James said to never open the skull. He said it was almost always fatal."

"Your Dr. James is not that far wrong. You have to be exceedingly careful that you don't further damage the brain when cutting or drilling into the skull. You must be very precise. Even if you do it perfectly, the wound will be terribly susceptible to infection. Very often the patient will take a severe fever that ultimately leads to death. But sometimes you have no other choice. If I hadn't relieved the pressure, he would most certainly have died."

"But you're saying that this patient survived?" asked Joshua. Dr. Hylton smiled.

"It's been two years and he's still aboard. Later I'll introduce you."

"It will be my pleasure," said Joshua, "though I doubt it will go very well if I ask him if I may examine his head."

"I don't think it would be a problem. Mr. Clavin has always been extremely grateful and considers his survival a miracle. He has as high an opinion of doctors as anyone I've ever known. I'm sure in the interest of furthering medical knowledge he'd allow you to examine the scar."

"Ordinarily perhaps, but…" Joshua's eyes looked down at his own black hands and forearms. "It's been my experience that folks aren't too eager about letting a black doctor lay hands on them."

Hylton nodded.

"I've known more than a few like that, though I wonder, if they were injured and their life blood was pouring out of them, would they object to your services then?"

In spite of himself, Joshua found himself smiling a bitter and ironic smile.

"You'd be surprised, sir. There are some folks that would sooner die then let a nigger doctor work on them."

Hylton nodded again.

"I'm afraid ignorance is one disease we'll never totally eradicate. But I think you'll find Mr. Clavin more civil then you're accustomed to. We British aren't quite as blinkered as our estranged American cousins, North or South." Hylton paused suddenly. He stared at Joshua as if wanting to ask a question but unsure how to ask it.

"Joshua, if I may ask,… how did you…come by the opportunity and resources to become a surgeon?"

How'd a nigger get into med-school. How'd a nigger get the money to go to med-school? Joshua had heard the question or variations of it a thousand times. Hylton's had been one of the most politely phrased. Joshua didn't really mind him asking. Even when Joshua had an intelligent conversation with a more open minded person like Hylton, such questions almost inevitably came up. That in and of itself said mountains about the prejudice in North America in general and the sad economic state of American negroes in particular.

Before Joshua could answer, a knock came at the open doorway of the sickbay. Joshua and Hylton turned to see a khaki uniformed negro soldier standing in the doorway. He looked so weak so as to be on the verge of collapse.

"Excuse me suh. I's feelin' mighty poorly. Cap'in Malcom, he send me up here."

"Come in soldier," said Hylton rising to his feet.

Joshua also stood, and went forward to help the soldier. The negro froze in his tracks when he saw Joshua, and openly gaped at him.

"I sees it but I don'ts believe it," he said weakly. "Josiah say der be a nigga docta on dis boat, but I tell him he be one crazy nigga. I done lost myself a pack o' smokes."

Joshua took him by the arm and helped him to his seat.

"What is your medical problem?" he asked. The negro gaped again, this time at Joshua's educated speech.

"I caint keep nothin down. I's done puked up everything. Thing is… my inside don't know it. Keeps trying to hurl even though dere nothin left."

"You are dry heaving," said Joshua. "Its motion sickness." Joshua spoke with a great amount of sympathy. He

109

himself had been tormented by sea sickness when they had set sail. He'd had no more experience on the sea than most of the other members of Whitmore's Legion. His own condition had improved, but he still hesitated to eat much.

"Mo' what?"

"You're sea sick," said Hylton turning around and opening a cabinet. "Its not exactly a medical remedy, but my father and grandfather swore by it." Hylton produced a small paper bag and handed it to the soldier who opened it to reveal what looked like flat dark brown biscuits. "They're a little stale, but they should help. Don't eat them to quickly, just munch on them a little at a time."

"What dey is?"

"Ginger nuts."

Joshua caught the faint smells of ginger and cinnamon coming from the bag.

"Thank you suh. I sho' do appreciate dis,"

"Make sure you try to drink some water too," said Joshua. "You need to stay hydrated."

"I try." The black soldier continued to gaze at Joshua. It was a look Joshua had seen at other times he had met fellow negroes. It was a look of disbelief mingled with reverence and awe.

"How you become what you is?"

Hylton smiled.

"We were just discussing that very question."

For a moment that seemed to stretch a very long time, Joshua regarded the negro soldier. He looked to be about his own age. Joshua reflected that nothing but God's grace and the circumstances of his birth separated him from this soldier and the millions of other negroes in America that were trapped in ignorance and injustice. A moment later he gave the soldier an answer to his question.

"I was blessed enough to have an educated father who worked hard and sacrificed much so that his son could go farther than the world thinks a negro should go." It was a generic answer, and it neglected to mention that his father and mother had made off with a small fortune in New Mexico gold at the end of the Second War of Rebellion. It was, however, a perfectly honest answer, and it seemed good enough for both the negro soldier and the ship's surgeon.

"What yo' name is?"

"Winslow. Joshua Winslow. What is yours?"

"Thaddeus."

"I'm pleased to meet you, Thaddeus."

Joshua reached into his front pocket and pulled out a pack of cigarettes.

"Here, these should make up for the pack you owe Josiah."

"Thank you suh, but you don't have to do dat."

"Think nothing of it," said Joshua. "I've tried them and haven't quite taken a liking to them."

"A pity," said Dr. Hylton and proceeded to pull a cigar from his own pocket. "The London medical Journals have had numerous articles on the health benefits of tobacco smoking."

After Thaddeus had made his way out of the infirmary, Hylton closed the medical textbook on his desk and handed it to Joshua.

"Yours with my complements."

"I couldn't possibly…"

"Nonsense. I have a bad feeling that you'll be dealing with far more head injuries in the immediate future than I will. Besides, I have another copy."

"Thank you, doctor."

"You say you haven't taken a liking to tobacco. I can't say I blame you considering the garbage that masquerades under the name in the United States. But you would have to lack all good taste not to enjoy one of these."

He reached into his pocket and pulled out another cigar which he passed to Joshua. Not wanting to offend his new friend, Joshua accepted it. He'd had cigars before when he'd been at school in Chicago and hadn't found them any better than cigarettes. Of course, he reflected, he'd never allowed himself to try any of the tobacco that had been imported from the CSA. He'd been told countless times that tobacco from the Confederates States was infinitely better than that which was grown in the USA, but he couldn't countenance enjoying a product that had been produced by the slave labor of the South. Hesitantly, he looked at the golden band around the cigar, fearing that he'd see a southern cross or a blood stained banner. Instead he saw the gold and red la rojigualda of Spain."

"Habana?"

"A little taste of where you're headed," said Hylton. "And I might add another small incentive to keep Cuba out of the Confederacy."

His conscience clear, and slightly curious about experiencing what was universally acclaimed as the greatest tobacco (even better than that grown in the CSA) Joshua cut off the end of the cigar, stuck it in his mouth, struck a match and proceeded to ignite it. He took several puffs on the cigar and…

"What did I tell you chap?"

Joshua's face said it all. He held out the cigar and stared at it in wonder. The flavor was amazing. He returned it to his mouth and started puffing happy clouds. Hylton laughed.

"Don't like it too much. They cost a King's ransom."

"I wonder why I've never seen one before?"

"As I understand it the Confederacy has just about cornered the North American tobacco market. Most of the Cuban tobacco is shipped to Spain and then sold throughout Europe and the British Isles."

The two men smoked and talked for the next hour and a half, until they had finished their cigars and the clock had struck 18:00.

"It's about time for dinner. Will you be joining us?"

"I'd better not," said Joshua. "Lunch didn't sit well with me, so I'd better not hazard dinner. But I will certainly join you for breakfast in the morning. In the meantime may I remain here and avail myself of your books?"

Hylton smiled and nodded.

"You are a glutton for knowledge. The medical profession needs more like you. My humble library is at your disposal for as long as you like."

Hylton may have called his collection of books humble. But he had a large collection of medical journals from London containing articles that Joshua would most likely never get the chance to read again. He wondered how much faster medical knowledge would grow if doctors from the various nations cooperated more in their research endeavors and were more readily able to share ideas and results. Setting aside the book that Hylton had given him on the human brain (he'd have plenty of time to read that later) Joshua delved into the medical journals. Dr. Hylton hadn't been jesting when he'd said that doctors in England were propounding the health benefits of tobacco. He found no less than three articles on the subject as he perused the journals. He was most fascinated by an article written by a British military doctor that had served on the front lines in Afghanistan. The article detailed the wounds likely to be caused by various calibers of bullets and gave detailed instructions on the extraction of the projectiles and the treatment of the wounds. Another article detailed various drugs used in anesthesia, a continually developing art that allowed more organized and less strenuous surgeries by rendering patients unconscious. In earlier decades most surgeries had been performed by giving the patient a shot of whiskey, strapping them to the operating table, and placing a piece of leather in their mouth to prevent them from biting off their tongue or crushing their teeth in pain, while the doctors cut and performed surgery on them fully conscious. Joshua had heard horror stories from some of his professors who had been practicing physicians before the various forms of anesthesia had been widely available. He'd heard stories too, about patients waking up in the middle of surgery.

No anesthesia is perfect...

The electric lights above him allowed Joshua to study far into the night. When he finally broke into a yawn and looked at the clock it was after two in the morning. He stood to his feet and stretched. He was young and healthy and strong, but sitting for so long was hard on both the body and the eyes not to mention the brain.

Much study is a weariness of the flesh. The passage from Ecclesiastes came to his mind as if by reflex. His parents had been engraining the scriptures in his mind and heart since his birth. At one point he'd considered the ministry, but felt that God had been calling him to another profession.

I need some air. Shortly after leaving the sick bay another scripture sounded the trumpet in his mind. He'd turned a corner in one of the corridors just in time to see Major Pershing and the nurse Jennifer Harper slipping quietly and discreetly into her cabin.

For this is the will of God, even your sanctification, that ye should abstain from fornication: Joshua knew that what they were doing was not only immoral but against regulation and protocol. He tried to remind himself that: *Lost people are going to act like lost people,* and that it was not his place to judge them. They would hardly be the first young couple to forgo the vows of matrimony because of impending military conflict. Joshua made a mental note to pray for an opportunity to tactfully and compassionately speak to the Major about the condition of his soul. *Especially since the bullets will soon be flying.*

Joshua made his way up on deck. The night air was cool and crisp but felt absolutely invigorating to his lungs. He breathed in the salty sea air, savoring its freshness as he walked to the starboard railing. About half a mile away he could see the masthead light of one of the other freighters of the convoy. Up in the sky the moon shown in a star studded and cloudless sky. A few minutes later, Joshua was startled as a man literally erupted, huffing and puffing, from a hatch to his right. Even in the depth of the night, Joshua recognized the scar that made its way down his face. Though he couldn't recall the soldier's name, he knew it was the same man that had disembarked the train along with Pershing, Harper and himself less than a week earlier. Though the man had apparently made efforts to conceal his emotions, Joshua had had a life time of experience in seeing past such facades in certain white people. He was reasonably certain that the man disdained negroes. Joshua seemed to remember that the man had claimed to come from Maryland—which in many ways would explain his hostility since Maryland had been one of the few slave states to remain in the Union. The inhabitants had been none too happy when the U.S. government had abolished slavery and many Marylanders were bitter to that day. With his peripheral vison, Joshua watched as the man made his way past him and aft towards the stern where he stopped and took tight hold of one of the lifeboat davits. The man was obviously winded and Joshua wondered why the man was up in the middle of the night and storming through the ship at breakneck speed. He didn't have time to wonder long.

Suddenly the deck trembled ominously underneath Joshua's feet, accompanied by a rumble like thunder. A few seconds later, the trembling became a violent shudder. A massive fireball burst through the deck at the bow. It erupted out of the main cargo hatch and various breaches in the deck planks. Then the whole ship lurched suddenly, and Joshua was thrown overboard and into the sea...

XVI

John Pershing lay quietly in bed. Under the covers his body was intimately interlaced with that of Jennifer. After making passionate love with him she had fallen fast asleep in his arms and he felt her quiet breathing against his chest. He had just about fallen asleep himself, when there was a loud noise as if a thunderbolt had somehow struck within the ship itself. The entire vessel shook violently and in the midst of the chaos, Jennifer woke suddenly as Pershing felt the ship lurch hard to the port.

"What's happening?" she asked in a terrified voice, holding him to her tightly.

In the darkness of the cabin he had no way to know for sure.

Did we hit something? Did someone fire on us? Obviously something had happened and he had no time to lose. Instantly metamorphosing from lover to military man of action, Pershing leapt out of the bed and rapidly began to dress.

"I'm not sure what's happened," he said, "but I'm sure that was an explosion."

"Are we going to sink?" she asked in a terrified voice that seemed on the brink of panic.

"I don't think so," he said as he fastened his pants and started to look for his shirt. Actually he was certain of no such thing. The ship was obviously lurching to the port. But he needed her to remain calm.

"You need to get dressed and get up on deck immediately," said Pershing. "Head to the lifeboats just in case."

"What about you?"

"I've got to find out what happened and see to my men. Now get moving."

She rose rapidly from the bed and embraced him tightly.

"I love you!" she said.

In less than a heartbeat and without even thinking he replied to her in kind.

"I love you." Saying the words for the first time to her sounded strange, as had hearing her say them to him. He had no doubt that it was genuine on both their parts. Their relationship had grown more and more intimate and serious. And though in the heat of the moment they'd engaged in the ultimate act of love that night, they'd not expressed what they felt in words until that moment. Taking her firmly in her arms he brought his lips down to hers in a passionate kiss. A moment later he forced himself to let her go. "Get dressed and get topside quickly."

He made his way out of her cabin and into the corridor. Almost instantly he caught the smell of smoke. Part of him wanted to immediately return to Jennifer—to see to it personally that she made it to safety—but his sense of duty prevailed. He rapidly headed through the narrow corridors, down gangways and towards the aft cargo hold where his men were berthed. The smell of smoke seemed thicker the deeper below he went, but it started to thin as he moved aft. The lights suddenly flickered. For a moment he was plunged into pitch darkness. A few heartbeats later, the lights returned. Pershing breathed a sigh of relief. The last thing he needed was to be trapped in the darkened bowls of a possibly sinking freighter, and he had no desire to feel his way through the labyrinth of corridors.

Pershing quickened his pace. As if to motivate him to move faster, the ship's list seemed to increase suddenly. She was very obviously listing to the port and Pershing now had the distinct feeling that he was walking slightly uphill. He also noted ominously that the smell of smoke seemed to be following him. The lights flickered again about a minute later. Once again, they came back on after only a moment.

Pershing entered the aft hold to discover that the men were already awake. He wasn't surprised. The explosion had sounded like the end of the world and he was certain that even at the opposite end of the ship the violent shockwave had been felt. He was pleased to see that Captain Malcom had ordered the men to gear up. The men still seemed groggy and they were moving at a yet dilatory pace, but Malcom's stern voice lashed at them like a taskmasters whip to keep them moving.

"What's going on, Major?" demanded Malcom as soon as he caught sight of Pershing.

"I'm not sure," replied Pershing. "We know there was an explosion, the ship is lurching, and there is a smell of smoke in the corridors. I don't think we've been attacked, we would certainly have been hit again if that were the case."

"Well there's enough explosive ordinance stored in the bow to blow this ship to the infernal regions and back but what could have set it off?"

"Only two options," replied Pershing. "An accident...or sabotage."

Malcom's face grew suddenly hard.

"I find that last option most distasteful."

"As do I. Finish getting the men ready. I'm going topside to find out what's happening."

Suddenly, the ship seemed to lurch again. A coffee cup on one of the tables slid off and shattered on the deck plating. Pershing looked Malcom in the eye.

"Don't wait on me. Don't wait on instructions from the Captain or crew. As soon as the men are ready get them topside."

"Understood, sir."

Pershing made his way out of the hold and back into the corridors. Smoke was slowly but surely beginning to permeate the air in the aft of the ship. He coughed several times as he went up the gangways and felt a rush of relief when he finally made it up to the main deck and into the open air. The deck seemed to be in chaos. Sailors seemed to be running to and fro. Several had uncovered the life boats and manned the davits.

Pershing grabbed one of the sailors by the shirtsleeve.

"Has the order been given to abandon ship?"

"Not yet, sir. We're just taking precautions."

"Where can I find the Captain?"

"He's in the wardroom with General Whitmore."

Pershing headed forward. The Capricorn was listing at least fifteen degrees forward and about five degrees to the port. When he came in sight of the bow he saw no flames but a large amount of black smoke was coming out of a large gaping hole where the main cargo hatch had once been and out of several smaller breeches as well. Pershing noted also that the front of the bow was much nearer the waterline than it was supposed to be. A few more degrees and the sea would start to over flow the foredeck.

Pershing was startled by a sudden bang and burst of light. For a moment he thought they were under attack or that another explosion had occurred but he quickly realized that an officer had fired a bright red flare into the sky, signaling the Capricorn's distress. Pershing hoped it was only a formality.

Surely the lookouts on the other ships of the convoy saw and heard the explosion. Pershing glanced hurriedly to the port. He was relieved to see that another ship of the convoy was sitting no more than a hundred yards from them. In the dim light Pershing could see its own sailors rapidly preparing their own life boats.

Just in case.

A hatch in the side of the superstructure led into the wardroom. The Captain, the First Officer, the ship's engineer, Joseph Whitmore, David Lovejoy, and Charles Landon stood around the table in tense conversation. The engineer pointed at a schematic of the ship that was spread out on the table.

"The fire thankfully is out. Though smoke is still pervading the lower decks, the influx of seawater we've taken on has extinguished the flames, but the weight of the water has begun to pull us down by the head."

"Haven't you sealed the water tight doors?" demanded the Landon. The representative of the British Admiralty looked not only disheveled but on the verge of a nervous breakdown.

"Of course, my lord," said the Captain. "One of my men nearly died of smoke inhalation by going into the lower decks and sealing them."

"It doesn't matter," interjected the engineer, and pointed forcefully to the schematics of the vessel upon the table. "The watertight bulkheads only go up two decks. When the explosion occurred, it ruptured rivets from the bow to the midships—mostly on the port side. The entire forward half of the ship has been opened to the sea. As the ship goes down by the bow the water will spill over the bulkheads one after another. The forward hold is already almost completely flooded." The engineer pulled out a pocket watch. "In less than an hour this ship will be at the bottom of the Atlantic."

"We have to get the troops and the crew off," said the Captain.

"The Santorini is already alongside and the Bresson is also standing by," said the First Officer.

The Captain nodded.

"Issue the order to abandon ship. The nurses and surgeons will be the first ones into the boats." The Captain then turned to Charles Landon. "Your lordship, you and Mr. Whitmore will also go over in the first wave of boats along with, however many troops we can fit. With the added boats of the other two ships we should be able to ferry everyone to the Santorini and the Bresson. But we must hurry. We have no time to lose."

A moment later the small party began to disperse. Whitmore caught immediate sight of Pershing. The elderly millionaire looked red in the face with anger.

"Pershing, you heard the man, get your men ready to abandon ship. Make certain they bring their rifles and as much gear as possible."

"I've already seen to it, sir. They should be up on deck soon."

Whitmore nodded. The old man then swore profanely.

"I tell you Pershing, there is a saboteur among us! First the mysterious explosion at my mansion and now this!" Whitmore blasphemed profanely. He was clenching the top of his cane so tightly that his fist was white. He stabbed the deck with it in a rage. "When I find out who's responsible I'll hang him myself!"

His aid, David Lovejoy took hold of the old man's arm.

"Sir, we must get to the boats"

Whitmore swore again.

"I'm coming, blast your miserable soul! I must retrieve a few things from my cabin first. We've lost the cannons and most of the spare ammunition, but I'm not turning back, you hear me?"

"I hear you, sir," said Lovejoy, almost frantically trying to urge his employer to hurry.

Even after Whitmore had exited the wardroom down the aft corridor, Pershing could still hear the old man's shouting, swearing, and fuming.

Pershing wasted no time, but quickly made his way back outside. The bow had now sunk completely beneath the water. Only the forward cargo crane remained above the surface and it too was going down fast. The ship was now at a much steeper angle. As he headed aft he literally had to walk uphill. When he reached the midships, he caught sight of Jennifer. He was glad to see that she was near the life boats but she didn't notice him. Along with another nurse and Dr. Hylton she seemed to be stooped over someone lying prostrate on the deck. As he drew closer he noticed that it was Joshua Winslow. The young negro surgeon was motionless on the deck. His clothes looked to be soaked.

"What happened?" demanded Pershing.

"Hypothermia and exhaustion. He was thrown overboard in the explosion. He tread water for nearly twenty minutes before the sailors threw him a line and pulled him out. Considering the temperature of the water it's a miracle he lasted as long as he did." Hylton then started barking orders at Jennifer and the other nurse. Get blankets and wrap him in them. We've got to get him onto one of the boats and over to the Santorini."

As he proceeded further aft, Pershing was glad to see that Malcom and the men of his company were all mustered on deck and standing calm at parade rest. Each man was fully uniformed, wore his full field pack, his ammo belt and carried his rifle. The men from the other companies didn't look nearly as well equipped or orderly. Most of them had their rifles, but their uniforms and gear were haphazard at best. Many of them didn't have their field packs or even their ammo belts. Whitmore would be furious, but Pershing's company had salvaged all it could.

This is what happens when civilians try to play soldiers. He'd resolved to worry about it later. For the moment he had far more pressing concerns. He turned to his second in command.

"The ship's going down."

Malcom motioned almost melodramatically at the steep angle of the deck. Whereas the bow was underwater, the stern had begun to rise out of the water and into the air.

"You don't say…" he said. He then tossed a duffle bag to Pershing and an ammo belt with Pershing's side arm. "I took the liberty of grabbing your things. I'm not sure if I got everything, but I wouldn't recommend going below to check. The smoke down there is nearly unbearable."

"Thanks Malcom." Pershing then proceeded to put on his ammo belt and side arm. He then turned to regard the lifeboats. The evacuation was underway. "As long as no one panics we should get everyone off before the ship goes down."

"How long do we have?"

Pershing pulled out his own watch.

"Maybe forty minutes."

The evacuation proceeded slower than it should have. The first wave got off fairly quickly. Pershing was glad to see that Jennifer was off the ship. Things seemed to go more smoothly for a short while as another wave of boats came in, but when the ship lurched forward again, and the stern rose several more degrees into the air, several of the men started to panic, and some of them didn't have to look far for an excuse to get off the doomed ship faster.

"White men before niggers!"

Several men from one of the white companies tried to force their way past Pershing's men. The negroes didn't take it kindly. A fist fight erupted just as a group of boats from the Bresson approached the sinking freighter.

Pershing pulled his army revolver, charged into the midst of the brawl, and brandished it at the men that had tried to force their way to the front.

"That's enough!" roared Pershing in a commanding voice as he pointed the weapon at the men that had started the trouble. "You men get back in your place or I'll save you the trouble of waiting on a life boat."

Staring down the barrel of Pershing's revolver the troublemakers fled to the back of the line like cowards. Pershing then headed back to his own place.

"Are you alright, sir?" asked Malcom.

Pershing nodded and breathed a sigh of relief. He then opened the cylinder on his revolver and proceeded to load it with bullets from his ammo belt.

Malcom's eyes grew suddenly wide.

"Well played, sir. Remind me never to play poker with you."

Pershing's men began to board the life boats. A half hour later, from the deck of the Bresson, he and Malcom watched as the Capricorn disappeared into the depths of the sea.

XVII

We will deal with that when we come to it…

Major Antonio Vega cursed the words he had spoken to his second in command when Captain Perez had warned him about the swamps that stood between his small company of soldiers and their goal of reaching Santiago de Cuba. Now they were waste deep in the muddy mire, trudging through the Zapata swampland. They were dangerously low on ammunition—so much so that Antonio doubted they'd be able to engage in any kind of sustained fire fight. If they encountered the enemy they would only get a few shots. Antonio wanted to make sure they at least got those few shots. The Spaniards moved with their rifles lifted high above them. Bloodthirsty mosquitos tormented them. Antonio swatted one on his neck. He suddenly found his muddy hand stained with red blood—his own. He swore profanely.

This is not what I had in mind! He'd chosen to go east as opposed to west, so that he and his men would not be cut off on Cuba's western tip (and so that they would have their best opportunity of escaping back to Spain). Unfortunately the swamplands were in his way and they were proving a greater obstacle than he ever imagined they would. He'd decided to go through, as opposed to around, the quagmire to avoid areas largely controlled by Cuban guerrillas. Until they were resupplied Antonio wanted to avoid all contact with enemy forces. The swamps were free from both Cuban bandidos and Confederados, but contained other enemies, and unfortunately for the ragged Spaniards they were worse than just blood sucking mosquitos. Antonio had already lost one man to a poisonous snake bite and another to a Cuban Crocodile. The men now moved with considerable caution— and trepidation.

"Perez! How much further!"

"I'm not sure, senor."

"I refuse to be swallowed by this cursed swamp!"

"I'm more worried about being swallowed by cocodrilo!" said one of the soldiers impudently.

"Shut up, Julio!" shouted Antonio, "or I'll feed you to them myself!"

Suddenly a rifle barked only a few feet away. In its aftermath several soldiers shouted in terror and also discharged their weapons—expending precious ammunition in the process.

"Hold your fire! Hold your fire!" cried Antonio as he sloshed through the muddy swamp water towards where the first shot had been fired.

"I...I...thought I saw a cocodrilo!" cried one of the soldiers while pointing at a black object only a few yards away.

"It's only a rotten log you, idiota! The next man who wastes ammunition will be sorrier than a toro about to lose his cojones!"

Hour after hour they pushed on through the swamp. They encountered no more Cuban crocodiles but one more man suffered a poisonous snake bite. Towards the end of the day they finally found a patch of ground firm enough to rest on and set up a makeshift camp. Finding wood dry enough to start a fire with proved something else altogether.

"Cono!," swore Perez as he ignited the third match in a row to try and set fire to a small pile of sticks and limbs he'd managed to gather. "San Nicolas, burned easier than this!"

Antonio sighed. He was beginning to wish his conscience was something he could have removed—though he found it was becoming increasingly easy to ignore. After executing the father of the young boy that had tried to shoot him, Antonio had had his men set fire to the entire village. At the time he'd thought he might have to shoot the rest of the villagers but they accepted their fate. Some had done so with eyes filled with tears others with eyes full of hate but they'd offered no further resistance.

That will teach them to rise up against holy Spain!

Three matches later Perez finally managed to get a small fire going. They had little food to cook but they did have a decent supply of coffee. Antonio longed for something colder to drink but welcomed the boost that the caffeine gave him after such an arduous march. After downing his mug, he pulled out the worn map and examined it.

"We're a little less than half way through," he said not without gloom. Captain Perez slid his aching body along the muddy ground so that he was beside his commander and could also see the map.

"If we swing north-east we'll be able to get out of the swamps a lot swifter than if continue south east."

"We risk running into guerrilla's," said Antonio.

"Si, Major. But if we keep on like this this swamp is likely to finish us off or at least leave us so weak that we are combat in effective. In my humble opinion, senor, we're no more likely to encounter enemy forces in the north east than in the south east. It would also get us to Cienfuegos faster."

Antonio reached up and scratched the black hair of his chin beard contemplatively. Cienfuegos was the most important port on Cuba's southern coast in that region. It was supposed to have a descent garrison and would hopefully be able to resupply Antonio and his men.

"The sooner we reach it the better," pressed Perez. "The Confederados will undoubtedly want to take it. If they do before we get their then we really will be cut off from western Cuba and Santiago with virtually no hope of getting through. We'll be trapped between the enemy, the sea and these accursed swamps."

Antonio sighed again, this time resignedly. Not long ago he'd seen and looked down on officers that rejected sound ideas for no other reason than it wasn't theirs. He'd been on the bad end of that situation more than once. Now that fate had placed him in command (albeit of an ever dwindling skeleton company) he wanted to make sure he made the best decisions for his men and for his beloved Spain.

I've just got to make certain it's the right thing to do. He looked his second in command in the eye.

"I will sleep on it, Captain, and decide in the morning. For now... get some rest."

By his tone he indicated that the discussion was over. Perez nodded and seemed satisfied with Antonio's answer. Antonio wanted desperately to try and get some sleep, but first he needed to check on his men. He forced himself to his feet. His aching legs cramped in protest but he forced them to obey. The firm ground on which they had camped was little more than a pseudo-island in the middle of the swamp. The ground was kept firm more or less by a large cluster of tall trees and their roots. Antonio made the rounds with his men to check on them. Predictably moral was not good. He really couldn't blame them. They'd been driven across Cuba by Confederados, shot at by guerrillas, then forced to march through a hellish swamp where they'd been attacked by both crocodiles and snakes. And to make matters worse they were still in the midst of it. Nonetheless, the men put up gallant fronts for their commander. He'd earned their respect after a fashion. The worst thing his inspection revealed was that three of his men were severely sick with high fevers. That more than anything made up his mind that the sooner they got out of the swamps the better.

Exhausted as he was, he was only barely able to get some sleep. The ground was muddy and the mosquitos were ferocious. In the end Antonio resorted to sitting up and leaning against the trunk of one of the trees in order to get some sleep.

The next morning he woke his company at the crack of dawn. Captain Perez looked at him without saying anything. Antonio met his gaze.

"We turn north east."

They pushed back into the muddy mire. The three sick men were too weak to carry their rifles and gear, but Antonio refused to allow anything to be left behind. He ordered their weapons and gear divided up amongst the men. Even so the three feverish soldiers had a hard time keeping up. Two of them vomited up their meager breakfast within fifteen minutes of starting the march. Even though it was hot and muggy, they shivered as though cold. At noon one of them literally collapsed. He would have drowned in the swamp water had two of his comrades not taken hold of him and pulled him up. One of the Sergeants swore, half-heartedly at the man trying to make him get back on his feet. Antonio needed only a moment's glance at the infantryman to know he would not be able to make it on his own.

"Scatter out!" he ordered. "Get some branches and vines. Use whatever scraps of fabric we can scrounge up. Make a stretcher. I'm not leaving anyone to die in this cursed swamp." It took a good twenty minutes but they made the stretcher.

"Let's get going! We have no time to lose!" The men pressed on with renewed determination. After another four hours of gruelingly sloshing through the swamp, the waters began to get shallower. In the course of an hour the mire went from waste deep to knee deep to ankle deep. By the late afternoon they were on firm ground.

"Should we stop for the day, Major?"

Antonio shook his head.

"We're still deep in the jungle. I want to get to the road before we stop. We push on."

The men weren't happy, but they marched on obediently. Finally, just as the day was coming to an end they entered a clearing and found the road. Actually it was more like a jungle trail at that particular place but it was what they were looking for. The road ran from northwest to southeast. Antonio ordered two scouts to take up guard positions in one direction and two others in the other while the rest of the men again set up camp. Antonio looked forward to a much nicer sleep than the one he'd endured the night before. He'd just curled up in his blanket when one of the scouts he'd sent towards the northwest came charging into camp.

"Major Vega! Riders are coming! They're about two and a half miles from here! They'll be here in a matter of minutes!"

"How many?"

"At least twenty."

"Did you identify them?"

"No, senor. Private Sanchez is trying to do that now but we wanted to let you know as soon as possible."

Antonio wasted no time.

"Captain Perez! Assemble the men! We'll divide into two elements. You'll lead one into the jungle to the left and I'll take the other into the jungle to the left. We'll move parallel with the road. If these riders are hostile we'll ambush them with what little ammunition we have left. Hopefully there are no more than twenty. I pray the blessed virgin that we can overwhelm them with the element of surprise or at least send them running!"

Perez nodded hesitantly then added.

"Let's just hope they're not a scouting party for a larger force."

"And I thought I was the one becoming a pessimist."

Antonio Vega and his men fanned out into the jungle. Antonio gripped his own Mauser tightly, his trigger finger extended but ready at a moment's notice to send the weapon into action. They moved as quietly and stealthily as they could. Antonio led his element from the front. When he heard a horse whinny up ahead he raised his arm signaling his men to halt and stand ready.

He and a Sergeant then moved ahead together slowly and cautiously. They halted and knelt just a few feet off the road and inside the jungle. Antonio peered ahead intently. It wasn't long before he caught sight of the lead riders. They were obviously military but at that distance he had trouble determining their uniform colors. His own sky blue uniform was so muddy, stained and faded you could hardly tell what its original color had been. The same was true with the approaching cavalry. They might have been wearing sky blue they might have been wearing gray. They'd have to get closer before he could tell.

I wonder where Sanchez is at? No sooner had that thought occurred to him than he spotted the private walking alongside one of the lead riders. A few moments later Antonio caught sight of a small, and dirty but perfectly recognizable red and gold Spanish cavalry pennant.

"Hold your fire!" cried out Antonio for both the benefit of both the riders and his own men. The men of his company then slowly but surely began to make their way out of jungle and onto the road way. Antonio approached the rider beside whom Sanchez walked. It turned out to be a Lieutenant Colonel. Antonio snapped to attention and brought his arm up to salute. The cavalry colonel grimly returned it. After brief introductions Antonio said: "We are ever glad to meet you, Colonel."

"And we you. You and your men look as though you've been through quite a lot."

Antonio nodded.

"We were in Havana when the Confederados attacked. I myself was on the La Cabana. We held as long as we could and we just barely escaped with our lives."

The cavalry colonel, Felipe Dominguez, nodded.

"In that case you are one of the only units stationed in Havana to have made it this far. Most of the others are trapped on the far western tip of the island. They are cut off by the enemy, under siege and with little hope of escape. We ourselves were stationed at Varadero, east of Havana. We have engaged the Confederados three times, once just West of Matanzas and twice between here and Jovellanos. We've lost two-thirds of our force and we have barely slowed the enemy's advance. To make matters worse we've been under attack by guerillas almost constantly."

Antonio nodded in sympathy.

"I take it Senor, that you like us are headed for Cienfuegos?"

"Si," said Dominguez.

"We have just prepared camp. We would be most grateful if you would join us. We have just crossed the Zapata swamps. We are exhausted and low on ammunition. In the morning we can go to Cienfuegos together."

"Si, we would be honored. We'd best move at first light, though. The Confederados and the Cubanos are undoubtedly on our tails."

Once again Antonio nodded, all too knowingly. As he began to lead Dominguez and his cavalry back towards their camp he clasped his crucifix and sent a prayer heavenward.

Holy Mary thank you for watching over us and bringing us these friends. Keep us safe tonight! Get us to Cienfuegos where we may carry on the fight against both the traitors and invaders! Forgive me of my sins and please keep me and my men alive. In the name of the Father, Son and Holy Spirit, amen!

XVIII

"What flag is she flying Mr. Brisk?"

"I'm not sure, sir, but it's definitely not Spanish."

Captain Blake Ramsey raised his own binoculars to his eyes.

"Portuguese."

Ray Brisk let out a sigh.

"I always envisioned commerce raiding as being a little more exciting than this. I'm starting to wonder if Spain has any merchant marine vessels to sink."

"They're out there," said Ramsey. We just have to be patient."

"I still think we should have gone into the Mediterranean. Most of their trade happens in there or through the Suez with their Pacific holdings."

"That would exceed our orders. Besides, after our last encounter with the British I have no desire to pass through the strait of Gibraltar. The Royal Navy would instantly know we had entered the Mediterranean and I have a sneaking suspicion that that information would conveniently find its way to the Spanish Admiralty. Most of Spain's ships may be dilapidated, but one Confederate battleship versus their entire Mediterranean fleet are not odds I'd care to take."

"I'm sure that France's own fleet is keeping them bottled up at Barcelona."

Ramsey nodded, conceding the point.

"After the way the French fleet bombarded Villa Cisneros I have no doubt of their abilities." The Texas had made a token bombardment herself just as soon as the British had withdrawn their people. They'd smashed the docks, wrecked most of the fishing boats, and pounded the fort with several shells. All of which was nothing when compared with what the French had done when they'd arrived. Three large French battleships, and nine cruisers had shelled the city for nearly thirteen hours straight until the Spanish had raised the white flag of surrender over the old fort that guarded the city. The French Tricolor had been flying over Villa Cisneros when the CSS Texas had departed. For all intents and purposes the Spanish Sahara had become the French Sahara. Despite the impressiveness of the French fleet, Ramsey still had no intention of taking his ship through the strait of Gibraltar.

"I'd still rather not risk being trapped in the Mediterranean. Especially with tensions as high with Britain as they are."

"I wish we had some more news," said Brisk. "As it is, if the Brits do decide to jump in the first we may learn of it is when one of their ships open fire on us."

"On that point, we are agreed."

A cold north wind came rushing suddenly in and Brisk shuddered.

"It's too cold for this Georgia boy."

Ramsey nodded. He was from Alabama, which like Georgia was far warmer than the middle of the North Atlantic where they were patrolling.

"Give me the Caribbean any day," said Ramsey. "Or even the anti-slavery patrol off the African coast."

Even Brisk couldn't argue with that. No matter how much he despised the Confederate States' participation in the patrol, he disapproved of the cold more.

"Explain to me again, why we're searching for Spanish ships this far north."

"It's fairly simple. Just about every nation on earth does business with the Yankees. With that in mind I drew a straight line from Cadiz to New York. We're cruising up and down that line."

Brisk nodded. It made good sense. Trying to forget the cold he pulled out a cigar and lit it. He took a good long drag and exhaled a cloud of smoke.

"Looks like our Portuguese friends are picking up steam. Look at all that smoke coming out of her stack. They must really be laying on the coal."

"Yes..." replied Ramsey, his voice tinged with sudden suspicion. "She's not only increasing speed she's turning away from us." He raised his binoculars back to his eyes and took a second look at the freighter. She was definitely flying the blue and white flag of the Kingdom of Portugal.

"Why would they run away from us? The Confederacy's never had any bad relations with Portugal that I know of. In fact from what I know they don't really like the Spanish all that much themselves."

"My thoughts exactly. But they're running so fast you'd think we were flying the Jolly Roger." Ramsey zoomed in on the freighter with his binoculars as close as possible. The vessel had completely turned her stern to the Texas and was moving away rapidly. Ramsey's gaze shifted from the Portuguese flag flying at the aft end of the ship, down to where the port of registry was written across the stern in fine gold letters.

El Puerto de Santa Maria

"I've got another good question for you Ray. Why would a Portuguese ship have one of Spain's largest seaports as its port of registry?"

"Maybe the Portuguese bought it from the Spanish and haven't bothered to change the lettering"

"Or maybe they're really a Spanish ship and their flying false colors."

Brisk blasphemed himself.

"If that's the case Captain, I sure don't see how we can prove it or what we can do about it."

"We can board her and find out the truth," said Ramsey.

"If we go after them and we're wrong there will be hell to pay. Are you sure you want to risk it?"

Ramsey smiled maliciously.

"Do you remember last night's poker game?"

Brisk swore again. The night before the chief engineer had gone all in. Brisk had folded. The Captain had called—and won.

Ramsey started issuing orders.

"Hard over, follow that ship. Mr. Brisk, inform the engine room we'll be needing all the speed they can give us—then order the marines to assemble on deck. I want a heavily armed boarding part ready to head over to that freighter."

"Aye aye, sir," they chorused.

Ramsey turned to his Yeoman.

"Jeb, spread the word to all compartments. See if there's anyone on board that speaks Portuguese and or Spanish. If so have them report to me."

"Aye, sir!" said Yeoman Ferguson and then left the bridge to carry out his orders.

The Texas came hard about. Smoke belched from her stack and the whole ship vibrated as her massive steam engines picked up speed. Ramsey had signal flags run up ordering the freighter to heave to and prepare to be boarded.

"She's not slowing down, sir, and we're not exactly matching her speed."

"I can see that. Sound general quarters. Put a warning shot across her stern."

"Are you sure, Captain? Boarding a neutral vessel is one thing. Firing on one is…"

Brisk's protest was cut short by Ramsey's stern glare.

"Aye, sir."

A moment later klaxons were sounding through the ship. At the bow, the Confederate battle flag was raised into position. Two minutes later, the Texas' forward twelve inch gun boomed. The shell screeched through the air and crashed into the sea about one-hundred yards away from the fleeing freighter. Ramsey watched the impact through his binoculars.

"Tell the gunners to fire again. Tell them this time to make sure they get the shell closer. We're trying scare them, not make them think we can't hit the broad side of a barn."

A minute later the main gun fired again. This time the shell exploded into the water a mere ten yards from the fleeing ship. The explosion sent a spray of water onto the deck of the escaping ship.

"That's more like it," said Ramsey.

"It's fine gunnery to be sure, sir. But they're still not slowing down, in fact they're pulling away from us."

The Texas was covered in armored plating. She was built for battle. Not pursuit.

"Then we'll try to disable her. Order the gunners to hit her in the heels."

A minute later the main gun fired again. The shell landed just aft of the ship, no more than five yards behind the stern. A few moments later the Texas' twelve inch gun fired yet again. This time the shell exploded into the rear of the fleeing freighter. The top of her aft deck was literally blown away in a massive explosion that sent flames and debris in all directions.

"She's not flying a neutral flag now," said Ramsey nonchalantly.

Brisk nodded solemnly. The freighter's forward momentum slowed considerably. A billowing plume of black smoke rose from her devastated stern. A moment later a white flag was run up her signal line.

"Mr. Brisk you'll lead the boarding party. Order them to surrender their manifest and their registration papers."

"What if nobody speaks English over there?" asked Brisk.

As if on cue Yeoman Ferguson entered the bridge with the Engineer's Mate.

"Captain, Mr. MacArthur here speaks both Spanish and Portuguese."

"Only a little Portuguese, sir," interjected MacArthur. "My daddy did railroad work down in Mexico and Brazil. I spent time in both places when I was a youngin."

"Just do your best, Mr. MacArthur."

"What if they give us trouble Captain?" asked Brisk.

"We just hit them with a twelve inch shell and you've got twenty armed marines going over with you. I don't think they're in a position to give you much trouble."

A short while later Brisk and MacArthur sat at the front of a longboat filled with an entire detachment of heavily

armed, gray uniformed marines that worked the oars in
perfect unison. As they neared the disabled freighter, Brisk
surveyed the damage. Her aft deck was completely wrecked
as was her rudder, but she didn't appear to be taking on any
water. A steady stream of smoke was still coming from the
gaping wound but the crew looked to have contained the fire.
Upon closer inspection Brisk noted that the ship was
absolutely filthy, and it wasn't just because he was judging it
by navy standards. He'd seen some sloppy freighters in his
day but the vessel they were about to board looked like it
hadn't been cleaned in a decade. A few sailors stared
menacingly and hatefully down at them. They looked no
cleaner than the wretched excuse for a ship that they manned.

 The marines brought the longboat up to the edge of
the freighter where a decrepit looking pilot ladder hung.
Brisk eyed it warily.

 "Better let us go first, sir," said the Gunnery Sergeant
in command of the Marine detachment. Brisk nodded.

 "Bull! Elkins! Head up that ladder."

 Two large, burly marines rose from their places, slung
their rifles over their shoulders and headed up the ladder. A
few moments later the rest started up. Finally, Brisk and
MacArthur made the climb. The marines had all fanned out
with their rifles at the ready. Brisk surveyed the small knot of
sailors that stood on the deck staring at him. He ordered half
the marines to start searching the ship and then he turned to
MacArthur.

 "Ask who the Captain is."

 "Quien es el Capitan?" asked MacArthur in Spanish.
No one stepped forward. MacArthur asked again—this time
in Portuguese.

 "Quem e o Capitao?"

 A large menacing man stepped forward. His dark
tanned complexion said that he'd spent a lot of time in more
tropical latitudes. The freighter Captain looked absolutely
enraged. He looked at Brisk as if he wanted to murder him.

 "Did he respond to the Spanish or the Portuguese?"
asked Brisk.

 "Portuguese," said MacArthur nervously.

 Brisk felt his heart leap into his throat. He uttered a
blasphemy. A sense of total dread came upon him. *Blake,*

you've messed up this time. We've fired upon a neutral vessel!

"Como sabia?" asked the freighter Captain in angry menacing tones.

"What did he say?"

MacArthur looked confused.

"He wants to know... how we knew."

"How we knew what? If they're Portuguese we were wrong and they had nothing to hide."

Suddenly, a breathless marine came running up.

"Commander! Sir, you'd better come see this!" Leaving the freighter captain and his men in the charge of half the boarding party, Brisk followed the other marine into the ship. Brisk instantly wanted to vomit. The inside of the ship stank of body odor and worse. When they entered the main cargo hold he discovered why. All in one instant Brisk was flooded with surprise, and a strange sense of relief. It all came together. The hold was packed with over one-hundred bound negroes. They were packed so tightly that there was barely room to walk. The floor was soaked in vomit, urine, and feces. Brisk swore profanely. He'd never seen anything so horrid, and despite a lifetime of looking down on and disdaining negroes, even he felt sorry for the pitiful wretches chained up in that living hell.

"This is why they were running," said Brisk. "They were smuggling niggers."

"It makes sense," said MacArthur. "When I was in Brazil with my daddy—their niggers were still slaves back then—they had a big problem with Portuguese slave smugglers bringing more of them in. When Brazil freed their slaves in the early eighties, those slave traders had to find another place to take them."

"And we're the only buyer left." Brisk tried to remind himself that the CSA's constitution forbad the importation of slaves from outside the Confederate States and it always had. Somehow, looking at the misery laying before his eyes, it did little to console him.

"Signal Captain Ramsey. We've got a big mess on our hands."

XIX

"Never in my worst nightmares did I ever even imagine such inhumanity," said Winston Churchill.

Cole Allens nodded while holding a handkerchief over his nose and mouth in a vain effort to keep out the sickening stench. He'd seen many horrors as a correspondent during the Second War of Rebellion. At the end of that bloody conflict he'd seen the results of cold hearted vengeance as Kentucky's secessionist leaders had been hung to a man. He'd also seen the results of the hatred man was capable of showing to his fellow man. The memory of a field of dead negro troops slaughtered by Nathan Bedford Forrest still haunted his dreams occasionally. All of it paled to the horror he saw before him now.

A vast field of human skeletons and rotting human bodies littered the ground over an area of several acres. The remains varied in size from adults down to what had obviously been children.

"They weren't even given the dignity of a common grave," said Cole. "How many do you suppose there are?"

"There has to be thousands," said Reginald Barnes. The young British officer pulled a cigar from his khaki uniform tunic and proceeded to ignite it. Cole followed his lead but soon found that not even the rich strong flavor of Cuban tobacco could block out the stench of so much death.

A few yards away a gray uniformed Confederate Captain that was serving as their guide stood holding their horses.

"There's a whole other field just like this one on the other side of the prison camp, if you'd care to see it."

Cole took a last look at the hellish scene before him and then turned to the Confederate officer.

"I've seen enough." He knew what he'd seen that day would be burned everlastingly into his memory and give him fresh nightmares to go along with the old ones.

Churchill gazed coldly at the field. Whatever feelings he had, he kept them hidden beneath his calm but cold demeanor. When Cole had first met the young British officer, he'd seen him as little more than a boy. He was beginning to see that there was much more to the young man than the youthful exterior.

"Take us back to the camp," said Churchill. "I want to talk to some of those people myself."

They returned to their horses and then the whole party headed towards one of the encampments that the Spanish had used to keep huge swaths of the Cuban population locked up. Lieutenant Barnes rode in front alongside their Confederate guide, while Cole and Churchill took up the rear. When he saw that Barnes was keeping the grey clad officer busy with conversation, Cole quietly addressed Churchill who was riding beside him.

"There's been reports coming out of Cuba for years about brutality and massacres. To be honest most people in the United States thought it had been blown way out of proportion by the Confederates to try and generate support for their own annexation of the island."

"That was the general view in Britain as well," said Churchill. "I'd read some of the reports myself but I had thought them far too terrible to be true."

"Now that we know these atrocities are going on, it may change the way our two countries look at this war," said Cole.

"I wouldn't be so sure," said Churchill.

"Why?" asked Cole. "Mr. Nelson made it perfectly clear that the Confederate States have no intention of returning slavery to the island."

"We have yet to see the details of that particular plan," replied Churchill. "Even if the Confederates somehow manage to annex the island without simultaneously bringing about the return of slavery, I still fear that London will be diametrically opposed to it."

"Why?"

Churchill sighed.

"Because the Confederate States are allied with France, and any expansion of Confederate influence is viewed as an expansion of French influence. I don't think the people in America realize just how great the gulf has become between London and Paris. Napoleon IV has challenged us in every arena of international affairs: political, military and economic. Ours is a Parliamentary system whilst theirs is a military dictatorship masquerading as a republic. Our two navies are engaged in the greatest arms race the world has ever seen. Our race to expand our colonial holdings is leading to great amounts of friction in several geopolitical hotspots around the world. And now, thanks to this spat between the CSA and Spain, France has taken advantage of the opportunity to spread its territory further."

Cole had noticed a change in the young Englishman's demeanor ever since news of France's entry into the war had reached Cuba.

"What are you trying to say, Lieutenant?" asked Cole. "That you think war between Britain and France is inevitable?"

"Many in my country believe exactly that. In the game of Empire, there is only room for one King of the mountain. There are those that believe the time has come to put the French in their place."

"If Britain and France went to war they would very likely drag most of the civilized world into the flames with them. Surely your two countries can live in peace?"

"Like your own and the Confederacy?"

"It's true that the United States fought two brutal wars with the Confederacy, but we've managed to keep the peace for the past twenty-five years."

Churchill nodded.

"And all you've had to do to keep that peace is let the CSA get away with whatever it wants."

"All we've had to do is mind our own business," said Cole, somewhat more harshly than he'd intended. Ever since the bloody war of 1869 he, like many of his generation, had been a staunch neutralist. He liked to think that the policy he'd so long supported had helped keep the peace. He eyed the young British officer. "Don't mistake scrupulous neutrality for timidity."

"Mr. Allens, I meant no insult but let us be honest. Your country was a growing juggernaut up until the 1860s. But ever since the two wars of secession your growth has stagnated. Your influence on the world stage has waned. The Confederacy has eclipsed you, not because it is larger and stronger than you, but because they are more ambitious, audacious, and active than you. They've hazarded war to reach their goals, made powerful alliances, and I must admit made cunning use of diplomacy to manipulate political circumstances as much as possible in their favor. You say that you believe in scrupulous neutrality. Do you think the Confederates take the same view with regard to the United States? The CSA maintains numerous forces and fortifications all along, your mutual border."

"As do we," interjected Cole. Churchill nodded in concession but then continued.

"But the Confederacy also has allies. France and Austria-Hungary have large numbers of troops in Mexico to supplement Maximillian's own forces. All those armies are ready to head north at a moment's notice. If war erupts between the United States and Confederate States the US will face the forces of not one but four nations. It seems to me that the CSA takes the idea of war against the United States as a very real possibility. You boast of neutrality and minding your own business, but in reality I think your country is simply afraid of having to fight another war. This is a tough world we live in. The countries that will be the most successful and powerful will be those that are willing to fight for their supremacy."

"Survival of the fittest then?" asked Cole.

Churchill nodded.

"England cannot allow herself to be outdone by France, nor should the United States allow herself to be outdone by the Confederacy."

Cole looked Churchill in the eye.

"My young friend when you've seen the horrors of war for yourself as I have, I believe that you will rethink its necessity for reasons as trivial as a nation's pride or economic prosperity. In any event, after what we've seen here today, I can't imagine your government or mine publically coming to the defense of Spain. Slavery pales in comparison with the crimes against humanity that the Spanish have committed against the Cuban people. As war correspondents our job is to report the truth. I intend to let my own countrymen know the full measure of Spain's atrocities, no matter how politically inconvenient it may be.

No matter how fierce the rivalry is between the United States and the Confederacy, I would not have my beloved nation allied with a country that can so ruthlessly and cruelly starve men, women and children to death—not even for the sake of scoring political points against our fiercest rival. I hope Lieutenant, that you'll not let your own feelings of animosity towards France, prevent you from fulfilling your duty to report the truth to your people."

"I assure you, Mr. Allens. I intend to do my duty, and report all that I have seen here. But please do not forget that neither my country nor yours is completely innocent when it comes to mistreating other peoples for the benefit of our own. I can hardly see how the United States' treatment of the Native Americans in your push from sea to shining sea is any different than how Spain has treated its own subjects here in Cuba."

In his mind Cole acknowledged the hit, distasteful as it was, that Churchill had made.

But j*ust because we've done wrong in the past, doesn't mean we have to keep doing wrong. The mistakes of the past do not excuse us from doing the right thing in the present.*

In any event, Cole did not care to be lectured on the proprieties of the strong exploiting the weak by a man whose own Empire had its own dark side. To his credit, however, Churchill went on.

"Our own treatment of the native inhabitants of India has been rather less than benevolent at times, but India is a vital source of resources for us. We can no more give it up than you could give up the vast swaths of western territory that makes up so much of your country. In fact we can afford to do so even less than you for we are an island nation."

"So once again it comes down to survival of the fittest?" asked Cole.

Once again Churchill nodded.

"Our mutual rivals form a massive power block. The alliance of the Confederate States and Mexico on this side of the Atlantic, with the French and Austro-Hungarian Empires on the other is a powerful combination. Individually any nation would be hard pressed to fight them as Spain is finding out. To guarantee our security Britain and the USA need to form our own alliance and in doing so we can't be too scrupulous in our choice of allies. We're going to need countries like Spain, Prussia, and perhaps even ruthless Russia if we are going to counter the alliance of hostile nations facing us."

From what Cole knew of Russia and its Czar, it was one of the most brutal nations on the face of the Earth. Russia kept serfs, much as the Confederacy kept slaves, and ruled over many other conquered peoples such as the Finns, Latvians, Lithuanians, and Poles with an iron fist.

He would really have us ally with such nations? To Cole the saddest part was that many in the United States thought the same way. In any event Cole doubted if the British could ever conclude a treaty of alliance with Russia. Spain and Prussia would easily join such an alliance but Russia was a different story. There had been bad blood in the past between the Bonapartes and the Czars to be sure, but the Crimean War had been fought four decades earlier and the British had had as much involvement as the French. Cole also knew that at that very moment there was a hot territorial dispute in the far north between British Canada and Russian Alayska.

Will the British cede territory in North America to secure an alliance in Europe? To Cole it was ludicrous to try to weaken a tyrant like Napoleon IV, by strengthening a worse tyrant like the Czar.

They soon caught site of the concentration camp. It was a roughly built prison. A fifteen foot high wall made of logs and topped by barbed wire surrounding an area of half a square mile. Inside, was nearly one-thousand people, Cuban men, women, and children that had been kept prisoner and literally starved for months on end. Most of the people were still too weak to leave. Those few men that had still had health and strength, had been given guns and allowed to join in the fight against the Spanish. When they had first arrived at the camp, Cole had thought the smell inside to be intolerable. Now that he had had a whiff of the field where the Spanish had been throwing the bodies, it didn't seem quite as bad.

The front gates were open. As Cole and the others entered on horseback, it became clear that the enclosure at one point had held three to four times as many people as it presently did. A high death rate followed by liberation at the hands of the Confederate Army had cleared out much of the camp. Filthy and emaciated people stared at them as they rode into the enclosure. Cole's eyes became locked with those of a small Cuban girl. The child was so thin that her bones showed through her olive complexioned skin. Though a believer, Cole had never been overly religious. But staring at the skeletal girl standing before him, Cole thought of the judgment that surely awaited the evil men that had committed such wickedness.

Cole and the other war correspondents interviewed many of the prisoners. For the most part they all had similar stories. They had been peaceful villagers. They had worked on coffee, sugar, and tobacco plantations. Then one day Spanish troops had shown up with guns, accused them of supporting guerillas, taken them from their homes, and then force-marched them for many miles over several days and locked them in the concentration camp to rot. Cole had no doubt that some of the villagers had indeed supported the Cuban rebels, but to him that was no excuse for the Spanish brutality to which there seemed no end. Though misplaced shame kept most of the women and girls silent, many of the Cuban men in the camp claimed that their wives, sisters, and daughters had been repeatedly raped both when the villages had been raided and then later by the guards at the camp. For themselves, the Cuban men claimed that most of them had been severely interrogated. Their bodies showed signs of torture—their flesh marred by scars from whips, burns from hot irons—and worse.

If Cole wasn't seeing it with his own eyes, he would not have believed it. He hoped his readers in the United States would believe him, and more than that, that they would once again recognize the horrors of war, and have no part in entangling alliances, with Spain, Britain…or anyone else.

XX

Riding across the Nevada desert at the head of a cavalry squadron, Nathan Audrey at last felt as if he were back in his element. The land behind him and over which he and his men had ridden was mostly a flat sandy plain. The only decoration had been the occasional boulder, cactus, or sun bleached animal skeleton. Just ahead and to the east, however, a labyrinth of large rocky hills loomed.

"That's ambush territory if ever there was such a thing," said Audrey.

"You think there are red skins in there, Colonel?" asked Lieutenant Philip Jergins, a young brevet officer that General Goldwyn had assigned to him as an aide.

For the briefest moment Audrey was taken back to his younger days when he had helped butcher Indians under the command of George Armstrong Custer. Considering the Lieutenant's age, Audrey reflected that his young aid had probably been eating sweets and playing cowboys and Indians the last time a major Indian attack had taken place anywhere on the continent. The USA, CSA, California, and Deseret had all three long since pacified their respective Indian tribes.

Of course each nation would have no compunctions against using its own Indians as weapons against its rival nations. Audrey turned to Jergins.

"If there are Indians in there, Lieutenant you can be certain they are working with the Mormons. The blasted fanatics have long utilized the Mericats as their pawns, but whether the red man waits for us in those hills or not is of no matter. The Mormons are just as capable of setting up an ambush as any band of Indians still living."

"So what are we supposed to do?"

Audrey spat a brown stream of tobacco juice onto the desert floor then pulled out his map. He then turned on his horse to regard the hills and ponder their rocky dilemma. He swore when he saw that there was very little detail on the map as to the proper path through the maze of rocks that lay before them.

"If we go in there in force we'll be sitting ducks," said Audrey. "I suppose I could send some scouts ahead."

"Alone into that big tangle of rocks? They wouldn't stand a chance!"

"Are you volunteering to lead the scout party, Lieutenant?"

Jergins gulped nervously.

"Relax son, I'm not in the mood to order anyone to their deaths today. You're right. If the Mormons are there in any strength they'd nab our scouts before they ever got the chance to report back."

"So what are we going to do?"

"We're not here to fight the Mormons over rocks. There's a town just a few miles south of here. Send a rider back to General Goldwyn. Warn him of possible ambush in the hills east of here and advise him that we are moving south towards…" Audrey glanced down at the map. "…Towards the town of Rattlesnake Cove."

"Sounds like a lovely place, sir."

"Get moving Lieutenant."

"Yes, sir." Jergins gave Audrey a half way descent salute and then rode off to carry out his orders.

Audrey shook his head. Not for the first time, he lamented the lack of formal training in the army of the Republic of California.

A mob, that's what we are. A half trained mob of civilians dressed up playing soldiers. There had been a time in his life when he never thought he'd long for the brutal discipline he'd endured at West Point or during his days as a member of the French Foreign Legion. Now that he was a Colonel, he did.

And if the Republic lets me stay in the army after this little war, I fully intend to bring some order to it.

After dispatching riders back to the main army, Audrey's cavalry squadron turned south and rode for seven miles when they spotted smoke rising from behind a small hill. Audrey raised his arm signaling his men to reign in.

"What's wrong, Colonel?"

"The town is just over that rise. For there to be that much smoke there's got to be something big on fire."

"You think there's trouble?"

"I don't hear any gunfire," said Audrey. "But there's definitely something wrong." He then drew his pistol and hollered to his men. "Listen up! We're charging over that hill. I'm not sure what we'll find but be prepared for anything. If the Mormons are there we go in shooting. Stick close to me and watch for my signal. If there's too many of them then we'll make this a hit and run, if not we'll take them! Now move!" Audrey set spurs to his horse. The animal reared and then took off like a thunderbolt. His men were little more than a few seconds behind him. If you couldn't follow a Colonel that led from the front, you couldn't follow anyone.

Audrey's heart raced with anticipation as his horse galloped forward. The cavalry squadron left a trail of dust behind them as they charged up the hill. They crested the top without so much as slowing, and an instant later they were moving downhill towards the smoldering remains of the town of Rattlesnake Cove. Most of the houses and buildings had burned down to cinders. Only one building still remained fully ablaze. It was by far the largest and stood at the west end of the town. From the tall charred black steeple that still stood atop the structure, Audrey could tell that it was the church. He didn't see any signs of life—hostile or otherwise. The squadron had just reached the bottom of the hill when they spotted the first body—a man lying face down in the dust. Audrey brought his horse to a halt and leapt down from his saddle. His men also reined in with their weapons at the ready. There was no sign the attackers were still present but they were taking no chances.

Audrey rolled the body over. He was indeed dead. There was a large bullet wound in his chest.

"Look, Colonel! Another and another!"

Audrey rose to his full height and looked around. Several more bodies littered the ground around the fire ruined buildings. While the green clad cavalry troopers checked for survivors, Audrey looked around with a mixture of rage and confusion.

"This can't have happened long ago!"

"Colonel!" cried Lieutenant Jergins. The boy's voice sounded terrified. Audrey turned to see that he was standing not far from the burning church.

"What is it, Lieutenant?"

The young officer simply pointed towards the smoldering house of worship. Audrey turned his own gaze on the church. His eyes grew wide with horror when he realized what his aide was pointing at.

"Great God in heaven…" Audrey crossed himself. The blackened remains of over a dozen bodies were clearly visible in the midst of the fiery blaze.

"How could anyone do such a thing?" asked Jergins.

Once again, Audrey's mind went back in time thirty years, when he had witnessed the wanton slaughter of Indians by George Custer and his men. Letting out a sigh he answered the Lieutenant's question.

"There are no limits to the brutality that man is able to show to man." Crossing himself again, Audrey reached up and felt the silver crucifix that he wore around his neck and under his shoulder. *Throw religious fanaticism into the mix and it's like putting kerosene on a fire. What part of Peace on earth, goodwill toward men, don't people understand?*

"Colonel! We found someone who's alive!"

Audrey ran to where his men had found the survivor. When he saw him, he quickly realized that the man would not be alive for long. He'd taken two bullets in the chest and blood was coming out of his mouth. Nonetheless, he just barely managed to speak.

"The women…they took the women… My daughter… please you must…" The man got no farther. He gasped loudly, and then closed his eyes in death.

"Fan out!" ordered Audrey. "Check the eastern perimeter. Find out which way these bastards went!" He then rounded on his aid. "Dispatch another rider to General Goldwyn. Inform him that the town of Rattlesnake Cove has been torched, its men murdered, its women taken captive. We are pursuing the brigands responsible!"

A moment later Audrey's suspicions were proved correct.

"Colonel! We've found horse and wagon tracks headed east!"

Audrey was already climbing back onto his saddle. A moment later he again set spurs to his horse and set off in pursuit of his quarry. They rode hard for nearly an hour before they had to slow down for the sake of the horses. As determined as he was to catch up with his enemies, and as angry as he was at what they had done, he was still clear headed enough to know that they would never achieve their goal if they ran their horses to death. Once they had slowed down, Audrey looked at the sky. The sun had begun to sink low in the horizon behind them. Ahead of them, darkness was fast approaching. Lieutenant Jergins urged his mount back up to a trot just long enough to ride beside his commander.

"Will we stop for the night?"

"Not as long as we're able to follow the tracks. There's not a cloud in the sky. Hopefully the moon will be bright enough tonight to light our way." Audrey pointed at the tracks. "They are travelling with wagons and presumably a large number of women. They can't be going that fast. With any luck, we'll catch up to them before dawn."

"What if they outnumber us?"

Audrey's grip tightened around the grip of the pistol he wore on his belt.

"The element of surprise is very often enough to make up for being outnumbered. But you listen to me Lieutenant. The men killed back there were Californian citizens—our countrymen. The women that have been taken captive are Californian women. I will not yield them unchallenged and by heaven itself we will bring these fanatics to justice or die trying."

"So you think it was the Mormons and not the redskins?"

"Lieutenant, regardless of the tales you might have been told as a boy, most Indians are not the ruthless savages they've been made out to be. The most ruthless men I've ever known were white men, not red men. Take my word, this is the work of religious zealots. Those Mormon fanatics butchered the men of that town and have taken their women with the intention of forcing them to become polygamous wives in their blasphemous false-religion."

They pressed on for another hour. Twilight gave way to night as the sun sank down below the western horizon. In its place, a nearly full moon rose into the sky casting its light over the desert plain, along with that of countless stars. A short while later they heard the baying of a coyote. Audrey brought his men to a halt. He dismounted so that he could get a better look at the tracks and not lose sight of them in the dark. Just a few minutes later, they caught sight of several campfires in the distance. Audrey signaled for his men to stop and be silent. He then slowly and cautiously made his way closer until he was within a hundred yards of the encampment. Inside the encampment, he was able to make out several men. Many of them were carrying rifles but none seemed to actually be on sentry duty. Beside the camp were five covered wagons and a large group of horses. From long practice at observing large groups of horses, Audrey deduced that they were dealing with about thirty Mormons.

Which means they outnumber us by less than ten men. He was confident that a sneak attack would more than compensate for the difference in numbers. *As long as we don't tip our hand.* Ever so carefully Audrey began to make his way back towards his men. He was nearly half way there, when a particular sound froze him in his tracks. It was a sound that could strike terror into even the bravest of men. It was the sound of a rattle. With his heart pounding in his chest, Audrey looked around warily. Sure enough a large rattlesnake was just over a yard away from him—well within striking distance. Its tail rattled in agitation and warning. Only then did Audrey remember that the only town in the region had been called Rattlesnake Cove.

And now I know the reason. His eyes were locked with those of the serpent. He could tell that the snake was trying to decide whether or not to strike. *No sudden movements...* Ever so carefully, he started to reach for his pistol but then stopped. Even if he managed to pull it and shoot the rattler without getting snake bit, the gunshot would instantly alert the Mormons to the presence of Audrey and his men.

Taking a deep breath, he took a judicious step back. The rattler didn't strike. Thus emboldened, Audrey took another breath and another step. He backed a good ten feet away before circling around and back to his waiting men.

"What are your orders, Colonel?" asked Lieutenant Jergins.

Audrey wiped cold sweat from his brow with his green uniform sleeve. His perspiration stood in stark contrast to the cold desert night air.

"We attack." He turned to one of his few veteran sergeants. "Take half the men around to the right. I'll take the rest to the left. Wait until you hear gunfire to launch your assault. The enemy's full attention should be focused entirely in our direction so they should be completely unprepared when you hit them from behind."

"Understood, sir."

Audrey turned to Jergins.

"Lieutenant, you're with me." Audrey liked the boy and had no doubt that one day he would make a fine soldier, but gold bar or no he was not ready to command an attack.

Audrey led his part of the force around to the north side of the enemy encampment. Once in position they remounted their horses and readied their weapons. With a quick silent motion of the hand, Audrey ordered his men to advance. Using the pressure of his legs and a flick of the reins he urged his own mount forward. They started at a trot but moved quickly to a canter. When they had closed half the distance they sped their horses up to a full gallop as they charged directly at the unsuspecting encampment. Rifle and pistol shots barked in the night as Audrey's men opened fire at the unsuspecting Mormons. Several of the Deseretans fell dead or else clutching bloody wounds while shouting cries of pain. A few of the Mormons returned fire, but they had been so taken by surprise that none of Audrey's men fell from the saddle.

The Californians surged into the encampment. Audrey leveled his pistol at a bearded Mormon and pulled the trigger. The revolver fired, and the man's head exploded—blood and gray brain matter flying in all directions. Audrey brought his horse about and shot another in the chest. He was about to take aim at yet another target, when suddenly a large burly man literally crashed into the side of his horse, took tight hold of him with enormous fists, pulled him from the saddle and slammed him down to the ground with tremendous force. Audrey hit the rocky desert floor hard. For decades he had lived a hard life. As a soldier, mercenary, bounty hunter, and lawman he'd been forced to fight countless times for his life, but at sixty years old, he just wasn't as good at it as he had once been. As he hit the ground, the wind was knocked out of him and pain shot throughout his body. Worst of all he lost his grip on his pistol. The large Mormon loomed above him, ready to leap upon him and finish what he'd started. But like an old gray wildcat that still had his claws and a few teeth, Audrey planned to show his attacker that there was more to him than met the eye.

His large muscular attacker fell upon him. His strong hands wrapped around Audrey's throat like chains of iron, fully intent on choking the life out of him. Audrey's vision began to grow blurry as he neared unconsciousness. With the last of his strength he pulled his knife from his belt and stabbed it into his attacker's side. The man screamed in surprise and pain. Wasting no time, Audrey ripped out the knife and stabbed him again and again. The Mormon released his death grip and rolled off of Audrey, trying to escape from his vicious blade. The man struggled to his feet. Blood was pouring from his mangled side. Audrey had also forced himself to his feet. Both men let out war cries that would have done justice to Apache Indians and charged one another. Audrey brought down his knife for a deathblow but the wounded and enraged Mormon managed to catch him by the wrist. For a moment the two men were locked in a dance of death. Audrey then brought his knee up in a savage blow to the man's groin. The man's eyes bulged, his knees buckled, and his grip on Audrey's arms loosened. As we went down, Audrey broke free of his grip, raised the knife high and then plunged it furiously into the side of the man's neck. A half second later Audrey ripped the knife back out. A fountain of blood erupted out of the Mormon's neck. A moment later he was lying face down in the dust.

Exhausted, Audrey took a moment to look around. The other half of his force had hit the opposite side of the camp and the last Mormon resistance seemed to be collapsing. A minute later, it was all over. Ten bearded men stood with their hands up. The rest of the Mormon force lay in the blood stained dust. By his count, Audrey's force had suffered only three dead and six wounded.

"What should we do with the prisoners, Colonel? Can we shoot them? They deserve it after what they did to that town!"

Audrey shook his head.

"No. At least not right now. They may have useful information. Tie them up, we'll take them back to General Goldwyn."

While the prisoners were being secured, Audrey made his way over to the covered wagons. As he lifted the back flap over a dozen feminine screams erupted from inside.

"It's alright! It's alright!" he said trying to calm them. "We're here to help you." A small kerosene lamp was lit within the wagon. By its light, Audrey was able to make out thirteen terrified women from as young as thirteen to as old as forty. Many of them were crying. Most of the others seemed to be in shock. The oldest of the women looked at Audrey and spoke.

"Thank you, sir. May God bless you for coming to our aid."

XXI

Major Antonio Vega found the fortress of Castillo de Jagua more comfortable than even the La Cabana had been. The Spanish fort that guarded the entrance to the Bay of Cienfuegos just south of the city resembled two large stone blocks—a smaller bastion set atop a larger base. Above that a large tower, from which flew the La Rojigualda, knifed its way into the air. Vega and his men had never been happier to reach a place. They had been fully resupplied and equipped and had been happy to join up with the city's large garrison. As Antonio inspected his newly oiled and cleaned rifle and secured a fully loaded ammo box to his belt he finally felt as if the war might actually be winnable.

At least we aren't running for our lives through the swamps!

Antonio made his way from the bowels of the fortress to the upper ramparts. He enjoyed the clean feel of his new sky-blue uniform. The sun glared down on top of him. There wasn't a cloud in the sky. He was thankful, however, for a cool refreshing breeze from the south that brought with it the salty and fresh smell of the ocean. Just to the north was the city of Cienfuegos. It wasn't close to being as large as Havana or Santiago de Cuba but it was as beautiful as either. Such was its beauty that it was called *La Perla del sur*—the Pearl of the South. At night its lights lit up the area north of the fortress so that one could walk there as though every night were a full moon. Seeing it, and the beaches, and palm trees made Antonio wish he had a Senorita to take on romantic night walks—and more. Cienfuegos also had plenty of churches and priests, so repentance would be close at hand.

But alas the Confederados must force me to keep all my focus on this accursed war!

A pair of binoculars hung from his neck. He raised them to his eyes and gazed out at the sea. Earlier in the day two Confederate light cruisers had been spotted steaming east along the coast. The shore defenses had been alerted but no shots had been fired by either side. General Vicente Eslava, the city's garrison commander, had dispatched Colonel Dominguez and his cavalry east to follow the cruisers and make sure that they had left the area. So far they had not returned.

Cienfuegos was a vital city for the Spanish war effort in Spain. It was the primary hub for all Spanish telegraph lines on the island of Cuba. Undersea telegraph lines ran on the ocean floor along Cuba's southern coast to Santiago and also south to Jamaica. Cienfuegos was therefore the primary link to the outside world for Spanish military forces in Cuba. As such the Spanish had fortified it as well as they could. Defensive works had been constructed north and east of the city. But Antonio knew better than most that it was also vital to fortify the beaches against amphibious landings and thus far that had not been done. He found the sudden appearance of the Confederate light cruisers as foreboding.

"Spot anything, Major?"

Antonio snapped to attention and saluted. General Eslava had joined him on the ramparts.

"Nothing yet, General."

"Bueno. The Confederados navy is not large enough to completely surround this island. Now that Havana has fallen, they will undoubtedly focus their attention on Santiago. I doubt we need fear a major attack here—at least not from the sea. Enemy forces attacking by land to the north of the city—that's a different story."

"Si, Senor," replied Antonio, hoping his superior was correct. The Confederate Navy had seemed plenty big to him when it had bombarded Havana.

"I thought you'd like to know. Orders arrived an hour ago from General Weyler in Santiago. Your men and several others are to be transferred to Santiago immediately to help reinforce the city. I think its fool hearty, but who am I to argue with the Duke?"

Antonio nodded. The King of Spain ruled by Divine right granted by Almighty God. That Divine authority channeled down to the noblemen under the King. It was not the place for men like Antonio or even General Eslava to question such leaders.

"We have prepared three transports. If all goes according to plan you will leave tonight."

Antonio gulped and felt his heart rate increase. To reach Santiago they would have to steam east along the coast—in the same direction as the Confederate warships. He didn't fancy the idea of being shot at by light cruisers, gunboats or worse. He was a soldier—not a fish.

Dear God, if I must be shot at please let it be on land where I belong!

"Still I wish I could retain the forces General Weyler is ordering me to send," continued. Eslava. "It will be difficult enough to hold onto Cienfuegos without sending a quarter of my garrison away."

A moment later one of the lookouts cried out that a rider was approaching from the east. Antonio swung his own gaze in that direction and quickly recognized the rider as one of Dominquez's cavalrymen. He turned to the General. Ever so respectfully he said:

"Senor, perhaps we should hasten down to meet the rider. He seemed in quite a hurry and every moment may be vital."

"Si, Major, you are quite correct."

To Antonio's relief the General hastened back down into the bowels of the fort. He made sure to be right behind him. They met the rider at the front entrance of the fortress.

"What is your report, Corporal?" demanded Eslava.

"Senor!" said the cavalryman while saluting, "the Confederados are coming ashore!"

"Where?"

"About four miles east of here!"

"Hostias!" cried Eslava.

"What is it General?" asked Antonio. For Eslava to invoke the Holy Mother Church as a swear word it had to be grave.

"That is where the telegraph comes ashore!"

"Then we must stop them!" declared Antonio. "If the Confederados come ashore there they will be able to severe our communications with Spain!"

The General shook his head.

"There is very little telegraph wire between here and there. Anything they tear up can be quickly and easily replaced or repaired."

"Colonel Dominguez said to tell you that there were a lot of Confederados coming ashore."

"How many?" asked Eslava. "Did you see them?"

The Corporal shook his head. The General looked at Antonio.

"Those two cruisers couldn't have carried a very large force."

"Perhaps they met up with other ships coming from the east," replied Antonio. "It could be a full scale amphibious invasion."

"Or a distraction to draw our attention away from the northern defenses," said Eslava. "Major, assemble your men. Follow the Corporal east, access the situation, and give whatever assistance you can to Colonel Dominguez. Send a fuller report back to me. In the meanwhile I'll put the northern defenses on alert and prepare to send you more reinforcements if it turns out to be necessary."

Antonio saluted.

"Si, Senor!"

It turned out to be a short march along the beach. Halfway there, the sound of rifle fire reached their ears.

"Everyone at the ready!"

They moved ahead at the double quick. The tide was out so the beach was wide and dry. Even double timing it, going over sand slowed them down. A short while later a rifle barked and a bullet cracked past Antonio and his men. He hit the beach hard, flattening himself out in the hot sand. The sun had heated it to a high temperature and he could feel the heat through his uniform—it was most uncomfortable. But when compared with taking a bullet somewhere in your soft vulnerable flesh he decided he'd deal with it. Up ahead a group of Confederate marines had landed on the beach and dug in. He recognized them by their gray uniforms and dark blue kepi's. Antonio wasn't sure how many of them there were, but he was now certain that this was no major amphibious landing. Off to his right he could clearly see the two Confederate light cruisers anchored offshore and no others.

It's some sort of raid! "Open fire!" cried Antonio. Up and down the beach the Spaniards opened fire. Up ahead and to the left, more fire came from the tree line where Colonel Dominguez and his Cavalry were positioned. The Confederates traded shots with both groups of Spaniards but didn't seem interested in expanding their beachhead.

What are they up to? Antonio pulled his binoculars from his haversack and risked raising his head just high enough to gaze at the sea. He quickly spotted several workboats between the shore and the cruisers. Each had about sixteen menm and they seemed to be working with grapples and hooks in the water.

They're trying to cut the telegraph lines in the water! Antonio knew very little about telegraph lines, but he was reasonably certain that repairing lines that had been cut out in the water would be a lot harder than repairing lines on the shore.

"Shoot at the boats!" he cried. "Shoot at the boats!"

The Spanish infantrymen bogged down on the beach began to send of hail of bullets towards the workboats with their Mausers. Antonio himself took aim, and squeezed the trigger. His rifle barked. He fired again and again until his rifle's magazine was emptied but was uncertain if he hit anyone. The boats were within range of the rifles but at such an extended range it was impossible to aim at a specific target. Antonio began to reload his rifle. Ahead and to the left the Spanish Cavalrymen increased their own fire on the Confederate marines on the beach, trying to keep them pinned down so that Antonio and his men could concentrate on the workboats. Antonio was just about to start firing again when he heard the familiar yet terrifying shriek of an incoming shell.

"Get your…" *Boom!* An explosive shell fired from one of the Confederate cruisers slammed into the beach with tremendous force sending lethal shrapnel in all directions and a plume of sand into the air that came raining back down on top of the Spanish troops. It was followed later by a second impact. Both cruisers had begun to bombard the shore. Not far away, the screams of a wounded soldier was added to that of the rifle fire and exploding artillery shells. Almost instinctively Antonio grabbed his entrenching tool and started to dig himself a hole on the beach. His men followed suit. In an artillery bombardment every little bit of protection helped—and it helped to stave off the terror. Antonio and most of his men had seen up close and personal what artillery could do to something as fragile as a human body. The second Confederate cruiser soon added its own fire to the shore bombardment. In what seemed like an eternity but was in actuality only a few hellish minutes, Antonio and his men endured a brutal bombardment. Every so often Antonio would dutifully pop up just long enough to take a pot shot at the work boats or steal a glimpse at them with his binoculars but for the most part he just kept his head down. The shore bombardment insured that the Spanish troops would be nothing more than a nuisance to the men on the work boats who were working feverishly to wreak havoc on Spain's primary line of communication out of Cuba.

Eventually, Antonio was able to determine that the Confederate marines were pulling back to their long boats.

He and his men sent several shots their way but the bombardment didn't let up until the gray uniformed marines had withdrawn and the workboats had begun to withdraw to the waiting cruisers.

In the aftermath Antonio cautiously walked the beach where the enemy Marines had come ashore. They had managed to destroy a small blockhouse that served as the junction of the land cables and those at sea. General Eslava had said that such damage would be easy to repair. As he watched the two Confederate cruisers steam away he found himself wondering just how much damage they had done to the cables on the sea floor. He had a sneaking suspicion that the Spanish army was now largely cut off from the outside world, and that this small Confederate raid had done far more damage than anyone would believe.

We'll find out soon enough...

XXII

"David, I'd always pictured hell as being a place of fire, but now I know it is made of mud," said Joseph Whitmore as he sat atop his horse surveying the disordered mass of men that constituted his mercenary Legion. His personal assistant nodded and then almost involuntarily swatted a mosquito that had dared to perch itself on his neck and partake of his blood. After washing away the blood and smashed mosquito Lovejoy looked upward. They were shaded by thick treetops which had grown up out of the muddy swamp. Earlier that morning in the hours immediately after they'd disembarked the ships, they'd been under the merciless sun. Though they were now under shade, the high humidity insured that the air itself held all the heat necessary to make them miserable.

"It is certainly hot enough here to qualify, sir," said Lovejoy, "though I must say my feet and legs are cool enough if not exactly comfortable." Lovejoy, was himself, standing almost waist deep in mud. He held the reins of his employer's horse, trying to lead the hesitant animal inland through a mire thicker than the mount cared to travel. Whitmore's Legion had landed in Cuba earlier that morning and had been attempting to push its way inland for several hours and link up with the regular Spanish forces.

"The Spaniards were supposed to be waiting on us!" snapped Whitmore. The elderly business man was in a dour mood. "If they can't keep a simple rendezvous than they deserve to lose this blasted war!"

"Any number of things could have happened, sir," replied Lovejoy. "They could have been delayed or blocked by the enemy, or perhaps they never even received the communiques. We are in a warzone. The island is surrounded by the Confederate navy. We should thank heaven that we were able to approach the coast and land without being discovered."

Whitmore let out a loud harrumph.

"The only reason that the Confederates weren't guarding that miserable counterfeit of a shore back there is that they knew only a fool would try to land there—and fools we are." The British freighters had come in slowly under the cover of darkness—always a risky venture for ships at sea. At dawn Whitmore and his men had disembarked. There really hadn't been a shore. The sea had simply given way to swamp and then mud. There had been little firm ground on which to place the crates of supplies. What little firm ground there had been was overgrown with vegetation. The wagons had been completely useless. In the end they had been forced to leave the vast majority of their supplies behind. All they had was what each man could carry and what they could pack on the few horses that they had.

"Look at the bright side, sir. This whole miserable business at least makes up in a small way for the loss of our artillery on the Capricorn. We never would have gotten those guns through this mess."

"No, I suppose not," said Whitmore with a voice of bitterness. "We should have landed in a port."

"Impossible, sir. Not without a naval force to get us through the Confederate blockade."

"I know that!" shouted Whitmore hurling a curse at his assistant. The old millionaire felt absolutely useless. He'd known that at his age he would not be up for much marching, but he'd counted on being able to use his horse. The animals were having a difficult time. If Whitmore's horse was unable to get through the mire, he wasn't sure what he'd do. For a moment he pictured the humiliating idea of his men carrying him through the swamp like an invalid. His fist tightened around the head of his cane which he kept at his side.

What a fool I am!

Sensing Whitmore's discomfiture, Lovejoy tried to reassure him.

"Don't worry, sir. We'll soon be out of these swamps and onto firmer ground."

They had landed over twenty miles east of Santiago de Cuba. Their plan was to head north where the swamps would give way to more mountainous terrain and then move west around the swamps and link up with the Spanish at Santiago. When they finally emerged from the mire and the cover of the trees the sun was well past high noon and moving into the late afternoon. As he watched his men emerge from the swamps, Whitmore's spirits improved slightly. He reflected that though it had only been a day, his Legion looked as though it had been in the field forever. The passage through the mire had insured that each man was covered from head to foot in mud. Their uniforms were so muddy they looked more dark brown than khaki. Their skin and faces were so muddy that he actually had trouble distinguishing the whites from the negroes. In an odd sort of way he wondered if their new uniformity would help their unity and moral. Their time in New York and the voyage from Canada had revealed deep fissures amongst his troops. While the whites from Canada and Britain made efforts to accept the negroes as fellow men, the whites from the USA looked down on them. Whitmore reflected that like him, most of his fellow countrymen from the United States were far more interested in killing Confederates then they were striking a blow at slavery.

Fortunately, the two amount to the same thing.

Whitmore felt for certain that getting out of the mire and onto solid ground had at least renewed their vigor. For a while they actually picked up the pace—until they realized that they had exchanged the swamps for a steep rocky uphill climb. They pressed on. By the time they reached the top of the first major rise they were little more than a disorderly throng. Whitmore pointed to the small, wooded valley below them. A small creek ran through its center, no doubt emptying into the swamp from which they had come.

"We'll camp down there, Mr. Lovejoy. See to it that guards are posted on top of each of the four hills that surround this basin. Once the sentry's are posted and the camp is set up have the officers report to me."

An hour later they had pitched camp under the cover of the trees. Almost half the men had left behind their tents, though most thankfully had (very muddy) bedrolls. While the men rested and ate their meager rations, Whitmore addressed his officers.

"I know that things haven't exactly gone as smoothly as we'd hoped. I know that today in particular has been extremely taxing on all of you. Pass along to your men that I am proud of what they have accomplished. It's been a long hard journey fraught with difficulty, but we are here! We are in Cuba!" As was his custom when he was excited, Whitmore began to pace back and forth holding his cane out like a sword. "Tomorrow we will push west with all speed. I want to be at Santiago by the end of the day."

"Sir," said Pershing. Though filthy, the young former US officer showed not the slightest sign of fatigue. "I strongly suggest that we send scouts ahead tomorrow well ahead of the main force. These hills are the perfect terrain for an enemy attack. And even if we run into the Spanish first, they could easily jump the gun and fire on us before they realize whose side we are on."

"An excellent suggestion, Major," said Whitmore. "You and your company have just volunteered to be the scouts."

Without any hint of disappointment Pershing nodded. "Yes, sir."

By his tone, Whitmore could tell he was eager to go forward and meet the enemy.

"We move out at first light, gentlemen. In the meantime, get some rest."

"Excuse me, General," said Joshua Winslow. "But I would like to make it clear to everyone here how important it is that the men use their chlorine tablets when they fill their canteens. I've already seen several men drinking from the stream. This environment is rife for malaria and yellow fever. If we don't take precautions the Confederates won't have to shoot us. Disease will do their work for them."

Several moments of silence followed in the wake of Joshua's remarks. It was Whitmore who broke it.

"You heard the man. I'll not have my army die of malaria before it sees combat. Do as he says!"

No sooner had the small crowd dispersed, than Whitmore shed his boots and uniform and crawled into the small tent that Lovejoy had erected for him. It was small and humble, but his bed in his upstate New York mansion could never have been as welcome a sight. The elderly millionaire all but collapsed onto the blankets and pillow. He fell asleep in virtually no time at all. He slept for a good seven hours. Nonetheless, it seemed like no time at all before Lovejoy was shaking him awake.

"It's time, sir. We'll be heading out shortly and you must eat some breakfast. You went to bed without dinner last night. You must eat something."

For a moment, Whitmore wanted to shout curses at his assistant, turn back around and bury his head in his pillow again. His entire body ached and not for the first time he wondered what kind of madman he was for trying to lead such an expedition in person. Nonetheless he forced himself to get up and get dressed. No sooner had he emerged from his tent than Lovejoy handed him a tin bowl of the grimmest looking oatmeal he'd ever seen and an open can of peaches. He also handed him a steaming cup of coffee. Whitmore's eyelids felt like lead weights, but the coffee gave him a sudden but welcome jolt of energy.

"Here sir, if you'll eat your breakfast I'll take down your tent and get your horse ready."

"If we get out of this, David, you're getting a raise when we get back to New York."

Lovejoy turned to his employer with a concerned look that was half serious half mocking.

"Sir, are you sure you're not coming down with Yellow Fever?"

Whitmore scoffed and then began to devour his peaches. One did not become as wealthy as Whitmore was without being somewhat tightfisted. In most instances, Whitmore was downright miserly. Lovejoy was certain his employer could have given lessons to Dicken's Scrooge.

A short while later, Whitmore watched as Pershing and his men headed west and out of camp. Most of his company was composed of negroes. Only one of Pershing's squads was made up of whites. After they had left the camp, Whitmore realized that he had only a few minutes before it would be time for the main body to move out as well. He quickly finished his coffee and choked down his oatmeal. He then made his way to the stream where he washed his mug and tin bowl. He also took the opportunity to refill his canteen, making sure to drop in a chlorine tablet with the water. He didn't like the idea of putting chemicals in his water, but he liked the idea of getting a tropical illness even less. At his age, he knew he would stand virtually no chance against either malaria or yellow fever. When he returned, he found that Lovejoy had finished packing his things.

"Your horse is ready, General."

Whitmore nodded. Lovejoy then helped him onto his mount. His backside was extremely sore from the previous day's ride. It sent a shockwave of painful protest throughout his body the second that he was in the saddle again. Nevertheless, they were headed west a short while later. At first it was a fairly simple affair. They had to head up steep rocky terrain, but the temperature was at least bearable. Whitmore reflected that the hills weren't as humid as the swamp. But as they passed from early to late morning, and the sun rose high into the air, the heat returned with a vengeance. The small wooded valleys provided shade when they passed through them, but they were exposed to the merciless glare of the sun every time they went over a hill. Still they pushed on. He'd told his men that he intended to reach Santiago by the end of that day and it was a goal he intended to reach.

Though they had sent a scouting force ahead, Whitmore and the other officers still eyed the hilltops and treetops around them warily, as if expecting Confederate raiders to open fire on them at almost any minute. They pressed forward. Whitmore was pleased to see that his men seemed as eager to reach their destination as he was. Then shortly after noon, Whitmore and the others suddenly heard the unmistakable sound of gunfire coming from the west. As they continued advancing, the sound grew louder and louder. A few minutes later a soldier in a muddy khaki uniform came charging over the next rise waving his hat excitedly in the air. He ran towards Whitmore at breakneck speed just barely managing to come to a halt without crashing into the front of his horse. The soldier brought his hand up in salute.

"Rebs, General! Major Pershing has sent me to tell you that he has engaged the enemy. Confederate forces appear to be present in battalion strength. He requests you come forward with all speed."

"Tell Major Pershing that we will be their directly," said Whitmore. The soldier saluted again and took off towards the west again.

Whitmore turned excitably to Lovejoy.

"It's time. Move the men forward."

"I advise caution, sir."

"This is why we are here, David!" said Whitmore. "This is why I started this venture!" The elderly millionaire pulled his pistol. "Let's go kill some Rebels!"

XXIII

Roger Connery took cover behind a large mossy tree as the thunderous sound of rifle fire resounded all around him and lethal bullets shrieked their way through the air—some striking trees, others flesh. After working the bolt on his rifle, his first thought was to shoot back at the men who were trying their best to kill him. But then he remembered that he was dressed in an enemy uniform. The soldiers in gray up ahead were his countrymen. Over the sound of the gunfire, Connery could hear the voices of Pershing and Malcom shouting for the men of the company to open fire. Most of them had already begun to do so.

This is not what I had in mind! Connery swore at himself. He hadn't planned on them encountering Confederate forces so soon after landing. He'd intended on slipping away and sending in a report to his superiors. In any event, his primary focus at that moment was to survive. A bullet slammed into another nearby tree, instantly snapping his full attention back to his precarious situation. For a brief moment, he considered playing dead.

If the boys in gray can drive Whitmore and his men back that might give me the opportunity to turn myself in to the army. Of course if they aren't able to do so, then these fools of Whitmore's might well discover that I was playing possum. Connery didn't care if they thought him a coward, but he didn't want to draw any more attention to himself than he already had.

I need to know what we're up against! If only I could get to higher ground. All at once an idea presented itself. He looked up at the tree behind which he was taking cover. It was overgrown with moss, vines, and stranglers. Driven more by adrenaline and desperation than by any particular skills at climbing, Roger Connery made his way up the trunk and into the thick evergreen branches. He perched himself near the top of the Florida Strangler amidst the thick green leaves. Without so much as stopping to catch his breath, Connery pulled his binoculars from his haversack and tried to survey the area ahead of them. The thick trees and vegetation made it somewhat difficult. He could make out only a small part of the hill that the Confederates had come over. What few of his countrymen he could see, he spotted by focusing in on muzzle flashes. The gray clad soldiers seemed to be as surprised as Whitmore's own troops.

This was no ambush, thought Connery deridingly. *We simply blundered into one another like a pair of blind beggars.* Wishing he had some way to more accurately gage the size of the Confederate force, he replaced his binoculars and again readied his rifle. His intention was to fire not at the gray clad soldiers to the northwest, but at Whitmore's men immediately below him. His easiest targets were certainly the Legionnaires immediately below his position. But Connery was wary of betraying soldiers that were positioned so closely to him. It would be too easy for them to discover what he was doing and what they would do to him if they discovered his treachery, paled in comparison to what they would do to him for cowardice.

Instead he gazed northeast along the line of Whitmore's men. The Legionnaires were virtually all laying prone. He followed the line of men until he spotted a khaki uniformed negro about one-hundred feet north of his position. Connery treacherously leveled his Enfield at the black Legionnaire who was very calmly and coolly discharging his rifle at the Confederates to the Northwest. It was a long shot, but Connery was an expert marksman. He took a deep breath, exhaled slowly and pulled the trigger. The Enfield barked, and the negro soldier's head exploded in a burst of blood and gray brain matter. Connery immediately ducked back into the branches and leaves atop the tree. It took him only a moment to work the bolt on his rifle to ready it for another shot, but he didn't want to push his luck by firing too often, otherwise the soldiers immediately below him might still figure out what was happening. A minute later Connery made his way back out onto the branch to search for another target. As he did so, the shrieking sound of the Rebel Yell made its way throughout the wood. Connery looked to the northwest and spotted a large number of gray clad Confederates charging downhill and into the trees at Pershing's thin Khaki line. His heart leapt. This is what he'd been hoping for. Connery's predatory eyes spied another negro. This one was not lying prone like most of his comrades but was taking cover behind a tree much the same way that Connery had been earlier. It offered the soldier good cover against the oncoming Confederate infantry, but against the assassin above it offered none at all. Connery took aim at the negro. The Legionnaire was a closer target than Connery cared for, but he was certain that the Confederates would be driving Whitmore's men back in short order. Once again Connery's rifle barked. The negro went down with a fountain of blood spraying out of the side of his neck.

The Rebel Yells suddenly sounded again, much closer this time and accompanied by a thick roar of rifle fire. Over the sound of the battle, Connery could again hear the voices of Major Pershing and Captain Malcom yelling orders.

"Retreat!"

"Fall back to the ridge!"

The company began to break and run. As they did so Connery searched ruthlessly for the two officers, hoping to snipe them while he had the chance. He caught sight of Malcom. The former British marine was not showing his back to the enemy but rather was engaged in a personal fighting retreat. He blazed away with two revolvers trying to give his men the time they needed to get to their fallback position. Connery took aim at him and fired. The shot missed. The Confederate operative worked the bolt on his rifle and took aim again. Connery's second shot caught Malcom in his left leg. He went down cursing with rage. Two negro Legionnaires quickly came to his aid. He roared profanities as they took hold of his arms and started to drag him away. Connery quickly worked the bolt on his rifle again, but was unable to get off another shot before Malcom had been moved out of sight. Thus cheated of his prey, Malcom instead shot another retreating negro in the back.

A moment later a line of gray clad infantry surged past the tree in which Connery was perched. The Confederate operative slunk back into the thickly grown green leaved branches. He didn't want to take a chance on being spotted by the gray uniformed soldiers below. Regardless of what side he was really on, he was still wearing the khaki uniform of the Spanish Foreign Legion and he had no intention of getting himself shot.

I need to wait for things to quieten down before I try to 'surrender.'

The Confederates didn't remain below him for long, but pressed their attack with vigor eventually pushing Pershing's company out of the trees and back up the ridge they had previously come down before blundering into the Confederate States' troops. Connery was about to climb down from his perch atop the tree, when suddenly another set of battle cries reached his ears. Connery made out a mixture of "Huzzahs!" from the British and Canadians and the more familiar "Hurrahs!" from those Legionnaires that hailed from the United States. The negroes of Whitmore's legion let loose war cries much closer to that of the Confederates they were fighting. It was not the sharp panther like scream of the Rebel Yell, but the deeper roar of a very different but equally determined group of men.

At first Connery thought that Pershing had ordered a suicidal counter attack. But he quickly realized that the entirety of Whitmore's force had begun to surge over the hilltop and down the ridge at the surprised Confederates.

Connery spotted a khaki clad rider coming over the hill top with the red and gold Spanish flag that served as the Legion's banner. Whitmore was hitting back with everything that he had. Connery was surprised that he'd been able to get all of his troops into the fight so quickly. Whitmore's Spanish Foreign Legion was doing far better than Connery been willing to give credit. Whitmore's counterattack was more than enough to stop the Confederate advance.

Suddenly finding themselves outnumbered two to one, the gray clad soldiers turned about and began a full retreat. Like the pendulum of a clock, the tide of battle had swung back in the other direction. Cursing the day, Connery again readied his rifle. The vast majority of khaki uniformed troops charging down the southeastern slope were now white. Connery could no longer afford the luxury of targeting the negroes that he so hated, but selected his targets as they presented themselves. Throwing caution to the wind he fired at the oncoming Legionnaires with abandon. A short while later, the retreating Confederates were once again immediately below him. As before they passed his position quickly. A few stopped to fire some shots at the oncoming Legionnaires, but most simply kept up a steady pace towards the rear. Connery hoped that perhaps the Confederates had more troops to throw into the fight. He was about to duck back into the obscurity of the trees thick leaved branches when he caught sight of Whitmore himself.

The eccentric Yankee millionaire had come over the ridge on horseback with a pistol held high.

If I didn't know better I'd think he was a real General. Being mounted made him an almost perfect target. For a moment Connery considered sparing Whitmore. He was certain the millionaire's insane venture was ultimately doomed to failure and was certain that living to see that would be far worse on the old man. But in the end he decided it was better to kill him. With the old millionaire dead the Legion would be demoralized, leaderless, and fractioned—all but insuring its eventual destruction. *Like chopping off the head of a snake.*

Connery leveled his Enfield at Whitmore and began to squeeze the trigger.

BILLY BENNETT

Suddenly a bullet slammed into Connery's left shoulder. The hot bullet bit into his flesh with a vengeance. Pain, worse than he'd ever known, shot throughout Connery's entire body. Involuntarily he groped for the bloody wound, inadvertently dropping his rifle as he did. The Enfield fell nearly sixteen feet and stuck barrel first into the muddy ground below. Connery clasped the wound trying to stem the bleeding. He suddenly realized he was extremely dizzy.

I'm losing too much blood! No sooner had the thought reached his mind than his legs lost their grip on the branch. As he fell from the tree his last reserves of strength kicked in. He fell a couple of yards and crashed into another branch. The impact was extremely painful but it slowed his fall enough so that as he fell another yard he was able to catch hold of another branch with his good arm. He managed to hold on for perhaps fifteen seconds before dropping the last seven feet to the ground. He was fortunate that the ground was soft and muddy. The impact, nonetheless, sent fresh waves of torment throughout his body.

Connery found himself starring blurry eyed at the tree tops above. For a while he felt pain everywhere- most severely in his shoulder which felt as if it were on fire. After a few painful moments that seemed to him an eternity, the pain began to subside as he began to grow cold and numb. The frantic noise of battle around him which at one point had been a strange symphony of gunshots and pain filled cries seemed to suddenly grow distant.

I'm...bleeding...to...death...

He became totally unaware of the passage of time. The sound of battle seemed to grow even more distant until he could barely hear it. The last thing he saw as darkness began to engulf him was the face of a negro. At first he thought one of the black Legionnaires, wise to what he had been doing, was poised above him like an avenging angel of death ready to finish him off. It was only at the last possible moment that he realized, with supreme irony, that Joshua Winslow was above him working frantically to save his life.

"He's lost too much blood! We've got to stop the bleeding! You, apply pressure to the wound. Miss Harper I need a bandage!"

XXIV

Distant thunder rumbled in the cloudy sky as Cole Allens sat under the cover of a large royal palm tree. It's broad, strong, green leaves blocked most, but not all of the steady rain that was drenching the entire area. An army issue oilskin tarp served to block the remainder of the rain as he strained to read the papers in his hand. The whole scene took him back to his experiences during the Kentucky campaign of the Second War of Rebellion which had been similarly inclement at times, though Cole didn't remember it being quite as humid. Not far away, his British companions— Lieutenants Churchill and Barnes—sat under a tree of their own. They'd been following the Confederate army east across Cuba for over a week but thus far had seen no combat. It seemed they were always a day or two behind the front lines. They'd passed several battle fields littered with the sky-blue clad bodies of dead Spanish troops. By all appearances the campaign was not going well for the Spaniards. Cole reflected that the Spanish not only had to contend with the Confederate Army in their front, but also with swarms of Cuban rebels in their rear.

Cole finished reading the papers and then stowed them in his pack. They were a copy of the treaty that the Confederacy was concluding with Cuba. As the Confederate officials had said, it offered Cuba what amounted to de-facto independence. The treaty declared Cuba to be a 'commonwealth' of the Confederate States, defining 'commonwealth' as belonging to, (but not being an actual part of) the Confederacy. The treaty was much more generous to the Cubans than Cole had expected from Richmond. The Confederate government would have no right to tax the Cubans (including tariffs and excises) except in time of war. The Cubans would have the power to determine for themselves whether or not slavery would be permitted on their island. That they would choose to maintain the ban on slavery was (to Cole) a forgone conclusion. Negro slavery had been extinct on Cuba for nearly thirty years and by all appearances even the Confederates did not want to deal with the political fall out that would come with returning slavery

169

to the island. The treaty also guaranteed the newly formed Cuban government full independence in all matters of internal civil law, a concession that would, among other things, exclude Cuba from the Confederacy's national ban on interracial marriage. From what Cole had seen during his brief stint on Cuba, was that Cuban people were an amalgamation of the original native islanders, Spanish settlers, and negroes. An enormous percentage of the Cuban population was mulatto and intermarriage on the island was already rampant. Cole did note that the treaty placed strict regulations on Cubans travelling to the Confederates States, but guaranteed Confederate citizens free access to Cuba. It also guaranteed to the Confederacy in perpetuity the right to station troops, and build and hold naval bases. In return the CSA assumed responsibility for Cuba's defense and security.

The Confederates aren't interested in this island for the territory or the people or even the resources. They're after its strategic location. Cole sighed, fearing that the Confederates were as paranoid of another major war in the future as many of his own countrymen. He knew that there were a few fanatics on both sides that probably craved war, but for the most part he felt that the vast majority of Americans both North and South had no desire for any further death and mayhem—even if everyone feared it to be likely or even inevitable. Cole sighed again.

The problem with everyone thinking that a war is inevitable is that it's all too likely to lead to self-fulfilled prophecy. Not for the first time, he hoped that the reports and stories he was sending home to the United States would serve to remind people that war was something to be avoided at all costs.

A sudden rumble came from the south and east.

Is that more thunder? Or could it be artillery? Though they had crossed most of Cuba without seeing any action, Cole knew that they were fast approaching the eastern end of the island. As the last major port under their control, the Spanish would most likely defend the city of Santiago de Cuba tooth and claw. Now that their backs were against the wall, they had nowhere left to retreat. Sure enough, it wasn't long before one of the Confederate officers assigned to be their escort came riding up on horseback. Cole pulled himself to his feet. A sharp pain in his back served to remind him that he was a middle aged man playing a young man's game. Seeing the grey uniformed Lieutenant approach, Churchill and Barnes also leapt to their feet and double timed it over to Cole's position to hear what their escort had to say.

"Good news—if you can call it that. There's a big fight brewing up just east of here."

"Bout bloody time we get to see some action," sad Churchill.

The Confederate officer nodded and spat a brown stream of tobacco juice onto the muddy ground.

"I've been ordered to take you fella's to the forward command post."

The three foreign war correspondents quickly gathered their things and mounted their own horses. As they plodded across the muddy terrain, the thunder-like sound grew louder and louder.

Definitely artillery.

They travelled east for nearly an hour. Towards the end of their brief journey, the ground became much firmer. The rain hadn't fallen as hard in that particular area. Cole and the others dismounted in front of a large canvas tent. A large Confederate Battle Flag fluttered above it and two gray uniformed sentries guarded the entrance with bayoneted rifles. They looked deadly serious. The roar of artillery fire and rifle fire was emanating loudly only a short distance away. Cole guessed they were no more than a mile from the fighting. He doubted that the Spanish would ever be able to get into the Confederate rear, but from the look of the guards outside the command post Cole could tell they were ready just in case.

The Confederate officer serving as there escort approached the sentries and handed them his papers. With no undo fuss they were all quickly ushered into the Confederate forward command post. A Confederate general stood in the corner of the tent with a field telephone gripped in his hand. With the other hand he held the ear piece to his ear. The General was a tall man. Though his gray hair and beard showed his age—he had to be sixty or over—Cole thought he carried himself with the vigor and strength of will of a much younger man. The general was shouting loudly into the receiver part of the telephone.

"I said, don't attack again until I give the order! You're sending your men in piecemeal! Wait until we can mass our forces!" Despite the exaggerated volume of his speech, a smooth gentlemanly Virginia accent made itself clear. To his left, Cole could hear Churchill and Barnes chatting quietly about the Confederates use of field telephones on the battlefield. Cole supposed that it made communications on the battle field quicker. He'd also heard that the navies of various world powers had begun to install the advanced technology on warships. In either case, Cole thought it a sad waste of something so marvelous. He looked forward to the day when common people would have telephones in their own homes. Theoretically you could talk to someone hundreds of miles away if the wires were long enough.

There was a brief moment where the general was obviously straining to hear what the person on the other end of the line was saying. "Just wait on my orders! We're bringing up some more artillery. That ought to soften them up a bit!" The general then jostled the earpiece back onto the receiver and all but slammed the phone down on the small wooden table beside the switchboard.

"Infernal machine."

Without taking note of the newly arrived war correspondents the general made his way over to a hastily erected map table around which huddled three other Confederate officers. Cole recognized one of them as General Wheeler, whom he'd met back in Florida. Pointing to the General that had been speaking on the telephone, Cole quietly asked their escort, "Who is that officer?"

"That's General Fitzhugh Lee," said the Lieutenant quietly. Cole nodded. He didn't need to be told that Fitzhugh was the famous nephew of the even more famous Robert E Lee himself.

"What are we dealing with here, gentlemen?" asked Lee as he joined the others around the map.

"It looks like we've got ourselves a tough nut to crack here, General," replied Wheeler. "According to my scouts we've encountered the first of three lines of defense that the dagos have built around Santiago. They've made good use of hills and woods. In some areas they've built field works and even dug entrenchments. They also seem to be fielding several modern Prussian artillery pieces—something we haven't seen before."

Cole wondered for a moment whether the Prussian King had somehow managed to deliver weaponry to Cuba for use by the Spanish.

Wheeler continued, "Both flanks are crawling with Spanish cavalry and the center of their line is resting on this large hill." He pointed to hill on the map with his gloved hand. Lee put on a pair of spectacles so he could read the lettering underneath.

"San Juan Hill…"

"Yes, sir. It appears to have been manned by a large force of Yankee, British and nigger mercenaries!"

Cole suddenly felt his heart leap in his chest. Beside him, Churchill and Barnes looked similarly disturbed.

They made it! Whitmore and his outfit actually made it down here!

"The mercenaries appear to be fresh, and both well trained and equipped. They've already blunted two major assaults," said Wheeler.

Lee nodded.

"I've just ordered Colonel Henry to halt his attacks until we can mass the forces we need to get around one of the flanks."

Wheeler shook his head.

"Both flanks are well anchored on even higher and rougher ground. The center is our best bet."

A Colonel next to Wheeler with red piping on his uniform then spoke up.

"We could hit em with a good artillery barrage and then hit them with an assault spear-headed by our toughest troops. My cannons will work them over good and there's a battalion of marines in position as we speak."

Lee shook his head. Both he and Wheeler had served as Generals all the way back in the Confederate War of Independence, and they were now both grey bearded old men. But there ended their similarities. Lee reflected that

Wheeler had always been a straightforward attacker and age had done nothing to temper his ardor. But if Fitzhugh Lee had learned anything from his famous uncle it was prudence.

"Never attack the center—not if you have any other choice. We'll make a diversionary demonstration in the center—make them think that's where the main attack is coming, then we'll launch our primary thrust on and around the right flank."

Wheeler didn't look happy, but Lee was the ranking officer.

"Shall I order the marines to make the demonstration?" asked the Colonel.

"Let's not waste our good troops on a diversionary attack," interjected Wheeler.

"The Cavalry then?" asked the Colonel.

Wheeler shook his head again.

"No, we can't afford to lose the horses." He eyed Lee. "Send in the niggers."

Reluctantly, Lee nodded.

"The marines are better suited to spearhead the main attack, and the proper place of the Cavalry is guarding our flanks, not demonstrating in the center." Lee then eyed Wheeler sternly. "Order the colored troops to make the diversionary attack but only enough to distract the enemy long enough for the main attack to get underway. I don't want unnecessary casualties. This army has already lost far too many of its men—more to disease than to bullets I might add."

Lee then pulled a gold pocket watch out of his grey great coat.

"The attack will begin in exactly one hour. I want readiness reports in fifty minutes!"

"Yes, sir!" chorused the men.

"By the way, sir, Major Dearman has been chomping at the bit to get those horseless carriages of his with the mounted machine guns into action. I told him I'd ask you."

General Fitzhugh Lee grunted audibly.

"More blasted machines. I'll not have the main attack disrupted and jeopardized by untested and untried equipment."

"Yes, sir." Replied General Wheeler. From his tone of voice Cole could tell that this was a matter about which both of the elderly Confederate commanders agreed. But then Lee continued.

"Tell Dearman, that if he has a mind to risk his neck, his unit has permission to join the diversionary attack in the center—if he can get those contraptions to move uphill."

"Yes, sir."

Lee suddenly chuckled—quite uncharacteristically.

"The attack is supposed to distract the enemy. When they see those things heading towards them, it aught to get their attention one way or another."

Wheeler nodded again. He then pointed at Cole and the two British officers who were still standing just inside the tent.

"Ahh yes. Our *neutral* war correspondents." Cole thought he put an undue and almost sarcastic twist on the word *neutral*. After brief introductions Churchill got straight to the point.

"We should like to move forward and observe the fighting," said Churchill.

Lee eyed the stout young British officer coldly.

"You do realize Lieutenant, that a large portion of the force we are about to attack and do our utmost to destroy, is composed of mercenaries from your own nation as well as that of Mr. Allens?"

"We do indeed, sir," replied Churchill. "As I'm sure you know they have no official sanction from Her Majesty's government. So far as we are concerned they are merely combatants under the Spanish flag. If any of our brave countrymen are killed or wounded in battle then that is a hazard they accepted for themselves. I'm certain that Her Majesty's government would never dream of holding any animosity towards the Confederate States on account of these men—provided of course they are treated in accordance with the rules of war to which the combatants of all civilized nations are entitled."

"You ask me we ought to shoot every last one of them," said Wheeler bitterly. "They're not Spaniards. This isn't their war. They're nothing but a bunch of abolitionist fanatics that…"

Lee raised his hand suddenly, and silenced Wheeler. He looked directly at Churchill.

"Richmond has already issued orders on this matter. The President has ordered that captured British and U.S. citizens fighting under Spanish colors be treated no differently than any other prisoners of war."

"Does that include negroes as well, General?" asked Cole.

"Mr. Allens, the Confederacy itself has utilized colored troops in this war."

"Yes, we heard," said Barnes, with only the slightest trace of sarcasm. Ignoring him, Lee continued to address Cole.

"The President's orders were specific. All prisoners will be treated in accordance with the rules of war, regardless of color."

Cole nodded. Once again he had to credit John Marshall Stone. The Confederate President was doing a masterful job of insuring the Confederate States would be viewed on the world stage concerning the war in the best possible light. So far he'd given the Confederacy's opponents as little as possible to hang around his country's neck, regardless of what some Southern hotheads like Wheeler wanted.

When Cole again nodded his acceptance, Lee turned again to the two young British officers.

"You gentlemen have boldly claimed that your government has given no official sanction to these mercenaries, and yet they are armed in part with British Enfields and have been kitted out with British uniforms and equipment. My scouts report that their uniforms are as butternut as your own."

Churchill looked down briefly at his khaki tunic then back up at Lee and smiled at the Confederate General. He might have meant it to be disarming but Cole thought it looked a little too disingenuous for comfort. He also doubted the elderly Confederate General was enjoying this verbal sparring match with the witty young British officer.

"Now General, surely you know that Britain sells arms and equipment to many different nations. But I digress, if Spain or the organizers of this mercenary group chose to buy British goods we can hardly fault them for they could have bought no finer materiel. Nor, dare I say could you fault us for selling to them since we have also sold to you on numerous occasions. I've seen several Maxims and not a few Enfields being used by your own army here in Cuba."

"Leave it to the British Empire to sell arms to both sides in the same war," said Wheeler. "So you're really here to see how well your guns and gear fair in a war?"

"We are here at your government's invitation," interjected Cole.

"You are correct," said Lee. "And I have no personal or official problems with you gentlemen fulfilling your duties here, but I'm afraid I simply cannot allow two British military observers onto the front lines when many of the men we are fighting are dressed in almost identical uniforms. To do so would not only be imprudent but criminally negligent. If things got hot enough it would be far too likely that one of my men might mistake you for the enemy and I fear the consequences might prove severe—especially for you."

"Under such circumstances, one could hardly fault one of your brave soldiers were we so foolish to go to the front so attired," said Churchill. "It just so happens we do have some civilian clothes."

Lee nodded.

"After you have changed your attire, I'll see to it that you are escorted to the front."

A short while later they were once again on horseback and headed straight for the sound of the combat. Above them the clouds had parted and the afternoon sun was shining brightly, heating the entire area to a steaming humid cauldron. They passed several columns of gray uniformed negro troops who were themselves marching towards the fighting. At the head of each column negro color bearers proudly held aloft the Confederate battle flags that fluttered in the breeze. Seeing the star belted St. Andrews Cross flying over negro troops still struck Cole as a strange sight, but the soldiers themselves seemed to carry it with pride. He supposed that in their view they were finally something more than slaves and field hands. At long last they were freedmen and soldiers.

Soldiers fighting for… their country, such as it is. Cole hoped and prayed that that country for which they were fighting and shedding their blood would come to treat them better. Cole reflected that Southerners were a confusing people. He'd traveled through the Confederate States from Virginia to Florida. The vast majority of people had been kind, polite, and for the most part deeply religious and pious. But when it came to black people, many of those warm people could and did become cold and harsh. Cole supposed it came from centuries of thinking of negroes as little more than beasts of burden—farm animals with a little extra intelligence—instead of thinking of them as human beings.

The sound of artillery fire was growing louder and louder. They were getting closer to the Confederate gun positions. A few hundred feet away a shell exploded into the ground throwing dirt and earth into the air. Not far away a gray uniformed soldier with a severed leg was screaming in pain. The Confederates weren't the only ones doing the shooting. The Spanish were shooting back. Cole suddenly felt a dread that was all too familiar. It was like a long forgotten nightmare that had come to terrify his dreams anew. It had been a quarter of a century, but the terror of being on a battle field with explosive shells raining down around him was now as vivid as it had ever been. No longer distant memory, it was now fierce reality—and it was as bad as he remembered it. Cole's horse reared slightly in fright but he quickly brought the animal back under control and soothed it by patting the side of its neck.

"Easy there, friend," he said. Off to his left Cole could see that the two young British officers were getting their own first look at what war was really like. Despite their youth, their army uniforms coupled with their remarkable bearing had made them seem far older than they actually were. Now, devoid of their military attire, dressed in plain civilian clothing, and shocked by the sudden reality of war they looked suddenly like little more than terrified and helpless schoolboys. Almost as much as the artillery fire, the sight of the two young men took him back to 1869 when he himself had been a mere teenage boy serving as a war correspondent.

They'll get used to it.

It wasn't long before the two young Englishmen had once again rallied their nerves and were once again their determined selves.

"It can't be much farther!" said Churchill.

"It's not!" shouted their escort. At his signal the party reined in and the Confederate Lieutenant then pointed at a hill just south east of their position. That's our primary artillery position and the dominant landform on our side of the battle field. From there ya'll should be able to get a view of everything."

It's also likely to be the primary target of the Spanish artillery, thought Cole but he kept it to himself. This was why he was there. He took a deep breath and addressed the gray uniformed Confederate officer.

"Take us there, Lieutenant."

The thunder of artillery fire seemed to grow in intensity as they once again got on the move. As they began to go up the northwest side of the hill they didn't see any more artillery shell impacts, though they heard several explosions. When they reached the hop of the hill, however, their view changed dramatically. Stretched before them on the southeast side of the hill was a large area of open grassy terrain that was roughly shaped like an oval. The area was completely surrounded by hills and small but thickly wooded patches of forest. Across this vast clearing stood another hill that had been heavily fortified by the opposing force. The flag that flew above them was the red and gold Spanish tricolor, but Cole and his fellow war correspondents knew without doubt that the men holding that hill were British and American mercenaries. They had only a minute for that thought to sink in when a boom so loud that it nearly burst Cole's eardrums resounded through the air. Not far away, a Confederate cannon had fired. The shell streaked though the air and exploded in mid air—just above the mercenary lines, and sent deadly shrapnel in all directions. It was followed a half second later by another shell and then another and another.

Suddenly a different but more terrifying sound reached their ears—a loud screeching sound that seemed to grow closer and closer.

"Get down!" cried Churchill. The young British Lieutenant went to ground, virtually dragging Cole and Barnes with him. No sooner had they hit the dirt, then a shell exploded into the ground a few yards away. In the aftermath of the explosion Cole thought he distinctly heard the sound of hot shrapnel flying through the air. After climbing back to his feet, he noticed that a couple members of the nearest Confederate gun crew were down. One was cursing a storm and clutching a bleeding arm. Cole feared the other gray uniformed artillerymen would never rise again. Even from that distance he could smell the metallic odor of blood from the massive amount of spilt blood, and the horrid stench of released bowels. Trying focus on something—anything else—Cole turned to Churchill.

"Where is that artillery fire coming from? I don't see any gun emplacements on that hill?"

"Most likely from the further behind the Spanish lines. General Wheeler mentioned the Spaniards were using the latest in Prussian Artillery pieces. If what I've read is accurate, the only piece in the Confederate arsenal with a prayer of hitting back would be Whitworth cannons, and I don't see any on this hill."

Churchill named the Whitworth with no small amount of pride. The breech-loaded rifled field gun was manufactured in Britain. That the finest artillery piece in the Confederate Army was manufactured in a foreign nation spoke volumes on the Confederate States' precarious position with regards to manufactured goods and armaments. Suddenly there was another shrieking sound. This time, Cole needed no help in hitting the dirt. He threw himself to the ground and waited for the inevitable explosion. When it came it was far more distant than the previous one had been. Not only that, but he hadn't felt the small tremor in the earth that usually accompanied a shell impact.

"There!" shouted Barnes after they had again risen to their feet. He was pointing up and to the northwest at a large gray artillery balloon that was hanging in the sky behind the Confederate lines. A long rope with an attached telegraph line tethered it to the ground. A black smoke cloud lingered in the air about two dozen yards to the right and below the balloon—marking where the shell had exploded. A minute or so later they again heard the screech of an incoming shell. As before they flattened their bodies against the earth. Cole was reasonably certain that for the moment the Spaniards were not shooting at the hilltop but had no intentions of taking chances with such things. He did keep his head lifted so that he could continue to gaze at the balloon. Sure enough, the shell exploded in the air, no closer to its target than it had been before.

"I guess hitting an airborne target is still an emerging science," said Cole.

"They don't have to hit," said Churchill. "All they have to do is get the shell to explode close enough and the shrapnel will bring it down."

Cole turned his attention back to field before them. Churchill and Barnes pulled out their binoculars so as to better survey the Spanish position atop San Juan Hill. After a moment, Cole borrowed Churchill's, and had a closer look for himself. Even from that distance he could make out their khaki colored British style uniforms and peaked caps.

"What I wouldn't give to go over there and interview those men," said Cole absently.

"The Southrons would never allow it," said Barnes.

"I'm not so sure about that," said Churchill. "That hill has already repelled a number of assaults." Cole's gaze came to rest upon several grey clad bodies that littered the front of the hill. Not all of them were completely lifeless. Some of those fallen soldiers were wounded but still alive and writhing in torment in the heat of the day. "If they withstand another assault and if the Confederates fail to flank the hill as General Lee plans, you may well see a lull in the fighting and a temporary truce to gather the wounded. If you were ever going to go over there that would be the time."

"If the Confederates let me."

Churchill nodded.

"I wouldn't worry so much about the Confederates granting your request. I'd be more worried about the blokes across the way receiving you. They may well take you for a spy and tell you to bugger off."

Suddenly, the Confederate artillery fire slackened. Off to the left they spotted several squads of gray uniformed negro skirmishers moving out of the cover of the trees. They were followed quickly by a large but loose formation of black Confederate soldiers. Only the handful of officers were white. Cole watched as the negroes formed up. They maintained their discipline, even as Spanish shells started to rain down around them. A few moments later to the rolling of drums they began to march up the slopes of San Juan Hill with the Southern Cross floating determinedly above them. Only then did the cruel irony of what was transpiring hit him. A large number of the mercenaries entrenched atop the hill were negroes from the USA that had signed up to strike a blow against slavery and the CSA. Now they were about to face off with their brethren from the South that had traded their chains for military service and their hoes and plows for rifles. Cole let out a sigh, and shook his head.

XXV

"When he'd first joined up with the Spanish Foreign Legion, John Pershing had honestly doubted whether the black men over whom he'd been placed in command, had what it took to be soldiers. Considering who their enemy was they'd had spirit enough, and he reflected that they'd more or less learned the rudimentary principles of soldiering they'd been taught in their short training time on the grounds of Whitmore's New York Mansion, but so far as he knew not a one of his men had ever seen the elephant before. He didn't doubt them anymore.

The beginnings of their campaign could only be described as a disaster. The transport ship carrying them to Cuba had literally sunk beneath them taking most of their supplies and all of their artillery with it. They'd only barely escaped to another freighter. They'd spent the remainder of the voyage crammed into every possible nook and cranny of that ship. When they'd finally 'landed' (a term he only very loosely associated with their arrival in Cuba) they'd been forced to move through swampland waist deep in mud and mire. Then they'd all but blundered into an advanced

Confederate scouting force. Pershing and his men had been screening the Legion's main force and were at the forefront of the counter attack that had sent the Confederates running. Shortly thereafter they'd finally made contact with the elements of the Spanish army that had been sent to meet them and as quickly as possible they'd been positioned atop San Juan Hill, in the ring of defenses that had been set up around one of the last major Spanish stronghold in Cuba— the port city of Santiago. Since that time, they had repulsed three separate attacks on their position. Regardless of the color of their skin, Pershing's men had earned his confidence, and his respect.

Pershing lifted his hand to help shield his eyes from the afternoon sun. The visor of his British style peaked cap wasn't quite up to the task. Pershing actually liked the dusty brown khaki uniform. It might not have been as dashing as the U.S. Army blue that he was accustomed to wearing, but he was certain it made him a lot harder to spot out in the field. When people were shooting at you that counted for more than good looks.

"Looks like they're going to hit us again, Major," said Dominic Malcom in his precise British brogue. Pershing nodded. For a brief moment he regarded the limp with which his second in command walked. Malcom had taken a bullet in the leg shortly after they'd arrived in Cuba. Fortunately, it had done little more than graze the limb. Still, it worried Pershing. In the short time he'd known Malcom he'd come to know that the former British Marine would put his duty first. It was an admirable trait, but Pershing didn't want it costing him a leg.

"The Reb artillery has slackened off," said Pershing. "You're probably right. It's been a while since they tried. They'll probably have their act together this time."

"I just wish these defenses had been prepared properly," said Malcom bitterly.

Pershing grunted his agreement. The Spanish had chosen a good hill to fortify. San Juan Hill looked as if it had been especially designed by God to be a defensive position. Unfortunately, the Spanish had taken poor advantage of it. Most of the positions were well concealed, but they had constructed their defensive line along the geographic crest of the hill as opposed to the military crest. The positions were totally unsuitable for plunging fire. San Juan was a steep hill. Attackers would be under fire as they approached, but eventually the hill itself would give them cover from the defender's fire, allowing the attackers to finish their approach unmolested until they were close to point blank range. Pershing and his men had done what they could to reposition some of the defenses in their part of the line, but in the end they had had very little time to do so. Most of the defensive positions were still as the Spanish had prepared them.

"I want an ammo check up and down the line. Get a runner back to the wagons—make sure it's that fella that speaks Spanish…"

"Jerkins, sir."

Pershing nodded.

"I don't want any mix ups this time." The Spanish field commanders had agreed to integrate the Legion into their own logistics system, assuring Whitmore that they could supply ammunition of the appropriate caliber and in sufficient quantity. Pershing's unit had found out the hard way that their very first batch of ammo from the Spanish supply train had been the wrong caliber. They had discovered it in the middle of a fire fight. Only the fact that the Confederate attack had been uncoordinated and without proper artillery support saved Whitmore and his men from being overrun. Pershing didn't intend to let it happen again.

While Malcom handled the runner, Pershing double timed it up and down his section of the line. A three foot high stone wall ran atop the crest of the hill, a feature which afforded Pershing's men considerable cover.

"Pershing!"

Pershing spun around at the sound of Whitmore's voice. Giving the millionaire industrialist all the respect due a real general, Pershing came to attention and brought his hand up in salute. The old man might have been eccentric, but Pershing liked him for having the guts and the patriotism to launch such a daring venture and to pay for it out of his own pocket. He also admired Whitmore's stamina. He only hoped when he was that old he'd have a similar energy level. Whitmore all but charged up to him with cane in hand. As usual, his aid, David Lovejoy was in tow. Pershing also noted that Whitmore was dragging another man in his wake—a mustachioed Spanish officer. From the elaborate gold braid and epaulets on his sky blue uniform, Pershing judged that he was a General. He was right.

"Major Pershing, may introduce General Arsenio Pombo, commander of the Spanish forces defending Santiago. General Pombo may I introduce, Major John Pershing, formerly of the United States Army." Less than a heartbeat later, David Lovejoy repeated Whitmore's words in Spanish to the General. Pombo let loose a string of Spanish.

"The General wants to know what you think of the defensive positions."

For a brief moment, Pershing considered asking the General if he had court marshalled and shot the idiots that had prepared those defensive positions. Since the General himself was likely one of those idiots, and in lieu of insulting a superior officer, Pershing simply said: "Tell the General we'll make good use of them." The response seemed to please the Spanish commander who quickly moved on with his inspection of the line. After they had moved on Pershing sighed and shook his head. Fighting someone else's war was hard enough without human stupidity and incompetence making it harder.

Captain Malcom came limping back towards Pershing.

"What was that all about, Major?"

"Nothing that we can do anything about now," replied Pershing and then explained his encounter with the Spanish general. For his own part, Malcom looked disgusted.

"Jerkins told me that he overheard two Spanish officers saying that the Spaniards have over ten thousand troops in reserve inside the city and less than one-thousand out here with us."

Pershing nodded.

"I've heard that myself. General Weyler, the Spanish governor of Cuba is hold up in Santiago. I guess he wants to keep those troops close on hand for his own personal protection. They don't want to risk an uprising in the city."

"If half the things I've heard about how General Weyler has treated the Cubans is true I'd worry about an uprising as well," said Malcom. "And about what they'd do if they got their hands on me."

Pershing never had an opportunity to respond. Off to the northwest, a bugle sounded, and drums started to beat.

"It's starting," said Pershing. "Take charge of the left wing. Open fire as soon as they come out of the trees. We're at long range right now, but we need to take advantage while we can—before they get so close to the hill that they've got perfect cover!" Malcom nodded and hurried off towards his position. Pershing took up his own position, cursing silently as he did so. Their rifles had the range to hit the enemy from the moment they first showed themselves, but at that long range their shots wouldn't be very accurate.

From a hill like this we ought to be able to murder those bastards the entire time they're coming across that clearing and up the slope.

Up and down the line, Lieutenants and Sergeants started shouting exhortations to the men. The officers and non-coms were all white, but many of them were abolitionists from England and Canada. It was relatively easy to fire up negro troops to fight Confederates. Virtually all of the black men under Pershing's command had been born to parents that had been slaves in Kentucky, Maryland, Delaware, and his own home state of Missouri. Lots of negroes had fled the latter when the Confederates had taken (to Pershing stolen) it from the United States. Since the Confederacy still held millions of their kinsmen in bondage to that day, they needed little encouragement to kill the gray coated Southerners. Pershing had also quietly noted that a few of the young negroes in his company bore scars on their backs, which meant that they weren't native US negroes, but rather escaped slaves from the Confederate States. The United States viewed such negroes as illegal aliens. If caught, they risked being shipped back to the Confederacy and returned to slavery. Such men had taken quite a risk in joining Whitmore's Legion.

I suppose striking a blow for the freedom of their people was worth risking their own. If they got back to the

Union alive, Pershing intended to do everything in his power to get the army to let them enlist.

At the first sign of movement across the field, the men of the Spanish Foreign Legion opened fire with everything that they had from behind the cover of the stone wall. The constant bark and crackle of rifle fire resounded up and down the line. Not for the first time, Pershing lamented the fact that they had lost their artillery when the Capricorn went down. Further to the rear the Spanish had a number of Prussian artillery pieces that had done a decent enough job of bombarding the Confederate positions, but they would be of little use once the oncoming wave of Confederate attackers got near his position. The Spanish had a handful of smoothbore artillery pieces on the hill that would go a long way towards hurting the advancing Confederates. Spanish artillerymen in sky blue uniforms were already working frantically to get them into action. Pershing also knew that some other companies in the Legion had been equipped with Maxim machine guns. They'd not been put into action in the earlier assaults. Pershing hoped they were ready for this one.

A few minutes later the first Spanish cannon on the hill belched flame and sent canister fire at the approaching Confederates. Through his binoculars Pershing watched as it exploded in the air above the gray clad troops and then nodded in satisfaction when he saw several of them fall to the ground, cut down by the shrapnel. He only wished the Spaniards had about a hundred times more cannons then they did.

Undaunted, the Confederates continued their advance. Even without his binoculars, Pershing would have had no trouble making out the Confederate battle flags fluttering in the breeze above them. As he stared at the approaching enemy troops, though, something seemed odd—something Pershing couldn't quite put his finger on. The Confederates moved forward in what could best be described as a giant skirmish line. Like his own U.S. Army, the Confederates had learned painfully the folly of using massed formations of troops against rifled and especially breech-loaded guns. Nonetheless the Confederates left a steady field of corpses behind them as they move across the clearing. They returned a steady stream of fire as they moved forward, but stooped as they were behind a stone wall, Pershing and his men made poor targets.

Suddenly, Pershing caught sight of something that made him do a double take. He lowered his binoculars, rubbed his eyes and then looked again. Sure enough it—or rather they were still there. A half dozen wheeled contraptions had emerged onto the field. The shouts and curses that Pershing was able to hear even over the roar of gunfire were more tinged with surprise and wonder than they were with anger or even fear. Pershing had, of course, seen horseless carriages before, but the sight of them on the battle field was something he'd never imagined. It made him wonder what kind of mechanical marvels would appear on future battle fields.

A bullet suddenly cracked past his head, and John Pershing left all such contemplations behind. The Confederates had reached the midpoint of their approach to San Juan Hill. Soon they would be shielded by the hill's own steepness. Pershing shifted his position a few yards to the right and then again brought up his binoculars. Five of the horseless carriages had made their way across the field parallel to Pershing's view. The sixth contraption seemed to be bogged down. Pershing wondered if his men had managed to kill its driver or disable it. The contraptions were soaking up rifle fire as a sponge sucked up water. Pershing zoomed in on it with his binoculars. It seemed to have a busted wheel. Pershing imagined the men in control of the horseless carriages were having a rough ride with such narrow wheels. They'd turned to face the Spanish lines and were now doing their best to follow along behind the Confederate infantry. Pershing made another sweep of the approaching enemy troops and then his jaw dropped. He swore long and loud and then cursed himself and uttered a blasphemy. The Confederate troops approaching them were negroes. The sight of them on the battlefield, dressed in gray, rifles in hand, and Southern Cross flying high seemed almost more unbelievable than the horseless carriages.

Suddenly a loud chattering sound like the ripping of a cloth caused Pershing's heart to leap in his chest. Far off to the left, one of the Maxim machine guns had opened fire.

Pershing took a deep breath and exhaled long and loud. When his men learned that they were not fighting white southern slave masters, but their own fellow negroes, he feared that their hearts would fail. Sure enough, there was a distinct drop off in the rate of fire as soldier after soldier spotted the black skin of their approaching enemies. There were shouts of dismay and anger from many of the negroes on the firing line. Pershing had little time to empathize with them. They'd had hard lives and now a cruel world had hurled in their faces yet another injustice. But they had a job to do. At Pershing's direction, the angry shouts of the Lieutenants and Sergeants lashed out at the negro troops with the ferocity of a task masters whip. Slowly and with an utmost effort of will, the black soldiers leveled their rifles at the approaching gray clad negroes and opened fire. Many of them had tears running down their faces. One young black soldier, in an attempt to bury his grief shouted in anger and rage at the oncoming black Confederates. He hurled curses and insults as he fired again and again until his rifle was empty. Then like a bursting dam, his grief returned. He dropped his rifle, collapsed to his knees, buried his head in his hands and wept bitterly and uncontrollably. A few moments later he collected his wits, grabbed his rifle, slammed in a fresh clip, and started shooting again.

XXVI

Joshua Winslow was more terrified than he'd ever been in his life. With artillery shells exploding around him, shrapnel and bullets flying through the air, the thunderous sound of cannons, the crack and bark of rifle fire, the torturous screams of dying and wounded men, and the stench of blood and death, Joshua finally understood what his father had been through years earlier and why he never talked about it. He also understood why Jethro had not wanted him to come.

Joshua had expected to be working at a field hospital further in the rear, but ever since arriving in Cuba he'd found himself on the frontlines in the roll of battlefield medic.

The negro soldier over whom he was working screamed and cursed as Joshua started to tie a tight bandage around his wounded arm. It was more than a graze. A bullet had ripped through his left bicep. The muscle looked as if something had bitten a chunk out of it. Still it could have been a lot worse.

"Your lucky," said Joshua. "The bone isn't broken and the bullet isn't buried in your arm. The pain your feeling is nothing compared to what you'd feel if I had to go searching for the bullet and pulling it out with a pair of forceps." Joshua finished the bandage and said: "Get yourself to the rear."

The soldier swore but obediently made his way to the rear as Joshua moved on to find the next wounded man.

Joshua carried no rifle. The only protection he had was a white arm band with a red cross and he'd already seen that it had no magical aura to protect him from harm. One of his orderlies had taken a bullet in the head. Joshua moved as quickly as he could down the line, trying to keep as low as possible. To his right, soldiers were huddled behind the cover of a short stone wall, and firing at the oncoming enemy. Joshua still could not fully grasp the fact that the Confederate soldiers attacking them were negroes. He'd read in the past that the Confederacy had a law on the books that permitted the arming of negroes during time of war and that in exchange it supposedly offered freedom. Never in a million years would he have believed it. But now it was staring him in the face.

I wonder if they really will free them? What about all the others back in the CSA that can't fight? A bullet suddenly cracked past his head far too close for comfort. It brought his attention squarely back to the situation at hand. A few yards away a negro legionnaire rose above the stone wall just long enough to fire a shot—and to get shot himself. He fell backwards with a cry. Joshua headed straight for him. Off in the direction of the enemy he heard a sound like a ripping cloth. Several nearby soldiers swore. One of the nearby white officers cursed and said: "Those things are equipped with machine guns!"

Joshua resisted the urge to poke his head up and look at the Confederate horseless carriages. For one thing it was a surefire way to get his head blown off. For another he had a much more important matter to deal with.

The front of the wounded soldier's khaki tunic was soaked with blood. He'd taken a bullet in the upper right quadrant of his chest. Joshua braced himself. This would be a lot worse than a wounded arm.

Joshua immediately applied pressure to the wound with one hand while holding the man's wrist with his other and feeling for a pulse.

"Can you hear me?" he asked taking hold of the man's hand. The sound of rifle and cannon fire was still resounding loudly around them but Joshua was just able to make out the soldier's response.

"Yesuh…" The wounded man's voice was weak.

"I'm going to help you. I need you to keep talking to me. What's your name?"

"I's Cliff suh…"

"Can you move your arms and legs?"

His limbs briefly moved. Cliff suddenly cursed and swore in intense pain.

"Yesuh…but my right arm, it hurt like hell, suh."

Joshua nodded and let out a small sigh. The fact that he was talking meant that, for the moment at least, his airway was clear. The bullet didn't seem to have hit his lung, though it couldn't have missed it by much. The fact that the man could move showed that the bullet more than likely hadn't hit his spine. The man started to shiver, a side effect of losing so much blood. He needed to be kept warm. Unfortunately time was their enemy. With his great strength Joshua ripped the man's blood soaked tunic open so that he could better examine the wound. The man's bare chest was soaked in blood. The bullet had entered a few inches above the right nipple. It hadn't missed his lung by much.

"Alright, Cliff, hang on this is going to hurt, but I have to see if there's an exit wound are you ready?" The wounded man looked straight into Joshua's eyes and nodded. Joshua heaved him. Cliff cursed and swore again.

No exit wound. That means the bullet is still inside him. Joshua eased him back down as gently as he could. Suddenly there was a shrieking sound in the air.

"Hit the dirt!" Up and down the line soldiers threw themselves flat. Joshua through himself over his patient. A half second later a Confederate artillery shell exploded in the air. Shrapnel flew in all directions and fresh screams of pain erupted. Trying to remind himself that he was just one man and that no matter how much he wanted to he couldn't be more than one place at a time, Joshua went back to work on Cliff. He did his best to tune out the nightmarish sounds of the battle that was raging around him. It wasn't easy. He took a deep breath trying to remember his training.

Okay there's no exit wound. So I don't have to worry about him losing blood any other place. It looks like the bullet is impacted somewhere between the scapula and the clavicle. Unless he starts massively bleeding internally he should be stable enough to move.

At that point Joshua briefly considered sending the wounded man straight to the field hospital. But earlier in the day after the first assault Winslow had sent some wounded negroes to the rear for treatment. Hours later when he'd paid a visit to the field hospital they were still lying on stretchers outside. Joshua didn't think it was the fault of the Legion's surgeons, but the Spanish had no problems putting negroes at the bottom of the list. Joshua had also seen some of the botched jobs the Spanish surgeons had done. Joshua didn't want to risk them getting ahold of his patients. He resolved to do as much as he could himself.

Suddenly one of the soldiers on the firing line just a few feet away caught a bullet in the face. The man's head exploded like a cantaloupe. Red blood and gray brain matter sprayed everywhere. For a moment, Joshua sat as though frozen in time. He turned to look at the just demised soldier. For him, there was nothing he could do. Joshua felt a massive sense of terror building up inside of him. A part of him wanted to flee madly for the rear, to get as far away as possible from the bloody carnage playing out before him. Slowly but surely he willed away the urge to run like a madman.

This is why I'm here.

He looked down at his patient. He had to get him away from the front line. Joshua turned to the orderlies.

"Alright, let's get him on the stretcher. We've got to get further to the rear. We're far too exposed here." He pointed to a small clump of trees that stood atop San Juan Hill about a dozen yards from their position.

Cliff winced in pain as they briefly lifted him and then set him on the stretcher. Joshua took the wounded man's hand and applied it to the blood stained surgical cloth that Joshua had been using to stem the flow of bleeding from the wound.

"Keep tight pressure. We've got to move you away from the front lines to some cover." The two orderlies heaved the stretcher and following Joshua they ran for the clump of trees. Several bullets whirred through the nearby air. After what seemed like an eternity—but in reality was no more than a couple of minutes, they reached the wooded area and Joshua gave thanks to God that none of them had been hit and that now they at least had some measure of protection.

"Alright, let's get that bullet out." He grabbed the forceps from his surgical kit and then looked the wounded man in the eyes and took tight hold of his hand.

"Cliff, I'm not going to lie. This is going to hurt—a lot. But I've got to get that bullet out and stitch the wound. Hesitantly he nodded. Joshua looked at the orderlies silently indicating for them to take tight hold of the patient.

When he entered the bullet wound with the forceps Cliffs entire body tightened. The man's back arched as every muscle in his body tensed in reaction to the extreme pain. He screamed and swore and cursed through gritted teeth. Undaunted, Joshua continued. Just as he'd suspected, the bullet had lodged itself between Cliff's scapula and clavicle. Neither bone seemed to be broken, but the muscles of the region had been mangled and mutilated. Using the forceps, Joshua took tight hold of the bullet and then expertly removed it. Absently, Joshua held up the bullet and stared at it.

Amazing how much pain such a little piece of metal can cause. Joshua tossed away the bullet and then hurriedly began stitching the wound and then dressing it with bandages. After the ordeal he'd just been through, Cliff barely reacted at all to Joshua using a needle and surgical thread to sew up the wound. Once the wound was stitched and dressed, Joshua turned to the orderlies.

"Get him back to the field hospital and then get back here immediately."

The orderlies nodded and moved to lift the stretcher. Cliff quickly clasped Joshua's blood stained hand in his own.

"Thank you, suh… Thank you and God bless you!"

"God bless you," replied Joshua and then they took him away. Joshua wasted no time but headed back towards the fighting. It was the last place in the world he wanted to go, but there were more wounded men that needed him. As he headed back towards the stone wall he noticed that the incoming fire had seemed to slacken considerably. Looking ahead most of the advancing enemy troops could no longer be seen. Either they had withdrawn or they were now in the shadow of San Juan Hill. If so then for the moment they were out of the defenders line of sight. Earlier, Joshua had heard several of the officers cursing up a storm about the poor positioning of the defenses.

But maybe they withdrew. He hoped that was the case. Either way, the young surgeon was just glad to have a few moments without bullets flying in his direction so that he could try to help the wounded without getting shot himself.

As he neared the line, he very quickly found himself in one of the worst predicaments a battle field surgeon could find himself. There were far more wounded than he could possibly treat alone and out of all the wounded he saw he had to make a choice. Taking a deep breath, and surveying all the wounded he could see he quickly tried to triage them in his mind into those beyond help, those that needed immediate attention, and those that while wounded could wait. Very few fell into that last category, and far too many fell into the first.

One man was gut shot. Joshua tried not to think about the long miserable death that awaited that man. Another man had a sucking chest wound. The man was trying to breathe but there was so much blood in his lungs and airways that he simply couldn't. Blood bubbled out of his mouth and the only sound he was able to make was a gurgling noise. Joshua's eyes came to rest on a man who had taken a bad hit in the arm. Two of his comrades were desperately trying to stop the bleeding. They weren't having much luck.

The well-meaning soldiers moved aside for Joshua as he stooped over the wounded soldier. They'd been trying to stem the bleeding with a ripped off uniform sleeve. Ordinarily putting pressure on the wound should have reduced the bleeding. The fact that the man was still bleeding profusely, showed that a major artery had been cut. If Joshua didn't act soon the man would bleed out. Wasting no time, he undid the man's belt buckle and pulled it from his trousers. He then looped it around the man's ruined arm, well above the wound, and pulled it as tightly as possible. The makeshift tourniquet did its job. The bleeding stopped. Joshua took a knife and cut a new hole in the belt and then fastened it into place. Joshua then looked around for the orderlies. They had just come into sight carrying the empty stretcher. The two orderlies hurried to Joshua's position. After placing the wounded man onto the stretcher, Joshua again sent them to the rear. He knew the poor man's troubles weren't over. After applying the tourniquet, he'd gotten a good look at the wound. The arm was ruined—the joint completely shattered. The tourniquet had temporarily saved his life, but Joshua was almost certain that they would have to amputate. Joshua started to move on to the next wounded man when suddenly Doctor Lowes came on the scene. He had several orderlies with him in tow.

"Winslow! You're done here. We'll take care of the rest. There's a big fight underway to the southwest, you're needed there!"

Joshua took a deep breath. Off to the southwest the raging fight sounded like distant firecrackers with an occasional thunderclap. He turned to his orderlies.

"Let's go."

XXVII

Sergeant Jefferson Case, felt more exhausted than he'd ever imagined possible. At one point every muscle and bone in his body had ached. Now, however, they had reached a kind of numbness and like the battle hardened veteran that he had become, Jeff had simply kept going anyway. He couldn't show any weakness to the men under his command. He'd landed in Cuba a Lance Corporal. In the short time since he'd earned himself another two stripes and more responsibility than he'd ever cared to have.

BILLY BENNETT

At the moment he and his men were resting in the soft grass off to the side of the road and under the shade of several trees. Jeff was off by himself—his back against the trunk of a large royal palm. Off in the distance the resounding noise of rifle and cannon fire served as a constant reminder that they were in the middle of a war. At the moment they didn't care. All they wanted was to get some rest while they could.

Haphazardly he reached into his canvas sack and pulled out his corncob pipe and his tobacco pouch. After striking a match and getting his pipe going, Case hesitantly reached into his uniform coat and for about the hundredth time he pulled out the letter he'd received from Biloxi. He hadn't opened it yet. It had no name or return address but with a Biloxi post mark it could only be from one person. It had to be from Ellie.

In the previous months he'd faced rifle fire, cannon fire, violent Spaniards who'd wanted nothing more than to wring his guts out with their bayonets and yet in a way this small envelope stamped with the Blood Stained Banner in one corner and an image of George Washington on horseback in the other, held more fear for him than any of those other things. He no longer knew exactly what he felt. His heart and his mind were a tempestuous storm of conflicting emotions, desires and fears. Back in Biloxi he'd been dumbstruck with Cupid's arrow. He'd been so infatuated with Ellie that he'd seen straight past her color, and at the time straight past all the consequences of her color. Every one of the thirteen Confederate States had strict laws against interracial marriage and the national government had outlawed it in the three territories that weren't states yet. Not only that but the Confederate government and all of the state governments had declared that they recognized no interracial marriage, even those granted by other nations. Richmond had even gone so far as to make it a felony for a Confederate citizen (or in the case of blacks Confederate 'permanent residents') to enter into an interracial marriage outside of the CSA. At one point he'd told Ellie he'd leave the CSA for her. If they went somewhere like Canada and married, then they could never come home. Then of course there were the social and domestic consequences. If word got out that he was involved romantically with a mulatto girl, he could be court marshalled from the Confederate States Marine Corps. That probably accounted for why the envelope had no name and no address. She was trying to protect him.

More than anything, Jeff feared his parents back in Norfolk. He knew how they'd react. They'd disown him. With all these worries baring down on him like a dark and dangerous storm, Jeff had almost resolved to forget Ellie. But there was another side to the battle raging within him. He loved her. He genuinely loved her. He'd tried to convince himself it had been nothing but physical attraction. She was gorgeous, and that last night in Biloxi she'd given herself to him in a storm of passion. Of course that was nothing that young women hadn't been giving young men going off to war since the dawn of human history. But had it been nothing but a momentary adventure, Jeff was certain he would long since have forgotten about her. But he hadn't. He loved her. One of the reasons he feared to open the letter was that he was scared she might be angry at him for not writing. While interracial marriage was outlawed, the CSA had no shortage of white men perfectly willing to bed a black girl. Ellie's existence, and her beautiful coffee and cream skin were testimonies to that fact. It struck Jeff as the height of hypocrisy that while such acts of animal like lust were turned a blind eye to, true genuine love was forbidden under penalty of law. No matter what, he didn't want Ellie to think of him as one of those men. Taking a deep breath, he moved to open the envelope.

"Sergeant!" Jeff was momentarily startled. He returned the envelope to his coat pocket and leapt to his feet. The call had come from their new platoon commander, a scrawny First Lieutenant about his own age named Jeremiah Fudge. Judging from the fine eloquent way the officer spoke, the fancy custom gold embroidery that covered his uniform, and the large feather in his broad brimmed hat, Jeff had no doubt he was one of those high born planter's sons.

Not far from Case one of the other marines quietly quipped: "Who does he think he is? Jeb Stuart?" Ordinarily such an immaculate uniform would have made Jeff believe the man hadn't been serving in the field long. But the man's boots shined radiantly. He had to have been in the field at least a few days. The only way his boots could have shined so radiantly is if they had just been shined. After weeks of campaigning across Cuba, Jeff's own uniform and those of his fellow vets were a wreck. A neutral observer might have been able to determine that they had once been a solid gray though they were now so stained from mud and grass they looked like a mottled cloth of grays and browns. He was pretty sure he hadn't shined his own boots since leaving Biloxi.

He's one of those clean fanatics. Case had heard of a few fussy officers that demanded garrison quality spit and polish even in the field. If he expected that from Jeff and his men then mentally Jeff decided that prim peacock of an officer could go to the infernal regions.

If he doesn't take that feather out of his hat a Dago is likely to send him there anyhow. While his thoughts were his own, the rest of the world was not. Jeff saluted. Lieutenant Fudge returned it and then proceeded to pull a carefully folded map out of his uniform tunic.

"The negroes are keeping the enemy busy on San Juan Hill." He then motioned to the map. "We've been ordered to launch an attack here on the enemy's flank." He looked up from the map and pointed in a southerly direction, "Our objective is that kettle shaped hill yonder."

Case didn't the like the look of "Kettle Hill." It wasn't as big as San Juan, but it was surrounded by woods and it was very steep. Fudge pointed back at the map.

"The Spanish are still holding this small village between here and our objective. It will have to be taken as well. Captain Fordice says that's our job. Get the men ready to move out." Case saluted and then went to work.

"Alright, boys, up and at them! On your feet! We've got Dagos to kill! Get moving! Make sure your ammo pouch is full then fall in! On the double! Move!" His voice held an edge of authority that hadn't been there before he'd come to Cuba. The handful of other vets knew and respected him and they got moving because of those things. The newer guys—especially the green horns—feared him. They moved with an urgency that said they thought that Jeff would shoot them if they didn't move fast enough. Still smoking his pipe, Jeff watched in satisfaction as the men snapped to it. Not for the first time, he reflected that it was the Sergeants that really kept things going.

A small squadron of cavalry rode ahead of them to scout out the village. It wasn't long at all before Jeff started hearing gunshots. He knew the cavalry squadron was armed with the latest repeating rifles. They put out a lot of firepower for their size. Still, their function was scouting, not assaults. A few moments later they came riding back. Jeff noticed that a couple of the gray clad troopers were clutching bloody wounds. A couple of men were laid across the top of their horses either dead or incapacitated. The Sergeant in command of the cavalry squadron reined in his horse and leapt from the saddle while the rest of his men trotted towards the rear. He, Jeff, and Lieutenant Fudge converged in the middle of the road to confer. The cavalry commander cursed and swore angrily.

"Yeah, they're hold up in that village alright." He then pointed at Fudge's map with a gloved hand. "They've placed a couple of wagons across the road here at the entrance to the village. There's a small church here. They've put snipers up in the bell tower, there's men hiding in the trees on both sides of the road, and they've probably got riflemen in most of the houses. Ya'll are gonna have a devil of a time routing them out."

"We'll take care of it," said Fudge. His voice radiated confidence. He turned to Jeff and spoke sternly and resolutely. "Sergeant, you will take half the platoon into the trees on the west side of the road while I take the other half on the east side. We will converge on the village like a pincer. I want it cleared within the hour."

"Yes, sir." After saluting, Jeff quickly took a few last precious puffs on his pipe before emptying the still burning remainder of its tobacco on the ground. As wet as it was there was little chance of it starting a fire but nonetheless he stamped them out with his boot. Jeff then stowed his pipe, grabbed his Richmond rifle, and detailed off his half of the platoon.

After taking his men into the woods, Jeff swung far to the west. The rattle of gunfire from the east reached his ears far quicker than it should have.

Either Lieutenant Fudge didn't swing far enough east, or there's a lot more dagos on that side then there are over here... Jeff was reasonably certain which was correct. Like most enlisted men, he questioned the common sense and general intelligence of anyone with one or two bars on his collar. If an officer lived long enough to make it to Major or above chances were he was smart enough. Captains were a mixed lot. As far as Lieutenants…well…it was common knowledge they were all idiots.

Jeff's party hit the Spanish troops defending the entrance to the village in the flank hard. There weren't near as many as he was expecting. It was apparent that Fudge's attack had drawn off several. What defenders remained, found themselves ambushed and overwhelmed. A few tried to fall back to the village, but were gunned down as they fled. Jeff led his men over their bloody sky-blue clad bodies. They emerged from the woods due west of the entrance to the village. The Spaniards there were waiting on them. The gunfight in the woods had let the defenders know in no uncertain terms they were about to have trouble from the west. As the scouts had said, the Spaniards had positioned a couple of wagons across the road to serve as cover. Unfortunately for them, they hadn't had time to reposition them to account for the Confederate attack on their flanks. Jeff brought his squads to a halt right inside the tree line so they could enjoy a small measure of cover. From behind a tree trunk, he worked the bolt on his Richmond rifle, leveled it at a sky blue target and pulled the trigger. A Spaniard crumpled over. Jeff worked the bolt on his rifle and fired again. The others followed his lead. Together they sent a hail of bullets at the enemy. It was apparent that they had the defenders outnumbered, nonetheless the Spaniards—those that were still alive at any rate— held their ground. But when Jeff and his men let out a screeching Rebel Yell which was answered by another screeching Rebel Yell from off to the east, the remaining Spanish infantry abandoned their position and fell back into the town.

The two Confederate forces converged on the wagons. To Jeff's surprise, Fudge was still alive. His eyes darted quickly to the church bell tower. Fudge's gaudy uniform may not have gotten him killed in the cover of the trees, but he would be a prime target for the sniper up in that tower. Jeff may have questioned Fudges brains, but a moment later he found he couldn't question his courage. The officer with the feather in his hat pointed his pistol at the enemy held village and shouted: "Let's clear them out boys!" He then charged, confident his men would follow. Case acted quickly.

"Smokey, you and your squad keep fire on that tower! Tiger, you boys come with me."

Fresh Rebel Yell's sounded from the attacking Confederates like the howls of a pack of wolves on the hunt. Case expected shots from the tower and the windows of the small huts but none materialized. A few shots came from the tree line to the south of the town, but these were simply in parting. The Spanish had withdrawn. As Jeff's eyes once again surveyed the Kettle Shaped Hill to the south, he decided he didn't blame them. If he was outnumbered and had to make a stand, he'd much rather do it on a hill like that than in a small vulnerable village.

It wouldn't be long before they would join the main attack on Kettle Hill. Until then their orders were to hold their position in the village. Case had no problem with that.

The Cuban villagers seemed glad to have the Spanish gone, though they regarded the newly arrived Confederates with a great deal of fear and uncertainty. All Case saw were women, children, and old geezers. He supposed all the men of fighting age were off somewhere bushwhacking Spaniards. That also suited Jeff just fine. After posting a few unlucky greenhorns to guard duty, Jeff ordered his men to once again snatch what rest they could in the short time they had. He found himself a comfy spot under a tree on the northwest side of the village and when he was once again settled and smoking his corncob, he pulled out the letter and opened it.

Dear Jeff. I need to tell you something. I...we...are going to have a baby... I'm so scared. I don't know what I'm gonna do. I don't know what to do. I know you at war. I pray for you evr'y day. I pray to Jesus you come back. I also pray the baby look more like you. Write me soon please. I loves you. I miss you. Love Ellie...

Reading the letter, Jeff felt as though his heart had stopped. Afterwards he'd felt as if he'd been hit by a freight train at full speed. At first he was mad at himself. He knew that actions had consequences and that night of passion and love with Ellie had come with one doozy of a consequence. Then suddenly his anger gave way to fear. How would she take care of a baby? How would the locals react? *Not well,* was his answer to the latter. As scared as he was, he could tell from her letter that she was terrified, and not just by the baby. The writing was wobbly, as though her hand had shook as she wrote. He could also read between the lines. *I pray you come back...* He had no doubt she hoped he survived the war but she also prayed he didn't go on with his life and pretend she never existed. Far too many men had done that in history, especially white men in the south who'd put a colored girl in a family way. As scared as Jeff was he didn't think of going that rout for so much as a second.

I also pray the baby look more like you. More often than not, a baby of mixed heritage was plain for all the world to see. Every so often one would come out full white. Ellie was a mulatto herself. At only one-quarter black, the baby had a better chance than normal of coming out white. As many doors and opportunities as that would open up, part of Jeff hoped the baby looked like Ellie. Her beauty along with her gentleness and sweetness was one of the things he loved about her.

Jeff wanted to write her right then and there. Unfortunately at the moment there was no time. When Jeff moved out with his men a few minutes later, he did so with new resolve. His exhaustion and fatigue was forgotten. No matter what, he had to survive. In his heart he made a promise both to Ellie and the child growing in her womb... *I will come back to you. If God keeps me alive, I will come back.*

XXVIII

Once again Antonio Vega's heart pounded as he knew that he was once again about to lay his life on the line for Holy Espana. He'd come perilously close to death far too many times now. He'd barely survived the attack on Havana. He'd been driven from Cuba's northern shore to its southern shore by Confederate forces. He and his men had suffered the scourge of Cuban guerillas. They'd crossed treacherous and crocodile infested swamps, and endured bombardment by Confederate warships on an open beach.

After the fiasco at Cienfuegos, they'd been put on one of the most rickety transports he'd ever seen. The Spanish navy called it a ship. In reality it had been little more than a leaky steamboat. He and his men had been crammed inside like sardines in a can. Together with two other similarly dangerous ships they had steamed east along Cuba's southern shore. They'd left at night. Once the sun was up they enjoyed good luck—until a few hours before sun down when the small flotilla had come under fire from Confederate gunboats. The enemy ironclads had sunk the other two Spanish transports from Cienfuegos. They went to the bottom with their crews and all the troops they'd been carrying. Antonio's transport had beached itself to avoid the same fate and all the troops had managed to get off and move inland before the slow moving Confederate gunboats had moved in to finish them off. Fortunately they had landed only a mere twenty miles west of their destination. They'd marched at the double time and arrived in the outskirts of Santiago de Cuba just in time to face the advancing Confederate Army that was moving in to lay siege to the city.

Antonio and his men were now stationed atop a large steep hill. To the northeast the Confederates had attacked another nearby hill being defended by foreign mercenaries in the service of Spain. Antonio was uncertain what to think of them at first. For him his duty as a soldier of Spain was no less than a duty to Almighty God. He therefore distrusted anyone who fought for money.

How can you trust someone whose loyalty can be bought?

But when he saw from his elevated position how the mercenaries withstood the Confederate assault, he could not deny their courage. Having apparently being repulsed from that attack, the Confederados now seemed to be preparing for an assault on the smaller but steeper hill which Antonio and his men occupied along with several other units of the Spanish army. Confederate shells had been screaming in for several minutes. Though Antonio and his men had thrown themselves flat (only and idiot would remain standing during a bombardment if he didn't have to) he wanted to laugh at its effectiveness. The shore bombardment he had endured on the La Cabana and then later on the beach east of Cienfuegos had been like being in the pit of hell itself. This by contrast was…

Mediocre…

The Confederate preparatory bombardment was not entirely ineffective. Not far away cries of pain erupted from a soldiers lip's just as another shell came screaming in. Antonio would have bet every peseta he had the poor bastardo hadn't been taking cover like he should have been.

Unfortunately the Confederates were quite punctual with their attack. No sooner had the screams of incoming artillery shells ceased than a new shrieking noise reached Antonio's ears. Rebel yells resounded through the air. They put Antonio in mind of wild Indians or fierce mountain lions. He gazed down the slope of the hill to see what must have been over one-thousand gray uniformed Confederates surging up at them.

"Open fire!"

Rifle shots resounded up and down the crest of the hill as the Spaniards fired their Mausers and sent a deadly hail of led at the oncoming Confederate troops. The Confederates returned fire in kind as they advanced but as they were attacking very high ground the Spaniards had the advantage. What the Confederates did have, however, were a lot of guns. More than once a bullet slammed into the ground near to where Antonio was perched or else flew above his head. To his left and right several of his men weren't so lucky, taking hits in the head, throat, shoulder or arm.

Antonio emptied the magazine on his Mauser then worked furiously to reload it. He fired again and again, each time working the bolt on the rifle to chamber the next round. By the time the Confederates were half way up the slope Antonio had emptied his magazine again. The ground behind the advancing gray coats was littered with bloody corpses and wounded and writhing men. But to Antonio's chagrin the enemy had the numbers to take such brutal casualties and seemed determined enough to press on with the attack. He estimated glumly that by the time the enemy reached the crest of the hill they would more or less be equal with Spanish defenders holding it.

Antonio fired furiously, once again emptying his rifle. By the time he had started reloading the Confederates had nearly made it up the hill. Fresh Rebel yells reached his ears like Panther screams.

"Bayonets! Fix Bayonets!" cried Antonio. He finished reloading his rifle and managed to squeeze off four more shots before leaping to his feet to meet the oncoming enemy. A Confederate lunged at him with his bayoneted rifle. Antonio shot him in the chest and then dodged the oncoming blade which almost instantly went crashing to the ground with its late owner's body. Antonio came about and shot another gray coat. He turned again and found a Confederate charging wildly at him. Antonio took aim and pulled the trigger but the Mauser didn't fire. He wasn't sure whether it had jammed or had run out of ammo. In any event, he didn't have time to figure it out at that very moment. He used his rifle to deflect the bayonet thrust of the Confederate soldier. He followed up the deflection with at thrust of his own right at the gray coats head. Antonio's blade ripped into the side of the man's face cutting a blood spattering hideous wound and ripping back a whole section of flesh. Wasting no time Antonio thrust again this time stabbing the Confederate in the throat. No sooner had he killed the enemy soldier then he spun around alert and ready to face the next attacker but this time none came at him. He allowed himself to take a deep breath and look around. Suddenly he heard a bugle sound. By the tune and pitch he knew it was a Spanish bugle, what he didn't understand was why it was sounding.

Not far away, Captain Perez also understood what it meant.

"What coward sounded retreat!"

Antonio quickly surveyed the line to the left and right. Sure enough in their section they had held off the Confederates and blunted their attack. Elsewhere along the line however...

"Look our forces a hundred yards that way are being pushed back... their line is collapsing..."

Perez cursed profanely. "If we don't fall back we'll be attacked in the flank or surrounded.

Antonio let loose a curse of his own then cried out to his company.

"Fall back!"

Obediently they did so, and sent a few volleys of fire to the left to make sure that the Confederates didn't flank them. The Spaniards fell back a little over a hundred yards then turned to face the enemy just behind the reverse crest of the hill. Off to the left, their countrymen that had given way to the enemy were rallying underneath the La Rojigualda. To the rear, a column of fresh, sky-blue uniformed Spaniards were coming up. A ferocious smile spread across Antonio's face.

We're about to counterattack. Up ahead, the Confederate advance had ceased. Having gained the top of the hill, the remaining Confederados seemed content to hold it. A large Confederate Battle Flag was being held aloft as a signal to those in the Confederate rear that the hill had been taken.

A few moments later the Spaniards let loose with a battle cry of their own, one that dated back all the way to the days of the Reconquista and that perfectly fit the city the Spanish army was presently defending.

"Santiago! Santiago y cierra, Espana! Santiago!" Antonio roared it along with all of his countrymen. Then with bayonets still fixed and their rifles fully loaded, the Spaniards charged forward ferociously. The Confederates holding the crest of the hill opened fire at the oncoming Spanish troops. A few of the gray coats turned and ran after firing only a few shots at the attackers but most courageously stood their ground despite the juggernaut coming at them.

Once again the fighting atop the hill entered into a phase of bloody melee. Out of the corner of his eye, Antonio saw a Confederate stab Captain Perez in the chest with his bayoneted rifle.

"No!" Antonio spun around, brought up his rifle and fired. A fountain of blood erupted from the Confederados throat and he fell over dead. Antonio rushed to Perez's side. The bayonet wound in his chest was gruesome. The Confederate bayonet had been notched. As such it hadn't come out clean but had ripped out huge chunks, of skin, muscle, bone and organ tissue, leaving an enormous gaping hole in his chest. He was dead in less than a minute. Antonio used his fingers to close his comrade's eyes. He then rose to his feet and again charged at the Confederates who had now begun to retreat back down the northern slope and towards the tree line from which they had come. The Spaniards were not merely content to retake the top of the hill. They crossed the summit and pursued the fleeing Confederates down the slope. Further north Confederate artillery hastily opened up on them but the new bombardment was totally sporadic. A few shells exploded into the Spanish troops chasing the Confederates down the hill but the CS artillery fire was largely ineffective.

Suddenly from down below a new cry reached Antonio's ears. It was similar to the Rebel Yell, but somehow different. It seemed deeper, but no less ferocious. All at once fresh Confederate troops erupted out of the tree line at the base of the hill and began charging up the slope. The Confederates were now counter attacking the Spanish counter attack. These Confederates, however, were negroes. Up the hill they charged with guns blazing and bayonets fixed. Above them the Southern Cross of the Confederate Battle Flag fluttered defiantly. As it had before the pendulum swung the other way. The Spanish attack came to a screeching halt and within a few moments had reversed into a retreat.

Antonio didn't want to fall back again, but he was once again cognizant enough to know that his unit could not hold off the enemy alone. The Spaniards withdrew to the top of the hill then turned to hold their ground no matter the cost. At that point the entire hill was soaked in blood and littered with the dead and dying of both sides. Suddenly more artillery shells came screaming in and exploded amongst the Spanish defenders.

Antonio gripped his Mauser tightly, ready to fight the oncoming Confederate negroes to the death. Suddenly the same familiar and lamentable bugle call that he had heard earlier sounded again. Antonio let out a deep sigh then called to his men.

"Fall back!"

He took one last pot shot at the oncoming wave of gray uniformed negroes then fell back with his men, cursing the day, and officers who had finally yielded the hill to the enemy after expending so much blood and treasure to hold it.

XXIX

Joshua Winslow's personal tour of hell had yet to come to an end. The Confederates had thrown even more forces against the slopes of Kettle Hill then they had against San Juan Hill only a short distance away. They had also, Joshua noted, paid a much higher price in blood. Like the resolute soldiers of the Spanish Foreign Legion on San Juan Hill, elements of the Spanish Army itself had stood atop their own blood drench pile of earth to defend it against the gray tide. Unlike the foreign soldiers of fortune in their employ, however, the Spanish had given way.

Joshua went from wounded man to wounded man. Sometimes he could help, sometimes he couldn't. Several times he applied tourniquets that, if they stayed in place, would probably keep the poor miserable souls he tied them on from bleeding to death. Sometimes there was nothing he could do. Some were just wounded beyond the help of medical science. He gave them morphine until he ran out.

Joshua was as confused as ever about the situation. The Spaniards had held the hill, the Confederates had kicked them off. Then the Spanish had counterattacked and retaken the hill. Both sides had spilled an ocean's worth of blood in the exchange. To Joshua that was more than enough butchery for one day if not for a lifetime. The Generals had disagreed with him. The Confederates had thrown in their reserves. To Joshua's everlasting chagrin those reserves had been composed of Confederate negroes. As it had on San Juan

Hill, seeing the black soldiers clad in the gray of the Confederate Army, rocked Joshua to the core. One of the reasons he was there as a part of the Spanish Foreign Legion was to contribute in some small way to what he hoped would be their eventual freedom. To every negro Joshua had ever known, anything that hurt the CSA or stood in its way was a blow for the freedom for those still held in chains within its borders. He couldn't understand how these gray clad negroes could fight for the Confederate States as they were.

The Confederacy can't really be offering them freedom can they? He knew that's what Richmond was saying, but he couldn't believe it. But the fact that hundreds of negroes had, under the banner of the Southern Cross, charged so gallantly and ferociously up San Juan Hill and Kettle Hill into the face of rifles, machine guns, and cannons, argued powerfully against his presuppositions. You didn't give guns to a people you intended to deceive and keep in chains. The CSA had not only given negroes guns they sent them to kill other white men. To most of the white people in the CSA, who were predominantly Anglo Celtic Protestants, the Spanish were a bunch of swarthy Catholic Dagos but they were still white European people. Black men who killed white men would never forget it and they would know and remember that if they could kill Spanish white men the white men of the CSA could be opposed and killed too. Part of keeping a slave a slave was keeping a sense of inferiority in the slave's mind. After what it had equipped, trained, and allowed its black veterans to do, the CSA was likely to pay a heavy price if they did indeed intend on double crossing them. If the CSA actually intended to keep its promise of granting its negro veterans freedom then...

Then what am I and the other negroes from the USA here for? What are we fighting for? It sure wasn't for Spain. As much as he loved his country, it wasn't for the United States either. All things now considered, the Confederate States' grievance with Spain appeared to be no business of the United States at least not in Joshua's eyes—not if slavery wasn't going to be returned to the island. Not if the war meant the emancipation of thousands of negro Confederate veterans. It wouldn't be the final end of slavery in the

Confederate States, but Joshua had a hard time seeing how it wouldn't be a major blow to a system that—God willing—was on its last miserable leg.

The Confederate negroes had driven the Spaniards from Kettle Hill. They had carried the Confederate Battle Flag to the top and with it claimed the massive blood soaked, body littered pile of earth for the Confederacy. Shortly afterwards the Spaniards had tried to take it back a second time. This time they failed.

Joshua hadn't fallen back with his own side—if the sky-blue clad soldiers could really been called that. He'd been in the midst of trying to save a wounded Spaniard's life. The man had been shot in the head but miraculously the skull had deflected the blow. Whether it was the angle of impact, the slow velocity of a bullet that had been spent or both, the young Spanish soldier was alive. If Joshua had anything to say about it he would stay that way.

The white arm band that Joshua wore meant that, according to the so-called rules of war, he was a non-combatant. He could not legally be fired upon intentionally or taken prisoner in the course of his duties. Of course bullets and artillery shells made no such distinctions. Joshua had already lost one of his orderlies. His other assistant, white armband with red-cross or no, had fled at the approach of the Confederates.

Trusting to God, his armband, and the fact that he was unarmed and huddled over a wounded man, Joshua worked frantically to save the soldier's life. A few of the Confederate negroes stared at him in wonder as they made their way past but none of them bothered him. They clearly understood what he was and they had more pressing concerns, like keeping the Spanish from retaking the hill. Ignoring the still roaring sounds of rifle and cannon fire, Joshua went about his work. The bullet had ripped open the man's scalp. He looked as if an Indian had started to scalp him but close to halfway through hadn't finished with the job. Through the ripped up flesh and blood matted hair, the white of the skull could have been seen had it not been for the massive amount of blood. No major artery had been opened, but the thousands of capillaries in the scalp delivered an incredible amount of blood.

Joshua skillfully stitched the man's scalp back together. In one sense he was glad the poor devil was unconscious. But Joshua also feared the tremendous blow he'd received to the head may have cause internal damage. The sheer force of the impact alone could have killed him. It easily could have caused bleeding on the brain. If so the man was doomed. Despite his extensive study on board the Capricorn, Joshua simply wasn't equipped to try such a procedure in the field. Afterward he dressed the wound and that was the end of all he could do. The young Spanish soldier would either live or he wouldn't.

Breathing heavily, Joshua rose to his feet and wiped sweat from his black skinned brow with his blood covered hands. For the moment most of the Confederate negroes had moved several yards to the south to give the retreating Spaniards one last kick to let them know they were whipped. Joshua saw that there were no Confederate medics on the scene—at least none that he could see. It was a big area and he had learned in gruesome detail that war could wound, maim, and mangle men far quicker than medics could tend to them. He also found himself hoping that when Confederate medics arrived they would be willing to take the wounded Spaniard to one of their field hospitals. With all the fighting to the south it would be virtually impossible to get him through the lines.

Joshua scanned the area looking for more wounded. As he surveyed the north slope of the hill, he was overwhelmed by the sheer number of gray clad bodies (both black and white), that littered the face of the hill. The Confederates had paid a heavy price for taking the it. Several yards away and downhill, Joshua caught a glimmer of movement amongst the still bodies. A wounded Confederate negro was painfully trying crawl back towards the Confederate lines. Joshua moved like lightning to get to him. He was so in earnest, that in his haste to reach the wounded Confederate soldier, he blocked out most of the rest of the world. He was therefore taken completely by surprise when he was challenged by an angry voice.

"Hold it right there, nigger!"

Slowly and surely Joshua turned around with his hands raised. He found himself staring down the barrel of a Richmond Rifle and facing a squad of grim looking white Confederates. After weeks of being in the field their uniforms were more brown than gray. Their kepis and trim, however, were a dark blue. The fellow who at that moment had the rifle leveled right at his head also wore a pair of dark blue chevrons on his uniform coat. Joshua spoke slowly and respectfully.

"Sir, I am a field surgeon. A non-combatant. I was about to give aid to one of your own soldiers." Ever so slightly Joshua motioned with his head and eyes towards the wounded Confederate negro. He didn't motion to the arm band on his arm but he caught the grimy corporal looking at it. Whether it was the arm band, Joshua's educated speech or both, he watched the jaws on the white southern men drop. The corporal cursed himself and uttered a blasphemy at the same time.

"That nigger talks better'n you do, Tiger! He must be from England." He pronounced it, Angland. Tiger wasn't amused.

"I say we take him back to the rear."

"Come on, Tiger, it aint likes he's carrying a gun."

"He could be a spy! I don't care how fancy he talks. There's no way a nigger'd ever be smart enough to be a doctor! I'd sure as hell never let one near me!" He then blasphemed again and said: "Might as well be a monkey!" When he turned to regard Joshua again he had murder in his eyes. Joshua feared at the slightest provocation, (or none at all) the man might happily kill him.

Please Jesus, get me out of this! Please. No sooner had he sent his prayer heavenward, then another Confederate arrived on the scene. To Joshua's great disappointment, it wasn't an officer though from the three stripes on the fellow's shoulder he could tell he was a Sergeant. The Confederate Sergeant was as filthy as his men. He wore a broad brimmed black hat that covered a shock of red hair. Joshua also noticed that he wore a bloody make shift bandage over his right arm.

"What's going on here?" growled the newly arrived non-com.

"We got ourselves a nigger prisoner!" declared Tiger.

The Sergeant looked straight at Joshua's armband.

"Looks like a field medic to me. Orders are we leave them alone and they leave ours alone."

Joshua felt his soul flood with relief. Tiger was dumfounded.

"But...but...but...he's......HE'S A NIGGER!"

To Joshua's surprise the Sergeant looked not only indifferent but also angry at the Corporal's so called logic. The senior non-com's face grew stern and his voice took on a hard edge.

"General Lee has ordered that all enemy soldiers, including negroes, are to be treated according to the rules of war. Those rules say he's off limits. Now get down that hill and kill some more dagos or I'll personally shoot your sorry hide myself."

With a look of absolute disgust Tiger tore himself away and tramped south towards the fighting. His comrades went with him and teased him as they did so.

"Hey Tiger, if anyone's dumber than a monkey it's you!"

"Shut the..." The enraged Corporal cursed and swore profanely. His comrades just bellowed hoarse laughter.

"Thank you, Sergeant! Thank you," said Joshua. And he meant it. Did he ever.

"You just go about your business. My company commander was just saying there's talk of a temporary truce to gather the wounded. If so that aught to give you a chance to get back to your own side. Till then be careful. I mean real careful, you understand me?"

"I will, sir, I will." Joshua needed no reminding but was intrigued the Confederate Sergeant seemed genuinely concerned for his safety. He looked at the Sergeant's wounded arm. He was wearing a pathetic excuse for a bandage but it was about as well as a wounded man could tie on his own. "If you like, sir, I can bandage that properly."

The sergeant, seemingly startled at the very thought, all but leapt away from him, as abruptly as if Joshua had the bubonic plague.

"That won't be necessary," he said awkwardly. "There's plenty of others that…need your attention." With that, the Confederate Sergeant turned and followed after his men. Ever so slightly Joshua shook his head. The sergeant had seemed so much more reasonable than the ignorant hicks under his command. But it seemed even he would rather risk death than allow a negro surgeon to treat him. Joshua hoped it didn't get infected, he sincerely did. He sent a quick prayer to heaven for the Confederate Sergeant that had gotten him out of his predicament, and then hurried towards the soldier he'd originally intended to treat.

The Confederate negro's crawl had ceased. Joshua rushed to him and carefully turned him over. He had been shot in both legs. He had three bullets in the right upper leg and one in the left shin. The only way Joshua figured he'd managed that was that he'd been cut down by fire from a Maxim machine gun. The man had lost a lot of blood, but apparently no major arteries had been cut. He'd have bled out much earlier if that had been the case.

"Is you a Spanish nigga?" asked the gray clad negro as Joshua hurriedly applied make shift tourniquets to the man's legs—one using the man's belt and the other using the strap from his ammo box.

"I'm a surgical student from the United States," said Joshua. "I'm serving as a field medic for the Spanish Foreign Legion."

"A nigga doctor…" said the man. "I sho done seen everything now!" The man smiled and even tried to laugh. But Joshua knew he was far from being out of the woods. "You need to rest. I've done all I can for you here. We need to get you back to… your own side's hospital." The man nodded. Joshua was about to move on to try and find another wounded man but then before he did he asked he wounded black Confederate the question that had been haunting him.

"Why are you here? I mean why are you fighting?"

"Fo' my freedom." He said it in a tone that indicated he thought the question absurd and the answer obvious. Yes, the Confederate negroes had been promised freedom.

But will they get it? Looking at how hard they fought, Joshua concluded that they believed they would.

But only time will tell…

XXX

The red and gold Spanish tricolor still flew defiantly over Santiago de Cuba. The warships blockading her harbor, however, flew the Confederate Blood Stained Banner. As he stood on the deck of the HMS Dasher, Charles Landon wondered whether those ships would shell the city now that the Confederate army—in large part thanks to Whitmore's Legion—had failed to capture it.

Not if I succeed in my purpose.

The Dasher had steamed from Jamaica at the head of a small fleet of freighters. In addition to the late Capricorn's two sister ships, there were ten other freighters that were much older. Landon had commandeered every civilian and merchant marine British ship in Kingston that he could lay hands on in the name of the Crown. Many of the Captains and owners had put up a fuss. But Landon had the full authority of the Admiralty behind him and with the promise of adequate monetary compensation had had no real trouble.

The British destroyer had made the short trip to Cuba from Jamaica smoothly enough, though Landon would not have wanted to cross the mighty Atlantic on the small ship. He would have preferred a larger, heavier ship, but a cruiser or certainly a battleship would have been far to intimidating for his purpose. The 195 foot destroyer boasted a single twelve pounder gun and three torpedo tubes. It was enough for Landon to show Britain's flag without raising the suspicions of the Confederates or alarming them.

Landon had told the Confederate admiral in command of the blockading ships that he'd been sent by the British government to evacuate any British civilians that might be trapped in the city (not that he knew of any) and if possible negotiate the withdrawal of the British members of the Spanish Foreign Legion. Landon had even hinted at the possibility of negotiating a deal whereby the Spanish might declare Santiago de Cuba an open city.

Thanks to British war correspondents serving in Cuba, Landon was in possession of very recent news from the island. The news was telegraphed from Cuba to the British Ministry in Richmond, from their it was forwarded to the British Ministry in Mexico City, from British Honduras and from there to Landon at Jamaica. From these cables Landon had learned that the Confederate invasion of Cuba had finally run into its first real obstacle. Thanks in no small part to Whitmore and his men, the Confederates had suffered massive casualties in their attempts to take the last major Spanish stronghold on the island. If the Confederates wanted the city, it would cost them yet more lives and the fighting would likely leave the city in ruins. The CSA wanted the port city intact. They also wanted to conserve the limited manpower of their army. When Landon had showed up and even hinted at the possibility of a negotiated deal whereby the Spanish might be convinced to give up the city without a fight the Confederates had jumped at the chance. Even if the Spanish refused, if Landon carried away just Whitmore's Legion it would make taking the city that much easier. The back and forth with the Confederate admiral had taken a while, but now Landon was steaming into Santiago. He only hoped that the speed of modern communications didn't end up working against him. By all appearances the Confederates with whom he'd been dealing had no knowledge of the impending French invasion of Puerto Rico. Landon didn't know if that was because the French had kept it from their ally, or because Richmond had failed to keep its forces in Cuba appraised. One thing Landon knew. Time was of the essence.

The news that a British warship had steamed past the Confederate blockade and into Santiago harbor spread quickly. A Union Jack normally flew at the stern of the destroyer. Landon had ordered a much larger version hoisted up the forward mast. He didn't want the garrisons of the Spanish forts guarding the entrance to the harbor mistaking them for a Confederate vessel. More to the point he did care to be blown out of the water before he could identify himself. Once safely within the large harbor the Dasher raised signal flags to announce that they were carrying a special British envoy. Landon was therefore not surprised to find himself greeted at the pier by two Spanish naval officers. Both men were in their mid-fifties. One introduced himself as Admiral Pascual Topete and the other as Captain Fernando Villaamil. Topete was the commander of Spain's Caribbean fleet. The

Captain was giving the Dasher an appreciative look. Landon had read reports that Spain had been negotiating with British shipbuilders to construct some modern destroyers for the Spanish fleets. Perhaps someday those plans would come to fruition. One way or another Landon knew they'd do them no good here.

After announcing his intentions, the Spanish navy men took him to the Alcade's mansion which General Valeriano Weyler had made his headquarters. As they rode through the city in a landau, Landon noted the strong contrast between the city's décor and the disposition of its inhabitants. The La Rojigualda seemed to fly or hang from nearly every building of prominence. The Cuban inhabitants of the city, however, were anything but patriotic about still belonging to an empire that they loathed. One way or another, Landon was certain it was a situation that would soon change. From the glares they gave the coach as it made its way through the streets of Santiago, it seemed they might not be patient enough to wait. If it hadn't been for all the armed Spanish soldiers stationed throughout the city the population would probably have already rebelled against their Spanish masters. Several of the Spanish soldiers worked furiously to erect barricades and other defenses. Yes, they were planning to fight for the city. It was very apparent, that most of the Spanish soldiers, however, were busy keeping an eye on the city's populous. If Landon had his way, those Spanish soldiers would soon have a far more important purpose than holding down a city of seething Cubans.

They entered the main square of Santiago. The Spanish army had turned it into an encampment. The north was dominated by an enormous double towered cathedral. Each tower was topped by golden Spanish crosses. Between the towers, a large golden statue of a winged angel stood proud and strong. It took some time. The square was crowded and they had to pass through three separate rings of guards. They made their way through the square.

The Alcade's mansion was massive. If it hadn't been for the even more massive Cathedral across from it, it would have been the dominant structure of the city center. Sky blue uniformed guards raised their Mauser rifles in salute to the

Admiral who, along with Captain Villaamil escorted him up the front steps and into the mansion.

"His Excellency, the General will see you in just a few moments, gentlemen," said the aid who sat at a not too small desk in the large foyer outside of Weyler's office. Actually it was the Alcade's office, but the governor and supreme commander of all Spanish forces in Cuba had had no compunctions about commandeering it from the city's mayor for his own use. When a few moments looked to be turning into a few minutes, Landon took a seat in a large velvet, stuffed arm chair. He'd long ago ceased to be a young man. He'd been in the service of the admiralty for decades, and though he could have retired years earlier, he loathed the idea of putting up with the idleness and mediocrity of retirement. All the trips, assignments, and long hours were hard on him. But he felt uselessness, not overwork, would be his utter undoing.

The room was well furnished. When the Admiral and the Captain also realized that it was going to be a longer wait than they'd been led to believe they also took seats. If they were put off by being made to wait they gave no sign. From all Landon had heard, Weyler was the kind of man who would have no problem keeping people waiting. He'd see them when he was ready. The entire mansion was the epitome of luxury. As he'd made his way down the corridors he'd seen beautiful paintings and elegant tapestries. The foyer in which they sat had a large tapestry depicting a group of stallions charging across a plain with green hills in the distance. He supposed it was supposed to help remind the Alcade of home.

After nearly half an hour, Landon suddenly heard a familiar voice echoing through the corridors of the mansion.

"I tell you, there'd better be a darned good explanation for pulling me off of the front lines at a time like this!" Landon allowed himself a smile as he recognized the man's voice and the sharp smack of his cane against the mansions beautiful hard wood floor.

"I'm sure the General has a reason, sir," replied another familiar voice. Landon rose to his feet just as Joseph Whitmore entered the foyer flanked by his assistant and a

Spanish General. At that point the naval officers also rose to their feet.

The sight of Landon standing there brought Whitmore up short. At last he said: "I'm not sure what I expected, but I sure wasn't expecting you."

"It's good to see you too, General Whitmore. I'm pleased to see you're still well."

"Yeah, I'm none the worse for wear. I take it this little get together has something to do with you."

"Yes, indeed. And the matters we discussed on the voyage here."

"Ahh," said Whitmore and left it at that. Landon hoped that was a good sign. On the Capricorn Whitmore had been adamantly opposed to the course of action the British government was proposing. Now that he'd had time to stew on it, and to satisfy his craving to kill Confederates and then some, he hoped that he'd be more open to reason. In New York, Sir Julian Pauncefote had managed to convince US President Grover Cleveland. But Whitmore was a private individual, for all intents a mercenary with no official connections to the US government. If he didn't want to play along, especially if the local Spanish officers didn't prove reasonable themselves, there would be virtually nothing that Landon could do about it.

"So what are we waiting for?" Without further preamble, Whitmore strode to the desk where General Weyler's assistant sat reviewing reports. Out of all the worlds millions of people there were very few that Whitmore would ever allow to keep him waiting. General Weyler was not one of them. As he approached the desk he cleared his throat loudly.

"Ahem…"

When the assistant didn't look up quickly enough to suit Whitmore he took his cane and loudly tapped it on the man's desk. That did the trick.

"The General will see you shortly, Senor."

Whitmore pointed the tip of his cane less than a foot from the man's face.

"He can see us now, by Jove. There's a blasted war on. We haven't got time to sit around. Now you either show us in, or I'll bang on the door until the General himself lets us in."

The stunned clerk must have thought he meant it. Landon was pretty sure he did. Not far away a nervous looking David Lovejoy certainly did. When the overrated secretary moved to open the door to the General's office, Landon smiled—at Whitmore's very American audacity and brazenness.

General Valeriano Weyler looked up from his desk in confusion as Whitmore all but pushed his way into the room. Weyler let loose a torrent of angry Spanish at the clerk who promptly raised his hands as though helpless and then sheepishly replied with a string of his own Spanish. Weyler waved the clerk out then rose from his seat to regard Whitmore and the others who had followed him in.

"You wanted to see us, General."

Weyler glared down at Whitmore. The General was well over a foot taller than the American millionaire, especially since he had the stoop of an elderly man. Whitmore wasn't intimidated. He'd faced bigger cats, and skinned them too.

After a brief but tense moment, Weyler seemed to relax and slowly but surely his face grew less dark. He turned to face Landon and spoke in heavily accented English.

"You I take it are the British envoy?"

"I am," replied Landon.

"Then perhaps you would do us the courtesy of telling us why you are here."

"Your excellency, I have come for a number of reasons. First and foremost I have come to warn you that a large force of French ships are preparing to leave Veracruz on a mission to capture Puerto Rico."

"Santa Maria!" declared Admiral Topete.

Weyler didn't flinch.

"Mr. Whitmore has already passed this information to me."

The Admiral suddenly looked daggers at the General. Apparently Weyler hadn't seen fit to inform him.

"Did he also inform you that the United States was seeking to purchase the island from your King with the full blessing and approval of Her Majesty's government?"

Not far away Whitmore fumed ever so slightly. As far as he was concerned the United States needed no other nation's approval or blessing to do what it wanted. But Whitmore didn't fume long. He knew what Landon meant. The US wanted to buy Puerto Rico and Landon was letting it be known that the most powerful empire on earth wanted the sale to go through.

"He mentioned the possibility," replied Weyler. "Inconsecuente! Su Majestad would never sell off a piece of our beloved country."

"I would not be so sure of that," said Landon. "King Leopold has promised to give the matter due consideration and, if I may be blunt, you are going to lose the island anyway, whether the French Empire steals it or you sell it to the United States. At least with the latter you gain a profit and salvage something from your lost empire. I do not wish to throw salt on a wound, but Puerto Rico is hardly your largest concern. In Africa the French have already taken the Spanish Sahara from you. In the Pacific they have invaded the Philippines. Spain itself is threatened. Reports from Europe indicate there is fierce fighting all along the Pyrenes. And need I remind you, the Confederates have virtually conquered Cuba. You and this city are surrounded on both land and sea."

Weyler's face once again began to grow dark. He looked the British envoy in the face.

"Is that all?" he asked in a cold icy voice.

Landon took a deep breath.

"I have also come to offer British mediation. Specifically I would like to negotiate your withdrawal from this city. You declare Santiago an open city, call a cease fire with the Confederates and relocate your fleet and land forces to Puerto Rico. Chances are if and when Leopold decides to sell, it will be too late for US forces to take possession of the island before the French arrive. If your fleet and army are there it will stand a much better chance of holding off the French until the US and British forces arrive."

"That's all very well and good for Britain and the United States," said Weyler. "But why should our soldiers and sailors fight and die just so you can take possession of the land they fight to defend?"

"In the first place, if Puerto Rico falls to the French, Spain will receive no compensation. But more importantly, if you manage to keep the island out of French hands long enough for the sale to be finalized and US and British forces to arrive and take possession, you will have dealt France and the Confederacy a harder blow than any you can hope to achieve by remaining here."

"How so?" From the tone of his voice, Weyler didn't think that last claim likely. Landon drove the point home anyway.

"Puerto Rico is situated perfectly to command virtually every sea lane in this part of the world most especially those leading to the canal that the French and Confederates have been building in Panama. The US is perfectly suited militarily and economically to build a major naval base in Puerto Rico and if the need ever arises to put it to great use against the French and the Confederates." Landon didn't have to connect the dots any further for Weyler to understand that if the cold war brewing between the more powerful nations of Europe and North America ever turned hot, having Puerto Rico would allow the US to project its naval power into the Caribbean and would also strengthen the Royal Navy's position there too. I can also tell you, unofficially of course, that there is a place for Spain in this new alliance that Britain and the United States are taking the lead in forming. Help us now, and perhaps one day we will be able to help you get back some of what is yours from both France and the Confederate States."

Instead of replying immediately, Weyler opened a large ornate box on his desk and pulled out a Habana. After lighting it and sucking in a mouthful of rich flavorful smoke, he again regarded Landon.

"If all this is so, why would the Estados Confederados allow us to leave… even if I were, hypothetically…to go along with your loco plan?"

"That is why time is of the essence. The French do not appear to have informed the Confederates of their plans to capture Puerto Rico. If we act quickly enough we might get away."

Suddenly Admiral Topete spoke up.

"Even were we so inclined we could never transport everyone in a single trip."

"I've brought a small fleet of transports with me. When combined with your own ships here, it should be enough to transport the vast majority of your men."

"Enough," said General Weyler all of a sudden. "I will consider the matter. For now leave me." He returned to his seat behind his massive ornate desk to signal the discussion was over. Whitmore, however, threw one last talking point his way whether the General liked it or not.

"Another thing to keep in mind, General is what is likely to happen to you if the Confederates do manage to capture this city. The locals don't exactly love you. I could easily see the Rebs handing you over to them to curry favor with their new Cuban lapdogs."

Landon wanted to clap his hands together but remained perfectly still. True to form, Whitmore had hit the Spanish General way below the belt. By all reports newspapers across the United States and the British Empire were ablaze with headlines decrying the ruthless butchery that Weyler had unleashed on the Cuban people during his tenure as governor. That was another reason why time was of the essence. When the CSA's war with Spain had started public opinion in Britain and the US had been squarely behind the Spanish and against the Confederates. Now that the horrors of Spain's brutal treatment of the Cubans had come out for all the world to see, the balance was shifting.

Whitmore of course had no way of knowing about the newspaper headlines in the United States and Great Britain, but Landon had the distinct feeling you didn't have to be in Cuba long to get the distinct impression that the Cubans did anything but loath and deplore their Spanish occupiers. The fact that the vast majority of Spanish troops were in the city holding down the population instead of on the front lines holding back the Confederates bore testimony to that sorry truth.

Weyler's face darkened even further. Landon wouldn't have thought it possible. He also noted that several beads of sweat started to appear on his brow and they didn't have anything to do with the Cuban heat.

Once outside of Weyler's office Landon turned to Whitmore.

"So you actually changed your mind?"

"Not exactly. I'll admit you were probably right about me and my boys not being able to get here in time to do any real good. But still I'm glad I chose to come here. I fulfilled my promise to the Spanish and got to kill a few thousand Rebs in return so all in all I'd call it a profitable venture."

Landon couldn't argue with that kind of American logic. He was glad that Whitmore was now willing to bring his mercenary unit to Puerto Rico. He only hoped Weyler would come to see it the same way.

As the two elderly men made their way out of the mansion, Whitmore reached into his khaki uniform coat and pulled out two Habana cigars of his own. He passed one to Landon who readily accepted. Once they were both puffing happy clouds, Whitmore asked: "So when will our forces arrive in Puerto Rico?"

"Our combined task force is anchored at Bermuda. They will sail just as soon as Leopold makes his decision."

Whitmore blew a ragged smoke ring.

"He'd better decide soon."

Landon nodded. Truer words had never been spoken.

XXXI

Roger Connery was alive. There had been times during the past few weeks that he'd wished otherwise. He'd taken a bullet in the shoulder and fallen out of a tree. That had left him with a few cracked ribs, but he knew he could have easily suffered several more broken bones. All in all he considered himself lucky—most of the time.

As it did every night, his wounded shoulder throbbed. Each beat of his heart sent a fresh jolt of pain into it as if someone were stabbing him there with a hot knife. He clenched his jaw and gripped his bed tightly. Pain filled moans and the occasional cry was common place in the ward at night. Unless you were the poor wretch doing the suffering you tended to tune it out. If you were…

He found himself wishing for more morphine. In the past he'd seen men addicted to it. Many had become little more than fat, overweight, drug addicts. Now he craved it as a man trapped in the desert craved water. It allowed him to forget the pain and sleep through the night. But it seemed the hospital was always out and when it wasn't they hardly gave him any at all. He probably didn't manage any more than a couple of tormented hours of sleep per night.

As much pain as he was in, he was cognizant of the fact that not too long ago it had been much worse. Thankfully he had only limited memories of his first few days at the hospital. The operation where they dug the bullet out of his shoulder and cauterized the wound seemed like little more than a distant nightmare. Afterwards he'd taken a fever and nearly died. Though at a few points he'd been delirious, he had a much clearer memory of that period of time. The pain in his shoulder had been far greater. His entire body had ached and he'd had the chills so bad his teeth chattered as though he were freezing to death—even though in reality his body temperature was dangerously high. The fever had peaked at just over 104 degrees. At that point his body had gone into seizures. He had a vague memory of the nurse, Jennifer Harper putting ice packs on his head and around his body in an effort to bring down the fever. It had been a long and difficult battle but she and other nurses had tended to him for hours at a time. Doctors had given him medicines that would supposedly bring down the fever. Some they injected him with and others they poured down his throat. They had tasted horrible and they wreaked havoc with his plumbing. If they didn't give him the runs they made him defecate adobe bricks. At one point, *damn them*, they had used hypodermic needles in his shoulder to draw out the infection. Large burly male orderlies had had to hold him down for that. He remembered the night he'd awoken drenched in a cold sweat which meant that the fever had finally broken. The wound had healed significantly since then but the pain was still excruciating. One of the doctors claimed it was some sort of nerve damage. The pain could last days, months, years, or even the rest of his life.

He let out a cry. Thinking about it made it worse. A tear forced its way out of his eye. There in the darkness of the ward he felt no shame. It hurt.

After what seemed an eternity the first rays of sunlight started to come through the ward's windows. Not long after came the nurses on their morning rounds. He allowed himself a smile when Jennifer Harper came by his bedside to take his temperature. She was the closest thing to a highlight his days had. Though he'd done his hardest to kill Pershing, (and would in the future kill him without hesitation if he had the chance) he found himself genuinely hoping that either Pershing or some other man would make her a happy woman someday. She'd done everything in her power to ease his suffering. For a man like Connery whose heart was made of iron, that kind of sentiment was not easy to come by, but she had managed.

More than once in the torment of the night the thought had occurred to him that God in heaven was punishing him for his many murders. Whenever it did he'd pushed it aside. He wasn't a murderer, he was a warrior—a warrior fighting for his country. His methods were different, unconventional, and at times unorthodox. It was true that at times he'd sacrificed innocent lives to serve a higher purpose, but the ends justified the means or so he told himself.

I'm fighting for my country, and not just for my country! I'm fighting for the supremacy and survival of the White Race! As far as he was concerned, the two were inseparable and the CSA was the only hope. Of course he'd learned that not all of his countrymen shared he and John Wilkes Booth's vision for the Confederate States of America. More negroes were free in the CSA than ever before. Because of the war with Spain still thousands more were getting freedom. Men who'd once championed slavery now opposed it and for what? For money—for a better revenue stream! He was beginning to think that Booth had spent too much time focused on the Confederacy's external enemies, instead of the homegrown ones inside.

Booth should have let me kill Jackson years ago!

As Jennifer Harper pushed the mercury filled glass thermometer into his mouth he hoped desperately that the fever was gone. He had no desire for further treatments.

Despite his pain he'd been virtually begging the doctors to let him leave the hospital. He claimed he wanted to return to duty. In reality he wanted to get through to Confederate lines. He wanted to go home. As much as he hated to admit it, he doubted he'd ever be good for field work again. Maybe Booth would let him work in Richmond.

He'd tried to leave the ward once. He hadn't even made it to the door. It was sick, twisted ironic justice that he'd done so much work to infiltrate the Spanish Foreign Legion and now he was for all intents and purposes trapped in it.

"You're at ninety-nine," she said and noted it on her pad. He nodded. As long as it didn't get up over a hundred they'd keep the hypodermic needles away from him. He was about to ask Jennifer Harper what the situation on the front lines were when...

"Jen!"

Connery recognized the voice and his blood ran cold. Jennifer Harper recognized it too. Her face lit up with pure joy and she spun around to see that John Pershing had entered the ward. She virtually ran to him. He took her in his arms and kissed her. His khaki uniform was filthy, but she didn't care. His embrace lifted her off the floor and he spun her around still kissing her. It wasn't proper. It wasn't polite. That didn't stop the wounded soldiers in the ward from whistling, jeering, and poking fun. Several clapped for them. Others made jokes.

"Hey, honey what about me!"

"To bad we don't get that kind of attention."

A few of the older nurses coughed or ho hummed indignantly but the kissing couple ignored them. Pershing reflected that when you spent your days dodging bullets and artillery shells you didn't tend to worry about such things. The Rebels hadn't killed him. He wasn't worried about a few sour old women. He'd decided that you lived life as you could and enjoyed its pleasures when you could. In his line of work there's was a good chance he'd never get the opportunity again, so he treated every such instance as though it might be his last.

When she finally let him go he said: "We're pulling out of here. All of us. The Spanish have made a deal with the Rebs. They're gonna let them have the city without a fight in exchange for free passage to Puerto Rico."

That got mixed reactions from the wounded men in the ward. Some seemed indifferent. Others looked excited to be getting out of Cuba. They'd had their fill of adventure and then some. Others cursed and swore angrily and bitterly.

"What we'd fight for then!"

"What'd I lose my arm for!"

Pershing didn't tell them the war wasn't over yet. He didn't tell them they wanted to go to Puerto Rico to help defend it against a French invasion. The Confederates didn't know that and he didn't want to risk them finding out before they could sail.

Roger Connery had turned away from them. He didn't think his misery could have gotten any greater until he heard Pershing's news. He was so close to his true countrymen and now they were about to put him on a ship and send him to Puerto Rico. He couldn't get away on his own. He couldn't ask them to leave him in Santiago. Such a request would have drawn the highest suspicion.

He took a deep breath. There was nothing he could not accomplish by the power of his will. He might go to Puerto Rico, but from there he'd eventually get sent back to the US. From there he could get back to the Confederacy. It would just take time and patience.

XXXII

Cole Allens gaped at Santiago de Cuba. All around the besieged city, the guns had finally fallen silent. He and his two British colleagues had passed through Spanish lines without incident. Churchill and Barnes had been summoned for a meeting with the British envoy that had negotiated the ceasefire. They in turn had invited him along.

For the moment the Spanish Red and Gold tricolor was still flying over the city. Cole wasn't sure if it was going to be replaced by the Confederacy's Blood Stained Banner, or by Cuba's own revolutionary flag. Either way at sunset, after over four hundred years of Spanish rule, the La Rojigualda would be lowered from over Santiago and by extension all of Cuba for the last time. The Spanish commander had agreed to surrender Santiago in exchange for his forces being allowed to go free. The Confederates had leapt at the offer to take the city without further casualties. All they wanted was Cuba. For them the Spanish departure from Santiago meant the final victory of the war. There were still a few other pockets of Spanish resistance on the island. The Confederate command was certain that now that Santiago's garrison had surrendered, the others would follow suite.

But part of Cole found it hard to believe that the Spanish were actually throwing in the towel. From what he'd seen they'd fought hard all over Cuba. In the hills outside of Santiago de Cuba he'd watched both the Spanish and their hired mercenaries repulse several major assaults. They'd inflicted major casualties on the Confederates. But they'd suffered major casualties themselves, both in being driven across the island and in holding off the fierce and determined assaults around Santiago. Cole supposed that, combined with being surrounded with their backs against the wall had convinced even the Spanish that discretion was the better part of valor.

Once they'd gotten through the Spanish lines, the war correspondents had flagged a horse-drawn taxi. Churchill and Barnes had been directed to report to the Hotel Grandiosa in Santiago where the British special envoy had taken up special though quite temporary residence. Like a lot of businesses in Cuba, the Hotel Grandiosa was owned by a Confederate firm. Cole imagined the owners would be glad to get their property back. For the moment, however, it was still firmly in Spanish hands.

As the landau pulled up in front of the hotel, Cole spotted both the British Union Jack and the Star Spangled Banner flying out front, just above the entrance. He wasn't surprised to see the British flag, but the Stars and Stripes took him pleasantly by surprise. He hadn't seen old glory in months. It made him homesick.

The British envoy was hold up in the hotel's finest suites. A royal navy yeoman served as the man's aid and was standing outside the British official's rooms. Churchill and

Barnes presented their identities and vouched for Cole. The yeoman gave him a stare, but went ahead and showed him into the suite along with the two young British officers.

Charles Landon was an older man. He was heavy set, clean shaven, and had a full head of closely cut, solid white hair. Another older man sat in the chair beside him. He seemed very familiar but Cole could not quite place him. With the khaki British style military uniform he was wearing, (and its Spanish insignias) it took Cole a few moments to recognize the man as Joseph Whitmore. Cole's journalistic excitement grew. He was now envisioning not one headline but two. Cole knew that Whitmore had a reputation for loathing reporters. He'd have to play his cards just right if he wanted an interview.

"Welcome, gentlemen," said Landon. "I'm please you received my messages. In a situation like this I couldn't be certain that my messages asking you to come here had gotten through. He put a little extra stress on the word 'you.' His cold dark eyes turned to regard Cole.

"This fine gentleman has been our companion during our entire time here in Cuba," said Churchill.

"Cole Allens, sir. Covington Gazette," said Cole extending his hand to Landon. He next extended it to Whitmore who looked suddenly agitated. He didn't accept Cole's hand but sat with both his hands resting atop his cane.

"Just what we need. A news jackal," he barked. He turned to Landon. "If we reveal our plans to this blood sucking reporter they'll be all over the papers in no time flat."

"We're sailing in the morning. I doubt he could get it out in time," replied Landon.

"Don't be so sure," said Whitmore growing even more agitated. Don't forget that anything he sends back to the papers in the United States has to pass through telegraph lines controlled by the Rebs. It doesn't have to hit the papers for the Confederacy to get wind of what we're doing. We can't risk it."

A lot of journalists Cole knew would have taken offense at the things that had been said. Cole also knew that Whitmore had a myriad of reasons for not liking reporters. His internal scoop alarm was ringing louder than ever. He decided if he had a hope of being able to stay and getting in on what looked to be a huge story, he had to act quickly but not rashly. He chose his words with care.

"Mr. Whitmore, sir, your dislike of the fourth estate is well known…"

"And well deserved!" barked Whitmore.

"Perhaps so…" allowed Cole. "But I must insist that I have always held myself and my paper to the highest standards of journalistic integrity."

Whitmore raised one of his bushy white eyebrows and the old millionaire grunted.

"I know who you are Allens," said Whitmore. "And you're right, I can't recall your paper ever specifically printing anything negative about me or my company." That just about summed up Joseph Whitmore's definition of journalistic integrity. Cole had the distinct feeling that had the Gazette ever published anything bad about Whitmore the old millionaire would have remembered it. He struck Cole as the kind of man who had a memory for such things, a man who never forgot a slight no matter how trivial. He also struck Cole as the kind of man who would exact vengeance whenever and however possible. The old millionaire continued.

"I have also had occasion to read some of your editorials and I have to tell you that I found them most distasteful."

Not surprising, thought Cole. Politics in the United States was firmly divided into two major parties. The Republicans still existed technically. They had a small handful of representatives in the House and a single senator. Other than that they had become irrelevant. The major parties were actually the two wings of the Democratic Party. The Democrats, while still under the banner of a single entity had been divided into two camps that were increasingly growing further apart from one another: The Hawks and the Doves. Politicians and pundits had been saying for years that eventually one branch or the other was going to split off and form its own party. It hadn't happened yet. Cole was unabashedly and unapologetically a dove and it showed through every editorial he wrote. In essence he favored scrupulous neutrality in foreign affairs and staying out of military conflicts unless the United States was directly attacked. Like a lot of Doves, Cole also favored the passage of fair labor laws. In addition to giving people a fair shake, Cole also wanted to slow the growth another small but growing party—the Socialists. Joseph Whitmore by contrast was as Hawkish as they came.

And not surprising, thought Cole. When you owned a company that made rifles, cannons, and warships, war was good for business. Cole may never have written anything against Whitmore personally or his company specifically, but he'd written a lot against the things the man stood for. The only thing on which they probably came close was on the danger posed by the reds, though even there they differed. Cole wanted to see their ideas defeated. To Cole the pen was mightier than the sword. Whitmore, however, like all the other industrialists and bankers of the United States wanted them locked up. To them the sword worked just fine. Knowing that Whitmore was firmly rooted in all of his positions, and that Cole himself would seem like a hypocrite if he tried to back peddle on any of his own convictions just to try and curry a little favor, he pressed ahead with the third and as far as he could see, only option.

"Mr. Whitmore I know it goes without saying that you disagree with me about a lot of issues. But one thing we both have in common is that we are Americans. We both love the United States. Unless I miss my guess Old Glory is hanging outside at your insistence. It's true I came to Cuba so I could remind our countrymen of the horrors of war in the hope that it would go a long way towards keeping us out of conflicts in the future. I've been against war since I was a boy. I lost my father and my brother in the First War of Rebellion. As a correspondent I saw it up close and personal in the Second. The things I've seen the past few months here in Cuba have not changed my views, on the contrary they have reaffirmed and strengthened them. I'll be honest, I don't approve of you or other Americans fighting for the Spanish and involving—even indirectly—our country in someone else's war. All that being said, sir, I do not question your integrity or your motives. I accept and believe that you are doing what you think is right. You feel we have become weak and in your own way you are trying to show us how to be strong again. I can respect that, even if I don't agree with it. I can't promise that I won't write what I believe in my editorials. But you have my word that when I write news about your exploits and your views I will write nothing but the cold hard facts and I won't twist them to fit my views or yours, I'll simply write them as they are. My late uncle taught me journalistic integrity, and I hold it dear. Now you want to make an impression on the American people. Wouldn't you prefer one of your own countrymen writing about your exploits? Wouldn't they more readily believe it from someone they know and trust? Whatever you are planning, if you will let me cover it, you have my word I won't report anything until you say it's safe to do so without alerting the Confederates." He couldn't begin to guess what this new story was all about, but the sudden thought that there was more to the sudden Spanish withdrawal than met the eye filled him with excitement.

Cole felt Whitmore's gaze boring into him. It wasn't a look of anger or disdain. Cole realized he was sizing him up and trying to determine if he was serious and sincere. He must have decided he was for he looked over at Landon.

"Allens can stay." He then turned to Allens and smiled maliciously. "But I warn you, you won't like what you hear and I intend to hold you to your promise regardless."

Landon then slowly and methodically outlined for the three war correspondents the budding alliance between the United States and Great Britain, and their plans for Puerto Rico. Whitmore had been correct. Cole didn't like it. Cole had thought Grover Cleveland at least a moderate dove. As President he had greatly expanded and modernized the US navy. Cole hadn't been entirely against that. He wanted to keep the United States non-aligned and neutral not defenseless. But Cleveland, like every successfully elected Presidential candidate of the past twenty five years had promised on a stack of Bibles as tall as he was that he would keep the US out of military conflict. Like a lot of politicians he'd obviously just been telling the people what they wanted to hear. Cole and his paper had endorsed Cleveland in 1892. That wouldn't be happening again in 96.

From the look on Whitmore's face he saw Cole's discomfiture. Part of him obviously relished it, but the eccentric millionaire's face held more pity than malice.

"Now I know you can't see it, sonny. But this is a very good thing."

"Mr. Whitmore, this is nothing but a recipe for a war—a war I might add that will be bigger than any before in our history if it happens."

"You can't make an omelet without breaking a few eggs," said Landon. "The Confederacy, France and their allies must be taught that they may not bestride the entire world like a colossus to the detriment of other nations.

As the British Empire has done for the past couple of centuries? Cole left the thought unspoken. Landon and Whitmore went on to explain that the US and Britain simply intended this new alliance to be a counter balance to that of France and the Confederacy but to Cole it simply seemed that Landon couldn't stand for Britain to play second fiddle to France and that Whitmore, like most of the old war hawks in the US simply yearned to be avenged on the CSA for the events of a quarter century earlier. Either way, Cole felt certain that the world had suddenly taken a turn for the worst and was now rushing headlong into disaster.

His promise to Whitmore and his loyalty to his country kept him from getting a message to Covington as quickly as possible in an attempt to rally people against it. Whether he liked it or not his President had made his decision. If he announced it at this point all he'd do is tip off the Confederates and French and make it that much more likely that the US and British taskforce would get into armed conflict. He didn't want any US soldiers' or sailors' deaths on his conscience no matter what the political leaders had decided. He still clung to the faint hope that King Leopold of Spain would refuse to sell Puerto Rico to the US, that way the task force would never sail. But Cole had to admit that it didn't look very likely.

He knew he'd be sailing to Puerto Rico in morning. This was too big not to cover. If an intercontinental war broke out he had to be there to witness it, and document the folly for future generations. Helen was still back in Havana. Somehow or other he'd have to let her know.

XXXIII

"Boy, it's good to be home," said Ray Brisk as he gazed at Charleston longingly. "Even if it is for a little while."

Taking a long drag on his cigar, Captain Blake Ramsey nodded, and then exhaled a small cloud of smoke.

"And a short stay it'll be. Just long enough to take on coal, stock back up on shells, powder and a few other things, and deliver our cargo and prisoners."

Brisk swore. They had the entire crew of Portuguese slave traders in the brig. After capturing their freighter, the CSS Texas had towed it all the way to Liberia, which is what had so dangerously depleted their coal. Liberia was a small nation state established by former slaves. For understandable reasons the Confederate States had had zero diplomatic contact with the tiny African country until they had joined the anti-slavery patrol under diplomatic pressure. Liberia had made an agreement with the nations that made up the anti-slavery patrol that they would accept any rescued slaves.

The images of the inside of that slave ship still haunted Ramsey. He'd gone over to inspect it after Brisk and the boarding party had secured the freighter and arrested the crew. Never had he seen such misery as he had in that cargo hold. They had set the negroes free but many of them had had no food for a week. During the voyage Ramsey had ordered food taken to the negroes aboard the freighter which was why the Texas was low on provisions. Once the freed slaves had been put ashore in Liberia, the CSS Texas set a course for home. They had also left behind the ruined freighter. The Liberians would make use of it. No one else would want it that was for sure.

"Where do you think they'll send us next?"

"Who knows? They could send us back to join the blockade force around Cuba or back out to hunt down more Spanish shipping."

Brisk swore disdainfully. "Just so long as they don't send us back on the blasted slave patrol. Seems like we can't get away from that one even when we try."

Ramsey shrugged.

As they entered Charleston harbor, all eyes turned to look at the Statue of Secession. The French Emperor Napoleon IV had given it to the Confederate States in 1885 to commemorate the 25th anniversary of secession and the independence of the Confederacy from the United States. The Confederates had turned Fort Sumter into the base for the massive statue which stood over 150 feet tall. The statue was of a woman, crowned with a wreath and holding aloft a saber in victory with one hand, and an unrolled scroll in the other. The woman, who had come to be known as the Lady of the South, was modelled on the image of Empress Josephine I. On the scroll in her left hand was written the date: December 20th 1860 as well as two phrases in Latin. The first was Deo Vindice—God Vindicates. It was the national motto of the Confederate States. The other was Unum Ea Enim Dissolvitur—The Union is Dissolved. As if to drive the point home even further, the French had sculpted the statue so that the Lady of the South stood astride a slain Eagle wrapped in the Stars and Stripes. Four massive Confederate flags flew from the four corners of the statue's base which had once been fort Sumter.

After cruising past the Statue of Secession, the Texas cut her engines. Naval tugs were already waiting to take her to her moorings at the naval docks. Ramsey and Brisk now stared at the city that was spread out before them. Charleston had expanded greatly in the previous twenty years. At eleven stories high, the PGT Beauregard building, was the tallest in the entire Confederacy, though it was only half the height of the tallest US building. At twenty-one stories high, New York's American Surety Building was the tallest building in the world.

The Texas was scarcely tied up at her moorings when Ramsey spotted Admiral John McIntosh Kell standing down on the docks. Ramsey ordered the gangway extended, and Kell immediately made his way up it.

"Permission to come aboard?"

"Permission granted, sir," replied Ramsey, giving the Admiral a brisk salute. "I apologize Admiral if I'd known you'd be waiting on us I'd have had a more formal welcoming prepared for you."

"At my age I've had enough pomp and circumstance." The Admiral was on the high side of seventy. Like most heroes of the Confederate War of Independence they would let him serve until he was senile and probably after. For the present, he was still as sharp as ever, even if age had slowed him down considerably.

"You must have been alerted quickly, sir."

The Admiral nodded. The look outs at Fort Moultrie telephoned the naval command post as soon as they spotted you. But that's beside the point, we've been expecting you all day."

Ramsey raised a curious eyebrow. He didn't have to verbalize the question for Kell to understand he was asking how the Admiral had known of their arrival. Kell smirked.

"I thought I was the old artifact and you were the modern sailor? Modern communications Ramsey. The French have a naval attaché in Liberia. He cabled Paris, Paris cabled Richmond, and Richmond cabled me."

"It would be nice if the French put the wires to more use. It would have been nice to know that the French had a whole fleet on their way to the Spanish Sahara."

Kell nodded. "France is a good ally, but Napoleon isn't usually in the habit of consulting anyone—not his own ministers and most certainly not his allies. When he wants to do something he does it."

"He'd do better to let us in on his plans," stated Ramsey.

"You don't know how right you are," replied Kell. "Our forces have more or less secured Cuba. The Spanish garrison in Santiago de Cuba agreed to surrender the city in exchange for free passage to Puerto Rico. For all intents and purposes the war is over—at least that's what we thought."

Ramsey sent him a quizzical look. The Admiral continued. "The French are screaming bloody murder right now because we allowed Spanish forces in Cuba to evacuate to Puerto Rico. Apparently they had troops and ships down in Veracruz ready to take the island. The French have used this war as an excuse to gobble up Spanish possessions around the world."

"Well if they had bothered to inform us of their plans, then maybe we wouldn't have allowed all those troops in Cuba to reinforce Puerto Rico. They have no one to blame but themselves."

"That's my sentiments exactly, but the President is of the opinion that the French must be appeased. They're the most important ally we have. We can't risk alienating them."

"They need us just as much as we need them."

"Again you and I are in agreement, Captain. However, President Stone has decided to placate the French by taking part in their campaign to capture Puerto Rico."

"And they get the island?"

Kell nodded. "Politics…" the Admiral turned it into a dirty word. Ramsey nodded vigorous agreement.

"Will my ship be taking part in this operation?"

Kell nodded again.

"You leave just as soon as you've taken on more coal and provisions. You're to sail by dawn at the latest, preferably before."

Ramsey was visibly taken aback.

"If I may ask, sir. What is the big hurry. I had hoped to allow my men at least one day's leave."

"I'm afraid that there is no time to spare. The situation is…" The Admiral looked about suddenly, to make sure there was no one within earshot. The men had finished securing all the lines and were happily and busily preparing for shore leave that they wouldn't be getting. He turned back to Ramsey and went on in quieter tones.

"Let's find someplace more private. The situation is far more complex than you know and there's a few things we need to discuss."

Ramsey led the admiral into the wardroom of the Texas.

"There's been a couple of major diplomatic earthquakes since you last put to sea and they complicate the hell out of this situation with Puerto Rico. Yesterday, the United States announced that it has purchased Puerto Rico from Spain for ten million in gold. Apparently Spain has agreed to the sale."

Ramsey froze. There was a long moment of silence which Ramsey broke with a ripe round oath. After twenty-five years of quiet neutrality and isolation, the United States had made its most aggressive and provocative act since the events leading up to the War of 1869.

"If we allow this to go through," said Ramsey "it will allow the Yankees to project their naval power right into the heart of the Caribbean, not to mention the threat it would represent to the Gulf Coast."

"You're forgetting the most vital threat it represents."

Ramsey thought for just a moment before it came to him.

"The canal."

Kell nodded. The French-Confederate canal project in Panama was nearly twenty years from completion but there were other nations that would not care to have such a strategic advantage held exclusively by the Confederate States and the French Empire.

"And that's only the half of it," said Kell. "Yesterday the United States and Great Britain announced a treaty of alliance. A "mutual defense act" not unlike that which exists between ourselves and the French. They've promised to develop their national defenses in consort and to come to one another's aid in the event they are attacked."

Ramsey uttered a blasphemy.

"I'll bet things are going nuts in Richmond right now."

"You have no idea. This completely broadsided everybody and now everybody's trying to figure out what to do. The problem is we don't have much time to figure it out. Britain has already recognized the sale of Puerto Rico to the USA, and a joint Yankee British task force is sailing for Puerto Rico this morning to take possession of it."

"That means they'll be there in less than a week."

"The French task force has already sailed from Veracruz. They arrived in Havana yesterday. They also sail in the morning, along with a small taskforce of our own. Our side should reach Puerto Rico first. The plan is to capture San Juan and Arecibo before the British and Yankees arrive."

By his tone, Kell didn't seem to think that very likely. Ramsey didn't blame him.

"Suppose the landing forces fail to secure the ports in time? Even if they do, suppose the Yanks and Brits don't care and demand we surrender the island anyway?"

"Don't forget we'll have a joint fleet with the French down there as well. It will be deployed defensively. If the Yankees and Brits want Puerto Rico they'll have to get past those ships. Unless they want to start a war I don't think they'll try it."

"What if they do?"

"That's what we're waiting on a decision from the President on. There's a lot of hotheads who say we should fire on them. But it's not that simple. Including the Texas, our combined fleet at Puerto Rico with the French will still be outnumbered by the Yankees and British by nearly two to three. If they want to get past us, chances are they'll be able to, but like you said, if they do it will mean war—a big one. The problem is, we're not ready for it. We have so many troops deployed in Cuba and Panama that our home defenses are not near as strong as they should be. Our fleet has just finished an extended sea campaign against the Spanish. We came out relatively unscathed but we've used up a large amount of our coal reserves. A steam powered navy is useless without fuel and we get a lot of ours from the Yankees."

Ramsey swore profanely. The CSA had domestic sources of coal, but they were much smaller than those of the USA. He wondered if it would be able to fuel the navy in the event of war.

And not just the navy, he reminded himself. But also the railroads and arms factories. If all out war with the USA erupted for the third time in the 19th Century, Ramsey doubted they'd have enough coal to feed all the new machinery of war. Wood could take up some of the slack as it had in the previous wars. The Confederacy had abundant supplies of timber. But wood burned neither as hot nor as long as coal.

If war erupts now, we're screwed… "What are the French saying?"

"I have a hard time believing Napoleon's prepared for all out war at this point, but I have a hard time seeing him backing down."

"And if he decides Puerto Rico's worth fighting a war for?"

"That's up to the President, who by the way is very pleased with your capture of that slave ship. You've given us another victory in the propaganda war. Between our giving thousands of negroes their freedom so they could fight, the Spanish atrocities in Cuba, our keeping slavery out of Cuba by making it a commonwealth, and your exploits in the Atlantic, we've given the abolitionist fanatics as little ground to stand on as possible. According to the papers there's plenty of people in the United States and Britain who are heavily and vocally opposed to the aggressive moves they've made towards Puerto Rico. You've undoubtedly had a hand in that. The President has put you and your exec in for Distinguished Service Medals. Though I'm afraid the ceremonies will have to wait until another time."

After seeing off the Admiral, Ramsey was approached by Commander Ray Brisk. "Excuse me, sir. But all lines are secure. The ship is fully docked. Shall give out the first assignments for shore leave?"

Ramsey sighed heavily then took a deep breath. He pulled a cigar out of his coat pocket, lit it and took a good long drag. After exhaling the smoke he turned to face his exec.

"Sorry, Ray, there's been a change of plans."

XXXIV

Nathan Audrey, cursed and swore as he sat down on a large rock and unfolded his map. Not far away, Mrs. Barbara Maye's head twitched ever so slightly at the profanity but she said nothing. She and the other women they'd rescued from the Mormons were still with them. Trying to ignore her, as he had since he'd met her nearly a week earlier, Audrey tried to focus on what his rag tag unit should do.

Neither of the runners he'd sent to General Goldwyn returned quickly, in fact, in the end only one had returned at all and he'd gotten lost in the desert along with another twenty men on horseback and a couple of cannons that Goldwyn somehow considered "reinforcements." Depending on how you looked at it, three days after catching the

Mormons that had torched Rattlesnake Cove, Audrey had found the runner and the reinforcements or they had found him. Goldwyn's dispatch said that they had received a message begging for help from a town called Elko, which was supposedly surrounded by Mormons. It was one of the biggest settlements in northeast Nevada. It wasn't a Californian town, it was on the far-east side of Nevada, closer to Deseret. Though it had been under the control of the Mormons for years, the townspeople had been there since the days when Nevada had been a part of the United States. They didn't like living under the Mormons. In the 1870s they'd been 'convinced' to 'convert' to the faith. Now that the Californian army was in the territory they'd had a change of heart—and religion. They'd risen up against the Mormons and Goldwyn had answered their call for help. It was a noble mission, but in the meantime Audrey had his own objective and too few men to accomplish it.

Goldwyn's orders instructed Audrey to proceed to the town of Pine City and if he found any Mormons there, to drive them out. He was then to await the return of Goldwyn's army. On the surface that was all fine and dandy. The problems, however, were that Elko was over a hundred miles away and with just thirty-five men capable of fighting and a couple of cannons there was a good chance if there were Mormons at Pine City, Audrey's rag tag force would be no match for them.

Not if they're there in great numbers. There was also the worry that they didn't know where the main body of the Mormon army was. If Goldwyn ran into it, he'd stand a fighting chance. If Audrey ran into them…

We're dead.

Desert rocks and dirt crunched under his boots as the Lieutenant came to stand behind Audrey and stare at the map over his shoulder. The boy had been grazed by a bullet when they'd attacked the Mormon encampment. He still wore a makeshift bandage on his arm. Another of Audrey's men had been similarly injured. Neither man had shown any sign of infections. They were lucky. The other four men who'd been wounded had taken fevers. Two of them had died. The other two were still kicking, but without access to a surgeon or medicines their chances were slim. Mrs. Barbara Mayes and the other women they had rescued were tending to them as best they could. Audrey supposed that was at least something, but he still considered that having the women along was more trouble than it was worth. For one thing they slowed him down. For another the younger ones distracted his men. And besides...

War is no place for a woman.

"What's our next move, Colonel?"

"We go to Pine City as ordered," said Audrey. He'd been there just before the war with Deseret started. He'd carried a message from the small town asking for help from the Californian Army. Now he was about to return in person with a force of green uniformed soldiers. Audrey was certain he was coming far later than the good people of Pine City had expected. He only hoped he wasn't coming too late.

"Let's break camp and get going. If we move all day, we should be in position to attack in the early hours of tomorrow." It shouldn't have taken that long. But travelling with the wounded, the women and prisoners in three captured wagons slowed them down. The ten Mormon prisoners had to be guarded at all times. After what they had done to Rattlesnake Cove, Audrey considered them bandits and war criminals, not prisoners of war. He'd considered dispensing with them, if for no other reason than to help speed things along. He hadn't done it yet.

By pushing hard they reached their destination just a couple of hours before sun set. After setting up camp just a few miles north of Pine City, Audrey personally took a couple of his best men and rode towards the town. The sun was low on the western horizon as they carefully crested one of the hills on the northern side of the settlement. Audrey surveyed the town through his binoculars. A large blue flag emblazoned with a golden bee hive flew from the large unfinished court house. Had Audrey been in command of the Mormons in the town, he'd have posted sentries up there. Heck, if he'd been commanding the Mormons in Pine City he'd have posted sentries on the very spot from which he was now surveying the town. The fact that they had done neither showed they either weren't expecting an attack or they didn't have a clue what they were doing.

Hopefully both.

As he surveyed the town, Audrey reflected that if it hadn't been for the large Mormon flag flying from the unfinished court house, he'd have no way of knowing the town had been occupied by Mormons. As the sky went from day to twilight, Audrey saw only a few people but they seemed to be wearing the blue uniforms of the army of Deseret.

We'll hit them at dawn.

Twilight turned to night, and Audrey and his scouts returned to camp and the smell of cooking food. Audrey didn't like having women around in a warzone and to get in the way of his men, but even he had to admit, ever so grudgingly, that the chow was better with females to cook it. As she had every night since he'd helped rescue her, Mrs. Mayes brought him his plate personally. Despite the Mrs. in front of her name, she was a widow. Her husband had died a few years earlier. She'd given just about every signal a proper lady could that she was interested in him. She'd asked if he was married. She'd asked if he had anyone special. She'd asked if he'd ever thought of settling down. She'd taken every opportunity to wait on him hand and foot. In a way he supposed he was flattered. She was nearly twenty years younger than him, and as attractive as any woman on the high side of forty could be. Her blond hair had only a few traces of gray. She was kind. The food she cooked made Audrey's own seem like horse manure by comparison. But Audrey had been alone his entire life. Between the U.S. Army, being an outlaw on the run, being a soldier in the French Foreign Legion, being a bounty hunter, being a lawman, and now a Colonel in the army of California, hadn't left much room for female companionship in his long hard life. Audrey reflected that the woman seeking his favor didn't even know his real name. Each time she called him Colonel Johnson, it reminded him of his dark history. George Custer's murder was nearly thirty years in the past but like a specter it was still there. General Goldwyn was proof of that. Audrey wondered what Barbara Mayes would think of him if she knew the truth.

Dawn came quickly. Audrey rose just as the first morning rays peeped over the horizon. He detailed off just three men to guard the women and the prisoners then proceeded with the rest of his force towards Pine City. He sent just three scouts to the top of the main hill north of the town. He didn't expect the enemy to be any more vigilant that morning than they had been the previous night but the hapless Mormons would be a lot less likely to spot three mounted men than thirty. Audrey took the rest of the force just to the east and around the hills and approached the town from that direction. It wasn't long before he started seeing things he recognized. Ahead and to the left he spotted the Sheriff's office, but there was no sign of the Sheriff...or anyone else. It was like riding into a ghost town. Audrey raised his hand, signaling his men to stop. He then dismounted.

"Keep an eye out." He made his way to the Sherriff's office. The front door was locked. Audrey motioned to one of his larger men to dismount.

"Kick it down."

It wasn't a very strong door. One good kick from the young cavalryman was enough to send it flying open. Audrey entered the office with his pistol drawn. He entered just in time to see the startled and confused look on the face of the Sherriff who was locked in one of his own cells.

"Sherriff!"

It took a moment for the lawman to recognize him.

"Marshall Johnson?"

Audrey nodded.

"Colonel now actually. Sorry it took so long."

"Well you know what they say: better late than never."

Audrey took tight hold of the iron bar cell door. Predictably it wouldn't budge. They wouldn't be able to get through it as easily as they had the flimsy office door.

"Where's the keys?"

"They keep them on them, but I got an extra pair. Move the chair behind my desk. There's a loose plank in the floor."

Audrey found the key and a moment later had the Sherriff out.

"Where is everyone, Sherriff? The town seems almost deserted?"

"When the Mormons invaded they hit Winnemucca first. A few folks got away and came here so we had a little warning. We knew we'd never be able to hold out against an army so we evacuated the town. Everyone's hiding in the old abandoned gold mines about four miles south of here."

"Then how'd they nab you?"

"We didn't want them figuring out where we went. I had everyone walk to the mines single file. Me and a few other fellas rode back the same way we'd come. We figured we'd try to create some false trails away from the town. Them Mormons moved quicker then we'd expected. We'd only laid two or three trails when their cavalry ambushed us. We made a fight of it or tried to. My horse got shot. I got thrown and took a lick on the head. I woke up here. I'm guessing my other men didn't make it."

"How many are here in the town."

"I don't know, but I don't recon it's too many. They didn't spend much time looking for the folks, otherwise they would have found them by now. They wanted to keep moving…"

Suddenly gunshots sounded outside. Audrey and the Sherriff rushed out of the office. The cavalrymen were exchanging shots with a band of blue uniformed men who were trying to make their way across the town square. There didn't look to be more than a dozen of them. Audrey mounted his horse and shouted to his men.

"Run them down!" Audrey set spurs to his horse and went charging down the dirt road towards the heart of the town. His men were right on his heels. A couple of them fell from the saddle clutching bloody wounds but the rest stormed fearlessly into the heart of the town with their guns blazing. The attack overawed the small group of Mormons. Several of them went down with gunshots. The rest darted from one piece of cover to the next trying to get to the stables. Audrey worked the lever action on his rifle and then brought it up to his shoulder. He pulled the trigger, the rifle barked, and one of the fleeing Mormons bit the dust. Audrey didn't want them getting away and he didn't want them getting word to the Mormon's that the town had been retaken.

A couple of suicidal Mormons, performed a holding action while their comrades entered the stables. Taking cover behind three large wooden barrels they made a stand and tried to buy time for their comrades to get away. A couple of bullets cracked past Audrey far too close for comfort but it wasn't long before the Californians threw so much suppression fire at the Mormons that they could not pop their heads up to shoot back. While the majority of his men rained led on them, Audrey led a handful of his men around to the right of the Mormon's position. From there they could clearly see the beleaguered Deseretan fighters. A single volley from Audrey and his party cut them down.

"Press on!" cried Audrey. They reached the stables just as four men darted out the back on horseback. "After them!" The Mormons rode their horses hard trying to get away. One turned for a Parthian shot. The Mormon's rifle barked and one of Audrey's men fell from the saddle dead. A moment later that same Mormon fell from his own horse with a messy hole in the back of his head. Audrey worked the lever on his smoking rifle and aimed again, this time at the lead rider. Audrey's rifle barked again. The lead rider met the same fate as the previous Mormon. Watching his dead body fall from the saddle, the remaining two Mormons decided they had had enough. They reigned in, dropped their weapons and raised their hands in surrender. Audrey and his men came to a halt and addressed the defeated Mormons.

"I take you prisoner in the name of the Republic of California!"

XXXV

"I can't believe I'm going to get to meet President Jackson himself!" said Florence Dumas as excited as a young school girl. She brought up her good arm to straighten her hair for the tenth time.

"He's not President anymore, Flossy," said Mansel Dumas with barely concealed frustration. *And thank heavens for that…*

"I'm looking forward to meeting Mr. Jones again," said Mitchell. Mansel looked over at his eighteen year old son who was riding a cantering horse alongside the rolling wagon in which he and his wife sat. Mitchell was wearing his gray militia uniform and he'd begun to grow a thin downy mustache to complement his blond hair.

"Doesn't our boy look so grown up, Mansel?" said Florence. Mansel sighed. Florence turned back to him with a smile. "And you look so handsome in your new suit." Mansel was dressed in an elaborately lined light blue coat with a silver sash. Florence had affixed a large white flower to one of his large lapels. He had matching dress pants and also wore a black string-tie on the collar of his white dress shirt. A broad brimmed light blue hat sat on his head. She'd purchased the suit for him on her last trip to Jackson. It made him look every bit the traditional Southern planter that he was.

Sighing again, Mansel turned to his son.

"It is fortuitous that you decided to return home in time to join us," said Mansel. He'd intended the comment to be sardonic. His son had stayed away from home for weeks, and Mansel knew why. Florence Dumas, however, was merely glad to have her son home, and had spent the previous two days trying to reconcile the two most important men in her life to one another again.

"Yes, it certainly was fortuitous," said Florence. "And we are so glad to have you home."

Mitchell smiled.

"I don't think I could have gone much longer without your cornbread, Momma."

Mansel took his ivory handled cane and tapped the driver's seat in front of him where a young black slave sat holding the reins.

"Let's pick up the pace, Raphael, I want to get their before dark."

"Yes, massa." Raphael flicked the reins and the two horses sped up.

Mansel still couldn't believe that he was going to Turtle Creek. When Lester Jones had driven up to the mansion in his horseless carriage and pitched his outlandish proposals and invited him to come and meet the most famous (and notorious) man in the entire Confederacy, he'd thought the man crazy and sent him on his way. But then he'd gotten the telegrams from New Orleans and St. Louis about his latest cotton sales. If he hadn't known his sales agents in both cities for years he'd have sworn they were cheating him. Prices were lower than ever. As he'd read the reports at the large ornate wooden desk that had once been his father's and before that his grandfather's—he honestly wondered what the future of his plantation would be. He hadn't slept well in the past couple of weeks. His dreams had alternately been filled with nightmarish visions of Twin Harbours either surrounded by piles of unsold worthless cotton, or of barren fields devastated by boll weevils. In both dreams he saw himself and his family having to abandon the mansion and the land that had been theirs for generations. He was quite certain the dreams had driven him mad—mad enough to actually think about the things that Lester Jones had talked about and to even consider them in the back part of his mind. Then he'd made the mistake of mentioning the whole thing to Florence. From the moment she heard that they'd been invited to meet and hear Stonewall in the flesh, her mind was made up and he knew from long experience that that was the end of the matter. And so there they were, on their way to Turtle Creek Plantation. When Mitchell had come home he too had leapt at the chance to go, though Mansel was reasonably certain that his son was as eager to see the horseless carriage again as he was to meet the former President of the Confederate States. As he turned to again regard his son who was riding beside them, Mansel decided that it was indeed a good thing that his son was coming along.

He's far more mechanically inclined than I am, and if our own cotton mill and textile factory are in our future he's going to have to deal with it much longer than I will.

Mansel sighed again, trying to push the image of a very Yankee-like industrial complex marring the picturesque beauty of his plantation out of his mind. A while later, Florence turned to him.

"How much longer will it be?"

"Not long, my dear," said Mansel setting his hand on hers. "Though I'm afraid going home later tonight will take a little longer." Even with lanterns to help guide the way, he knew they would have to travel much slower on their return journey.

"I do wish we could have brought the girls," said Florence.

"They'll be fine with Mammy," said Mansel. "I don't believe we would have ever heard the end of it from her if we'd kept them out so late. You know what a stickler she is for keeping the children on their schedule."

"She is very good with them," said Florence. She looked down at her crippled arm and legs. She'd had her stroke right after Connie had been born. "I don't know how I'd keep up with them without her."

They continued down the dirt road. They passed a couple of riders, and three carriages laden with goods and driven by negro slaves from other plantations. The blacks smiled large white toothy smiles at them and tipped their hats. A short while later they passed a couple of grim looking riders armed with guns and whips. Mansel recognized them as the county slave patrol. It was their job to stop negroes and check their papers. A negro had to present his freedom papers if he was a freedman or a valid pass from his master if he was a slave. The two mean looking white men nodded respectfully to Mansel and paid no attention to Raphael. They weren't overly concerned with negroes who were travelling in the company of whites, especially those travelling with obviously wealthy planters. Mansel acknowledged them by lifting his cane and they responded by tipping their hats.

A short while later, they started passing the wrought iron fence and green hedge groves and flowerbeds that marked the boundaries of Turtle Creek plantation. The main gate was wide open, and Raphael turned the carriage down the main drive that was lined on both sides by beautiful magnolia trees. The grounds in front of the large white mansion was already filled with the carriages of other guests that had arrived. Mansel recognized most of them as local planters and their wives.

The look on Lester Jones face when he saw the Dumas come down his drive was priceless. He'd obviously not expected the master of Twin Harbours to show. Mansel's proud face flushed slightly but he maintained a dignified and prideful countenance.

I may have come, but you and Mr. Jackson are going to have to do a lot of convincing if you want me to buy into this scheme of yours...

Meanwhile back at Twin Harbours plantation, Ebenezer was preparing for the most important moment of his life—a moment that he had dreamt about and longed for. After years of quiet patience it had finally arrived.

From this moment on, I am no longer a slave. From this moment on I will never be a slave again...

Ebenezer, Cap, and several other former Sharp Stone slaves made their way down to the wooded area of the river bank and began to uncover rifles and ammunition. Ebenezer grabbed one of the Enfield's and slapped in one of the clips. He then gripped the rifle tightly and again felt the surge of power that it gave him. Ebenezer then turned to his comrades who were looking to him for leadership. Caesar was not there. He'd gone on to personally oversee the uprising on Sharp Stone itself. After dealing with Twin Harbours, Ebenezer and his force were to join Caesar at Sharpstone and then they would link up with armed bands of slaves from various plantations. They would then seize the militia armory.

And den, de' real uprising start! De revolt will spread all over!, he thought with vicious ecstasy. Like a raging fire over a parched cotton field they would consume the entire South.

Ebenezer took a deep breath. The moment of truth for the slaves of Twin Harbours had arrived. Ebenezer and the others were about to force their hands, but first they had to deal with the overseers.

Most of the white men had already retired to their cabins for the night. They lived on the other side of the plantation behind the stables. Slowly but surely the band of armed negroes made their way across the plantation grounds.

Beside Ebenezer, Cap glared at the mansion as they walked past, angry that fate had conveniently removed the planter from their grasp. He'd looked forward to paying Dumas back for the lashing he had received. He'd settle for burning down his mansion, though he hoped that revolting slaves on another plantation might dispense justice for him. In any event, it was their former master—Fitch Haley that Ebenezer, Cap, and the others most desperately wanted vengeance against. Caesar had promised to wait for them to arrive at Sharpstone so that they could be present when the fierce black hand of justice finally fell upon the master of Sharpstone plantation.

After passing the dimly lit mansion, the band of armed negroes made their way past the stables and the workshops. They then followed a short trail through a lightly wooded area to the cabins of the overseers. Despite the large number of slaves on his plantation, Mansel Dumas only employed a handful of white overseers. The man was confident in the loyalty of his slaves.

And de' sad part is he aint dat' far wrong, thought Ebenezer. There was a reason he and Caesar had only included former Sharpstone slaves in their plans thus far. To Ebenezer, the Twin Harbours negroes seemed far too content with their lot and much too devoted to the white family that owned them. *Hopefully, what happen to Cap wake dem' up!*

Seven clapboard cabins with dimly lit windows stood in the clearing. Gray smoke puffed from their chimneys. The familiar smell of stew and cornbread reached Ebenezer's nose. The overseers were poor whites who were, at least economically, little better off than the blacks they watched over. Their families labored in the fields alongside the slaves, and most of the modest pay they received, they paid back to the Dumas' for room and board.

With Ebenezer in the lead, the armed band of negroes made their way cautiously towards the cabin of the head overseer, a man named Michael Melton Slater. It was Slater that had whipped Cap. Just as they neared the cabin, Ebenezer raised his hand to signal the armed slaves to halt. He then turned to face his charges and spoke in a voice just barely above a whisper.

"Yall divide up and git by de' door of each cabin. When you hear me knock on Slater's cabin yall knock on da others. Two of ya be ready to grab de' buckra when dey come to de' door. Make sho' you keep yo' guns ready but don't shoot dem' unless you gots too—not yet. We takes care of dem together."

"What bout da womens and chilluns?" asked Cap. "We gone kill dem too?"

Ebenezzer sighed loudly. He'd put off thinking about what to do about them. As much as he hated white people for the way he'd been treated, he couldn't stomach the idea of killing women and children.

But if we let dem' go, den' dey raise de' alarm. He looked at one of the younger negroes in his party.

"Guthrie, git back to de' shop and git some rope." The young black man nodded and then headed back out of the clearing at a fast run. Ebenezer, Cap and another negro then headed for Slater's cabin. They came to a halt right in front of the door. Ebenezer took a deep breath, knocked on the door firmly three times and then like a lion about to pounce on its prey he waited. A few seconds later the door opened. For exactly one second, Michael Slater stood in the doorway of his cabin completely flabbergasted to see the black men outside of his cabin. He had no time to react in any way. Six strong black hands seized him, pulled him outside and then through him to the ground with tremendous force. Slater tried to get back to his feet but a quick kick to his ribs from Ebenezer knocked all the wind out of him.

The rush of exhilaration that flooded Ebenezer when he struck the white man was overwhelming. It felt as though a lifetime of grief, misery, and rage had finally begun to escape from his soul.

And it only jus' beginin.

Cap and the other armed Negro charged into the cabin brandishing their guns. A woman's terrified scream came from inside. A moment later the two armed negroes emerged from the cabin with Slater's wife and thirteen year old son. From the terrified looks on their faces they looked as if their worst nightmares had come to life right before their eyes.

And it has.

At most of the other cabins, the almost exact same scenario had played itself out at each one. Events at the eastern most cabin, however, had gone differently. Ebenezer watched as a tall muscular white man fought ferociously against the negroes that had grabbed him. He sent one of his attackers flying towards the tree line, then with a hammer like fist he gave one of the others a smashing blow that knocked him to the ground. Ebenezer was about to send Cap and another negro to assist in subduing the final overseer but suddenly there was a gun shot. Screams erupted from the terrified white women and children. Blood erupted from the white man's mouth and nose as he toppled over dead. No sooner had the echo of the gunshot died then Ebenezer swore loudly and profanely. It was too soon for the alarm to spread. Ebenezer hoped the gun shot didn't end up causing them undo attention.

At Ebenezer's direction the whites were divided into two groups, women and children on the right and men on the left. Guthrie came bounding back into the clearing with a large amount of rope and a few of the negroes went to work tying up the women and children while the other armed black men dragged the overseers to their feet and held them securely.

"You are some dead, niggers," said Michael Slater as two blacks took tight hold of his arms. Despite his predicament, the head overseer was red faced mad. His fellow slave drivers, however, were not as defiant. Their eyes rested solemnly on their dead friend at the eastern end of the clearing.

"We gone kill dem now?" asked one of the negroes anxiously.

"I don't want no mo' gunshots yet. Dey might alert other buckra," said Ebenezer. One gunshot in the night wouldn't be that out of the ordinary. A whole bunch of them could easily gain the attention of whites living on other nearby plantations.

"Don't worry," said Cap. He suddenly pulled a knife from his tunic and grinned a big toothy grin. "Dis do de job nice and quiet like." The eyes of the white men focused on the cold steel in Cap's hands. Its old blade was rusty and slightly dull but it could still be put to lethal use. Without waiting for Ebenezer's permission, Cap made his way towards Slater. A large toothy grin spread across the negroe's face as he approached his moment of vengeance. Slater's face went from rage to terror. He started to fight against the two negroes holding him, but he could not break away from their firm grip. Cap reared back, ready to stab his blade into Slater's gut. Suddenly the overseer's teenage son broke away from the group of women and children just as one of the negroes had reached for him to tie him up.

"John Victor! No!" cried his mother.

The thirteen year old charged towards Cap ferociously but he couldn't get there in time. Cap plunged the knife into Michael Slater's gut.

There was yet another scream from the women. Cap ripped back his knife. Blood dripped down its blade. Slater fell to the earth, clasping the wound in his gut. Blood poured from his mouth. Cap then turned just in time to see Slater's son, John Victor Slater charging him.

"I'll kill you, you filthy nigger! Leave my daddy alone!"

In one quick motion, Cap reached out and grabbed the charging boy by his shirt collar. He then held the bloody knife up to him.

"Yo' daddy git' exactly what he deserve." He then threw the boy back towards the women and children where the other negroes proceeded to tie him up. Cap then turned to Ebenezer.

"What we do next?"

"We set fire to de' Plantation. Guthrie, you take yo' group and set fire to de' big house. Agamemnon, you take yo' group and set fire to de' warehouse and docks. I goin' down to da' cabins ta let de' Twin Harbours niggas know what goin' on." Ebenezer then pointed at the other six overseers. "Cap, you and yo' group stay here and finish off the rest o' these buckra, den you come join me at de' cabins."

When he arrived at the ramshackle slave village he found that most of the negroes had been roused. The vast majority of them looked both confused and terrified. Flames were already belching from the warehouse and from the docks. The light of the flames bathed the assembled negroes in an eerie glow. Ebenezer noticed, however, that the Dumas mansion had not yet been set ablaze. Ebenezer wondered what was taking Guthrie so long to set it afire. He had no time to worry about it at that moment. It was time to rally the slaves to fight for their freedom. It was time to start a revolution. Ebenezer climbed atop an old wooden crate and held his Enfield rifle high for all to see.

"De day o' jubilee has come! It time to break de chains! It time to make de' white man pay for what he done!"

"You one crazy nigga," said an old field hand suddenly. "De white folks gone kill you. Dey probably gone kill us because o' you."

Ebenezer rounded on him with a fury.

"Not if we kill dem' first! We gots guns! And dis aint jus' happenin here. De' niggas is risin' up all over! De white folk aint gone know what hit em!"

"It aint gone work!" said the elderly negro. "You may gots guns, but de' white folk dey got lots mo' and dey knows how to use dem'. I'm gone tell ya agin. Dey gone kill you."

"I's tired of being a slave!" roared Ebenezer. He felt like a raging volcano. Part of him wanted to level his rifle at the old field hand. "I's been one my whole life and I's tired of it. I wants to be free! And if I cants be free den I's gone die and take as many o' de' buckra wit me as I can!"

"De good Lord, he wouldn't want us to kill," said another negro. He pointed at Ebenezer's rifle. "Dis aint de' answer, Ebenezer."

Ebenezer clenched the weapon tightly.

"Dis is da only answer dat dey understand! De white folks gots to be forced to let us go! It aint gone work no ways else!"

"Things is changin', Ebenezer," said the old field hand. "Lord knows deys changin' slow, but dey's changin. Dey are settin' niggas free and lettin' dem serve in de army. White folks all over is talking about de gov'mint payin' dem to set us free. Where we spose to go and what we spose to do if they does dat' I don't know. I don'ts understand it all, but I know dis' dey didn't ever talk dis way back when I was yo' age."

"Cain't you niggas understand? It time to fight back! Get off yo' knees! You can either take de scraps dey throw you like a bunch o' dogs or you can win yo' freedom fo' real! You aint gots much choice." He pointed at the elderly field hand. "Like dis ole nigga said, dey probably gone kill you no matter what now. De' white folks aint gone care what side you on. Dey gone kill every nigga dey can. Yo' only hope is fo' us to win. Now whoever wit' us come stand behind me!"

At first no one moved. But then, slowly but surely, many of the terrified negroes began to fall in behind him. Some came because they'd been convinced by Ebenezer's words. Most came because they felt they had no choice. Ebenezer had expected all of them to join him. He was surprised and angry that nearly half of them had refused to join the uprising. Ebenezer glared at the slaves that had refused to rise up.

"You niggas is nothing but cowards and traitors to yo' own kind. You gonna regret this, you jus' wait and see!"

Suddenly, Guthrie came running up to Ebenezer.

"Why aint de' big house on fire yet!" demanded Ebenezer.

"Berry and de other house niggas... de won't get out so's we can burn it."

Without a word Ebenezer jumped down from the crate and headed towards the mansion. Most of the other negroes followed in his wake. Berry and two other butlers were standing on the massive porch that encircled the mansion. Several maids were also outside on the porch or looking down from the balcony above. Most of them looked absolutely terrified. He saw Rosy among the ones on the porch.

Berry and the other two butlers were standing at the top of the stairs that led up to the porch. In his hands Berry held Mansel Dumas' double barreled shotgun. At the moment he wasn't pointing it at anyone but he had it at the ready.

Ebenezer approached the base of the stairs flanked by Cap and Guthrie.

"It time for yall to git out. We gone burn dis big house to da' ground," said Ebenezer sternly.

"No you will not," replied Berry in equally stern tones and inched the shotgun over a little. He still wasn't pointing it at anyone but the motion was a not to subtle reminder that he was armed. "Dere are womens and chilluns in dis house."

Ebenezzer looked up and saw Mansel Dumas little girls Connie and Nancy on the top balcony, their Mammy's arms wrapped protectively around them.

"We aint hurtin womens and chilluns," said Ebenezer. "But we did kill all de buckra and we is destroyin' every bit o' dis plantation so it caint be used again."

"You is foolin' yo' self," said Berry. "Even if we let you burn it dey jus' rebuild it. Dey gone kill you, Ebenezer and everyone that follows you. You not doin nothing but bringing mo' misery down on all of us. A lot o' niggas is gone die because of you."

"You just a good, well trained house nigga aint you?" Ebenezer turned his Enfield on Berry. "Now git outa our way or I swears I will blow you guts out."

Berry responded by aiming the shotgun straight at Ebenezer. That in turn caused all the Sharpstome negroes to raise their own rifles at the butler.

"I gots you out gunned, Berry," said Ebenezer.

"Dat may be so, but I promise you dis, if anyone shoots, you gone git blowed away yo self, no matter what." Berry then shouted at the mass of slaves standing on the front lawn of the mansion.

"Don't listen to dese Sharpstone niggas! Dey's angry cause o' de way ole Fitch Haley treat dem, but Massa Dumas, you all know he aint like dat. If you follow dem' you gone wind up dead wit em'." Berry then looked Ebenezer straight in the eyes. "Go back to Sharpstone. You wanna kill somebody, go kill Fitch Haley. But git off Twin Harbours!"

Ebenezer started to squeeze the trigger on his Enfield, but suddenly the old field hand that had stood up to him earlier stepped out of the crowd, walked half way up the stairs and then stood between Berry and Ebenezer. A few moments later another joined him. A few moments after that several more stepped forward and stood between the Sharpstone negroes and the house. Ebenezer could tell from the amount of talking going on behind him that most of the Twin Harbours slaves were having second thoughts. He turned to Cap. "We's runnin way late. Dese niggas wont ta stay slaves, den let dem stay. Once we whip de buckra, we come back and deal wit dem." Ebenezer then spat in Berry's direction and stomped off.

"Whoever's comin wit us, git down to da river and git yo self a gun! We gots a lot o' work ta do!" A frantic female cry came from behind him.

"Ebenezer! Wait!"

Ebenezer turned to see Rosy running towards him as fast as she could.

"I's comin wit you…"

XXXVI

"Mansel Dumas!" said Lester Jones with a broad genuine smile! "I am pleasantly surprised, sir!"

"Perhaps not as surprised as I myself," replied Dumas as he climbed down from his carriage. "But all things considered I thought I'd at least here Mr. Jackson's proposals from the man himself. I'm not one to judge a man or his beliefs by what others say about him. I prefer to see for myself."

"A wise and noble philosophy, sir," replied Jones.

Dumas turned to help his wife down from the carriage. Seeing her, Lester Jones instantly metamorphosed into a fair version of a European nobleman.

"And this must be your lovely wife," he said removing his hat.

"May I present my wife, Florence. My dear this is Mr. Lester Jones."

"It is an honor and a privilege, Madam," said Jones as took her good hand and kissed it.

"It is a pleasure to meet you at last Mr. Jones. I regret I did not get the opportunity to do so at your last visit to Twin Harbours." For an instant she looked sternly at her husband before turning back Jones. "Be assured that when next you visit you shall see how happy we are to have visitors at Twin Harbours."

"What my wife is trying ever so delicately to say is that she is sorry if I offered offense in not being more hospitable when you came by to see us."

"Not at all," he said with a large genuine smile. "I admire a man who speaks his mind and holds to his convictions and I admire even more a man whose open minded enough to question his preconceptions. And I assure you, you will not regret your decision to come here."

Suddenly Mitchell Dumas cleared his throat in a rather melodramatic fashion.

"Oh yes," said Dumas. "Mr. Jones I believe you have met my son, Mitchell."

"Yes indeed," said Lester taking Mitchell's free hand. "Jonah! Come over here and stable this young soldier's horse!"

"Yassuh!" A short stocky negro took the rein from Mitchell and led his horse away.

"Mr. Dumas, if it pleases you sir, you may tell your nigger to park yall's carriage on the west lawn and unless you need him for anything we've got a special area out back set up where our guests servants may wait."

"You heard the man, Raphael. Get moving. We'll send for you when its time to go."

"Yes suh."

As the carriage rolled away, Lester turned back to Mitchell.

"As I recall young man you were somewhat fascinated with my horseless carriage."

Mitchell lit up like a Christmas tree.

"Yes, sir. I surely was."

"Well then how would you like to take it for a spin on the south lawn?"

Mitchell's smile grew wider than the grand canyon.

"That would be fantastic!"

"Not yet," said Mansel Dumas sternly. "First you'll pay your respects to Mr. Jackson. A former President of our glorious Confederacy deserves no less."

The look on Mitchell's face radiated disappointment and bordered on mutiny.

Lester Jones smiled broadly and put his arm around Mitchell.

"I'm afraid father's outrank even Lieutenants, my friend, but you have my word you'll not leave here without taking my carriage for a drive. And now if yall will kindly follow me, it will be my privilege to introduce you to President Jackson. He should be out in just a few minutes.

Jones then proceeded to lead them across the grounds and towards the mansion. With her one good arm Florence took hold of her husband's arm and together they followed as quickly as her crippled legs could move. Three quarters of the way there, Lester Jones suddenly realized to his embarrassment that he had left his guests far behind.

A large crowd of Lester Jones' wealthy guests were gathered in front of the mansion. Planters, lawyers, and politicians from across Mississippi stood in fine suits alongside their wives who were dressed in hoop skirts. The men smoked cigars while the ladies used parasols to shade their own delicate complexions. White rattan tables and wicker chairs had been set up across the front lawn for use by the guests. Black slaves in fancy clothes hustled to and fro among the guests carrying trays of hors d'oeuvres or serving Champaign, wine and other drinks.   Mansel Dumas reflected that Turtle Creek Mansion was even larger than Twin Harbours though in his less than impartial opinion it lacked the latter's grace and elegance. As he surveyed the rest of the plantation, Dumas also noted two groups of militiamen dressed in immaculate gold embroidered gray uniforms.

"Looks like some of your friends, Mitchell."

"Colonel Norman was kind enough to provide us with an honor guard and a band for this momentous occasion."

Suddenly a tall man with a pencil and pad approached Lester Jones.

"Excuse me, sir, my name is James Bullock and I'm with the Daily Clarion Ledger."

"I've already issued a statement to the press."

"I only have one question, sir, and then I'll be out of your way."

Lester Jones let out a martyred sigh and motioned for the newspaper man to ask his question.

"Even if you are able to convince enough influential people of the wisdom of your plan, how exactly do you plan to get around our revered constitution's provision protecting the institution of slavery?"

Dumas perked up his own ears. It was a question that wanted answering. Lester Jones didn't shy away.

"What we are proposing in no way denies or impairs the right to own negro slaves. My goodness man, look around this plantation. Do you know how much it costs to feed and care for all these niggers? Have you seen how bad the cotton market has become? I'm not asking the Confederate States to force me and my fellow property owners to give up our niggers. I'm asking the Confederate States to take them off of my hand for monetary compensation so that I can better invest the capital in ventures more profitable than simply growing cotton. Surely you're not suggesting that the constitution forbids me to do what I will with my own property? The constitution does not forbid my right to sell my slaves to whomever I choose, nor does it forbid the government from buying them from me and setting them free."

"You say you want the money for more profitable ventures?"

"Yes like cotton mills and textile factories. Do you realize how profitable a textile factory would be here right next to the source of the cotton!"

"But if your slaves are gone how will you grow the cotton?"

Lester Jones laughed.

"These niggers aren't going anywhere. Oh a few might go off but they'll be back once they realized there isn't any work for them except working in the cotton fields. I'll have to pay them a little something since they'll be free. But they'll have to pay it right back to me for food and shelter."

A few of the surrounding men laughed. Bullock's pencil scratched rapidly across the pad. He looked back up at Lester Jones.

"So you're saying nothing is really going to change?"

"Oh I didn't say that," said Lester Jones. "They'll stay similar for a while. But we are on the verge of a new century—a new era that will be dominated by machines and technology. Mark my words. In a few years we'll have machines that can do the work of a thousand niggers in one-tenth the time! In short we won't need them anymore. "

"What will we do with them?"

"The deal was one question, Mr. Bullock. I've already answered three. You'll just have to wait to hear what President Jackson has to say on the subject."

Lester Jones then headed for the stairs that led up to the main porch of the mansion but was intercepted by a distressed looking white man. From his work clothes, Dumas deduced he was not a guest but one of Jones' own hired men. From the whip at his belt, he deduced that he was an overseer. Lester Jones looked not too pleased at the new interruption.

"I'm sorry, sir, but we have a small situation."

"What is it, Ford?"

"Well, sir, we've got a large number of uninvited guests that just arrived at the front gate."

"Who are they?"

"Just a bunch a plain folks that wanna see Mr. Jackson, sir. Word done spread far and wide that he'd be here. Some of these folks said they done traveled for days just for the chance to see him."

"Well they can just travel for days back to where they came from," said Jones. "This is a private event. I won't have my guests startled and made uncomfortable by...by...rift raff. Send them away at once. These Yeomen are probably here just to cause trouble." The non-slave holding, small land owning, largely uneducated, white subsistence farmers who composed the majority of Confederate citizens were amongst the fiercest opponents of the government compensated emancipation being espoused by Jones and his like-minded planters. There were various reasons why that was so. The poorer whites resented the wealthy upper classes being paid with tax dollars to have their negroes set free. Some of them harbored dreams of one day owning slaves for themselves. Many feared the increased competition that would come with the freeing of the slaves. And perhaps most powerful of all, the common white people of the CSA did not want to lose one of the only things that made them feel special despite their miserable condition. Most of them were dirt poor with little to no prospect of bettering their lot. But the one thing they had that made them special was that they were white and free. The aristocratic planters that made up the

263

Confederacy's smallest, but also its richest and most powerful population looked down on the Yeomen almost the way medieval nobles looked down upon the peasants. But as long as those same poor whites could in turn look down on the negroes, it somehow made their own lives more bearable and meaningful. If the negroes were set free, that sense of superiority and specialness would be gone, and so the vast majority of the Confederate States' common people were violently opposed to emancipation.

"Begging your pardon, sir," said Ford, "but I don't think these particular folks are here to cause any kind of trouble. A lot of them are old vets dressed up in their old uniforms. Some of them say they served under Mr. Jackson. But sir, all the old grays say they aint leavin till they see Stonewall."

Jones swore fiercely, but thinking about the reporter, relented.

"The last thing we need is to give our adversaries ammunition to use against us. Very well, they may come on to the grounds but see to it that they keep to the back."

After that Jones finally ascended the stairs to the massive front porch of his mansion. A few moments later a large crowd of common folks came on the scene—men in overalls with their young sons on their shoulders, women and girls in homespun dresses, teenage boys with straw hats, and over twenty old men dressed in the same worn out gray uniforms they'd fought in decades earlier. Taking a deep breath, Lester Jones leaned against the railing and addressed the people gathered on the lawn of his plantation.

"Thank you for coming, my friends! Today it is my great pleasure to introduce to you a man who needs no introduction. A man who along with Robert E. Lee himself, helped to preserve the independence of our great Confederacy and under whose leadership our flag was carried to the shores of the Pacific Ocean. Ladies and gentlemen, I give you former President Thomas Jonathan "Stonewall" Jackson!

The crowd erupted into cheers and applause. At Jones' signal, the militia band struck up Dixie. Spontaneously, but not all together unexpectedly, the entire crowd—young and old, men and women, rich and poor, erupted into song.

Oh I wish I was in the land of Cotton!
Old Times there are not forgotten!
Look Away! Look Away! Look Away! Dixieland!
In Dixieland where I was born, early on one frosty morn!
Look Away! Look Away! Look Away! Dixieland!
And I wish I was in Dixie! Hurray! Hurray!
In Dixieland I'll take my stand, to live and die in Dixie!
Away! Away! Away down south in Dixie!
Away! Away! Away down south in Dixie!

As the last verse of the chorus sounded, Jackson stepped out onto the porch as the band played on. A few people kept singing, but most simply erupted into cheers and applause. The old vets let loose with screeching rebel yells. Jackson inclined his head to them.

Dumas stared curiously at Jackson. He wasn't disappointed, but Jackson seemed different then he'd always pictured him. He had a full head of gray hair and a long thick gray beard. His eyes radiated with confidence and strength of will. In a way he looked like an aged and dignified lion. And yet, there was still a sense of meekness about him.

As the cheers and applause continued, the old vets took up the chant "Stonewall! Stonewall! Stonewall!" Jackson, bowed his head slightly, and Dumas saw genuine humility on his face of a sort not generally seen in most men of power. Dumas reminded himself that Jackson had never really and truly been a politician, but a General who had dutifully stood at the side of his great commander Robert E. Lee when a grateful Confederacy had all but demanded he serve as President. Had fate not removed Lee, and elevated Jackson to the highest office in the land, Dumas doubted that the General would have sought the presidency for himself.

He's far too honest. Jackson's views on slavery and emancipation, though unpopular had never been hidden. Perhaps no other figure in the Confederacy, save Lee if he were still alive, could have held to such views, and yet retain the loyalties and affections of so many Confederates. Anyone else would long since have been ostracized and rejected. But Stonewall was Stonewall.

Jackson moved with a slow but deliberate stride. In his left hand he gripped an ornate cane while with the right he took tight hold of the bannister as he descended the steps from the front porch of the mansion to intermingle with the assembled guests. Several gentlemen and their lady escorts quickly stepped forward to meet and greet the former Confederate President. Jackson was almost but not completely swarmed by the enthusiastic guests. Neither were the plain folk shy about approaching him. Whether they agreed with his ideas or not, the assembled planters, lawyers, and other high society people greeted him warmly and politely. The grey uniformed vets, however, approached him with hats in hand and they clasped his hand solemnly and gazed at him with so much reverence and awe that it was as if they'd seen an angel of the Lord. For his part, Jackson returned their reverent affection. They enjoyed a bond that none save others that had served could ever understand.

Florence was simply not able to keep up with the crowd. The Dumas were, therefore, amongst the last to get to meet the President. They made their way forward slowly. Florence Dumas kept tight hold of her husband with her one good arm but moved her crippled legs with a spree that was seldom shown. When at last their turn came, her face was alight with joy. Mansel reflected that whatever his final verdict on Jackson and Jones proposals, the smile on his wife's face was worth the trip and then some. They were introduced by Lester Jones.

"Mr. President, may I present Mr. Mansel Dumas and his lovely wife Florence."

Ordinarily a lady extended her right arm when greeting a gentleman. Since her right arm hung limp and useless at her side, she instead released her grip on her husband and extended her left hand to the former President. Jackson, ever respectful, courteous, and true to custom, accepted it with his right and kissed her gloved hand.

"It is an honor and a privilege, my dear lady."

Florence blushed as Jackson turned to shake her husband's hand.

"It is indeed an honor, sir," said Dumas in spite of himself.

Lester Jones turned to Jackson.

"Mr. Dumas here is one of the men here today that is most skeptical of our plans."

Dumas felt his face redden. It was not something that happened often nor something he cared for. He wanted to glare at the younger plantation owner but maintained his composure. He then addressed Jones.

"If my mind were not open, Mr. Jones, I assure you I would not be here. Like a good lawyer you have elucidated greatly on the economic and industrial benefits of emancipation."

Jones bowed to Dumas.

"As I am indeed a law school graduate I'll take that as a complement, sir."

Dumas turned his gaze upon Jackson.

"I would like to hear from you yourself, sir, why we should abandon a system that has worked for us for hundreds of years."

Jackson returned his gaze man to man.

"I shall be happy to do so."

"To that end," interjected Lester Jones, "I have arranged a place where we can all sit down and discuss these matters more fully. That is after all why we are here. If you gentlemen would care to accompany me into the mansion?"

Dumas exhaled heavily, then turned to his son.

"Take your mother and see that she finds a place to rest comfortably."

"Yes, father," said Mitchell taking his mother's arm. Dumas then followed Jackson, Jones, and several other men up the stairs and into the mansion.

The south wing of Turtle Creek contained a large library which doubled as a smoking room. It had several overstuffed chairs, and sofas. Lester Jones directed Jackson to the most ornate chair while most of the other men took seats around the room. Dumas was one of the few left standing, and just as well, for he doubted he could have remained calm, if forced to sit. He stood in the corner of the room beside a fine wooden writing desk with his arms crossed, waiting to hear what the former President had to say. Jackson didn't keep him waiting long.

"Gentlemen, I have no doubt that Mr. Jones, as the leading member of our society in this state, has well stated the case for the nationally compensated emancipation of negro slaves. It is for no small reason that our organization is known as the Confederate Society for Prosperity and Industrialization, though our enemies viciously attack the name as a ploy to distract from the real issue. It is not my intention here today to dwell upon the disastrous state of the cotton industry, or of our international relations. You gentleman no doubt feel the pain of those two inexorably linked issues than do I. But moving beyond the economic reasoning, I should like to point out what the emancipation of the negro does not mean. It does not mean caving into the demands of foreign nations such as the United States or Great Britain nor does it mean acknowledging that the system upon which our society has been based for nearly four hundred years is in any way more unjust or evil than the social stratifications that exist in those countries. I have said many times that slavery as it exists in the Confederate States is an honest system that acknowledges slavery for what it is. The truth is that the lower classes in Britain and the masses of impoverished immigrants in the United States are hardly freer than our negroes. If those oppressed masses are free from the industrialists of London and New York then they are free in most cases merely to starve. They labor in conditions far worse than the slaves of our plantations and what little pay they receive is swindled from them in exchange for food and shelter no better and often worse than any we provide for our slaves. So gentlemen this is not about being more moral than our opponents, though I think you'll find that much of the animosity we face abroad will vanish when we take these first serious steps towards emancipation. But most of all, gentlemen, this is about preparing for the future, and it is about the security of our great nation.

I perhaps more than any man alive in the Confederacy today, am aware of the unique challenges that will face our nation when the next war with the United States comes…"

Olen Jamison, one of Duma's neighbor's, took that moment to interrupt the former President.

"You speak as if another war with the North is inevitable, sir."

Jackson replied in deep tones of absolute confidence.

"I have never been more certain of anything in my life. The Yankees have never been able to stomach our independence. Twice they have attempted to invade and conquer our land and twice we have repelled them."

"Excuse me, sir," said James Bullock (Dumas hadn't noticed the newspaper man had entered the room), "but it seems to me that things with the Yankees have been relatively quiet for the past twenty-five years. As you say, they attacked us twice and we licked them twice, but they haven't tried again since. Why then must another war be inevitable?"

Without hesitation, Jackson answered the reporter's question.

"If you were old enough to have faced the Yankees in battle, you would know what I'm talking about, when I speak of their determination to have dominion over us. Those people have merely been biding their time. Look at recent events. The United States maintains massive forces along our border forcing us to do the same. Their President, Grover Cleveland, has been expanding their navy. As we speak Union mercenaries are in Cuba fighting for the Spanish against our boys in gray. The United States has belligerently purchased Puerto Rico from Spain, knowing it will bring a confrontation with ourselves and Spain, and they have signed a treaty of alliance with the British Empire, ensuring that the next war, whether it comes sooner or later, will be larger than any we have ever even imagined."

Dumas could no longer contain himself.

"Sir, I do beg your pardon but what does all of this have to do with why we should set the negroes free?"

"The point at which I am driving, Mr. Dumas, is that the United States have always outweighed us in population and industrial output. That is true now, more than ever despite the limited advances our industry has made in the last thirty years. Statistically speaking if we went to war today those people could field nearly three times as many men as we could."

"You're saying you want to set the niggers free so that we can put guns in their hands and make them fight Yankees," said Dumas.

"They form over a third of our population and would go a long ways towards evening the balance."

"Only a fool would put a gun in the hands of a black," said Jamison. Dumas wondered how the former President would take the insult. He'd seen duels fought over less offensive remarks. Jackson turned a fierce gaze back upon the planter.

"As a Christian man, I'll not take offense at your calling me a fool, sir, though I must wonder whether or not, if President Lee were here today, you'd say such to his face. He too was in favor of emancipating slaves to help in the defense of our sovereign states as I might add was George Washington long before him. The negro conscription act for which I am so often vilified was drafted by President Lee himself at the height of the War of 1869 when the Union armies were at the gates of Richmond. We barely held off the Yankees then. If we are to do so again, we must have all available men. Furthermore, we must greatly expand our industry. We have more factories now than any southerner in 1860 could have ever dreamed and yet it is still not enough to match the industrial might of the United States. For the security of our Confederacy we must find a way to end our reliance on imported goods. We must gain the ability to manufacture all the necessities of war for ourselves and in sufficient quantity."

"Let us assume that you are right, sir," said Dumas, "and that another war with the United States is inevitable. Let us also assume that all the economic benefits stated by Mr. Jones are true. I get a massive influx of government funds, I build myself a cotton mill and maybe a textile factory, the foreign markets all open back up and business is as good as it was in the old days. There is still one very important question that must be answered. And unless you can answer it satisfactorily, you'll never have my support. What do we do with the negroes after we free them?"

Jackson sighed.

"At first they will have nowhere to go and so the vast majority of them will stay with you as free laborers. You'll pay them wages and they in turn will pay you back for the food and shelter you will continue to provide them. Our symbiotic relationship will continue, much as it has for the past four hundred years, though in modified form—not far different from the one I described that exists in the US, England and other parts of the world, though I hope that in Christian charity and Southern honor we would treat our former slaves more graciously than those other nations treat their working classes. However, in the very near future, I have no doubt that technology will advance to the point where we will no longer need thousands of field hands to bring in the crops. At that point the current system will end by default. We must prepare for that day. There is no sending the negroes back to Africa nor anywhere else. The logistical requirements of such an attempt would be astronomical and utterly unfeasible, to say nothing of the injustice of turning millions of negroes who have faithfully served us into poor homeless refugees in a foreign land. The negro is here to stay gentlemen. We must prepare him to take care of himself. My vision is that in the future each Confederate State will set aside land on which their respective negroes may live, care for themselves, and even govern themselves—segregated from—yet under the guidance and protection of the Anglo-Celtic race." *Until the day that, by heaven's grace, we are at last ready to live together as children of God.*

Silence filled the room in the wake of Jackson's words, as the assembled men pondered what he had said. It was broken by a planter named Jacob Populis.

"I don't know if the future described by Mr. Jackson will ever happen. Who knows if technology will ever indeed advance to where we no longer need negroes to bring in the crops. If such a scenario comes to pass, we will deal with it one way or another. Speaking for the present, I can indeed see the benefits economic, political, and military that Mr. Jones and Mr. Jackson have described. I also see the potential for great danger. We must tread carefully and not act rashly for once this is done, it cannot be undone."

Nods and grunts of agreement resounded around the room. Olen Jamison swore.

"There's already more free-niggers running around then I'd ever care to see."

"And sufficient laws have been enacted at both the state and Confederate level to insure that they remain in their place," said Jones. "Naturally, those laws would be greatly expanded if our plan for emancipation went forward."

"Now wait just a minute," said yet another planter. Dumas didn't recognize him so he presumed he must have traveled from some distance away. "We're not talking about setting them all loose right away are we?"

"No, sir," said Jones. "It will be completely voluntary, that by the way is what makes this plan constitutional. If any man cares to hold onto his negoes he may do so, though I'd wager he'll change his mind when he sees the success and profits the rest of us experience."

"So you're not in fact trying to force anyone to give up his niggers?" The man spoke as if he was for the first time understanding the plan being proposed.

"No, sir. All we're asking is that we be allowed to emancipate our slaves and receive government compensation. The only instance in which slaves can be forcibly emancipated is in time of war which as we all know is already law."

"And we all know who to thank for that," said Olen Jamison, and shot a dagger like look at the former President.

"I didn't know that it wouldn't be mandatory," said the other planter stroking his beard. "That makes a lot of difference." Several of the other men nodded. Lester Jones, rose to his feet.

"Well gentlemen, I suggest we let it mull over for a little while." He pulled out a gold pocket watch. "Dinner will be ready in just over an hour. In the meantime I suggest we return to the ladies."

Dumas made his way out with the other planters. He found his wife and son sitting at a table under an umbrella and enjoying glasses of lemonade.

"How was it, Father?"

"Interesting," said Dumas, and left it at that. It wasn't long before Lester Jones appeared again. He addressed Mitchell.

"Now my friend, I do believe I promised you an opportunity to drive my horseless carriage." Mitchell's face lit up with excitement. He turned momentarily to Mansel who hesitantly nodded his permission. As his son walked eagerly away with Jones, Mansel turned to his wife.

"Infernal machines, Flossy. To hear some folks talk they'll be doing everything one day."

"Well if so I do hope they'll invent machines to fight the wars, so our young men will no longer have to be in danger."

Suddenly, a deep voice spoke from beside them.

"I'm afraid, Madam, that in my experience technology has only made warfare even more deadly. Man is constantly seeking to invent more and better ways to slaughter his fellow man. If the weapons of war grow even more terrible, then God help us."

"Mr. President," said Dumas rising from the table. "May I join you?"

"Please, sir."

"Did you serve in the wars, Mr. Dumas?" asked Jackson.

Mansel nodded.

"I was 21 years old in 1861. I served in the 1st Mississippi Light Artillery. I'm afraid we enjoyed little of the glory that you won in Virginia. At the end of the war, we were surrounded in Vicksburg. I imagine we would have starved to death had you and General Lee not won at Gettysburg."

Jackson nodded, as much as in sympathy as in agreement.

"Our forces here in the western theater were outmatched even more so than we were in Virginia. You should be proud that you held out as long as you did."

"I'm afraid I have little to be proud of, sir. I spent more time in the sick hospital than I did in the field though I did see action at Corinth and then later at Vicksburg. The Yankees ravaged Mississippi during the war. Many of the friends of my youth died in the defense of our rights, our independence, and our way of life."

"Now your own son wears the uniform. Let me ask you this, Mr. Dumas. Do you trust the negroes on your plantation?"

"Yes, for the most part," said Dumas.

"The vast majority of them were born and raised on Twin Harbours and have been part of our family all their lives," added Flossy.

Jackson nodded again.

"Now, Mr. Dumas, let us suppose that one day, heaven forbid, your son shall find himself in a situation similar to the one you faced in your own youth—outnumbered and outgunned by the Yankees. Would you trust those negroes, who have served you all their lives, to bear arms and fight alongside your son?"

Dumas shifted uncomfortably in his seat.

"In such desperate circumstances, I suppose I would, but there is far more to this matter than you are intimating, sir. While I do indeed trust most of the negroes in my service, I cannot say the same for those of other men. I consider myself a fair man. I hope you won't consider it bragging if I say that in my opinion I treat my people well. That being said there are men who don't. The few slaves with which I have had trouble are negroes that I procured from such men. On top of that, abolitionists in the United States and England are constantly trying to stir up the slaves against us. Make no mistake, there are plenty of negroes who would happily rise up against us and even murder us if they got the chance."

Instinctively Jackson quoted the Bible.

"'Even as I have seen, they that plow iniquity and sow wickedness reap the same.' Shortly after being elected to a term of my own, I introduced to the Confederate congress a bill prohibiting the cruel treatment of negro slaves as cruel and unchristian."

"I remember, sir," said Dumas. For a moment Dumas felt a tinge of shame. Here he was warning of the danger of mistreating slaves, and yet when Jackson had tried to prevent it years earlier, he'd been as vocal as any in opposing it. "Men don't like to be told what to do with their property," said Dumas. "Whether a dog, a horse, a mule or a negro, a man's property is his property. That is one of the principles our Confederacy was founded upon." Dumas spoke with a conviction ingrained in him for generations.

Jackson nodded. Dumas thought he sensed a slight trace of bitterness.

"That bill never made it past the committees. I was ridiculed in the press across the nation. But you and I know that there is a great deal of difference between a negro and a beast. Though enslaved, the negro is still a human being, made in the image of God. Even a dog will bite back when it is treated cruelly. Why should we expect any less from a black man? Slavery existed in biblical times. The word of God admonishes the masters to treat their slaves with compassion, we would do well to heed it."

A short while later a fancy dressed negro began to ring a dinner bell to call all the guests in to the mansion. The Dumas and Jackson rose to their feet. Jackson looked at Florence.

"It would be an honor and a privilege madam if I could be allowed to escort you to the dinner table." He then hefted his own cane. "I'm afraid, however, that at my age I am fortunate to keep myself on my feet."

"Think nothing of it, Mr. President," said Florence. "I have enjoyed getting to meet you and look forward to the rest of our evening."

Slowly but surely the guests made their way into the mansion. An enormous dinner table, fit for a palace stretched across the entire dining hall. It had chairs for forty-two people—twenty on one side, twenty on the other and one at each end. As host, Lester Jones took his seat at the head of the table. Jackson, by virtue of his status, was seated at the other. As Dumas and his wife took their seats not far from Jackson, Florence asked, "Where do you suppose Mitchell is?"

"No doubt, he's still messing around with that infernal machine," said Dumas in a disapproving yet unsurprised tone.

In short order, negro servants brought out large platters of ham and baked chicken, bowls of vegetables and rice, pans of cornbread and many other delicious dishes.

"It's almost like Christmas!" said Florence. "This party must be costing Mr. Jones a fortune," she said quietly.

Dumas nodded.

"Which tells me one thing of which I am at least convinced. Lester Jones really believes there is profit to be made in his plan."

"Do you really think people will go along with it?"

Dumas, sighed.

"There's a good possibility. If they do, I just hope we don't end up regretting it."

Suddenly from outside there were several large bangs.

"Are those fireworks?" asked Florence.

Mansel shook his head.

"I don't think so. They sounded like gunshots."

All at once the sound reached their ears again, this time louder and closer than before. The front doors of the mansion were swung open violently and the assembled Southern elites then saw the substance of their worst nightmares. A large number of negro men—field hands by their ragged clothes—stormed into the great plantation house brandishing military grade rifles. Several of the women screamed—a few even fainted. Like most of the men Dumas was speechless, virtually paralyzed by rage and fear.

Lester Jones rose from his chair and addressed the large negro who stood in front. The plantation owner was literally red in the face. He swore blasphemously.

"Spartacus what is going on here!"

The negro's eyes filled with hate and anger. He let out a loud fearsome cry of rage, raised his rifle and pulled the trigger. The rifle barked loudly. Jones' chest exploded into a fountain of blood. The plantation owner stood in shocked silence for a few seconds and then fell down backwards never to rise again. The vengeful black man worked the bolt on his Enfield and then brandished the still smoking barrel at the other whites and answered his late master's question.

"The day of Jubilee!"

XXXVII

Mitchell Dumas had been having the time of his life driving Lester Jones' horseless carriage all over the grounds of Turtle Creek plantation. At first Jones had ridden with him. But eventually he'd had to return to his guests, though he made it perfectly clear that young Mitchel could drive the contraption as much as he wanted, or at least until his father or mother hunted him down and ordered him off. Mitchell had happily taken him up on the offer. After his third lap around the plantation, he was already formulating how to persuade his father to get one. As the carriage crested a small rise on the western end of the grounds, Mitchell pulled the break lever and brought the carriage to a halt. The sun was getting low. It wouldn't be much longer before the dinner bell rang if it hadn't already. The mansion was off to the east. To the west was the river, Turtle Creek's slave shanties, and...

Negroes. Mitchell saw a whole bunch of black field hands headed east towards the mansion. Something was out of place, though at first he couldn't quite put his finger on it. Finally, it dawned on him.

Guns! They're carrying guns! He released the break lever and spun the large and almost vertical steering wheel to the right. Jones had showed him how to increase the carriage's speed by pushing another lever forward a single notch while simultaneously pushing a special pedal on the floorboard. Sure enough the carriage picked up speed. The engine also became louder. *What are they doing with rifles?* No matter what he'd seen he still had a hard time believing it, much less imagining them doing anything menacing with them. All his young life he'd never seen negroes do anything but obey white people. A few were uppity, but most just did as they were told. He'd always taken their obedience for granted. He'd certainly never seen a black openly defy a white. Not until now.

The unmistakable sound of gunshots reached his ears. The negroes had opened fire at the gray uniformed militia band that still stood on the grounds in front of the mansion. A few of the militiamen that actually had guns reached for them but were gunned down before they could so much as draw back the hammers. Mitchell watched in horror as the gray uniformed men went down with sprays of blood. A cold chill went up his spine and he felt sick to his stomach. He'd known guns could kill people. He'd imagined being a soldier his whole life. He'd imagined it being exciting. Seeing it in real life turned out to be both frightening and disturbing. He sat frozen at the controls of the still moving horseless carriage. Another second and he would have crashed into an ornate stone bird bath. The sudden sound of more gunshots and of bullets cracking past him, snapped him back to reality. He turned the horseless carriage to the right, away from the negroes who were shooting at him, and towards the plantations main entrance. He turned so fast, he very nearly turned the carriage over. He felt the left wheels leave the ground, and breathed a sigh of relief when they came crashing down again.

More bullets chased after him. Thankfully, none of them hit him—or the engine. He sped out of the main gate and down the main road. He felt horrible leaving his father— and especially his mother—behind, but he had to get help. His first thought was to get help from one of the other nearby plantations.

But if the niggers here have guns, those could have guns too…

He didn't know how the negroes of Turtle Creek had gotten their hands on rifles but he was smart enough to know it was unlikely to be a fluke. *They couldn't have gotten them on their own. They must have had outside—foreign help.* He'd listened to his father and other men for years talk about the insane abolitionists of the North and of England.

I've got to get to get to Fort Rosalie! The small outpost on the Mississippi where he had done his drill and training was manned by a small unit of regular soldiers. But it was also the center of the militia command for all the local counties. One glance at the sky told Mitchell he'd never get their before dark. The night was almost upon him. Hesitantly, he slowed the horseless carriage and then applied the break lever. He looked warily over his shoulder. There was no sign of pursuers. He leapt down to the ground and made his way to the front of the carriage where two carbide lamps were mounted. Jones had mentioned them in passing, but he'd not explained how they worked or how to light them. He looked at the sky again. Night was coming quickly. If he was going to light the lanterns he had to figure it out quickly. He fumbled in his uniform coat for some matches. He ignited one and then held it up to the orifice from which the flame was apparently supposed to emanate. Nothing happened. He swore and tossed the used match aside. Taking a deep breath he surveyed the lanterns again. A small valve sat atop each of them. Mitchell turned the valve and he suddenly heard a faint dripping sound. Some sort of liquid was falling from the upper chamber in to the lower one. Deftly, he struck another match and held it up to the orifice.

There was a bright flash that both startled and pleased him at the same time. A bright white flame was issuing forth from the orifice. Mitchell repeated the process on the second light and a few moments later the horseless carriage was once again chugging down the road. He didn't push up to full speed again. For one thing the dirt road was far too uneven and crooked. He'd do neither his parents nor any of the other poor people trapped back at Turtle Creek any good at all if he crashed into a tree or a ditch. For another he didn't know how much fuel the contraption had left and he didn't want to use it up faster than he had too.

He made his way steadily and cautiously down the road. The carbide lights did an excellent job of lighting the roadway. Every so often he would glance behind him, but it was so dark he could see nothing. Sighing, he decided all he could do was press on. He came upon a bend in the road. He made the tight turn as carefully as possible, but as he came about he saw something that made his heart leap. He jerked the break lever so suddenly that the inertia threw him forwards into the steering wheel. Taking a deep breath he looked up in horror. Three bodies swung from the trees by the neck. Mitchell recognized them almost instantly. It was the county slave patrol. Gulping and filled with fear, Mitchell released the break and got underway again.

After about an hour he passed an old abandoned church. That let him know he was only a mile from a crossroads. A left turn would take him into Natchez, a right turn would take him to Sharpstone plantation. Going straight would take him to the fort and eventually home to Twin Harbours. Mitchell considered heading to Sharpstone. Fitch Haley and his men would have guns...

If his niggers haven't gone all up in arms... For the first time he thought about the slaves on his own plantation and his little sisters. He tried to shake the picture of the negroes at Twin Harbours rising up with guns as he'd seen the ones at Turtle Creek do. No matter how hard he tried he couldn't form that picture. He doubted Lester Jones could have either before it happened.

About half a mile from the crossroad, the engine started to sputter. A few moments after that it went dead and the horseless carriage came to a rolling stop. Mitchell let out a curse, but wasted little time climbing down and heading down the road as fast as his legs could carry him. When he finally reached the cross roads he stopped to catch his breath.

I need a horse... He knew that every moments delay was another moment his parents would be in danger. He hoped and prayed the Turtle Creek negroes wouldn't hurt them. He was about to turn right towards Sharpstone, when suddenly he caught sight of a large group of people carrying torches coming from up the road. Until he knew who they were he didn't want to be seen. He quickly dashed off the road and into the trees to watch from cover. He was very soon glad that he had done so.

Down the road came a large groups of blacks carrying torches and rifles. Mitchell thought a few of them looked familiar, and then he got a look at the ones who were leading the pack. Ebenezer, and Cap each carried Enfields. The looks on their faces said that they were eager to use them. Next to Ebenezer, Mitchell spotted Rosy, one of the house slaves. His heart sank and his thoughts went to his little sisters who'd been left behind at Twin Harbours. Mitchell had never before been filled with so much anger, fear, and confusion. He was unsure what to do. One thing was certain, he wouldn't be going to Fitch Haley's plantation. The whole band of armed negroes made the turn that would lead them to Sharpstone. If he hadn't already, Fitch Haley would be getting a nasty surprise. If his own family hadn't been in such danger, Mitchell might have hoped the negroes gave the mean old snake what he had coming to him. As it was...

He made his way as quickly as possible towards the fort. He ran harder and faster than he ever had in his life. When he finally reached the fort two hours later he was ready to collapse. The gates were locked and the guards were either asleep or else doing something other than keeping watch. In any event he shouted like a madman and a few moments later the main door opened. The sergeant and corporal that came out to meet him looked as if they thought him deranged when he told them what was going on. Nonetheless, his Lieutenant's bars were enough to get him an audience with Major Fife.

"Calm down son! Calm down!"

"I'm telling you the niggers have got guns! They were shooting people at Turtle Creek! My parents are trapped back there. I passed more with guns on the way here!"

No matter how he explained it the Major looked as if he couldn't believe it. Had he not known who Mitchell was he might not have listened at all. Fortunately it was only a short while before another man came up to the fort screaming about niggers with guns and about how the plantation where he worked as an overseer was burning. Major Fife looked like a man in a daze, but he gathered himself quickly and went into action.

"Sergeant, sound assembly! Get the men ready to move out!" He then turned to Mitchell. "You come with me, Lieutenant." Mitchell followed the Major and his second into the interior of the fort. They made their way into Fife's office where the Major spread a map onto the desk.

"Show me where, Turtle Creek is at."

Mitchell pointed.

"And you are certain, that President Jackson himself is there and is being held hostage?"

"He was there when I left, sir."

Fife sighed and turned to his second in command.

"Captain Renwald, I want you to send an all out alert over the wire! Contact Jackson, Vicksburg, New Orleans every county within a hundred miles. In the meantime we'll head north ourselves, and sweep the plantations until we reach Turtle Creek. Tell the boys to shoot any nigger they see on sight, understood?"

"Yes, sir. But with the war on in Cuba everything is likely to be poorly manned. It could be a while before we get any help."

"Just send the wire. And let's pray help is able to get here in time."

XXXVIII

The sun was getting low in the sky as Fitch Haley rode his horse through the main gate of his plantation. The master of Sharpstone considered himself an excellent horseman, and of course a horseman of his caliber deserved the finest horse. His solid white mount was a thoroughbred Stallion he had imported from Spain. It had cost him a small fortune. He had purchased the horse a few years earlier. The Confederacy had been at peace with Spain then, and the finances at his plantation hadn't been nearly as bad. In the past year he'd been forced to sell off nearly a third of his slaves and at outrageously diminished prices. It was Haley's custom to take a short ride in the evening after having dinner. Normally he'd found that it helped him calm his nerves and relax. Not this night.

He brought the horse to a halt right in front of the mansion. As expected, a negro waited nervously to take the horse back to the stables. If he hadn't been there just when Haley wanted him he would have paid dearly. The jittery slave came forward to take the reins just as soon as Haley dismounted.

"You take good care of him, you hear me boy? That horse is worth more than you are."

"Yes, Massah! Don't you worry. I takes good care ole' Forrest here."

Haley menacingly pointed his horse whip at the negro.

"You had better."

He then turned and stormed up the steps onto the front porch of his mansion where another nervous looking negro, this one dressed in a fancy butler's suit waited to open the door for him. No, Haley's horse ride had done nothing to brighten his mood.

I guess I'll just have to ride something else... Haley turned to his butler.

"Eliab, get your black ass down to the cabins and tell Sally May to get up here and get my bed ready for me." The tone of his voice and the smirk on his face said he wasn't sending the young negress up there to change the sheets and turn down the mattress. She wasn't even a house slave. But she was his property. He could do what he wanted with her and or to her. And so he blasted well intended to. It would hardly be the first time. Like a lot of slave owners, Haley had never had any compunctions about taking a master's privilege with his young female slaves. He'd had to be discreet about it when his wife had been living. Now that she was gone, well... he took his privileges a lot more often. He still had to be a little discreet. He still had one daughter living with him that he hadn't yet managed to marry off. Predictably she was waiting for him in the parlor, and she did nothing to improve his mood.

"Daddy!" Her voice was plaintive and petulant. "You should have let me go to the ball at Turtlecreek!"

"We've been over this, Beth! Lester Jones has got that damned black Republican as his guest of honor and together the two of them are trying to get everyone to turn loose their niggers! We will have no part of it!"

"But everyone else is gonna be there! Mary, and Joanna, their husbands took them!"

"When you find a husband as foolish as theirs... *and the sooner the better...*then you can go to all the 'set the niggers free' parties you want to!" Whereas he had been merely shouting at her angrily, he now shouted at her at the top of his lungs. His angry voice echoed though out the house. His face was blood red. A vein on his forehead bulged.

"NOW I DO NOT WANT TO HEAR ANOTHER WORD!"

His angry outburst silenced her, but it didn't frighten her. She merely stuck her nose in the air and spun on her heels.

"Come on Zuendy, I've got to figure out what I'm going to wear tomorrow." A frightened looking negress house slave followed Haley's daughter out of the parlor and towards the mansion's west wing. Beths's voice trailed behind her.

"...not that I expect a negress to have any fashion sense, but they both have little tears that need mending. I guess you'll just have to sew both of them before morning…"

Haley rubbed his eyes and made his way over to the liquor cabinet. He poured himself a good dose of amber liquid and knocked it back. Mentally he made a note to start inviting more suitors to the mansion. He started to pour himself another, but then stopped. He wasn't exactly a young man anymore and if he still wanted to have fun that night he didn't want to hamper his performance with too much alcohol. Suddenly excited, he was able at last to put away his financial troubles and all the changes happening in the world that he hated. There'd be time enough for all that later. For now…

He made his way to the mansion's left wing and up the stairs. He may have been getting older, but he had a spring in his step nonetheless. He opened the door and just as he expected, there was Sally May standing in front of the bed. Unexpectedly, she was still in her clothes.

I'll take care of that by, thunder. She was a beautiful teenage girl. Her skin was a light coffee and cream color—a testimony that not too far back a situation similar to the present one had helped bring her into being.

Haley walked lustily towards her.

"Come here, honey…"

Bam!

For Fitch Haley, everything went black. When he finally awoke he had a splitting head ache and his vision was blurry. He was dazed and confused, unsure what had happened. Then he tried to move, only to discover that he was tied to a chair. He tried to speak but found that he was gagged. Slowly but surely his blurry vision came painfully into focus and he realized he was still in his bedroom, but there was no sign of Sally May. Instead he saw on older negro that looked somehow familiar.

Caesar!

Haley's eyes grew wide with shock, fear, and anger.

"Hello, Massa Fitch. It be a long time eh?"

Haley tried to speak but the gag completely muffled his words.

"You save yo' strength now," said Caesar with a malicious smile. "You sho gone need it." Caesar began to pace the room. "When I was a young man, yo daddy owned me and beat me. Then later you owned me and beat me. I was yo' servant. I was yo' creature. I was yo' animal! When I rans away you chased me down wit dogs and guns but I beat ya. I gots away. De' underground railroad, dey gits me out a the CSA, through the USA and into Canada. I be a free man all dese' years but you be sure I never forget Sharpstone, where I comes from."

Haley was red in the face. A few loud angry noises escaped the gag but nothing was coherent.

"You wants to know why I come back? I come back to sets my people free and to see to it that those who oppress them pay fo' their crimes." Caesar suddenly pulled an old rusty knife and pressed it against Haley's face just below the eye. He spoke in a slow, but deep and menacing tone. "And believe me, white man, you is going to pay."

Caesar's hand trembled as though it longed to drive the knife up into Haley's eye or slash it across his throat, but his discipline and patience won out.

First things first. He put the knife away and returned to his pacing.

"You remember my sister, Aurelia? You used to haul her up here to your filthy bed chamber and defile her just as you've done to countless other of our women since. It seems you haven't changed in all these years. Well now you gonna know what it like."

Caesar suddenly pounded the bedroom door. A moment later Haley heard a feminine scream. He recognized it has his daughter. A moment later the bedroom door flew open and she was thrown violently through the door way and onto the floor. Seven large black men walked in after her. Haley recognized them as some of his strongest slaves. All seven of them wore enormous and sadistic smiles. Caesar nodded to them and they took violent hold of Haley's daughter and began to rip her dress off of her. Haley fought against the cords holding him to the chair but it was futile. He tried to yell in rage but the gag kept him muffled. He watched helplessly as the seven black men stripped Beth naked, and then one after another beat, raped, and sodomized her. Her screams and cries and then later her moans and groans filled the entire mansion. The whole time Caesar stood watching Haley's face, taking nothing but pleasure in his former master's misery. The old negro soaked up the fallen plantation master's sorrow with relishing glee. He watched Haley's face go from contorted rage to panicked and helpless despair. When Haley tried to close his eyes so he wouldn't have to watch anymore, Caesar walked behind him and then pried his eyelids open with his fingers.

When, after what seemed an eternity, the black men had finished with her, Haley was forced to stare at her naked, motionless, abused body lying there on the bed. She made no noise nor did she move. He was unsure if she was alive or dead. He never got the chance to find out because one of the black men subsequently punched him in the gut, knocking the wind out of him. At Caesar's direction they untied him from the chair, bound his hands behind his back and then literally dragged him by the hair of his head out of the bedroom, down the stairs, through the parlor and the front door, and out onto the grounds in front of the mansion.

As he staggered to his feet, Haley had the distinct impression that he had died and gone to hell. All around him his plantation was burning. The rebelling slaves had set fire to the docks, warehouses, barns, and stables. No sooner had they'd thrown him from the mansion then the angry negroes also set fire to the big house. With tears in his eyes, Haley watched as the flames engulfed the mansion.

Beth!

Haley found himself completely surrounded by angry, slaves who jeered and shouted, and cried out for his blood. The eerie light of the burning plantation made them look like fiery demons ready and waiting to torment him and so in a way they were. Haley suddenly found himself being dragged away and towards the ramshackle village where his slaves had lived so long. Once there he caught sight of several dead bodies. His heart started to pound as he recognized them. They were his overseers. They had been stripped and beaten with whips until every last square inch of their bodies were covered in lacerations. Haley could still hear feminine screams. Maybe it was latent mad memories of what had happened to his daughter or maybe it were the cries of his overseer's wives and daughters suffering the same fate.

Haley was tied to the whipping post that he'd used his entire life to beat his slaves. The angry negroes stripped him naked and then backed away. Caesar stood over him in judgment like the Almighty over a hell bound sinner. To Caesar's left and right stood Ebenezer and Cap like Apostles at his side. In his arms Cap at last held his woman Jemima and his son, Zeke. To Haley's utter amazement and disbelief all the negro men held guns. Caesar held up a large black leather book.

"The Bible says, whatsoever a man sows, that shall he reap! You, Fitch Haley have spent yo' entire life sowing nothing but wickedness, misery, pain, and sorrow. Now you shall pay fo' yo' sins, eye fo' eye, tooth fo' tooth, burn fo' burn' stripe fo' stripe!"

Haley's gag insured that he was silent before his accusers. At Caesar's signal, Sally May, Jemima, and several other negresses came forward and each in turn kicked Haley between the legs as hard as they could. Blow after blow sent waves of pain through Fitch Haley such as he had never known. With each blow, a cry of pain tried to escape his mouth. The gag prevented it. In the aftermath, Haley clenched his jaw so tightly that he cracked his teeth. Tears of pain forced their way out of his eyes. When the other women had finished with him, Sally May took a knife knelt before him, and viciously unmanned him. She held the ruined bloody remnants of his manhood in her hands just in front of his eyes and then slapped them in his face. She then spat on him and walked away.

Though at the moment he could have scarce imagined it, Haley's torture had just begun. Vengeful negroes came forward with glowing red iron brands. Haley had used such brands for years not only to mark his horses and livestock but also to punish his slaves. Now several of the slaves he had branded paid him back all at once. He tried to scream every time that the hot metal branded his flesh. When they finished he was a broken man. He hung helplessly from the pole, crying like a baby. The vengeful negroes showed him not an ounce of pity. Ebenezer, Cap and several others went to work on him with whips. They whipped him again and again and again. Fitch Haley found himself longing for death, long before it came.

XXXIX

Virtually, all of the white people in Turtle Creek Mansion cowered in fear on the far side of the dining hall. Former President Thomas Jonathan Jackson, was not one of them. He glared menacingly at the negro that had murdered Lester Jones there in front of everyone. Jackson knew he could die. He also knew it could not happen until God sovereignly decreed it.

"What do you think you can possibly accomplish with this madness!" demanded Jackson. Several of the negroes spun their rifles towards him. Jackson didn't so much as flinch, but continued to fix Spartacus with that same commanding glare.

"Be quiet, ole man! Fo I blows yo' head off!"

"Do you have any idea what you've done?" demanded Jackson. "We were finally making headway, finally bringing your people one step closer to freedom. It was on the horizon! Now, you have all but guaranteed that slavery will continue! This rebellion has no hope of succeeding. It will end in fire and blood. The authorities and the army will not stop until they have hunted you down and destroyed you, and I fear that in their zeal to crush this rebellion many innocent negroes may be caught up in the fighting. In any event those who survive will have to live with the consequences of your foolish and selfish actions."

Spartacus's eyes narrowed savagely. He jerked his rifle slightly.

"This is all you white folks understand!" he shouted angrily. His finger started to tighten on the trigger. A deep rich voice suddenly shouted: "Spartacus!"

The slave turned to face another armed negro but kept his rifle leveled at Jackson. This one was tall with a smoothly shaved head and face. When he talked, his voice was not only rich and deep, but also educated.

"Are you going to kill our most valuable hostage?"

Spartacus raised a questioning eyebrow.

"That is former President Jackson himself you are about to kill."

Spartacus lowered his rifle and turned back to regard Jackson.

"I...I didn't know..."

"Oh don't go apologizing to him!" said the educated negro angrily. "He's to be kept alive because he's a bargaining chip, and for no other reason." He walked up to Jackson and stared menacingly down at him.

"Who are you?" demanded Jackson. The black man was young but from the way he spoke he was both educated—and Northern.

"If you must know, my name is William Du Bois. Of course I know who you are—the great white hope. Well as you can see, Mr. President, we don't need your help. We are perfectly capable of taking what is rightfully ours."

"What do you intend to do with us?"

"We have no intention of killing so prestigious a person as yourself, Mr. President. As I said, you are a hostage. To be used in negotiation. As for these... people..." he turned to look at the disheveled planters and their wives, "They will face the justice of those they have so long tyrannized and oppressed."

"I'll ask you, what I asked Spartacus," said Jackson. "What do you hope to achieve by this?"

"In a word Mr. President: 'Freedom.' More specifically we are intent upon following in the footsteps of the Confederacy itself and seceding to establish a nation of our own."

"That is madness," said Jackson. "It will never succeed."

Du Bois spread his hands.

"From here across to South Carolina—we want a black homeland on the American continent and the freedom of all our brothers in bondage!"

"It will never happen," replied Jackson. "Not that way."

"You would certainly have never gotten us our freedom," said Du Bois bitterly. "Not real freedom at any rate."

"You don't know that," said Jackson. "It would certainly have been far better than what you are about to bring upon yourselves and your people."

"Your threats are meaningless to us."

"I'm not threatening. I'm telling you the sad honest truth whether you want to hear it or not." Jackson pointed to the Enfield that was slung on Du Bois shoulder. "The foreigners who have incited you to rebel and who have provided you with arms, they know that you will ultimately fail. They know you don't have a chance. They are merely using you as pawns—whether to strike a blow for their fanatical cause or to distract the Confederacy from its current endeavors I know not—but either way, it is you and your people who will pay the highest price. Do you have any idea how many soldiers there are stationed in the forts and bases all up the Mississippi? How many along the coasts?"

"Our supporters have assured us that this uprising will be happening everywhere! All across the Confederacy! Most of your army is off fighting in Cuba."

Jackson shook his head.

"The river and coastal forts are still garrisoned as are the ones on the border with the USA. There are plenty of reserve forces. Even setting aside the army and the state militias, every white man in the south will oppose you with arms. And as far as this notion of an uprising happening everywhere it's simply not possible." *Or at any rate, not very likely.* "Before dawn the telegraph will have alerted the entire Confederacy as to what is going on here. If by some chance this rebellion is widespread it will make no difference. You'll be up against artillery, machine guns, repeaters, and overwhelming numbers. It will mean the virtual extinction of your people in the South. Richmond would stop at nothing to put you down. Here in this area you won't just be facing the county militia, or the militias of the surrounding counties. The army could have thousands of heavily armed troops here by river and by rail in a matter of days—especially if this uprising is as confined as I believe it to be. Either way, you and your people will be slaughtered. I implore you to end this folly while you still can."

Du Bois turned his back on him and started to walk away. Before leaving the mansion he turned back to Jackson menacingly.

"Perhaps we will be, Your Excellency. But if we are slaughtered, know that you and these people most certainly will be as well. That I promise you."

XL

John Wilkes Booth studied the map of the Confederacy on his desk with trepidation and anxiety. He still had no idea as to the exact area in which the foreign abolitionists were attempting to incite a slave revolt, though he was certain it would be within one-hundred miles of Vicksburg and somewhere on the Mississippi. Nearly one-hundred marines and over two hundred reserve army troops had been stationed in Vicksburg along with several ironclads and transports. Booth had convinced President Stone to order Navy Secretary Hilary Herbert to order the concentrations in conjunction with the War Department. Booth had informed the President that he had received intelligence about a massive smuggling cartel that was bypassing Confederate tariffs and importing foreign manufactured goods illegally by bringing them ashore at remote areas of the Mississippi. It was technically the truth. Booth had received such reports, but it was a much smaller problem than he'd made it out to be. The marines and troops were in Vicksburg awaiting deployment orders. Booth had hoped that the revolt would take place sooner. As it was the troops and marines were ready but the commanders were confused as to why they were not yet being deployed to hunt for smugglers and search for contraband. Thankfully President Stone and Secretary Herbert were far too busy with the war with Spain and the newly announced alliance between the USA and Britain to pay much attention to the operation.

But I can't keep them on station indefinitely. Eventually the wrong people are going to start asking questions.

Sighing, he rolled up the map. He had other duties that needed attending to, no matter how obsessed he was over the simmering slave revolt. Setting aside the map he opened a report detailing a counterfeiting operation in Georgia. Like its counterpart in the United States, the Confederate Secret Service had many different areas of responsibility. In addition to gathering intelligence, counter intelligence, and special operations abroad, it was also charged with hunting down counterfeiters. The Confederate economy was suffering enough without the inflation and lack of faith in the country's currency that was caused by the printing of counterfeit money. Such people were waging economic warfare on their own nation. Booth and his men had narrowed down the counterfeiters to a single county about thirty miles outside Atlanta. He had undercover agents combing every town, village and hamlet in it. They had orders to take the counterfeiters alive if possible, but Booth had a higher purpose in capturing them alive than merely bringing them to justice.

He reached into his desk drawer and pulled out what, at first glance, looked like a Confederate gray back. In reality it was one of many counterfeit one-dollar notes that his men had seized. Booth reached into his wallet and pulled out a genuine note, then set the two side by side. The counterfeiters were good. Just about everything matched: the lines, borders, numbers, writing—even the seal and the signature of the Secretary of the Treasury. The only real difference was in the feel of the paper—genuine currency was slightly heavier and more coarse, and a few subtle differences in the portraits of Jefferson Davis. The counterfeiters had produced a good image of the first Confederate President, and it was nearly identical to the one on the genuine note. There were however, subtle—and incriminating differences. The shading was slightly darker and the eyes looked different. The average person would probably never notice.

They're good. And I have the perfect use for them.

When he finally captured them, Booth intended to give them a choice: life in prison or work for him. With their counterfeiting skills and the resources Booth had at his disposal he hoped to be able to duplicate and mass produce the currencies of the Confederacy's rivals and enemies. In the event any of them carried out their economic threats against the CSA (and probably even if they did not) he envisioned leaving envelopes with thousands of dollars or pounds in counterfeit currency all over the United States or Great Britain—millions of dollars or pounds in total. Of course those nations had anti-counterfeiting agents of their own. *Which means we need the best counterfeiters.*

After reading the reports from Georgia, Booth searched through the stack of paper work looking for anything about agent Connery. He'd heard nothing from him since Whitmore's mercenaries had left Canada on British flagged transports. He had reliable intelligence that one of those transports had sunk enroute to Cuba. At the time he had been reasonably certain that Connery had been responsible. But it had been weeks since Whitmore and his Yankee and British mercenaries had arrived in Cuba. Now by all reports a truce of sorts had been reached in Cuba.

The Spanish army was declaring Santiago an open city and in exchange the Confederate forces were allowing both their troops and ships to withdraw unmolested. Cuba was now completely controlled by the Confederacy, the war—for all intents and purposes—seemed won. Ordinarily Booth would have been pleased. It was— after all— his personal plan that had set the war in motion by destroying the CSS Mississippi and blaming the Spanish. By having Connery destroy his own nation's warship, Booth had provided the Confederate States with the cassus beli for declaring war on Spain and seizing the island of Cuba.

But where is Connery now? Booth rose to his feet and walked to the wall of his sanctum. He'd long since moved the gold pin that represented Connery from Canada down to Cuba.

Did he sink with the British ship? Has he been killed? Captured? It was the last possibility that worried him most. Connery was a strong man but Booth knew from close personal experience that information could be forced from even the strongest men—if proper techniques were employed. Booth was not alone in his expertise. The Union, Britain, and even Spain had men just as willing to do what was necessary to extract information from the enemies of their respective nations. If it ever got out that Booth was the mastermind behind the war, it would have major repercussions—both for the Confederate States, and most especially for he himself. Booth tried not to dwell on such things. He returned to his desk and resumed his work.

The hours passed, but Booth was so consumed in his work he hardly noticed. There in the basement of the Treasury building there were no windows for him to see that the sun had set. The electric lights which illuminated his sanctum were constant regardless of the hour. When Booth finally looked up at the clock on the wall it was after midnight. He was just about to leave for the night when candlestick phone on his desk rang.

"This is Booth."

The man on the other end of the line stifled a yawn.

"Director, Samuel Lamont here."

Booth recognized the exhausted man's voice as that of President John Marshall Stone's personal secretary.

"Yes, Mr. Lamont?"

"Sir, the President must see you immediately at the Presidential Residence it is a matter of some urgency."

"Tell him I'm on my way."

Booth rose from his desk. After securing his sanctum he climbed up the stairs that took him out of the basement and then made his way out of the treasury building and onto the streets of Richmond. Since it was the middle of the night it was as quiet as a grave yard save for the sound of a few crickets. The streets were well lit by electric lampposts but were entirely deserted. It was a good fifteen minute walk to the Presidential Residence on Shockoe Hill. Booth arrived at the front gate to the mansion grounds just as General Edward Porter Alexander, the General in Chief of the Confederate Army came riding up on horseback. Alexander leapt down from the horse with the gusto of a much younger man. Booth envied him his spryness. At age sixty, General Alexander was in remarkably good physical condition.

"Good evening, Mr. Booth."

"Good evening, General. Any idea what this is all about?"

"I'm afraid not, but we'll undoubtedly find out in short order."

The two men were almost instantly let in the gate by a gray uniformed soldier of the Presidential Guard. Samuel

Lamont was waiting for them at the entrance of the gray stuccoed mansion.

"This way, gentlemen. The President will see you immediately."

He led them across the bottom floor of the mansion and up a large staircase that led to the second floor where every President since Jefferson Davis had maintained a private / secondary office in addition to the main executive office in Confederate Hall.

John Marshall Stone rose from his desk looking both haggard and exhausted. He frantically brandished what looked like a telegraph dispatch at them.

"We have an emergency! According to this dispatch from Natchez there is a massive slave insurrection underway!"

Both Alexander and Booth looked stunned. Alexander because it was genuine and Booth because— despite being out of the theatre business for years—was still a natural actor.

"Are you certain, Mr. President?" asked Booth.

The President thrust the dispatch at him.

"Yes, I'm certain! According to this report they have guns, and we're not talking squirrel guns we're talking military grade rifles!"

"How is that possible?" asked Alexander.

"I don't know. But the insurrecting niggers are burning plantations, murdering their masters, killing white men, raping white women..."

The President collapsed into his chair in despair and unless Booth missed his guess shock. Mississippi was Stone's home state. He was himself a former governor. The news was a staggering blow to him.

It will also be a staggering blow to some of your policies. I wonder what the people will think of your giving niggers guns after this? Booth was reasonably certain that the insurrection would send Stone's political popularity plummeting—not that a President of the Confederate States of America had to worry much about that. He was only eligible for a single six-year term.

295

"Has the militia been activated?" asked General Alexander.

"Of course! Governor McLauren is calling up every available unit in the state but many of the best men are away from their districts filling vacancies along the national border to make up for all the troops we have in Cuba. Louisiana has also activated its militia, but they are as shorthanded as those in Mississippi."

The President then looked directly at Alexander. "How long to get regular troops down there."

"As thinned out as we are...at least two days, maybe even three."

"Mr. President," interjected Booth. "You may recall that some time ago you had the navy and the war department concentrate over three hundred marines and soldiers in Vicksburg, as well as a good number of ironclads and transports to assist the Secret Service in intercepting smugglers..."

Booth got no further.

"You mean they are still there?" asked the President in disbelief.

"Er.. yes sir. The operation had to be postponed because..."

"Never mind that!" said Stone excitedly. "They're still there! That's what's important!" The Presidents face was now lit up with both excitement and hope. "Maybe we can contain this fire before it spreads any further!" He turned back to General Alexander. "Dispatch a wire to Vicksburg at once! Send those forces to Natchez immediately! Order them to do whatever it takes to put down this insurrection!" The President's face suddenly grew cold and hard. "And tell them to show these niggers no mercy! Let them find out what it means to defy their rightful masters! We must make an example of them! I want every nigger in the world to see the price of rising against us so that nothing like this will ever happen again!"

"I will see to it, Mr. President," said Alexander grimly and turned to go.

"One other thing General."

"Yes, sir?"

"According to this report former President Jackson was a guest at one of the plantations where the niggers are risin' up! He's either dead or being held hostage."

A vicious smile spread suddenly across Booth's face.

Now that is what I call ironic justice... thought Booth with relish.

As an old veteran of the Army of Northern Virginia, Alexander's look couldn't have been more different. It showed a combination of worry and fierce anger.

"Do we know at which plantation, General Jackson was a guest, sir?"

John Marshall Stone handed him the dispatch.

"It's in the report."

Alexander hurried away frantically. The War Department was in for a long night. The President turned to face Booth.

"I want you to find out who's responsible for this. Those niggers couldn't have gotten guns on their own! I want to know who's responsible for giving them to them."

Booth nodded somberly.

"Don't worry, Mr. President. You may be assured that the Secret Service will use every measure at its disposal to discover the truth."

XLI

Ebenezer basked in the light of the glowing flames that were consuming Sharpstone plantation. He'd dreamed about that moment all his life. Now he had found revenge was as sweet a dish as he'd always imagined. Now that Fitch Haley and the other white people on Sharpstone had been dealt with, Caesar was ready to get on with their plan. He approached Ebenezer.

"Where are de rest of the nigga's from Twin Harbors?"

"Dey wouldn't join us," said Ebenezer with disgust.

"What do you mean dey wouldn't join you!" asked Caesar in a rage. The flames of Sharpstone house, were still raging in the background.

"Berry and most of de' house niggas, and an ole field hand, dey'd rather fight us den de' buckra!" said Ebenezer angrily. "Most a dem nigga's too dumb and scared to know when it time to finally strike back! I told em' dat dey would pay!"

"And dey will," said Caesar. "But first, we gots to win. We needs to get to Turtle Creek."

Ebenezer and Cap nodded. They'd settled with their previous owner. What was left of Fitch Haley's body hung lifeless from Sharpstone's whipping pole. Their other former owner was there at Turtle Creek along with a whole lot of other oppressors.

"We takes care o' dem just like we did ole massa Fitch," said Cap. Caesar shook his head. "No, not yet. Dey are much more valuable to us alive. Especially President Jackson. He be a valuable hostage. The buckra, dey might bargain fo' him. But regardless we gots to get organized and join up with others. Get everyone together. We's moving out."

Ebenezer surveyed the burning plantation with satisfaction one last time. He'd spent virtually his entire life there at Sharpstone. It had been a life of misery. He took one last gratifying look at Haley's corpse. It brought a smile to his face.

Cap had his woman and his boy. Ebenezer looked around for Rosy. He spotted her by a tree, her face buried in her hands.

"What wrong?"

"What ya'll do to dat man… it not right."

"Shut yo' mouth!" yelled Ebenezer. "You don't know! You don't know what he did to us!"

"I don't wanna watch you do de same to massa Mansel and miss Flossy…"

"Dey, gots to die," said Ebenezer savagely. "All de' oppressors gots to die."

Rosey turned away from him and made to cover her ears. Ebenezer's voice softened a little. "But we be quicker wit dem den wit Fitch. Maybe we not even kill em. Caesar said we gone use em as hostages."

"I never wanted this…" said Rosy.

"What did you want?" asked Ebenezer.

"I wanted freedom...and I wanted love. But after what I've seen tonight... I don't know if I want the freedom...and I don't know if you can give me love..."

Ebenezer reached out to touch her, but she pulled away from him. Angrily, she started to walk off.

"Nigga's like you is gone have to learn. Dis is de' only way. De white man is never gone give us our freedom. We gots to rise up and take it. We gots to hurt dem so bad dat dey's lets us go!" Then he walked away. Behind him, Rosy broke down crying.

A short while later the entire group of armed negroes began marching away from the flaming ruins of Sharpstone. Just as they reached the cross roads, several mounted negroes came riding up on horseback."

"What news?" asked Caesar.

"The niggas on Monmouth and Melrose are wit us. Dey done burn de plantations and is headed dis way."

"Dat's good!" said Caesar.

"We gots some bad news too. It don't look like dere's any uprising at all on Dunlieth, Auburn, Rosalie or any of the other plantations."

Caesar was momentarily speechless. He rallied quickly.

"Dey'll join us soon enough. We jus' gots to get to em' and sho' em what's goin on!"

"We gots one other problem too. De' buckra in dat fo'te is stirrin. Dey marchin dis way!"

"Dat aint no real surprise," said Caesar. "They jus' doin it a little sooner den we thought dey would." Caesar then turned to Ebenezer.

"I need to git to Turtle Creek and talk wit William. He de nigga from up north' who come down to hep us. You and Cap take most of the men here, join up wit de niggas from Monmouth and Melrose and slow down dem' buckra. De rest of us will take de women's and children's to Turtle Creek. We send you some mo' fighters soon."

Ebenezer nodded and gripped his rifle tightly.

"We'll give them buckra a taste o' steel!"

Caesar nodded.

"I know you will. You were always strong. Even when you were a boy I had you marked fo' greatness. You haven't let me down!"

Cap turned to Jemima he held her by the hands and looked into her tear filled eyes.

"Take Zeke and go wit Caesar and the other women."

"We not be separated from you agin," she said.

"You have to," said Cap. "Zeke is too small to be near shootin' and fightin'. You go and no matter what you stay safe."

"We're not leaving you!"

"I said, you go! I be back soon!"

He took her in his arms and kissed her.

Ebenezer looked for Rosy. He didn't see her. Letting out a sigh he hefted his rifle and turned back to Cap.

"Let's go kill some mo' buckra."

XLII

From the floor of the dining hall, Mansel and Florence Dumas watched the exchange between the negro leader and President Jackson with trepidation. Dumas admired Jackson's calm nerves and brave demeanor, but he doubted they would do any good.

"Are they really going to kill us?" asked Florence in a frightened voice. Dumas let out a sigh. No matter what he thought, he wanted to reassure his wife. But he couldn't very well answer her question with no when Lester Jones bloody body was still lying atop the ruined dinner table. The negro, Du Bois, had made it clear that the insurgents had no intention of letting them live if their demands weren't met.

Fat chance of that.

To his wife he said: "I don't know what they are going to do Flossy. All we can do sit tight and wait."

"Do you think Mitchell is okay?"

"I don't know." Mansel was also worried about his boy. Mitchell had been wearing a gray uniform. There had been a lot of shooting outside when the uprising started. So far they had seen none of the honor guard that the militia had sent, which had to mean…

He was off on that contraption. Maybe he had sense to get out of here when the shooting started... "I'm sure he's fine, Flossy."

"I do hope so." For a moment she seemed to relax but then she nearly went into a panic. "Our little ones! Nancy and Connie are back on Twin Harbours! They said this nightmare is happening everywhere, we..."

"Calm down!" said Dumas. He wasn't the only man having to calm down a frantic wife. The armed negroes standing guard seemed to be enjoying their captive's distress. Nevertheless, Dumas got the distinct impression that they didn't want anyone doing much talking.

"We've got to stay calm," he said quietly. Then he whispered in her ear. "I don't care what these niggers say. The girls are with Mammy, and Rosy, and Berry and all the rest of our people. They would never hurt them."

With tears in her eyes Flossy nodded. Mansel held her and rocked her until she finally fell asleep. Outside the sun had long since gone down. Dumas had removed his coat and hat and used them as a pillow for his wife. A few feet away he could see Jackson sitting in abject silence, staring away into empty space, and completely lost in thought. Mansel Dumas wondered what was going through his mind. Despite the precariousness of their situation, part of Dumas wanted to gloat, to throw the whole thing in the President's face. To tell him what a fool he'd been for thinking negroes could be trusted. But not now. In a way, Jackson had been proven correct. He'd been warning for years that allowing a few ruthless men to treat their slaves barbarously could lead to disastrous consequences. Dumas had honestly felt that he'd always been a fair master.

But heaven knows Fitch Haley isn't. Dumas didn't have any trouble imagining an uprising like this on Sharpstone. Dumas had no idea what kind of master Lester Jones had been, but he knew which way he'd bet now. He'd seen the look on Spartacus' face when he'd killed Jones. He'd never heard talk of the master of Turtle Creek wantonly beating his slaves with whips, branding them with irons, or any of the other nightmarish stories he'd heard about Sharpstone over the years.

301

But physical torture is hardly the only way a master could earn the hatred of his slaves. Dumas suddenly remembered that he had seen a number of light skinned young pickaninnies on the plantation. Dumas shook his head and sighed. Whatever the truth was it was far too late now.

After checking to make sure that the guards weren't watching he crawled quickly and quietly over to where Jackson sat.

"Mr. President, are you all right?" he asked quietly.

"Yes, Mr. Dumas, as well as can be. Yourself and Mrs. Dumas?"

"She's asleep, now. I'm afraid the stress of all this could give her another stroke."

"I do pray God, that is not the case," said Jackson gravely.

"Who do you think is behind this?" asked Dumas. "Like you said, they couldn't have done this without outside help."

"Does it really matter now?" asked Jackson. "Slavery is and always has been an unarmored and exposed weak spot on the surface of our nation. We have failed to cover it in time, and now one enemy or another has taken the opportunity to plunge in a dagger."

"The question is what do we do about it?"

"I'm afraid all we here can do is wait and pray. As far as what to do about slavery in general now, I fear that what has transpired here tonight may well place the peaceful abolition of slavery in our country beyond our reach forever."

Dumas couldn't tell him he was wrong. The vast majority of white people in the South would never forget, and never forgive an uprising like what they were seeing. Especially if it was as widespread as the negroes were claiming.

"After what has happened here, sir, do you still really think that slavery should end?"

Jackson looked him in the eye.

"I do. What we are seeing here is not a result of our considering the end of slavery. It is a result of slavery itself and of our failure to end it before now. I have no doubt we will put down this rebellion with fire and sword. But in the aftermath, if we don't learn from this, and get the albatross of slavery off from around the neck of our nation, I fear it will eventually pull us under and drown us."

Jackson suddenly hung his leonine head in the deepest despair.

"I fear that we are only reaping what we have sown." He suddenly looked up at the armed negroes standing in the room. His eyes radiated sadness. "And soon, so will they."

XLIII

Ebenezer had been nothing but a slave his entire life. Other than the fact that he had been taught to read in secret as a boy by Caesar, he had no education to speak of. He certainly had no training as a soldier. Caesar had had to teach him the basics of loading and firing his rifle in the secrecy of his cabin. The first time Ebenezer had ever gotten to fire the weapon had been in anger. Now he was trying to lead a band of armed, insurrecting, slaves against and an approaching group of soldiers. Ebenezer may have lacked education. As far as being a soldier was concerned he lacked experience. But he was very intelligent.

Before burning the stables at Sharpstone, they had taken the horses. In fact they had more horses than negroes who knew how to ride them. On any given plantation, only a few trusted slaves were ever allowed to leave to carry out business for their masters. Those who did had passes, and usually drove a horse pulled wagon. There were a few, however, who had worked in the stables and whose duties had included taking the horses out for rides on the plantation grounds. What few horsemen he had, Ebenezer sent forward to find out where the buckra were. Another problem they faced that also stemmed from the fact that most slaves were never allowed off of their plantations was that there were very few who knew the basic geography and road layout of the region they'd lived in most of their lives. Most negroes never left their plantations.

Even though they had torches, the fact that they were operating at night didn't help matters at all. When it finally became clear that they were in danger of getting lost, Ebenezer finally brought the group to a halt. He looked at Cap.

"We wait. Till de horse niggas git back or de sun rise." He posted guards and then ordered the others to get some rest. He took part in the first watch. They had no way to tell time exactly, but about half way through the night he woke a few other negroes and ordered them to keep watch till dawn. He then leaned against a tree and tried to get some rest himself. It seemed no time at all before Cap was shaking him awake.

"Ebenenzer... de horse niggas is back."

Ebenezer leapt to his feet. It was still dark. He had to grope and feel his way out of the trees but the horsemen carried torches. The firelight made them look menacing on road.

"We ran into de buckra. Dey comin dis way with torches and guns."

"How many?" asked Ebenezer.

"Too many. Some of dem is soldiers. Most of dem is buckra from Natchez and dem plantations where de nigga's didn't rise up yet."

That last part made Ebenezer want to curse and to swear. It infuriated him to no end. But there was no time to worry about it now. He pushed it to the back of his mind. He had more pressing matters to deal with at the moment.

"How long fo' dey git here?"

"Not long. Befo' sunrise. We also see dem split up. One group headed off east, so maybe mo' nigga's risin up over dat way."

Or maybe they takin another rout around behind us… Ebenezer hoped the slave on horseback was right, but he feared, that before long he'd have enemies both before and behind him. He issued orders to the scout.

"Yall git back dat way and give de buckra as hard a time as you can, den git back dis way as quick as you can. We be ready fo' dem when you git back here." As they rode off, he turned to the armed negroes that made up his band. "Grab branches and logs. Drag dem across de road. We gots to block it. Den grab mo' and pile dem up in de trees to de left and de right so we has somethin to hide behind."

The negroes worked harder and with more zeal then they had ever shown for their masters. They were fighting for their freedom…and their lives. Ebenezer reflected that the two now went hand in hand. No matter what, they'd never go back to being slaves. Even if they had wanted to the buckra would have never allowed it. As far as whites in the CSA were concerned there was only one thing to do with niggers that opposed them: kill them. Ebenezer hoped that knowledge was soaked into the head and heart of every negro that was taking a position on that firing line. They'd fight harder if it was. Though there was no time to set up defenses in the rear, Ebenezer did post a handful of fighters there.

Just in case.

About an hour before dawn they caught sight of a few torchlights coming down the road. Ebenezer had ordered most of the torches extinguished. He held one of the few remaining ones in his hand.

"Don't shoot till I say so!" shouted Ebenezer. He squinted in the darkness trying make certain they were his own side's scouts.

"Who dat!" he shouted.

"It us!" came the familiar reply. "De buckra is right behind us!"

"Git over here and git dat light out!"

The horsemen dismounted and led their horses off the road, into the trees and behind the makeshift barricades as quickly as possible. A couple of minutes later all the torches were out and they were in pitch darkness. Other than his breathing and that of the fighters nearest to him, all Ebenezer could here were crickets and frogs. He felt a sting on his neck and slapped a mosquito. A few moments later and they caught sight of more torchlight coming down the road. It was a large band of white men. A few were mounted but most were on foot. Ebenezer took aim with his rifle. He hoped no one opened fire before he gave the signal. He felt for certain the closer they got, the more of them they would hit…and kill. The whites were probably no more than thirty yards away when they spotted the barricade in the road.

"Now!" Ebenezer's rifle barked. A half second later guns to his left and right followed suit. The forward-most white men were cut down by the hail of bullets. Ebenezer worked the bolt on his Enfield, took aim and fired again. He grinned savagely as one of the mounted buckra fell from the saddle dead. The remaining buckra started to move off of the road into the cover of the trees. Their torches, however, drew bullets from the insurrecting negroes like moths to a flame. Only a few haphazard shots came back at the slaves. The whites were too busy trying to put out their torches. Ebenezer fired until his rifle was empty. He started pulling bullets from his ammo pouch but discovered that reloading the Enfield in the dark wasn't easy. There was a noticeable slacking of fire all up and down the line. He wasn't the only one having trouble feeding rounds into the magazine. Over the course of a minute that seemed to last an eternity, he finally managed to load eight rounds in the dark. He worked the bolt and looked for a target. The buckra had finally managed to put out their torches.

"Stop shootin!" cried Ebenezer. Slowly but surely the negroes who'd managed to reload their rifles ceased fire. Up ahead, Ebenezer saw a couple of muzzle flashes, but by and large there was almost no fire coming from the whites. Several cries of pain echoed through the night as wounded men called out for help. Ebenezer was certain that most of them came from white throats.

He took a deep breath. They had given the white men a bloody nose but he was certain they hadn't killed all the buckra that had been in that group. He peered hard into the darkness trying to see any sign of their enemies.

Either dey waitin, or dey pullin back. Ebenezer let out a sigh and wiped sweat from his black skinned brow. *Either way, we stopped dem fo' now.*

XLIV

Thomas Jackson had gotten very little sleep during the night. Long ago, in the army, first of the United States and then of the Confederate States, he'd known quite a bit of hardship. But it had been quite a while since he'd been forced to sleep on something as uncomfortable as the floor of Turtle Creek Mansion. At his age, his bones and back complained enough when he had a proper bed to sleep on. The night had not been pleasant.

The negroes had kept armed guards around the assembled hostages all night. Conflicts with them started when nature started calling on several of the prisoners.

Jackson would have bet that none of the wealthy men and most especially women being held captive had ever been escorted outside by a slave to relieve themselves. To what they thought of as their everlasting shame they had now.

At one point during the night Jackson was certain he'd heard a commotion outside, as if several men were marching away. Sure enough, when the first rays of dawn came in through the mansion windows, there seemed to be fewer armed slaves around then there had been the night before. Shortly after first light another loud commotion started outside. Jackson could hear the frantic shouts of several negro insurrectionists but he couldn't make out what they were saying. A moment later he heard two loud booms, one right after the other. Jackson recognized them immediately as cannon fire.

It's begun. Outside the sound of artillery shells exploding onto the plantation grounds reached Jackson's ears as did the terrified shouts of several negroes. Jackson was certain they were shouts of fear not pain. Once one had heard the screams of men wounded and ruined by artillery fire, one never forgot. Jackson wasn't surprised the negroes were scared. They'd undoubtedly never encountered anything like this before.

Suddenly, Du Bois came into the room looking angry and confused. He ignored Jackson and the other prisoners and made his way towards the mansions front door. Caesar and several other negroes nearly ran into him in their haste to get inside the mansion.

"I thought you said that field hand from Sharpstone had managed to stop the enemy's advance!" said Du Bois angrily.

"He did!" said Caesar irately. Maybe he was simply under pressure, but Jackson thought the older negro disliked taking orders from the much younger but obviously more educated Du Bois. "Ebenezer and his men stopped de buckra several miles south of here!"

"Then where is that artillery fire coming from!"

Caesar swore and cursed furiously.

"From de gun boats in de water!"

Du Bois raced to one of the windows facing the river. Sure enough, two Confederate river ironclads were just off the river bank along with three other boats. The ironclads were toys compared to their ocean going cousins, but their guns were plenty deadly. At the moment they were raining shells onto the armed negroes that had been encamped on the plantation grounds. The slaves moved away from the river banks, but the shells seemed to follow them.

"They won't risk shelling the house," said Du Bois. "Get everyone either in the mansion or behind it!"

"We be sittin' ducks if we do dat!" protested Caesar. "Besides dey got soldiers in dem' boats! Dey could come ashore any minute! We gots to git outa here and hook up wit Ebenezer and de others."

"What about dem'," asked Spartacus, motioning at the prisoners with his rifle.

"We'll take Jackson and a few others with us," said Du Bois.

"Shoot the rest!" said Caesar savagely. He and Du Bois then made a hasty retreat out of the mansion.

Two large negroes made their way towards Jackson. He offered what resistance an unarmed man his age could. He tried to hit them with his cane. They deflected it easily, took it away from him and cast it aside. They grabbed hold of Jackson while four others grabbed a couple of the wealthy planters and dragged them all away from the other prisoners. Screams and protests erupted from the hostages on the floor as several armed negroes spread out and leveled their rifles at them. Mansel Dumas rolled atop his crippled wife to shield her with his body. Suddenly, there was a gunshot and one of the negroes dropped dead. One of the planters on the floor had pulled and fired a pistol that he had kept concealed until that moment. He tried to fire again but was cut down by a hail of bullets from the other negroes. Several other planters saw their chance and though they were unarmed threw themselves at the armed negroes. Three of them were shot dead but two others became locked in close quarters combat with the negroes they had attacked.

Suddenly there was a deafening explosion. An artillery shell had landed just in front of the house. The blast blew in the front door and most of the windows. A large sharp piece of glass imbedded itself in Jackson's right hand. He let out a cry of pain and an angry curse forced its way out of his lips. His memory shot back in time thirty four years to the first battle of Manassas, where he'd caught a bullet in the hand. He'd cursed that day too. He could count the number of times he'd used profanity in the intervening three decades on one hand.

Several of the negroes had gone down with wounds far worse than his own. Because most of them had been huddled on the ground, most of the prisoners were unhurt. Several more men took advantage of the opportunity and leapt to their feet. A vicious battle erupted inside the dining hall. Jackson never got to see the outcome of the contest. He was dragged out of the mansion.

Outside the shells were still coming down. The negro insurrectionists were now abandoning the plantation as quickly as they could. Even if he'd given them his cooperation, Jackson never would have been able to keep up with his captors. They would have to drag him, and drag him they did—almost like a rag doll. Jackson caught a brief glimpse of the plantation grounds. The brief bombardment had already left it scarred and cratered. The bodies of several dead negroes were strewn about. Yes artillery was just as deadly as it ever was.

Another shell came crashing down. The blast threw Jackson and his captors to the ground. Jackson felt intense pain as his elderly body smacked the earth, but he didn't think anymore deadly shrapnel had cut into him. The same could not be said for one of his captors. The negro had been have decapitated by a flying piece of shrapnel. Jackson knew the black man would not rise again until judgment day. His other abductor leapt back to his feet. Jackson was in no condition to resist as the strong black man pulled him to his feet and once again started to drag him away.

They were getting close to the front gate of the plantation grounds when suddenly the shelling stopped. In its place came the high pitched shriek of the rebel yell and the sound of rifle fire. Confederate marines had come ashore. Jackson's negro captor suddenly stopped and threw him to the ground hard. The impact completely knocked the wind out of him and the pain was so great he thought he would die. His chest grew extremely tight as though his heart were in a vice. His vision became blurry.

I am yours, Lord. I am yours... All at once the pain in his chest eased. He heard several gunshots. Time seemed to stretch out indefinitely. Slowly but surely his senses began to return to him and he once again felt strong hands on him. He nearly broke down in despair before he realized they didn't belong to his captor, but to a couple of gray uniformed marines.

"Are you alright, sir?"

Absently Jackson nodded.

Suddenly one of the marines recognized him. The young man swore profanely in his excitement.

"It's Stonewall!"

"He's wounded! Someone find a medic!"

Jackson suddenly remembered his wounded hand. As though triggered merely by the thought it started throbbing. He paid it no heed. He felt some of his strength returning and he had much to do.

XLV

Mitchell Dumas had always envisioned being a soldier as something exciting. A day earlier he'd thought he was one. He'd joined the county militia and because his daddy was a rich planter he got to wear a fancy uniform and be a Lieutenant. Since then he'd learned the hard way that reality was a lot different. Being shot at had a way of changing your perspective.

He'd wanted to be a hero. He'd wanted to impress his friends. He'd wanted to impress the girls. Now all he cared about was making sure his loved ones were okay. He still didn't know what the situation was with his sisters at Twin Harbours. Major Fife hadn't allowed him to go check it out for himself. There wasn't time and they'd needed every man. Shortly after setting out they'd met up with a band of armed civilians from Natchez and several surrounding plantations where the negroes apparently hadn't risen up in armed rebellion. That fact alone would have greatly eased his worries about Twin Harbours had he not recognized

Ebenezer, Rosy, and Cap in the band of negroes that had been marching towards Sharpstone the night before.

Shortly after meeting up with the civilians the troops from fort Rosalie had gone their own way. They'd taken a detour off to the east because Major Fife and Captain Renwald wanted to "get around the niggers' flank." It had been hard going in the dark and the movement had taken the entire night. Mitchell was glad he'd been issued a horse at the fort. Now that the sun was up they were moving much faster. Mitchell had been sent out ahead of the main force as part of a small cavalry screen. Captain Renwald was in the lead but Mitchell knew the area well. He'd been riding horses through these woods most of his young life.

About an hour after dawn, they reined in atop a small hill. Captain Renwald surveyed the area. Though he couldn't see it, Mitchell knew that the Mississippi river was only a few miles west of their position. Just off to the north they'd heard both gunfire and cannon fire. The cannon fire had ceased. The rifle fire had continued and seemed to be getting closer. Mitchell knew that that was the direction of Turtle Creek Plantation. He hoped and prayed fervently that his parents were okay.

Off to the west they could see a large clearing where the main road passed between two small yeoman owned farms. Mitchell didn't have any binoculars, but his eyes were young and sharp. He could clearly see several negroes making their way hurriedly down the road, and across the farm fields apparently fleeing the fighting to the north. Most of the black insurrectionists were on foot but a few were on horseback.

Captain Renwald drew his pistol.

"Let's get those niggers!" He set spurs to his horse and started charging down the hill. A second later, Mitchell and the others were charging along right behind him. His heart raced as he pulled his own pistol. A brief stretch of woods separated the farm fields from the base of the hill. As he cleared the trees, Mitchell came into sight of a short split rail fence that marked the yeoman's property. He urged his mount up to a rushing caricole and leapt the fence. Renwald and several of the other cavalrymen had done the same. They started blazing away at the surprised negroes that were running through the fields. Mitchell leveled his own pistol at one of the armed slaves and pulled the trigger. The black man clutched his chest and crumpled to the ground. Though it was the first man he'd ever shot, Mitchell had no time to feel either excitement or guilt. Several more were making their way across the field. Mitchell took aim at another and fired again. The negro went down clutching a bloody wound but as he did so another shot rang out. A bullet graze Mitchell's right arm. He swore loudly and clasped the wound with his left hand. He just barely managed to keep hold of his pistol. The gray haired negro who had shot at him was busily trying to reload his rifle. Mitchell spun around on his horse and fired three hasty shots at the slave that had fired at him. Two of the shots missed. The third hit the negro in the shin. The older black man let out a cry of pain and started hopping up and down on his unhurt leg. For a moment Mitchell thought about finishing him off with his last shot but the wounded negro had dropped his rifle and he had no desire to kill an unarmed gray haired man. Captain Renwald had no such qualms. He reined in just behind the wounded negro, leveled his pistol and the man's head and pulled the trigger. Blood and brain matter sprayed everywhere.

Mitchell didn't waste any tears. He had other worries. Cautiously, he removed his hand and inspected his wounded arm. Though it hurt like a firebrand, it looked to be little more than a very bad bleeding scratch. He'd live. Trying to ignore the pain, he opened the cylinder of his pistol and started to reload it. He'd just finished doing so when a black man on horseback came charging across the field from the trees to the north. Mitchell's horse was in the way. Both riders tried to move their mounts out of the way but there was no time. Both horses reared up as they hit one another and both riders were thrown from the saddle. Mitchell hit the ground hard but once again he just managed to hold on to his pistol. With a nimbleness and stamina only an eighteen year old boy could possess, he leapt back to his feet only slightly the worse for wear. He brought his pistol to bare on the black man with whom he'd collided. He was tall, rugged and young with a clean shaven head and face. Though his clothes were dirty, they weren't the usual raggedy garb worn by most negro slaves.

"Just kill me," he said in a voice filled with bitterness and hatred. "Come on white man, kill me." Mitchell's eyes rose in surprise. Only a few times in his entire life had he ever heard a black man speak with anything other than the uneducated speech of slavery.

"I think I'll just take you prisoner," said Mitchell.

Several gray uniformed Confederate marines began to emerge from the tree line. They were obviously the ones from whom the negroes had been running. Their kepis, uniform trim, and paints were a dark blue. They eyed the stand-off between the young Lieutenant and the negro but didn't interfere. Once again, Captain Renwald had no such compunctions.

"Dumas, what are you doing?" said the Captain angrily as he reined in beside Mitchell. "Nigger's don't get to surrender son! We either shoot em like dogs or we hang em! Now as much as I'd like to string this coon up, we haven't got the time. There's too many more to kill!"

He brought his own weapon to bare on the black man. He was just about to pull the trigger when he was frozen still by the most commanding voice that Mitchell Dumas had ever heard.

"That will be enough, Captain! Stand down!"

Renwald spun around and found himself face to face with Stonewall Jackson. The former President was on horseback and was flanked by two irate looking marine officers on horseback. Renwald stuttered trying to find his words. Eventually he managed.

"Sir, this... this... nigger is..."

"Is under arrest," said Jackson in a voice that radiated exhaustion. The former President paused a moment to catch his breath before continuing. "Mr. Du Bois is under arrest for insurrection and high treason against the Confederate States of America." Jackson turned to the Marine Lieutenant beside him. "Take him. Put him on your ironclad and take him back to the naval outpost upriver. I don't want anything happening to him until he can stand trial, am I understood?"

"Absolutely, sir!" At the Lieutenant's direction two large marines took Du Bois into custody and led him away.

Officially speaking, as a former President and retired General, Jackson had no official authority. In reality, he was Stonewall and as such he had an authority that transcended official sanction. He would be Stonewall long after he passed from the world of the living. Mitchell stared at him, realizing he'd remember this moment for the rest of his life. His eyes fell on the former Presidents wounded hand, and he suddenly remembered his parents.

"Sir! Do you happen to know if my father and mother are okay? Mansel and Florence Dumas?"

Jackson turned to regard Mitchell.

"No, my boy I do not. I'm afraid I was parted from them amid much chaos and fighting. I do pray God that you are reunited with them safely."

Mitchell wanted nothing more than to head straight for Turtle Creek at that very moment. Unfortunately fresh gunfire erupted to the south… the opposite direction.

"Mr. President I must insist that we get you out of here!" said the marine Lieutenant. He and the other officer left Jackson little choice.

Mitchell found his horse and remounted him. After a longing look northward he brought his mount about and rode towards the south and the fighting.

XLVI

Months earlier when Nathan Audrey had suggested to the sheriff of Pine City that he could have strung up Black Dog himself without a word from higher ups, the lawman had objected that it would have set a bad precedent. How could you stand up for the law if you took it into your own hands? But as he surveyed the ten Mormons standing atop the scaffolding around the unfinished courthouse, with black hoods over their heads and ropes around their necks, the old sheriff offered not a single objection. For one thing there had been at least a semblance of due process. As the highest ranking military officer present, Audrey had ordered a military tribunal established. It hadn't taken long. He'd appointed Lieutenant Jergins and the Sheriff as his fellow justices, read the charges out to the prisoners, pronounced them guilty without so much as asking for their version of events and ordered them summarily hanged. A fair trial it was not, but Audrey had far more important things to do then waste time observing the rights of murderous war criminals. Because it was wartime and Audrey was in command, and because the men being hanged had torched a town, murdered its men, and kidnapped its women with the most nefarious of purposes, the Sheriff had made no undo fuss.

The women from Rattle Snake Cove certainly didn't have any objections, seeing as they were the ones who had been kidnapped and their menfolk the ones that had been murdered. When Audrey's green uniformed troopers used their bayoneted rifles to force the condemned Mormons to step off of the edge of the scaffolding and fall to their deaths, those women did not clap or cheer but neither did they flinch away. Their otherwise feminine faces radiated nothing but cold satisfaction as they watched the now dead Mormons swinging from the ends of the ropes.

For his own part, Audrey finally knew part of the exhilaration Judge Hingle must have felt every time he watched prisoners he'd condemned hang. Audrey didn't feel like an instrument of God, but he did get gratification from watching the miserable bandits meet their end. Audrey hadn't hung the few Mormons he'd captured when he'd liberated Pine City. They'd fought fair and (so far as he knew) they'd done nothing to warrant hanging. For the moment the Sheriff had them locked up in the jail cells at his office.

Most of Pine City's residents had come back to town from the old gold mines to the south. Audrey was pleased that most of the men were armed. Their Winchesters, shotguns, and six-shooters, weren't as good as military grade rifles and carbines, but they were sure a lot better than nothing. All told, Audrey now had over fifty men with which to hold the town, and he'd put every one of them to work building defenses. Audrey hoped that Goldwyn and his army would come before the Mormons showed up, but if the miserable fanatics came back first, he intended to be ready for them.

It hadn't been hard to determine that the Mormon army had moved north. Such a large force couldn't very well hide their tracks even if they had tried. If they came back from that direction the defenders would have a chance—at least at first. The hills to the north of Pine City were the most defensible pieces of ground around. The Mormons would have a devil of a time trying to push them off of it. If they approached from some other direction or if they decided to flank the town to the east or west… that would be a much different story.

If that happens we'll have to fight them building by building. Audrey feared it was not a question as to *if* it happened as opposed to *when*.

Audrey mounted his horse and rode up to the top of the hill just to the north. He brought his horse about and stared at Pine City not through the eyes of the man who defended it but of one who would be attacking it. A moment later, Lieutenant Jergins reined in beside him.

"Everything okay, Colonel?"

"Just trying to put myself in the enemy's shoes," replied Audrey. He pulled a cigar from his uniform coat, struck a match and got it going. That wasn't something a stuffed shirt Mormon would have done, but Audrey found that good tobacco helped him think. He exhaled a small cloud of smoke and then looked to the north. "If the Mormon's attack this hill they'll only do us the favor of making that mistake once." Whereas he had pointed north he brought his mount around and pointed south at the town with his cigar. "Afterwards they'll just move around us and attack the town in one of the flanks."

"That's about the size of it," said the young Lieutenant. Audrey looked at Jergins with the eye of a West Point instructor who was about to announce a surprise test.

"On which flank would you expect the enemy to attack, Lieutenant?"

For a moment the young Lieutenant looked surprised at the question but he didn't balk at it. He took a deep breath, and a moment to marshal his thoughts.

"Well sir, the buildings on the western side of the town are much closer together than those on the east and there's a dry riverbed running the length of the western side as well. Since we could defend that a lot better than we could the eastern side, I'd say they'd attack from the east, sir."

Audrey nodded in approval. He pulled another cigar from his coat pocket and handed it to the young officer as though it were a prize.

"Here. Consider this part of your command qualifications." The Lieutenant accepted the proffered cigar. After lighting it he choked on his first puff but afterwards dutifully took another. Audrey again turned to regard the town. "As you say, Lieutenant, the most likely place for an enemy attack would be from the east."

"It's not very defensible Colonel. True the enemy would have to advance over open ground but the only defenses we'd have would be a row of clap board buildings and there are some pretty big gaps—especially that one in the middle between the hotel and the saloon."

Audrey nodded.

"We'll have to close them up with barricades, but you're right—that one gap in the center will be the major weak spot. We'll just have to turn it to our advantage."

"Begging the Colonel's pardon, but how are we supposed to turn a gap in the defenses that big to our advantage?"

"By setting a booby trap, Lieutenant. I'm thinking some explosives either buried in the ground or put into some conveniently placed barrels with nails and other nasty surprises."

"You've got a gruesome mind, Colonel, but I'm sure glad you're on our side. Where are we supposed to get some explosives?"

Audrey took a last drag on his cigar and then tossed away the butt.

"Let's go talk to the Sheriff. There's some old mines south of town. Where there are mines, there's usually dynamite."

Talk to the sheriff they did. As Audrey suspected there was indeed a stash of old dynamite nearby. There wasn't as much as he wanted, but there was plenty to give an attacking force a few nasty surprises.

Audrey supervised the placement and burial of several sticks of dynamite as well as the laying of the fuses. He also supervised the construction of four barrel bombs. A

barrel full of nails and glass with a core of five sticks of
dynamite was more than the equivalent of an explosive shell
fired from a cannon. Afterwards they began constructing
barricades to fill the gaps between the different buildings. On
Audrey's orders they did so on both the east side and the
west just in case the Mormon commander turned out to be a
lesser strategist than Lieutenant Jergins. At first they left the
big gap in the middle where they had placed the dynamite
and the barrel bombs completely open. After all, they wanted
an attacking force to come in that way.

"That would be too obvious," said Audrey. "We don't
want to make them suspicious. Make it look like we're at
least trying to defend it."

They wheeled two wagons and several more barrels
to create a make shift barricade across the gap, much as they
had done at the others.

"That's good," said Audrey. He knew that to make
the ruse complete he'd have to position men in the center to
give the enemy the impression they were trying to defend the
gap. Whoever it ended up being wouldn't have long to get
away and under cover before the dynamite and the barrel
bombs went off. Audrey warned the owners of the tavern and
the hotel that their buildings would likely suffer heavy
damage from the explosions. To his surprise both had
shrugged it off. If the Mormons won they'd probably lose
everything anyway—that is unless they converted. That of
course would do their businesses no good. Mormonism had
no place for taverns and the owner of the hotel was a woman.
She had no desire to become one of a dozen wives in some
Mormon's harem.

Late in the afternoon Audrey again rode to the top of
the hill to survey the town. He was very pleased with the
town's defenses but he had the eerie sensation he'd been in
this situation before. He was reminded of the Foreign
Legion's last stand at Fort Moultier down in Mexico over
twenty-five years earlier. Audrey suddenly pulled out his
silver crucifix and kissed it. He'd been the only Legionnaire
to survive.

A lot of brave men had died in that hellish siege.
He'd lost a good friend.

With a sigh he lit himself another cigar. Audrey hadn't thought of Doug Appleton in years. He wondered with irony if some vengeful person still had people hunting Doug even though he'd been dead a quarter century. He wouldn't have been surprised. Hate knew no boundaries. According to Goldwyn, Tom Custer hadn't given up on catching Audrey and paying him back for killing his brother... and for other things.

It'll be different this time.

He rode back into town. Unsurprisingly, Barbara Maye was waiting on him. Surprisingly she wasn't holding a bowl or plate of food for him. If the way to a man's heart was truly through his stomach, she would have reached her destination much earlier. She kept trying though. Today, however, she held a large folded cloth.

Now she's taken to sewing something for me. He sighed. He didn't want to hurt her feelings. But at the same time he didn't want to take advantage of her. She was a lonely woman. She was a good woman.

Too good for me. But she's not going to give up, not without me hurting her. He sighed mentally. *I guess I'll just have to marry her.*

"Good evening, Colonel Johnson."

"Good evening, mam."

"The ladies and I made something for you."

"For me?" He tried to sound surprised.

"Actually it's for all of us." With the help of another woman she started to unfold it. It turned out to be a flag—a large white and red Californian flag. They'd taken one creative liberty. Instead of a bear, the flag bore a coiled rattlesnake. Audrey smiled. He ordered it flown from the top of the unfinished court house, the tallest structure in the town. Once upon a time, thirteen fledgling colonies had won some seemingly hopeless battles under a similar flag. He hoped the town of Pine City could do the same. The new flag was billowing in the wind as the sun set. Taking a deep breath, Audrey removed his hat and approached Barbara.

"Mrs. Mayes...Barbara...would you care to walk with me this evening."

"Why Colonel…" she said smiling. "I thought you'd never ask."

XLVII

At dawn the buckra facing Ebenezer and his fighters again tried to advance. Hours earlier, in the dead of night, the white men had been betrayed by the light of their torches. At least then they'd been able to put them out and take some shelter behind the cover of darkness. But there was no escaping the sunlight that filtered its way down through the trees and into the wood. Of course the newly arrived daylight also allowed the white men to see the negro defenders. However, the buckra soon found out it was much harder to route defenders out of entrenched positions in the woods than the other way around.

Ebenezer worked the bolt on his Enfield, leveled it at an advancing white man and pulled the trigger. A fountain of blood erupted from the buckra as he went down, never to rise again this side of judgment day. No words could describe the exhilaration he felt. For the long oppressed slaves, killing white men was almost intoxicating. Ebenezer worked the bolt a second time and took aim again. Once more his rifle barked and once more a white man went to the earth clutching a bloody wound. When Ebenezer had fired his eighth round, he had no trouble at all reloading. Having learned to feed bullets into the magazine in the dead of night, he had no trouble doing it in the early morning light.

The light also let them get a good look at their enemies. The buckra facing them weren't soldiers. Not only did they not have uniforms, but they were armed mostly with pistols, shotguns, and hunting rifles. Ebenezer and his men also didn't have uniforms. They fought in the same kind of rags that they slaved away in their entire lives. The rifle in Ebenezer's hands, however, was a state of the art military weapon. The buckra's attempt to advance that morning was bloodily and mercilessly repulsed. For the second time, Ebenezer and his negro fighters had held the line. But like so many other soldiers in history, Ebenezer learned the hard lesson that just because you won the battle on your front, it didn't mean that your side couldn't lose the war on another. When the first negroes started streaming towards his position from the rear, Ebenezer at first assumed that Caesar had sent him more reinforcements. Their terrified reports quickly told him he was wrong.

"De buckra! Dey comin! Dey comin wit lots o guns!"

"De boats! Dey shoot us wit de big guns!"

"De buckra! Dey come by de river!"

"Dey comin on horses!"

It was hard for Ebenezer to get a clear picture of exactly what had happened. All of the newcomers were confused and near a state of panic. It was obvious that Caesar and Du Bois' group had been attacked at Turtle Creek—and not just attacked but routed. One other thing was also unmistakably clear. The buckra were coming with a vengeance.

"Let dem come!" shouted Ebenezer. He and his fighters who had held off the white men the morning and the night before were ready to face whatever came their way. Victory bred such confidence—in most people. Cap was a nervous wreck.

"Jemima! Zeke! Dey was back at Turtle Creek!" Ebenezer had to physically take hold of his friend to keep him from running at full speed to the north.

"Hold it, you damn-fool nigga! You gone git yo' head blow'd off! We gots to stick together! Dey aint dere no mo' anyways. Look at all de' womens and chilluns comin' dis way. Dey's out dere somewhere. You try an find dem, you end up missin dem."

Cap started looking frantically around. Half the negroes streaming into the woods where they had their defensive position were women and children. As much as Ebenezer sympathized with his friend, he realized they had no time to lose. Soon it wouldn't be terrified negroes coming from the north, but white men with guns.

Ebenezer turned a wary eye back to the south. He didn't think the buckra would attack again from that direction. Still, he couldn't risk completely turning his back on them. He left a third of his men on the line, then took the rest to the northern edge of the wood where they hastily began erecting more defenses. As they had the night before, they dragged branches, tree limbs, and even fallen tree trunks across the road way, then extended the makeshift barricade to both the east and the west. They'd held with such defenses twice already. Ebenezer was confident they could do so again.

And when we do, de other niggas, dey will see dat de white man, he can be killed. He can be stopped. Den dey join us! Den dey rise up!

More negroes continued to stream towards them from the south. When Ebenezer finally saw someone he recognized he asked him, "Have you seen Caesar?"

The slave nodded.

"One o' de buckra's on horseback, blow'd dat ole gray haired nigga's head off! It happen jus no'th of here. De also capture dat uppity smart nigga boy dat talk like de buckra!"

Ebenezer hung his head in despair. His old mentor was dead. Worse than that the uprising had lost both its leaders. With one dead and another captured (as good as dead) that meant…

Dat means I in charge… Dat mean it up to me…

"Jemima!"

"Cap!"

Ebenezer looked up. Jemima was running towards the tree line with little Zeke in her arms. Cap ran to meet them. Ebenezer let out a sigh of relief. His friend had endured enough pain. He was glad that he had yet again been reunited with his family. He hoped they would not be parted again. He thought suddenly of Rosy. His heart sank. He hadn't seen her since they'd left Sharpstone. He couldn't get how she'd looked at him out of his mind. She'd looked at him like he was a…

Like I was a monsta… With a fierce grimace he pushed her from his mind and his heart which he endeavored to make cold and hard. Caesar and Du Bois had been right. Blood and fire were the only answer! Violence and force were the only language that the white man would understand. He worked the bolt on his rifle then turned to Cap.

"Get dem, to de middle wit de other women and youngins, den git back here. De Buckra be here soon!"

Suddenly gunfire erupted to the south. Jemima took Zeke further into the woods to the south while Ebenezer and

Cap rushed to the new firing line. Bullets whirred through the air and smacked into trees as the incoming gunfire increased in intensity. Not far away, one of Ebenezer's fighters caught a bullet in the face. One thing was instantly clear: they were no longer facing white bushwhackers with squirrel guns. Militia soldiers in solid gray uniforms and marines wearing a mixture of gray and dark blue advanced on their position with military grade rifles of their own. From the cover of the trees, Ebenezer and his fighters sent a hail of lead at them. Several of the advancing buckra went down with bloody wounds. Several of the militiamen through themselves flat even though they hadn't been hit—a few even ran. But the grim looking Confederate marines advanced into the negro fire relentlessly and sent back their own storm of bullets as they did so.

Ebenezer worked the bolt on his Enfield frantically. A bullet slammed into a felled tree trunk behind which he was taking cover. Another bullet cracked past his head so close he felt the wind of its passage. Still he continued to fire. When he had fired the last round in the chamber, he feverishly began reloading the magazine with bullets from his pouch. Suddenly there was a loud thump to his left. A half second later the negro beside him was screaming in pain. He fell to the ground. Blood was spraying out of his upper left breast. A few seconds later his screams became gargled as blood began to flood his lung. Ebenezer let out a howling scream of rage. He was unsure if he was screaming because he was going mad or to keep from going mad. He had within him a ceaseless raging fury. He fired again and again and again. His rifle clicked empty. Up ahead rebel yells sounded like panther screams. More gray uniformed soldiers and marines came charging out of the trees as did cavalrymen on horseback. A few yards from Ebenezer one of the negro fighters turned and ran. Then like the breaking of a dam, those around him started to flee as well. Ebenezer turned to look for Cap, but he too had fled for the rear. Ebenezer couldn't blame him. He was trying to get to his family—to protect them—if such a thing were possible. As for himself, Ebenezer had no intention of being captured. He let loose a war cry that would have struck fear into the hearts of a band of Apache Indians. He worked the bolt on his Enfield, leapt to his feet and took aim at on oncoming soldier. His rifle barked, the buckra went down. He worked the bolt again. *Bang!* Down went another.

Bang!

He felt suddenly light headed. He looked down to see a large spreading wet red spot on the front of his dirty cotton shirt. Strangely enough it didn't even hurt. He dropped his rifle and fell to the ground with a loud thump. The world grew distant and dark.

At least I died…a free…ma…

Free from slavery, free at last from a world of hatred, prejudice, and violence, Ebenezer went to a place where no slave master would ever touch him again.

XLVIII

Mitchell rode south until he once again found himself in a patch of woods. His horse picked its way carefully through the trees and thickets. He kept his revolver at the ready. Off to his left was another gray uniformed cavalryman. To his right he could hear the steady bark of rifle fire. It let him know that all of the negroes were not yet defeated. A dozen yards ahead of him a rifle barked. A bullet cracked past Mitchell's head. Instinctively he fired back. Up ahead someone fell into the bushes. Whether, he'd hit him or the negro was simply taking cover, Mitchell was unsure. Wanting to make himself a smaller target, he slid out of the saddle and quickly tied his horse's rein to a nearby branch. He then made his way forward slowly and cautiously, his revolver at the ready.

Suddenly another shot rang out. Once again, the bullet missed him by only a few inches. Mitchell fired three shots into the bush and a pain filled cry erupted out of it. He once again moved forward cautiously. When he reached the bush he discovered the body of a black boy—no older than fourteen—which helped explain his poor shooting.

"You alright, boy?"

Mitchell spun around and found himself face to face with the other cavalryman—a grizzled sergeant. The non-com took a glance at the single bar on Mitchell's collar and awkwardly amended his question.

"Uh, *sir*."

Mitchell didn't mind the awkwardness. He felt as strange having a forty something year old man call him sir as the militia sergeant did saying it.

"It's safer if we work as a team. If you'll get back on your horse and we'll move forward together."

Mitchell remounted his horse and together the two cavalrymen moved ahead again. The fighting off to the right seemed to be slackening. Mitchell caught sight of a couple of negroes fleeing through the woods from that direction. One of them was a black man with a gun the other an unarmed negress. Mitchell took aim at the armed negro and fired off several shots. The black man went down clutching a bloody wound. Suddenly another shot rang out. The Sergeant had fired at the negress. A fountain of blood erupted out of the woman's chest. Her body crumpled forward to the ground. Mitchell stared in shocked awe. Seeing a woman shot dead, even a black one, was overwhelming for him.

The negro fighter Mitchell had shot was still alive, though on the ground writhing in pain. The cavalry sergeant wasted no time in finishing him off. He galloped forward, leveled his pistol at the man's face and pulled the trigger.

Mitchell sighed.

When is this going to end?

He wiped sweat from his face with his gray uniform sleeve. He was perspiring from more than the heat. He took a deep breath and then took a few moments to reload his revolver. As he slammed the reloaded cylinder closed he suddenly heard a noise to his right.

Mitchell cocked the hammer on his army revolver, slid down the saddle and made his way towards a small bush. His heart was pounding. With his gun at the ready he made his way around the bush. Hiding behind it were three negroes—a woman, a very young boy, and a wounded man. Mitchell's eyes grew wide as he recognized Cap. The slave had taken two hits in the arm. At the moment he had no gun, though Mitchell had seen him with one the night before. The small family of three stared at him in terror but said nothing. Cap's eyes locked with Mitchell's and the young planter's son knew he recognized him.

"Hey Lieutenant! You find something!"

A few seconds went by that felt like eternity before Mitchell answered.

"Just a possum, Sergeant! Let's get going!"

With that Mitchell turned around, remounted his horse, and rode south with the Sergeant.

XLIX

Mansel Dumas had a hard time remembering the last time he'd driven his own carriage. It had to have been years earlier. He wasn't sure what had happened to Raphael. The slave might have joined the insurrectionists or he might have been killed by the insurrectionists. From what he'd heard quietly spoken, the rebelling slaves hadn't taken kindly when their fellow negroes refused to join them. In any event, Raphael was nowhere to be found. One way or the other he was most likely dead. The military forces had put down the slave revolt quickly and brutally.

As he awkwardly drove the carriage down the road that led to his plantation, Dumas was perfectly cognizant that there was a possibility none of his slaves would be found. It was, he reflected, entirely possible that his plantation was no longer standing, and that the mansion his family had called home for nearly a century was nothing but cinders. For the moment, none of that mattered. All that mattered was whether his two little girls, Nancy and Connie were okay. Many whites had been killed by the revolting slaves and while Dumas tried to push the worst from his mind, it stabbed into his consciousness like a dark knife.

"How can this have happened?" lamented Florence in a voice hoarse from tears. "It's as if the world is coming to an end!"

"Get ahold of yourself, Flossy!"

"But our precious little ones!"

"We're going as fast as we can! We're almost there."

"And our boy! Off fighting murdering renegade niggras."

Dumas' heart sank. His son had not been amongst the dead militia found on the grounds of Turtle Creek plantation, but what had become of him he had no idea. He'd convinced his wife that Mitchell was off fighting the uprising.

"When did so much meanness get into the world?"

Part of Dumas wanted to tell his wife the world had always been a mean place. But she was already seeing and enduring things that no southern woman should. As if to drive that point home they rounded a bend in the road and came into sight of a dozen dead negroes hanging from the trees.

Florence screamed. Dumas reined in the horses and gaped. They had already seen more scenes like this on their trip from Turtle Creek then they could stand. They had passed fields of negroes killed in battle. Those the militias hadn't shot they had hung. Blacks hung from trees, lampposts, and even telegraph poles. Even Dumas winced at this latest bunch. Several negro women and what looked to be young teenage boys had also been lynched. Florence screamed again—this time louder than before as she recognized one of the black women.

"Rosy! Why would the militia do such a thing?"

"It's a slave revolt, Flossy," said Dumas in a voice like ashes, as if that explained it. In reality, even Mansel Dumas had no words to describe what they were seeing. They had also passed a few whites hanging from trees that had not yet been cut down, mostly members of the slave patrol. From what he'd heard, what had happened on many of plantations was as a near a description of hell on earth as could exist. His mind went to what Thomas Jackson had said the day before about sowing wickedness and plowing iniquity. He couldn't imagine a more bitter harvest than all the death and destruction they were seeing. With a sigh he flicked the reins and got the carriage moving again.

They pressed on for several more miles, passing yet another scorched plantation. Finally they approached the bend that would bring them into sight of Twin Harbours. Dumas felt as though his heart were in a vice.

Rosy is one of our house slaves...if she's been killed... They rounded the corner and the mansion loomed into sight. They turned down the main drive and passed through the front entrance of the plantation grounds. The smell of burnt timber reached his nostrils. The mansion might have been standing, but the docks and warehouses had been burned as had the cabins of the overseers and most of the fields. He spotted several of his slaves. They stood still as statues, their heads hung low, their shabby hats in their hands. None of them looked him in the eye. He could sense the fear that radiated from them.

As they neared the big house, several of the slaves came out onto the front porch. Mansel and Dumas watched them with trepidation. Just as they were about to rein in at the base of the mansion, Mammy came out onto the porch with the girls in tow. Dumas jerked the horses to a halt and then all but leapt from the carriage. Mammy let loose the children and the two little girls ran down the front steps of the mansion and went careening into the waiting arms of their father.

"O my darlings!" said Dumas.

"Daddy! The bad niggers tried to burn down the house!" said Nancy.

"Berry chased them away!" said Connie.

"Did he?" said Mansel.

"Uh huh. With your gun!"

Mansels eyebrows rose. Up on the porch, Berry's already dark skin grew darker. The negro butler lowered his head, not in shame, but fear.

"Come to me my dears!" cried Florence suddenly.

"Momma!" they chorused.

While the girls climbed up into the carriage with his crippled wife, Dumas made his way up the front steps of the mansion.

"Berry…"

"I's so sorry, Massa Mansel…It was de Sharpstone niggas. Dey burn de docks and warehouses…and de fields. Dey kill de overseers. A few others join em, but most didn't. Dey try to burn up de house but we stop em…"

"You used my gun?"

"I's sorry, Massa," said Berry almost frantically. "I didn't have no choice…I…"

Dumas put his hand on Berry's shoulder. He'd never before shown such affection to a slave.

"You did well. You protected our home, and my little girls. And you better believe I'll never forget it. You want your freedom…it's yours. You want to stay with us…you can."

Berry breathed a sigh of relief. On the grounds below the slaves had begun to gather. Dumas raised his voice to address them.

"Listen to me all of you. I'm sorry you were all caught up in this tragedy. I'm not angry with any of you. I'm proud of you for your loyalty to this family. We're going to do our best to move on like this never happened."

Even coming from his own lips the words sounded hollow. Deep down he knew that neither he, the slaves, nor the entire Confederacy would be able to "move on" as though the revolt had never happened. As for the slaves, they simply seemed glad that they weren't in trouble.

And aren't going to be killed.

Mansel helped his wife out of the carriage, up the stairs and into the house. He let out another sigh of relief. All was as he'd left it. He turned back to Berry.

"You said the slaves from Sharpstone killed the overseers?"

Berry nodded nervously.

"What about their wives and children?"

Berry shook his head.

"Ebenezer had dem tied up. We set em loose as soon as the Sharpstone niggas leave. Dey was here until dis mornin' when de militia show'd up. De militia took dem away."

"The militia was here?" asked Dumas. Berry nodded.

"De only reason dey didn't kill us all is dat de overseers families, dey admit we weren't part of the uprising and little Connie and Nancy, de tell de Major we good niggas. De Major, he tell us to stay on the plantation or we be some dead niggas."

Dumas found himself breathing a sigh of relief. From what he'd seen, Berry and the others were lucky to have escaped the noose—innocent or not.

Dumas wanted to track down the wives and children of the overseers. They needed and deserved any help he could give them. He also needed to check the grounds and appraise the damage. Rebuilding wouldn't be cheap.

BILLY BENNETT

But it could be worse. So much worse…

Mansel made his way to the liquor cabinet, pulled out a bottle and poured himself a small glass of amber whiskey. He rarely drank straight liquor but at that moment he needed a drink more than ever. The bourbon felt like fire going down his throat and it exploded in his stomach. All at once he felt warm and relaxed. He really needed to get some sleep. It had been well over thirty-six hours since he'd had any. But sleep would have to wait.

"Where are you going?" demanded Florence as he grabbed his gun and headed out the front door.

"To find our son!"

If Florence Dumas had been about to voice any objections to his leaving so soon they vanished in an instant. Dumas hollered for his horse but then remembered that the stables had been burned. A slave brought him his personal mount all the same.

"Dey set loose de' horses fo' they set fire to de' stables. Dey didn't go far though. I's afraid all de saddles done burn up though Massa Mansel."

"Not all of them," replied Mansel. "Berry! Fetch my grandfather's saddle from the top of the staircase!" It was a family heirloom. Duma's grandfather had used it during the War of 1812. In the present situation, it was about to get pressed back into service. No sooner had Berry emerged from the house with the keepsake, then a horse whinnied some distance away. Mansel turned and looked down the main tree lined drive way of the plantation towards the main gate. A gray uniformed horseman was making his way rapidly down the drive. It took only a moment for Mansel to recognize him as his son. Relief flooded his soul.

"Flossy! Girls! Mitchell's home!"

Mitchell came galloping up at full speed and reined in just as his sisters came bursting out of the mansion. He leapt down from his horse, fell to his knees, and opened his arms just in time for Nancy and Connie to leap into them.

When finally able to extricate from the arms of his little sisters, Mitchell rose and found himself face to face with his father. The two men stared at one another in silence for a moment, then embraced one another as father and son in a way they hadn't done for years.

"Thank God, you're home safe and sound son!"

Mitchell looked his father in the eye and Mansel saw a look of near desperation.

"Momma?"

Mansel smiled and pointed at the mansion. Mitchell looked and saw Florence waiting in the doorway. He all but charged up the front steps of the mansion. Florence wrapped her one good arm fiercely around her son and kissed him again and again.

"My boy! Oh my sweet boy! Thank you, Jesus! Are you okay?"

"I'm fine, momma!"

"Are you sure?" she said looking at his bandaged arm.

He nodded.

"Thank the good Lord for keeping us all safe through this nightmare!" she said.

Mitchell turned and surveyed the plantation grounds from the front porch of the mansion. The damage was extensive, but reparable. Mansel and the girls soon joined them. Mitchell sent a quizzical look at his father.

"It was the Sharpstone negroes, most of our people remained loyal. Berry defended your little sisters from Ebenezer and the other cutthroat niggers that wanted to burn our home to the ground."

"So what do we do now, Father?"

By his tone, Mansel could tell his son was talking about the slaves. Mansel sighed. Nothing seemed to make sense anymore.

"I don't know, son. For now we carry on as we always have."

"You'll forgive me for saying so sir, but isn't that what brought us to this point in the first place?"

"This never would have happened if it hadn't been for foreign agitators and ruthless snakes like Haley. We treated our people well and it showed in their loyalty." That most of the Twin Harbour slaves had refused to join the insurrection out of justifiable fear as opposed to true loyalty never entered his mind. Nonetheless, Mansel Dumas found himself thinking and saying something he never imagined he would.

"Perhaps it is time we give due consideration to some of President Jackson's ideas, namely a law prohibiting the brutal treatment of negroes. I opposed it years ago. But I declare, I would not now. Discipline is one thing, but torturous brutality…that more than anything made this disaster possible."

Mansel brought his hand up to his son's face.

"Your generation will certainly have to deal with the consequences of what has happened here. I have no doubt you will still be dealing with it long after I am gone. I don't know how things will turn out. But I do know I'm very very proud of you and that one day Twin Harbours will have a bright future with you at its head."

With that the family made their way inside the mansion. For the time being, the nightmare was finally over.

L

Cole Allens had read a great deal about battleships. When he'd been merely reading about them he'd found them fascinating. After three days at sea aboard the *Leopold I*, however, he didn't think he'd ever want to be aboard one again. The trip from the Florida Keys to Havana had given him no trouble at all, he had after all spent most of the short eighty mile trip in a cabin with his beautiful young wife. There had been plenty of motion, but not the kind that caused sea sickness.

The voyage from Cuba to Puerto Rico was turning out different. Sea sickness had struck him shortly after they'd sailed out of Santiago. He'd spent more time kneeling over a toilet than he'd ever thought possible.

"Poor bloke. Are you all right?" asked Barnes on the morning of the third day.

"I'll live." The sound of his voice didn't give much reassurance.

"Don't worry, Mr. Allens. We're supposed to be arriving in San Juan today."

Cole missed Helen more than ever. He feared she'd never forgive him for leaving her behind in Cuba. It wasn't that he didn't think she was safe. He'd left her with good people and she was undoubtedly safer in Havana then she'd ever be with him in Puerto Rico, and he'd left her plenty of money to last her until he returned for her. She could literally enjoy what amounted to an extended vacation on the tropical island. All the same, he feared she'd never forgive him for putting himself even farther away from her.

If she even knows...

After losing the small breakfast he had attempted to eat, he made his way to his bunk to lie down. He breathed deeply and steadily in an attempt to settle his stomach. Another thing nagging him was that he had no way of being absolutely certain Helen had received his message. Before sailing, with the Spanish he'd re-crossed the Confederate lines and posted a letter to her in Havana via the Confederate military postal system. Since he'd promised not to reveal what was going on, (especially to the Confederates) he had given his wife very few details. He trusted her implicitly. What he didn't trust was the Confederacy's military postal system. In his letter he'd simply said that the Spanish were withdrawing from Santiago and he'd been given the opportunity to conduct some "special interviews" in Puerto Rico. He had no doubt she'd be able to read through the lines especially since the news about the USA purchasing Cuba would certainly break shortly—if it hadn't already. Assuming that one of the largest wars in human history didn't break out, he'd tentatively promised to return to Havana by the end of the month. If it did break out...

Then I've left my wife in enemy territory... Back to the toilet. Hello, toilet. He was now dry heaving. He had nothing left inside to give up. He let out a moan that might have come from the lips of a dying man, and then took a small sip of water from a tin cup he'd kept in the sink. *Even if war breaks out she's safer there than in Puerto Rico.*

A few hours later, he finally felt a little better. He left the small cabin he shared with Churchill and Barnes and made his way up to the deck. Like all modern ships the *Leopold I* was made of steel. She had two large smoke stacks and two masts that still boasted sails though they had almost never been unfurled. They were merely a back up to the steam engines. Cole wondered why they bothered putting them on ships at all anymore. He supposed it was because many of the Captains still remembered a time when nature's wind and not man's mechanization was the primary means by which ships moved. He suspected some men of the sea just wouldn't feel right without sails on board. He also suspected the next generation of warships would have no sails at all.

The decks were crowded. The warship had a crew of over two-hundred and in addition they were also transporting a couple of hundred passengers—mostly surviving members of Whitmore's Spanish Foreign Legion. It might almost have seemed like the deck of a passenger ship if not for the large gun emplacements at various points along the deck, the large number of negroes and of course for the very small number of women. There were a few to lighten the mood and of course they all had more than enough men to give them attention.

Because they were so near their destination, most of the passengers were on deck either in anticipation of their arrival, or for a last look at the sea. Cole had to look hard for a place where he could stand and look out at the horizon. He squeezed in just beside a young couple that seemed so enamored with each other that they seemed to tune out the rest of the world. The young man appeared to be an officer in Whitmore's Legion, the woman appeared to be a nurse. Cole smiled. They reminded him so much of himself and Helen. It wasn't long before the love birds went off to try and find a place more private. That suited Cole just fine. He finally had room to get a look at the ship's surroundings.

From his place on the port railing, Cole spotted several other ships of the Spanish Caribbean fleet travelling along with the *Leopold I.* They were probably just as crowded if not more so. Named after Spain's current Prussian descended King, the *Leopold I* was the flagship of the Spanish navy. As such it carried General Valeriano Weyler, himself. Cole desperately wanted to interview him. The voyage would have been the perfect opportunity assuming the General would have agreed to see him, but he'd been too sick to try. Now it looked to be too late. The whole ship was abuzz that they'd being putting into San Juan in just a few hours. He didn't think they'd ever let him have an interview on such short notice. That didn't stop him from trying.

A few inquiries let him know that Weyler, Whitmore and the other high mucky mucks were holdup in the wardroom. He managed to find the main entrance. Unfortunately a large Spanish sailor, armed with a rifle stood sentinel outside it.

"I'm Cole Allens. I'm an American correspondent with the Covington Gazette. I'd like to speak to General Weyler if he'll see me, please." The guard apparently didn't speak English. Though Cole couldn't understand any of the Spanish babble the sailor threw at him, both his tone and the harsh way he looked at Cole said he wouldn't be allowed to pass. Taking a deep breath, Cole threw his hands in the air and walked off. He doubted the interview would have lasted long anyway. He had a feeling that once he started asking Weyler questions about why he'd seen fit to lock up tens of thousands of Cubans in the most inhumane conditions imaginable (and allowed those same tens of thousands to literally die of starvation and disease) that the General would have brought the questioning to an abrupt end.

When San Juan finally came into view, Cole was impressed in spite of himself. The city was situated on a broad island that lay just off the Puerto Rican mainland and just in front of a large natural harbor. When he'd sailed into Havana the old but once majestic Spanish fortifications of Morro Castle and the La Cabana had been reduced to ruins by Confederate bombardment. As he looked at San Juan, he could not help but see the Castillo San Cristobal and its associated fortifications. It was a magnificent fortress that guarded much of the shore. Like Havana, San Juan had its own fortification called Morro. Standing at the western tip of San Juan, the Castillo San Felipe del Morro was an older and smaller fortification than the Cristobal, nonetheless it was quite formidable in its own right. It protected the primary harbor entrance with large guns. It was also only a first line of defense. If enemies made it past Morro they would next have to face the La Fortaliza. It was a beautiful and ornate fortress that had served as the governor's executive mansion since the sixteenth century. The eastern tip of San Juan was guarded by another fortress known as the San Geronimo. It guarded a second, smaller entrance to the main harbor on the eastern side of the city. Most impressive of all to Cole was that each fort was interconnected by fortified walls that completely surrounded the city. Thinking back on what he'd seen at Havana, Cole reflected that the San Juan fortifications, like their sisters back in Cuba, had been built in a time when fixed defenses were much more effective.

Before the advent of modern artillery. If French forces did arrive to seize the island as Cole was certain they would, he had no doubt that the port city's formidable defenses would cost the attackers a heavy butcher's bill. He was also certain that unless relief forces arrived modern guns would slowly reduce the walls and probably much of the city inside them to rubble.

The red and gold La Rojigualda fluttered proudly above the main fortification that stood sentinel beside the western entrance to the harbor. Cole tried to imagine the Star Spangled Banner flying there instead. The image didn't want to form. He'd never seen his country as being an imperial power and He didn't want it to become one. He feared that what he, and many of his other countrymen who shared his views wanted, no longer mattered to those who presently held the positions of power in the USA. Cole sighed. Even if the USA obtained Puerto Rico without instantly instigating a major intercontinental war, it would undoubtedly be viewed as both a threat and a challenge by the Confederates—a point of contention that could eventually lead to war down the road, even if not immediately.

Especially if this becomes the first of many overseas acquisitions.

When Cole finally set foot on Puerto Rico, he'd never been so glad to set foot on dry land. The port city of San Juan was one of the oldest in the new world. The name had been given by Christopher Columbus himself when he first discovered the island. The famous explorer had actually named the entire main island San Juan then later another famous explorer Ponce de Leon had named the port city Puerto Rico or "Rich Port." In an ironic twist, in the centuries since the names had somehow been swapped. The island was now Puerto Rico while its chief port city was San Juan.

Cole found it a largely run down and neglected place. Even so it had both a little of Havana's charming beauty and

Santiago's orderliness. It also had an unpleasant stench that the other Caribbean cities had thankfully lacked. Cole decided it was because the city and its inhabitants were so cramped. Old San Juan was broad from east to west but not very deep north to south. It was completely surrounded by water, with the ocean to the north and the vast harbor to the south and channels to the east and west. Adding to the cramped conditions were the thick fortification walls that completely surrounded the city. The Spanish had actually made plans to dynamite most of the defensive wall to give the city a little more breathing room. As Cole made his way down the cobblestone streets, he reflected it was a good thing they hadn't gotten around to it yet. If French forces arrived, the defenders would be glad they had those walls, even if they were antiquated.

The Puerto Ricans themselves looked little different than their Cuban counterparts except that, in general, the average Puerto Rican looked to be poorer than the average Cuban. The entire island was stricken with poverty. Everywhere Cole looked he saw kids with raggedy clothes, and no shoes. Cole wondered if the USA was getting more than it bargained for. Puerto Rico would be the Union's first overseas territory. *Assuming of course that a French task force doesn't seize the island before we can take possession.*

Cole's first order of business was to find the telegraph office and send a wire to his wife and to see if there was any news about the pending sale of the island to the U.S. Unfortunately, he arrived to find that the telegraph office was closed. There was a sign posted on the office door that probably explained why, but because it was in Spanish Cole could not read it. He tried again the next day but it was still closed. When he remarked on it to Churchill and Barnes, they quietly filled him in.

"Leopold has agreed to the sale," said Churchill. "The taskforce is on its way from Boston. The Spanish government ordered the telegraph here in Puerto Rico closed down because they want neither the population nor the garrison to know that the island is being sold to the USA."

"Why?" asked Cole. "They're going to find out soon enough."

"Madrid, is afraid that their troops will not fight if they know they are fighting for an island that is no longer their soil."

At first Cole was incensed that Whitmore and Landon had kept him in the dark that the news had been announced to the outside world. He hid well though, and granted that they may simply have not yet had the opportunity to inform him. He wasn't happy that he couldn't send a wire to his wife, but he understood the Spanish governments desire to keep a lid on the sale from their soldiers. Risking your life to protect your country and its territory was one thing. Risking your life just so another country could come plant a flag on ground you'd bled to protect was quite another. He didn't think it would go over very well if Spanish troops fought and died for Puerto Rico only to see it turned over to the USA right after. He shrugged. It was Leopold's problem, not his.

Unless of course the French get here first.

By all appearances the Spanish were doing everything they could to make sure the French didn't take the island. The Spanish forces that had left Cuba were a significant boost to Puerto Rico's garrison. The day after Cole arrived, a Prussian freighter pulled into dock and troops in dark Prussian Blue and leather Pickelhaubes started to disembark. When he saw the spike toped leather helmets, Cole at first thought that King Wilhelm had made a major military commitment to his cousin and fellow Hohenzollern but Churchill shook his head.

"The troops are Spanish. King Leopold has been trying to 'Prussianize' the Spanish home army for years now. He hasn't had much luck. From what I understand he's faced resistance from old guard Generals like Weyler."

Cole nodded. Upon closer inspection the troops themselves had the same swarthy complexion common to most Spaniards, not the light fair complexion common to most of the North European Prussians. While the new arrivals were clearly Spaniards, the dark blue Prussian style uniforms stood in stark contrast to the light blue uniforms of the Spanish Colonial troops not simply because of their cut and color, but also because of their cleanness. The troops from Cuba looked as though they'd been through a war—and so they had. The garrison of Puerto Rico was about as clean as anything else on the island. The troops getting of the ship, however, were obviously fresh garrison troops from the home country. The island garrison, and especially the veterans from Cuba, looked on them with undisguised disdain. Such was common in most armies.

"If you ask me, old Leopold would do better to teach them to fight like Prussians as opposed to dress like them," said Churchill.

"I don't know about that," replied Barnes. "Remember the Prussians lost in 1879."

"And I'm not surprised. They were fighting the French, the Austro-Hungarians, and there at the end the Russians."

"And of course the French had Napoleon," added Barnes. At the tender age of twenty-three, the fourth French Emperor to bear the name had proven himself a military genius in the tradition of his great uncle, by routing the Prussians at Sedan, driving them back across the Rhine and then marching on Berlin. For his part, Churchill was not impressed by history's latest version of "Bony the Ogre."

"It would have been no great wonder that Prussia lost, even without Bonaparte. They were outnumbered on three separate fronts. If Russia hadn't stabbed them in the back at the last minute, things might well have gone better at Sedan."

Barnes shook his head. "A united Germany— especially one dominated by Prussia—would have been a great threat to both France and Russia. There's not much love between the Bonapartes and the Romanovs, but even they could see that."

Cole wasn't as well versed in European politics as the two Englishmen. For him, like most Americans, it was a far away thing. What he did know was that the eagle emblazoned black and white flag flying from the freighter was most certainly Prussian. Wilhelm might not have contributed the troops, but he had certainly agreed to transport them under the diplomatic cover of his own flag. Cole wondered grimly if Washington and or London had had any hand in that.

Cole tried twice more to get an interview with Weyler. Both times he was turned away. The Spanish

General's staff shielded his office from reporters the way the Holy Cherubim guarded the gates of heaven against the devil.

Over the next three days he observed the construction of additional defenses along the coasts to the east and west of San Juan as well as the undeveloped inner coast of the harbor. Walking the beaches, Cole couldn't help but think again of his wife. She loved beaches and sunsets and the sea.

During his inspection of the defensive positions, Cole learned that the khaki uniformed mercenaries from Britain and the United States were stationed to the east of the city while the new arrivals from Spain were stationed to the west and south. The veterans from Cuba joined the city garrison in the Castillo San Cristobal and its sister fortifications. Regardless of where an attacking force landed, Cole was certain that they'd receive a warm reception.

Cole made his way back to the city. He passed the only major structure outside the city wall—a brand new and unfinished train station. San Juan was connected to mainland Puerto Rico by the San Antonio bridge. There was only a single large gate in the wall by which people, horses and wagons could enter and leave the city and cross the bridge. The route was crowded with traffic going in and out at all hours of the day. That was one of the reasons so many wanted to demolish the wall, it would give room to build more bridges. It took him a good ten minutes to get across the bridge and through the gate on foot. Had he been trying to get in with horse or even worse a wagon it would have taken considerably longer.

The hotel he had found was nothing compared to what he had experienced in Havana or even Santiago. Nonetheless it was a comfortable room. He made his way upstairs, ready to crash. He worked the key, entered the room and made to hang up his hat.

"I thought you'd never get here," said an amused, beautifully feminine voice. Cole whirred around in shock. There in the bed lay his wife. She was covered by a white sheet and *only* by a white sheet.

"Helen! How…."

"Sshh…," she said. "That's not important now." She tossed aside the sheet and motioned him to come to her.

LI

Joseph Whitmore stood atop the highest battlement of the Castillo San Cristobal. With his pair of binoculars, the elderly millionaire stared in all directions. To the north was the sea. He lingered there for a long while, looking for any trace of an approaching armada. There were two such armadas on the way. He feared the enemy's would arrive first. To the south, the walled city of San Juan was spread out so that he could see it almost like looking at a map. To the south and west was the vast harbor. To the south and east, the one bridge that connected San Juan with the rest of Puerto Rico. The walls of the Spanish castle on which he stood reached out to embrace the city like protective arms. Heavily fortified gun emplacements guarded both harbor entrances as well as the city's entire sea front to the north. When the tide was in, the castle's forward wall doubled as a seawall. When the tide was out, there was only a very narrow stretch of beach on which attacking troops could land. All along the sea facing fortifications were large rectangular projections known locally as "garitas." At the forward facing point of each garita was a stone guard tower. The garitas offered defending soldiers much better vantage points than a simple straight wall would have. If enemy troops were so foolish as to try to land at the base of the castle, they would find themselves facing enfilade fire from not one but three sides.

"I doubt even the frogs would be dumb enough to try to attack the city directly," said Whitmore. He turned to General Arsenio Pombo and then nodded to his own assistant David Lovejoy who repeated his employer's words in Spanish to the General. The newly minted commander of the San Juan garrison let out a string of Spanish. Lovejoy translated.

"The General says, he agrees with you, but with the French you can never be too sure."

Whitmore's grip tightened on his cane.

"Please tell the General that my men are stationed in the most likely enemy landing zone. They are brave and they are strong, but they will not be able to hold the beach if the enemy attacks in full force."

341

Lovejoy did. It was followed by yet another torrent of Spanish from Pombo.

"He says, the cannons they have placed to the east should enable us to hold off any assault, but that if it becomes necessary they will send reinforcements from the city."

"That will take too much time!" thundered Whitmore. To Lovejoy's relief he didn't lift his cane as though he were going to clobber the Spanish General upside the head, but he did raise it and bring it crashing down on the fort's stone floor in frustration. "Whether we hold the line or it collapses could be determined in a matter of minutes." He looked at Lovejoy, "Don't bother translating any of that. There's no point in arguing with a blasted fool." Whitmore turned his attention to the large red and gold Spanish Flag flying above them.

"Ask the General again, if we can fly Old Glory instead. If the French or Confederates see the Stars and Stripes they may not have the guts to attack."

Lovejoy sighed, but obediently asked the question. Whitmore didn't have to understand Spanish to know that the General's reply was in the negative.

"He says it would dishearten his soldiers to fight under a foreign flag, sir."

Whitmore's fist tightened around the head of his cane so tightly that his knuckles turned white. He sighed heavily, and turned to stare at the sea again. A fresh sea breeze hit him in the face, and ruffled his large white whiskers. He breathed deeply. It helped him relax—a little.

"All right, by jingo, if that's the way they want to play the game, that's how we'll play. Come on let's get out of here."

With barely a cursory fair well nod to General Pombo, Whitmore came about and marched himself away. Lovejoy gave the General an improved formal adios, and then hurried after his employer who had already descended into the bowels of the fortress. Whitmore made his way down the winding spiral staircases and through the narrow downward sloping corridors far more nimbly than most men his age would have. Lovejoy hoped none of the Spaniards stationed in the fortress could understand English because the entire time Whitmore proclaimed loudly what he thought of Pombo, Weyler, the Spanish, and Spain in general. His curses and tirades echoed throughout the Castillo San Cristobal. When they at last emerged from the castle's interior and into the streets of San Juan, Whitmore was still venting.

"How in the devil are we supposed to hold this wretched colony?" He used his cane to point at the battlements and fortifications around them. "The frogs are going to push ashore in the east, drive to the bridge and by thunder they'll have cut off San Juan from the rest of Puerto Rico and trapped the entire stinking Spanish army inside. Assuming we aren't dead, captured, or driven from the field we'll wind up trapped in here with them. And once the enemy brings artillery to bear from all sides this place and these walls won't be worth spit!"

"Even cut off, sir, I imagine the Spanish and we ourselves could last quite a while. Surely long enough for our fleet and that of the British to arrive."

Whitmore and Lovejoy climbed into a waiting coach that had been put at his disposal by the governor. Whitmore gave the roof a loud bang with his cane.

"Back to my command post!"

"Si, General."

"David, why are there so very many idiots in the world?"

Lovejoy wondered for a moment how many times the eccentric millionaire had demanded an answer to that question from either himself or from the world at large. The industrialist usually asked it when confronted by the obstinacy of those few individuals he could not coerce or bend to his will. He reflected quickly that usually his employer ended up being right. The men he considered fools, usually were.

"Too many, sir."

Whitmore uttered a blasphemy.

"You've got that right, by thunder!"

The coach rattled over the cobblestone streets as the horses pulled it through San Juan. They passed a column of marching Spaniards.

"This is Weyler's doing. That gaudy fat clown wants to keep as many troops around himself as possible!"

"Could it be he wants this venture to fail, sir?"

After a moment's thought, Whitmore shook his head.

"I don't think so. Weyler did the same thing at Santiago. He kept most of his troops in the city around himself while we and a token force under Pombo held out the rebs."

"The Spaniards were worried about the Cubans. Could the Puerto Ricans pose a similar threat?"

"There have been a few minor revolts against Spanish rule, but not nearly as bad as Cuba. In the past the Spaniards and Puerto Ricans fought off both English and Dutch attacks. That's probably why the British want us to take possession of this blasted place instead of doing it themselves. They think we'll have an easier time of governing. According to the new treaty their navy gets to use this place in any event."

Traffic came to a slow crawl as they neared the one gate that led out of the city wall and across the bridge to the mainland.

"I swear, Lovejoy, if there was a fire in this city the vast majority of its inhabitants would perish for want of a proper escape route." A few minutes later they passed through the gate and onto the bridge, they went from a crawl to a dead stop. Whitmore swore profanely. "They'll never be able to get us reinforcements in time."

"I'm sure that in a military emergency the Spanish troops could clear the bridge rather quickly, but yes, sir, I see your point."

Whitmore shook his head.

"What kind of idiot builds a wall around a city with just one gate and one bridge to get out?"

"A Spanish one, sir."

Whitmore lit a cigar. It was going to be a long wait.

LII

When John Pershing was given an order about anything, he did his best to carry it out. They'd drilled that into him at West Point. When the lives of he and his men were on the line, he threw himself into his task with abandon.

"That's it men! Dig those rifle pits deeper!" The khaki uniformed negroes let the dirt fly. Each black man had undoubtedly dug plenty of ditches. Save for Joshua Winslow and a precious few like him, very few negroes had any work to do other than back breaking manual labor. Nonetheless, the men of Pershing's company went about their task with uncommon zeal. These were not common ditches. These were trenches to keep them alive when the bullets started flying.

Pershing's orders from the Spanish commander had been to occupy the beaches east of San Juan and set up defenses. Whitmore and Pombo had inspected the work two days earlier and had been pleased.

They can be pleased all they want. Until the enemy gets here, we keep digging!

The other company commanders in Whitmore's Spanish Foreign Legion weren't quite as zealous as the West Point graduate. They'd worked until the Spanish higher ups had said the defenses were good enough. All Pershing had had to do was think back on the poorly prepared defensive positions his men had been forced to use on San Juan Hill to know that the Spanish commanders had no idea what they were talking about. When he insisted they keep digging and setting up defenses, and his fellow company commanders refused, one quick visit to Whitmore was all it took for Pershing to get his way. The Legion had been set to work again and with the added bonus that Whitmore had placed Pershing himself in overall command of the defense preparations. Going over his fellow company commanders heads had earned him some animosity. They'd started calling him "Nigger Jack" both because he commanded a unit that was mostly made up of negroes, and because they said he worked them like niggers. As long as they dug trenches, Pershing didn't care.

"The secondary lines on the right flank are nearly done, Major," said Captain Dominic Malcom. Pershing nodded. He was proud that his second in command had stood by his side. The former British Marine knew as well as he did the importance of having a well prepared defensive position.

"After the blood baths on San Juan Hill and Kettle Hill, I'm surprised we had any trouble at all convincing these bloody fools that they needed to dig in more," said Malcom. "I've got to hand it to our glorious leader though, the old man knows a good idea when he hears one."

Again Pershing nodded. Like most men in the Legion, Whitmore had no previous military experience (though thanks to the campaign in Cuba they now had more than most men in the US Army). In addition to Whitmore's audacity and patriotism, his willingness to listen to and follow the advice of professional soldiers was yet another reason that Pershing admired the man.

Pershing lifted his binoculars and scanned the beach to the north.

"I wish we had some land mines," he said absently.

"Underground bombs?" Malcom shook his head. "You have an uncommon gift for imagining ways to make life difficult for the poor buggers who have to make the amphibious assaults." As a former Marine, he was more used to planning amphibious assaults as opposed to defending against them. As he peered through the binoculars, Pershing smiled a wry grin. "Considering it's the enemy I'm wanting to blow up I'd think you'd be happy."

"Oh don't get me wrong," said Malcom. "Anything that sends Boney's minions down where they belong is fine by me. I just don't fancy the idea of someone using the idea against us later. War's hard enough without us constantly inventing new ways of killing ground pounders."

"It's not as new a concept as you think," said Pershing. "The Rebs used them as far back as 1862 during the First War of Rebellion. My own country's army has been experimenting with them in recent years. I'd sure love to have some now."

"Well I don't know about land mines," said Malcom, "but here's something now."

He motioned to several approaching supply wagons that were approaching from the direction of San Juan. To his surprise he spotted Joseph Whitmore on horseback.

"Beware Greeks, bearing gifts," said Whitmore. The commander of the Legion looked at the expanded and improved defenses and nodded vigorous approval. "You boys have done well, by jingo!"

Pershing saluted his commander.

"Thank you, sir." He then turned to regard the tarp covered wagons.

"I don't suppose you've got some land mines there, sir?"

Whitmore raised one of his bushy white eyebrows. "No I'm afraid not."

"That's alright General," said Malcom. "We'll settle for some more Maxim machine guns or even some old Gatling guns."

"Sorry, boys. Nothing quite as extraordinary as all that, but I'm sure you'll find it useful."

Whitmore motioned with his hand, and the Puerto Rican teamsters driving the wagons hopped down and pulled back the tarps to reveal...

"Barbed wire!" said Pershing.

Whitmore nodded.

"One of the gifts from the Prussian army to the Spaniards. Predictably they've made little use of it, so I was able to convince Weyler and Pombo to let us have it. I trust it will be of use?"

"Of that you may be certain, sir." Pershing looked a silent order to Malcom who started barking orders for the men to stop digging and start unloading the wire. Whitmore stayed a while and observed as Pershing and Malcom supervised the deployment of the wire. They laid most of it on the upper beach, just in front of their forward most trenches, and inland enough to not be washed away at high tide. Nodding in satisfaction, Whitmore took his leave. They spent most of the rest of the day deploying the wire and finishing the trenches. Afterwards, Pershing again surveyed the beach.

"Now that's more like it," said Pershing. "That wire should slow them down."

"And give us time to blow them to old Hob," said Malcom viciously.

Pershing lowered the binoculars and let out the sigh of a man who'd labored and accomplished much in a short but difficult period of time.

"Tell the men to take it easy. They've earned a rest."

"There not the only ones, John."

Malcom's use of his first name surprised him. Pershing didn't mind. They'd been through a lot together and he'd started to view the hard bitten former British marine as a friend as well as a comrade. He was just so used to him being strict and proper all the time and so it took him by surprise.

I'm glad to see there's a human being under all that discipline after all.

"Go get some rest yourself, Malcom. You've earned it as much as any of the men. I'll man the command post."

"Actually, sir, I was thinking you might care to go inspect the field hospitals in the rear. You can rest assured I can take care of things here. I highly doubt the Frogs will be attacking tonight. Besides… you haven't seen her since we got off the boat four days ago."

Pershing had made certain not to allow his relationship with Jennifer Harper to interfere with his duties. He'd done his best to avoid even the appearance of distraction. He'd also taken advantage of every possible opportunity to be with her without compromising his duty.

"I'm serious, John. Go see her. Life's too short, especially in our business. And besides, don't think I haven't seen you tinkering with that little box you picked up just before we left Santiago. I'm surprised you didn't ask her on the ship."

"I wanted too. I just couldn't find the right moment."

"Don't worry about it. Some of the bravest men in the world turn into cowards when it comes to women."

"You sound like you speak from experience. Have you got anyone back in England waiting on you?"

Malcom shook his head and looked suddenly sad.

"Not anymore. But once upon a time, I did. But as Britain's great poet, Alfred Lord Tennyson said, 'tis better to have loved and lost, then never to have loved at all.'"

"I never would have pictured you as a student of poetry."

"I am full of surprises. Now with all due respect, sir....get out of here."

He slapped Pershing on the shoulder and then headed off to the command post.

Pershing mounted his horse and rode a mile to the south until he spotted the tents of the field hospital. Most of the nurses and field staff ignored him as he rode into the small encampment. Joshua Winslow was the sole exception. The young negro surgeon was, predictably, reading a book by what little daylight remained. Pershing admired his ferocious appetite for knowledge. Joshua looked up from his reading and greeted Pershing with a smile.

"If you're looking for Miss Harper, Major, her tent is over that way."

"Thank you, Joshua. What are you reading?"

Joshua held up a battered book with a dull golden cross on the front.

"I'm afraid my Bible went down on the Capricorn with the rest of my books. I picked this one up at a shop in San Juan. The prints small but I count my blessings."

Pershing nodded his thanks. His mother had taken him to church when he was younger, but he didn't consider himself a particularly pious man. He'd had a violent life. His earliest memory was of Union loyalists and Rebels shooting at each other in the fields of his family's farm during the First War of Rebellion. Just a few years later during the Second War of Rebellion Rebel raiders had killed his father and burned his brothers and sisters alive in the family farm house. Later that year he'd killed his first man at the tender age of eight. He'd killed a lot of men since. He'd never known peace—until he'd met Jennifer.

"Hello, Miss Harper," he said formally.

Jennifer Harper spun around excitedly to see her beloved looking down at her from horseback.

"Good afternoon, *Major*," she said with a smile and mock formality.

"Would you care to take a ride with me this evening?"

She accepted his invitation by way of offering her hand. He helped her up onto the horse. Her split nurses skirt allowed her to straddle the horse just in front of him. He gave the reins a flick and they rode off together towards the east. After about three miles they turned north until they reached the beach. They were well east of the trenches and the beach was empty. They rode east again, along the shore and with the setting sun to their backs. The sky was a beautiful orange-red. To the north east, a full moon was already visible. Presently, Pershing slowed the horse to a trot. He wrapped his arms around her waist and held her tightly. He put his head up to her ear to speak and breathed in the sweet fragrance of her hair.

"Do you remember when you made the crossing into Iowa from Missouri?" He asked softly.

"How could I ever forget," she said. "If it wasn't for you, the border guards never would have let me in."

"Do you remember what I told them?"

She turned in the saddle and gazed into his adoring eyes.

"You told them I was your intended." She said it with a quiver and so softly it was almost a whisper. Slowly, almost magnetically their lips met in a passionate kiss. He brought his hands up to her hair and she brought up her own hand to the side of his face. Afterwards, Pershing slid nimbly off of the horse and then helped down Jennifer. They walked a short distance more hand in hand and then Pershing stopped suddenly and turned to face her. He took both of her hands in his and then went down on one knee in front of her and gazed up into her eyes. For brief moment he was worried. She was crying, but they were tears of joy. His heart was pounding. Her heart was pounding.

"Ever since I met you, I've looked at life differently. You've brought my life peace and new purpose and I can't imagine my life without you."

He reached into his uniform coat pocket and pulled out a small black box. He opened it to reveal a small gold ring.

"Jennifer Harper…will you spend the rest of your life with me? Will you be my bride?"

In a voice hoarse with tears she said, "yes!"

Pershing leapt to his feet. He lifted her into the air, and spun her around. As he lowered her, she wrapped her arms around him and their lips met again. Alone with their love, the light of the setting sun, and the sound of the ocean waves, they forgot the world and all its troubles and thought only of each other and their future together.

LIII

"Dare I ask how you managed to get here?" said Cole to his wife. He hadn't had a chance to ask her the night before.

Helen Allens smiled over the breakfast table in the lobby of the Hotel' San Juan. She took a cautious sip of coffee.

"I received your letter, the same day the news broke that we had purchased Puerto Rico from Spain and that President Cleveland had signed a treaty of alliance with Great Britain. I instantly put two and two together and realized why you'd come here. So I resolved to get here as fast as I could."

"Even though this is likely to be the starting point of the greatest war in our country's history?"

Helen set down her coffee cup.

"My darling you may be more right than you know. The Confederates were totally incensed. I heard several of their officers demand war. I don't know how serious they were but they sure sounded angry."

"They were serious," said Cole and took a bite out of his toast.

"Do you think the Senate will confirm the President's treaty?" asked Helen.

Cole raised a curious eyebrow. He hadn't expected his wife to be so politically astute.

"Well I certainly hope not. In my book Cleveland has betrayed the pledge he made to those who supported him during the election."

"Yes, dear. But do you think it will pass?"

Cole sighed heavily.

"If this gamble pays off and we get Puerto Rico out of it then probably. But that's a big if. From what you've told me about the Confederate reaction in Havana, I can only imagine how the hotheads in the Confederate war department are taking it."

"Well I'm sure there are hot heads in every country's army," said Helen. "What's important though is whether President Stone will call for war. I don't think he will."

Cole lit a cigar.

"Since when are you an expert on the Confederate government?"

"I read your editorials," said Helen.

Cole smiled.

"Well in this case I think you're right, after a sense. John Marshall Stone is many things, but a hothead is not one of them. He won't call for war over this. But that's not the danger."

Helen looked at him quizzically. Cole continued.

"President Stone believes that the CSA's alliance with France is essential to its security. France and Austria-Hungary have a large number of troops down in Mexico ready to come to the Confederacy's aid in the event of war, that is an enormous comfort to Richmond because no matter what we are still larger and stronger than the Confederate States. President Stone may not want war over Puerto Rico but Napoleon might. If France goes to war, Stone will probably insist that the CSA meet its obligations to its ally. In his view certain war now with France and her allies on his side is better than possible war in the future with the CSA standing alone. If Paris decides to go to war, Richmond will find itself between a rock and a hard place. This is why George Washington said to stay out of entangling alliances."

His wife gave him an amused look.

"Washington was a Virginian."

"All the more reason the Confederates should have heeded his advice," replied Cole quickly. He then smiled at her amusedly. His wife never ceased to amaze him. "I don't know why I keep encouraging you on your artwork, I should put you to work at the paper writing about politics and world affairs."

He took a long drag on his cigar and exhaled a small cloud of smoke.

"You never answered my question about how you got here."

"Well if you must know I went down to the docks and started to inquire about different ships and where they were headed. I found a small British freighter whose Captain was willing to grant me passage in exchange for forty dollars in gold."

Cole momentarily choked on his own cigar smoke. Helen simply smiled amusedly. She reached out and took his hands in hers.

"Wasn't it worth it to have me back with you?"

He melted like butter.

"Yes," he said reluctantly. "I suppose if a bigger war does break out I'd rather have you here with me then trapped in enemy territory."

"My thoughts exactly," said Helen.

Suddenly church bells all across the city started ringing frantically and constantly.

"It's not Sunday..." said Helen confusedly.

"No it's not. They're not calling for worship, they're sounding the alarm!"

Cole pulled out a Morgan and placed the coin on the table. US currency wasn't generally accepted in Puerto Rico (not yet at any rate) but silver had value regardless of whose face was stamped on it. Without waiting for change, he and Helen rose from the table and made their way towards the exit.

"Darling, please do me the favor of returning to our room and waiting for me."

"Cole, please. I need to see this and I don't want to be separated from you."

Cole sighed heavily and looked at her wryly.

"I never could tell you no. Come on. Let's get going."

They made their way out of the hotel and down the narrow cobblestone streets of San Juan. Cole had instructions to report to the governor's residence when and if the enemy arrived. Several criers were shouting at the populace in Spanish, undoubtedly announcing whatever it was that was going on, but neither Cole nor Helen understood Spanish. Several times they had to get out of the streets as a column of soldiers or wagons driven by soldiers rushed past them.

The La Fortaleza was situated on a hill that faced San Juan harbor. The castle was built of white and blue stone and was the oldest fortification in San Juan. For centuries it had housed the island's governors. The grounds surrounding the La Fortaleza were covered with lush green vegetation and palm trees. Light-blue uniformed Spanish soldiers had the entrance to the governor's residence cordoned off. Cole pulled out the credentials he'd been given. The lead Spaniard scrutinized it closely. Finally he handed Cole back his papers.

"Entrar!"

Cole motioned to Helen and together they made to enter the castle.

The soldier's suddenly blocked their path. The fellow that had inspected Cole's papers pointed agitatedly at Helen. Cole couldn't understand what he said, but he was certain he had a general idea. His papers didn't say anything about Helen. In lieu of merely saying she was his wife in a language they wouldn't understand, Cole also held up her hand, pointed to her ring and displayed his own. To his surprise the lead Spaniard at least understood what he was trying to convey.

"Ah…Si." His tone had softened slightly but he still didn't let them through. He did however yell at his underling in Spanish and send him running into the castle. A couple of minutes later he returned with an officer in tow. Thankfully, he spoke English.

"What seems to be the trouble here, Senor?"

"I'm afraid my papers were issued before I knew my wife would be joining me in San Juan."

"And you are?"

"Cole Allens, sir. Special correspondent for the Covington Gazette, Louisville USA."

"I see." He turned to face Helen, took her hand and as only a dashing Spanish officer could do, bowed over it and kissed it."

"Welcome, Senora, to the La Fortaleza. If I had such a beautiful esposa, I too would take her everywhere with me."

Helen blushed, smiled, and giggled all at once, obviously delighted by the Spaniards charm.

"Thank you so much, Senor," she replied.

The officer smiled broader, this time at both of them and led them into the Castle.

"If I may ask, sir, what exactly is going on?"

"The Frances and the Confederados have arrived with many ships. I would be happy to show Senor and Senora before I take you to the Generals."

Helen looked suddenly nervous.

"Isn't there a danger they'll...fire on us?"

"I think not, Senora. Even now the Confederados and Frances are sending in a boat under a blanco...eh....a 'white' flag." The Spanish officer led them up a set of stone stairs. They took them very cautiously. To the left was the castle's outer wall. To the right was nothing. Helen tried to not look down as they ascended to the upper rampart. Once there the view of the sea was breath taking. Off to the east the sun was still low in the horizon. But as they looked north west out of the harbor's main entrance they could clearly see a large number of battleships, cruisers, and other vessels. Cole thought the warships in particular looked far larger and more formidable than the ones docked inside San Juan's harbor. They also spotted a motorized skiff, making its way into the harbor under the cover of a banner of truce."

"Where do you think that boat is headed?"

"Truly, I do not know Senor, however, there is a small dock on the harbor side of this castle. I believe the generals are waiting there."

"Take us there please. Gracias."

Take them there the officer did.

Whitmore and Landon were waiting there, as were Churchill and Barnes. Cole also noticed the presence of General Valeriano Weyler and his aids. His two British colleagues noticed him but at the moment there was no time to talk. To Cole's surprise, Whitmore was not dressed in his custom made khaki Generals uniform. He wondered why.

Suddenly one of Weyler's men fired a flare into the air to signal the approaching boat. No sooner had the flare soared into the air then the motorized skiff came about and headed for the docks. As it came near the General's guards readied their rifles. Weyler quickly snapped at them.

"Como Eras!"

The guards quickly returned to attention. The motorized skiff slowed as it approached the dock and slowly made its approach. Cole expected to see men in dark gray Confederate naval uniforms. Instead he saw men dressed in the dark blue of the Imperial French Navy. The skiff cut its motor, and a French sailor tossed a line to a Spanish soldier at the end of the dock. Two French officers climbed out of the boat and made their way down the dock to where Weyler and the others were waiting.

The Frenchmen saluted Weyler who gravely returned it. The higher ranking French officer then began to address Weyler in… French.

Cole sighed. It was virtually impossible, (and for a man in his position endlessly agitating) to be unable to understand the things he was supposed to be reporting. A moment later, however, he was pleasantly reminded that his lovely wife, spoke French. She quietly began to translate for Cole.

"Ahh Monsieur General, I am Capitaine Ernest Francois Fournier, and this is Capitaine Pierre Ronarch."

Weyler then surprised both Cole and the French officers by replying in French.

"If you have come to ask our surrender, then I would advise you to return to your ships immediately, you are wasting your time."

"Monsieur General, Admiral Fournet, simply wishes to avoid the large scale destruction of this beautiful city and to insure the safety of the people inside. We have come to you with an overwhelming force at our disposal. However, even though we are at war, Admiral Fournet, and His Imperial Majesty, the Emperor Napoleon, offers you generous terms. Surrender Puerto Rico to the French Empire, and we will allow you, your army and your fleet to withdraw to Spain unmolested. I have also been authorized to inform you that if you accede to these conditions, His Imperial Majesty's government will immediately be open to negotiations between our two neighboring countries and will seriously consider granting Spain compensation for the territories you have lost in this late unpleasant little war."

Weyler's face went suddenly hard.

"In other words you want us to let you have this island without a fight, and then maybe you will deign to give us some pesetas for it and all the other territories you and the Confederados have stolen from us. Know this: Spain does not negotiate with a pack of dirty backstabbing thieves. If you were to try to take this island by force, know that my gallant soldiers would defeat you and drive you back into the sea."

Cole could watch the Frenchmen's face darken as Weyler went on and Helen translated for him. Then suddenly, Weyler dropped what Cole supposed was supposed to be the coup de grace.

"In any event, Monsieurs, it no longer matters. This island no longer belongs Spain. His Majesty, King Leopold, has seen fit to sell it to the Estades Unidos, who at least had the honor to pay for it with a handsome price in gold and to ask before taking it."

Now Cole noticed a definite change in the French officers. Ronarch looked worried but Fournier looked as angry and contemptuous as ever.

"I see no, Union flag, flying over this island." His eye looked up at the red and gold Spanish la rojigualda which flew over the La Fortaleza and by extension all of Puerto Rico. Joseph Whitmore chose that moment to step forward.

"This is Mr. Joseph Whitmore. He has been appointed by Presidente' Grover Cleveland, as special representative extraordinaire, and empowered to take possession of this island on behalf of the American government."

Cole found himself wondering how a Confederate officer might have responded to that statement. From all he'd seen the Confederates also laid claim to the title American. He'd seen them become fussy when the word was used to describe the North to the exclusion of the South.

Well too bad. They're the ones that wanted to break away and form another country. Cole shook his head. For the moment, it was neither here nor there. He refocused his attention on the tense discussion between Weyler and the French officers.

"France does not recognize this," replied the French officer. His Imperial Majesty's declaration of August the 1st,

1895 clearly lays claim to this island. The claim of the French Empire precedes that of the United States."

Now Weyler smiled a savage smile.

"Even as we speak a fleet of American and British warships are on their way with a large force of troops to take possession of this island. Before all history I swear you will not take this island while I live and breathe. And I'm certain that even a couple of *debiles* like you must realize that you will certainly never take this port or this island before the British and Americans arrive."

Cole watched the faces of the Frenchmen fill with rage. But then suddenly, Capitaine Fournier's face softened. Cole admired the man's ability to master his temper. The French officer smiled and bowed politely to General Weyler.

"We shall see, your excellency. We shall see."

Without further ado, the Frenchmen returned to their boat and a moment later the skiff was speeding its way out of the harbor. It wasn't long before the shells started falling.

LIV

Captain Blake Ramsey stared at the city of San Juan from the bridge of the *CSS Texas.* Along with the rest of the task force, the Confederacy had sent to join the French in their assault on Puerto Rico, they had arrived the night before as had the French fleet. The inhabitants of the city had awoken to an armada of steel warships off of their coasts. Church bells in the city had loudly sounded the alarm. The people of San Juan had obviously expected the French to start bombarding the city. After what he'd seen the French do to Villa Cisneros on the coast of the former Spanish Sahara, Ramsey was equally surprised. The *Texas* and the other Confederate ships were prepared to bombard the city as well, but their orders were to follow the French lead. This was their show.

Starboard of the *Texas* was a handful of Confederate warships and troopships. To her port was a much larger French fleet. Ramsey stared at the *Andre Massena,* the flagship of the Imperial French Navy. She was over fifty feet longer than the *Texas* and much more heavily armored. Other than that Ramsey was not as impressed as he might have been. The French flagship had several more smaller guns than the *Texas* but like the Confederate battleship sported only two twelve inch guns. She was also bulkier and top heavy. Ramsey wouldn't have wanted to try to maneuver her. The *Andre Massena* and her sister ships had been built by France in response to the Sovereign and Majestic classes that had been built by the British. But Ramsey knew that the British battleships (in addition to exceeding the length of the French ships by over fifty feet and the Confederates by more than one-hundred) each mounted four main guns, not two. And the Royal Majestic class sported thirteen and a half inch guns which was larger than anything in the Confederate or French navies.

"If the French had bothered to let us know what they were up to we might have been able to bring more ships and troops with us," griped Ray Brisk.

Ramsey nodded.

"We also wouldn't have let the remnants of the Spanish fleet and an entire garrison of troops leave Santiago and reinforce Puerto Rico."

"I heard the French went ballistic when they heard about that."

"I wouldn't be surprised," said Ramsey. "I also wouldn't be surprised if President Stone sent Napoleon word that we'd appreciate being kept informed about what they're up to in this hemisphere. Allies are supposed to support each other's interests but that's kind of difficult to do when you are kept in the dark."

"Why don't you think they told us?"

"Who knows? Maybe they thought we wanted Puerto Rico for ourselves, or maybe some diplomat or military attaché dropped the ball."

"If that's the case," said Brisk, "then somebody's head needs to roll."

Ramsey nodded. He then pulled out a Cuban, stuck it in his mouth and lit it with a match. A moment later he blew out a small cloud of smoke and swore.

"Never underestimate the power of human stupidity."

He suddenly caught sight of a small craft off to the south, coming from the direction of the harbor entrance.

"Is it them?" asked Brisk. Over two hours earlier the French had sent a representative in a motorized skiff under a white flag to parley with the Spanish commander in San Juan. Ramsey clenched his cigar tightly in his teeth and raised his binoculars again.

"It's them."

"What do you think?"

"That they say no."

Brisk sighed and lit a cigar of his own. "If you're right this won't be like Havana. The guns on those forts have the range to hit back at us."

"Then we'll just have to knock them out."

The motorized skiff sped back towards the *Andre Massena.* A few minutes later the French battleship ran up signal flags.

"What do they say?"

Ramsey read the pennants through his binoculars.

"Commence fire…"

No sooner had the words escaped his mouth then the first shots erupted from the guns of the *Andre Massena* and her sister ships. The shells screamed through the air and came crashing down on the fortifications that surrounded San Juan. The Spaniards were ready. Almost immediately their own artillery responded in kind. Several shells splashed into the sea around the French ships.

"Let's join the party, Mr. Brisk. Order our gunners to open fire."

"Aye aye, sir."

Within a minute the *Texas'* own forward gun belched fire and smoke. The sound was deafening. Ramsey watched San Juan through his binoculars and nodded in satisfaction when the shell from the *Texas* exploded into the Castillo San Cristobal. A minute later a shell splashed down in the sea about one-hundred yards out of the *Texas* position.

"Raise anchor!" ordered Ramsey. He turned to Brisk. "Let's not sit here like a bump on a log. We'll be a much harder target if we're moving. As soon as the anchor is secure take us ahead two-thirds and come to course 090, that'll let us bring both twelve inchers to bear."

"Aye sir."

A few moments later Ramsey felt the ship vibrate as her steam engines picked up speed. The Confederate battle flag billowed in the breeze as the bow of the ship came around to the east. About that time another Spanish shell came crashing down. It exploded into the sea about fifty yards south west of the *Texas*. The Confederate battleship responded with full a broadside. Two twelve inch guns, and three six inch guns roared. Ramsey felt the *Texas* list slightly to the port as they did so. The two twelve inch shells found their mark as did one of six inchers. The last two shells fell just short of the target.

Ramsey swore.

"Tell those gunners to sharpen up!"

A minute later a second broadside rocked the ship. This time all the shells but one hit. Ramsey nodded.

"That's more like it."

A few more shells came crashing down around the *Texas* but only a few. The vast majority of Spanish fire was being thrown at the *Andre Messina.* In addition to being the ship that fired first, she was also the largest target the Spaniards had, which meant she drew artillery fire the way a beautiful woman drew stares from men.

Smoke belched from the French flagship's two large smoke stacks. Like Ramsey, Admiral Fournet had no desire to allow his ship to be a sitting target. Unfortunately the *Andre Messina* was just too slow and unwieldy. A Spanish shell slammed into her aft deck. Fresh smoke came from the French battleship but it emanated neither from her funnels nor from her guns. Despite the hit the *Andre Messina* responded with another full broadside. It would take a lot more than a single shell hit to silence the pride of the France's Imperial Navy.

Ramsey swept his gaze from the damaged warship and back towards the besieged city. Shells exploded all along the sea facing fortifications. As they had at Villa Cisneros, the French didn't try to confine their fire to the Spanish defensive positions. Rising smoke gave evidence that several shells had landed in the heart of the city. The Puerto Ricans and the city of San Juan were paying a high price for Spain's refusal to yield the island.

Suddenly off to the north east a deafening explosion reached Ramsey's ears. Another French battleship had taken a hit. Unlike its larger sister it hadn't continued on its merry way. The Spanish shell had penetrated the ship's powder magazine. The hull had literally been blown apart from the inside. The ruined remnants of the ship quickly flooded and within five minutes had slipped into the sea. Ramsey sighed heavily. The Spaniards weren't the only ones paying a price and the battle for San Juan was just beginning.

LV

"La Garita del Diablo, that's what the garrison calls this sentry box," said Major Antonio Vega as he peered northward towards the sea and the French and Confederate armada. Of all the fortifications Antonio had had the pleasure of manning during his time in the Spanish Army, the Castillo San Cristobal was, in his considered opinion, the most formidable and the Garita del Diablo, was the apex of its defenses. It wasn't as large and grand as the La Cabana, but its sea facing triangular projections (known as garitas) and the guard towers at their apexes would make sure that any force that dared land on the shore would face enfilade fire from not just one but three sides.

"A worthy name, Senor," said his newly promoted second in command Captain Pancho Seville. "If the Gabachos and the Confederados try to land here we'll make sure they think they've run into the devil."

Antonio nodded.

"And with God's help we will then dispatch them down to infernio to meet Satanas himself."

Antonio raised his binoculars and surveyed the battleships flying the French Tricolor or the Confederacy's Blood Stained Banner. His mind went back to the bombardments he'd endured on the La Cabana and the beach of Cienfuegos. In addition to the battleships he also spotted the same motorized skiff that had made its way into San Juan harbor, a short while earlier under flag of truce, speed its way back to the French battleship from which it had come.

"What do you think they wanted?"

"Probably for us to give them Puerto Rico without a fight. I hope General Weyler told them where they could stuff it."

Captain Seville nodded vigorous agreement. He turned to his left and right to survey the artillery emplacements that had been prepared up and down the sea wall.

"Why don't we just open fire!"

"Patience, Senor. You'll get your wish soon enough. But I too look forward to seeing these guns in action. They are so much better than the ones we had at Havana." Antonio then sighed a martyr's sigh. "If only we had received such guns before the Confederados attacked us. We would have given them a much better fight at Havana."

A few moments later, Seville got his wish. A sound like thunder boomed to the north. Half a second later three more booms followed in its wake. A moment later there was a screaming noise as the shells came crashing in. Most landed in the sea just short of the shoreline, but a few exploded into the Castillo San Cristobal and other defensive positions along the coast.

"Take cover!" cried Antonio a second before one of the shells exploded into the sea just short of the Garita del Diablo. Most of the sky blue uniformed soldiers of Antonio's company were hunkered inside the fortress in relative safety. Antonio himself and Seville took cover in the forward guard tower of the garita. He doubted the stone tower would survive a direct hit, but he hoped the chances of that were slim. It would be perfectly suited for protecting him from the flying shrapnel of exploding shells.

As they ascended the stone spiral staircase that led to the top of the tower, Antonio heard more thunderous booms, these from much closer.

"We're shooting back, Pancho!"

"Si, Senor!"

They reached the top of the tower. There was a long horizontal firing slit in the front of the upper compartment that allowed Antonio to resume his observation of the enemy armada. His radius of vision was decreased in the tower, but because of the increased height he could see just a little further. He watched in satisfaction as one of the Spanish shells slammed into a French battleship, wreaking havoc with its crew and superstructure. He wanted to shout and jump for joy. A moment later, however, several more enemy shells came crashing in and this time the majority did not fall short.

Several shells exploded into the forward defensive wall sending centuries old stone and mortar flying in all directions. Several others crashed into or exploded above the fort's upper ramparts. Up and down the fortification the Spanish guns continued to thunder in reply, but it quickly became apparent that the enemy armada was throwing far more at the beleaguered Spanish fort, than the fort was at the armada. But like a contest between a hammer and an anvil, the Fort seemed to hold up better.

With a pounding heart, Antonio watched as two more French ships and one Confederate one took direct hits from the Spanish artillery. One of the French ships exploded into a magnificent fire ball. Antonio watched in awe as its ruined hull began to flood and sink. The other two enemy ships seemed to be limping away from the fight.

"We're making the enemy battleships pay!" said Seville proudly.

"Si, but I wish the gunners would go after those troops ships."

Several of them, both French and Confederate were steaming east at high speed. Others seemed to be holding station—just off the shore line of San Juan and the Castile San Cristobal.

More shells came screaming in. One struck the shoreline just in front of the Garita del Diablo and another exploded in the air just above. The guard tower shook violently, and the sound of lethal shrapnel could be heard slamming into the stone walls.

Ave Maria! cried Antonio and crossed himself. "That was too close!"

"Look Major!"

Antonio once again turned his attention to the enemy. Through his binoculars he gazed a large number of boats, filled with enemy troops and marines heading directly for them.

"They are coming!" cried Antonio. He turned to Seville. "Alert the men! All troops to firing positions!"

Seville gulped and as Antonio had only a moment earlier, he crossed himself.

"Si, Senor…"

Seville climbed down the spiral staircase of the guard tower to the bottom where for a moment he sheltered just inside the door of the tower.

You must move! He told himself. *We're running out of time.* His brain tried to tell his legs to move but they didn't want to listen. As he looked out the entrance of the tower the upper level of the garita was strewn with debris. Seville had to cross the garita before he could enter the fort and order the men out. If a shell came crashing in at just the wrong moment…

Seville crossed himself again and said a Hail Mary. He then took a deep breath and headed out the door. He heard the shrieking sound of incoming shells. A moment later he heard the sounds of their impacts and explosions. Thankfully, none of them were in his vicinity. Nonetheless, he very nearly soiled his trousers before getting across the garita and all but leaping into the entrance to the fort.

Back atop the sentry tower, Antonio continued to watch the slow but steady approach of the enemy's landing boats.

Several of the Spanish guns had been silenced by the enemy barrage but many were still in action. But to Antonio's chagrin they were still targeting the enemy warships, not the incoming landing craft.

"Why aren't the gunners targeting those boats!" he cried to no one in particular. "Are they blind?"

Down below, the men of his company began to man the ramparts of the garita del Diablo. Seville readily re-entered the tower, climbed to the top and saluted Antonio.

"Senor! The men are deployed!"

"Bueno. Go below and take command of them! And send a runner to the artillery commander! Tell them to start shooting at those *maldito* boats!"

A fresh bead of sweat broke out on Seville's brow but he saluted and hastened to obey. Antonio turned back to the approaching enemy ships. Through his binoculars he noticed that the lead boat was flying the French tricolor and it appeared all the troops in all the approaching boats were dressed in dark blue coats with red trim, red trousers, and red kepis.

"So, this time we face the Gabachos!"

A few minutes later the Spanish gunners finally turned their attention to the incoming French boats. Shells began to explode into the sea in the midst of the small flotilla. One of the boats took a direct hit and it exploded in a burst of wood, flesh, and bloody red mist. Men and pieces of men flew in all directions. Up and down the heavily fortified shoreline, Spanish troops opened fire with their Mausers, from the garitas, ramparts, and sentry towers, sending a torrent of lethal led flying towards the oncoming Frenchmen. Despite it all, the boats continued to advance. Antonio and the handful of troops in the sentry tower of the Garita del Diablo, added their own fire to the deadly hail.

As the boats started their final approach towards the rocky shore, Antonio rushed down the spiral staircase and out onto the garita.

"They are about to land! No mercy! No mercy to the enemies of Espana! Shoot the gabacho perros!" As the sky-blue clad Spaniards fired away at the oncoming landing boats, the approaching Frenchmen at last came close enough to return fire. Antonio heard the familiar sound of bullets cutting their way through the air. Not far away one of his troopers caught one in the chest and fell from the garita, hitting the rocky shore below.

Because of the proximity of their landing boats, the French and Confederate fleet had ceased their bombardment of the Castillo San Cristobal, though they had begun to fire over it and into the city of San Juan itself. Up and down the ramparts and garitas, Spanish anti-infantry howitzers opened up. Several of the approaching boats and the men inside them were ripped apart, but for every boat they destroyed, two more hit the rocky shore. French marines leapt from their boats and fired their rifles at the Spanish defenders above them while sloshing ashore. The layout of the garitas was a nightmare for the attacking force. The dark-blue uniformed marines now took fire from three different directions. The

Spaniards mercilessly poured in rifle fire from the garitas and ramparts.

Suddenly, a chattering sound like the steady ripping of a cloth reached Antonio's ears. The French had a maxim gun mounted on the front of one of the landing boats. It stitched an arc of death across the Spanish positions. The Spaniards dropped down behind the edge of their ramparts to take cover, giving the French Marines the chance they needed to advance. They dashed up the small stretch of rocky beach. Ordinarily they could have taken relative cover at the base of the fortification, but the lay out of the garitas insured that no matter where the enemy tried to take cover, they would take fire from another angle.

"Up!" cried Antonio. "Concentrate all your fire on that gun!" Leading by example, Antonio leapt to his feet, and leveled his rifle at the boat with the Maxim gun, trying to target its gunner. The machine gun cut a swath of death across the garita and Antonio took two bullets in his upper gut. He dropped his rifle, clasped his wounds, and tumbled forward. One of his men tried to catch him but was himself cut down by the machine gun. Antonio fell headlong from the top of the garita. He landed on his back—hitting the rocky beach with tremendous force, and breaking bones throughout his body.

Antonio lay sprawled on the rocky beach. He was vaguely aware of the enemy marines around him fighting a desperate battle with his countrymen above. He tried to move but found he couldn't. But he could feel. Pain like he'd never known radiated from every part of his body. He opened his mouth to cry out, to shout for help, but all that came forth was a blood curdling cry of agony. Soon he lacked even the strength to do that. With men slaughtering each other all around him, Antonio looked up to the heavens above, and with his last breath on this earth spoke a prayer.

"Dios te salve, Maria. Llena eres de gracia…"

LVI

Sergeant Jeff Case and his men had brand new uniforms. The raggedy remnants of the uniforms they'd worn for the entirety of the Cuban campaign had been exchanged in Santiago just before they'd been shipped off to Puerto Rico. They had new accoutrements too. The old ones had gone to newly arrived negro conscripts. The only original equipment he had left was his Richmond rifle and his notched bayonet.

I guess they wanted us to look good when they send us in to help the French. The thought made his want to laugh out loud. *We look like a bunch of green horns that have never even seen the elephant.*

The guns of the French and Confederate fleets were still booming and raining fiery death and destruction down on San Juan and its defenders. Spanish guns thundered in return. Most of the enemy shells were directed at the battleships and cruisers for which Case and the other Confederate Marines thanked God. Troop ships were pathetically armored.

Jeff reached up and touched the three stripes on his gray uniform coat. Being a Sergeant meant he had far more responsibility then he cared to have. Occasionally though, it had its benefits. At that particular moment most of the men were still below but Jeff had the privilege of standing on deck. Of course with explosive shells being thrown back and forth even that was up for debate.

Captain Fordice, Lieutenant Fudge, and the other officers of the company stood on the starboard side of the foredeck watching the bombardment and surveying the coastline that they would soon be assaulting. Case and the other Sergeants were there too. They needed to know what was going on just as much—if not more than the platoon commanders. Nonetheless, they were silent observers. Sergeants didn't usually get to make plans, they just got to make sure they were carried out.

"We're not gonna try to assault that place directly?" asked one of the Lieutenants in dismay. Jeff whole heartedly shared his concern. Even he could tell that San Juan was much more heavily fortified than Havana had been. Assuming their boats even survived the trip ashore, if they tried an amphibious assault directly on the city they would end up landing at the base of a fortified wall and face enfilade rifle fire. Thankfully, Captain Fordice shook his head.

"The French Marines get that honor. This is their show so they get to get the glory."

They get to do the dirty work, translated Case. That suited Case just fine.

"We'll be landing to the east of San Juan in conjunction with another force of French Marines. They'll be going in first. We're just back up this time." He pulled out a map. Jeff crowded in with the other officers and non-coms to see. The Captain had marked the map at the point where they were supposed to land, and drawn an arrow that showed which way they were supposed to drive and finally circled what their objective was. "Our job is to hit the beach and drive off any defenders. We are then to push south, swing west around the eastern harbor entrance and seize the one bridge that connects San Juan with the rest of Puerto Rico. If we do that we've cut them off and no matter how many men they've got in that city it's only a matter of time."

They steamed east, with the rest of the Confederate troop ships. As they moved past the eastern harbor entrance, Case noted that the beaches looked bare. There were certainly no heavy brick and mortar fortifications like what surrounded San Juan itself. Beyond the beaches looked to be open ground. He spotted a few trees, but it couldn't compare to the heavily wooded areas that had been past the beaches east of Havana.

A large number of French troop ships were already lined up in front of the beach and disembarking troops when the Confederate ships took up position beside them. By then the Marines had all been assembled on deck. Jeff screamed for his platoon to fill the longboats assigned to them. The men clad in gray coats, with dark blue trousers and kepis filled the landing craft like sardines in a can. As Jeff's boat was lowered into the water a shell screeched through the air and exploded into the sea. Whether he'd seen them or not, the Spaniards obviously had artillery on shore and in this area and the vulnerable troopships and even more vulnerable landing boats, would be the primary targets.

Jeff's boat was amongst the first lowered into the sea. Ordinarily the first boats would not head straight for the shore but would wait for all the other boats to get in the water

so that the whole company could go in together. You didn't
want to assault a beach piecemeal. In this instance, however,
Jeff ordered his men to put out oars and row for shore
immediately. A wave of French Marines had already gone
ashore. Case's orders were to get there as quickly as possible
to back them up.

Jeff swore viciously at his men.

"Row!" The twenty marines in the boat worked their
oars with a fury. The slower they were the easier they would
be for Spanish artillerymen to target. "Row!" he thundered
again. For the moment the men in the boat were nothing but a
human engine. Jeff continued to heap angry curses and
profanities upon them the way a coal heaver hefted coal into
the furnace of a steam engine. It did the trick. The boat
picked up speed. Jeff turned to look at the approaching
beach. There was a raging fire fight going. Muzzle flashes
and the familiar roar of rifle fire let him know right away that
the beach wouldn't be taken easily.

"The French are catchin' hell! Let's get in there and
show em how it's done!"

Suddenly an artillery shell crashed into the sea to
their right. The blast was close enough to rain sea water
down on top of them. The men's pace slacked off for maybe
a second but then it picked up even higher than before. As
long as they were in the water they were little more than
sitting ducks. If they could get ashore at least they'd have a
fighting chance. A few dozen yards behind them another
longboat wasn't so lucky. A shell burst in the air directly
above it and fiery hot shrapnel rained down on the men
inside. Several of the marines were killed or wounded. Those
that weren't went into a panic and the boat quickly capsized.
Jeff bowed his head. His own boat picked up yet more speed.

The beach was now much closer. The French were
easy to spot. Their uniform coats were a dark blue, but their
trousers and kepis were red.

Jeff swore and blasphemed out loud. He couldn't
believe his eyes.

"Red? The poor bastards are just asking to get shot!"
Bullets started cracking through air. Jeff swore again. They
couldn't shoot back without the risk of hitting the Frenchies
in the back. They had to get ashore and quickly.

"Come on boys, row were almost there!"

The waves started to whitecap and their surge helped push them more quickly towards the shore. Jeff felt the keel of the boat hit the sandy bottom.

"Out!" he roared. The Confederate Marines leapt from the long boat into the knee deep water and started to splash ashore. To Jeff's relief no one tripped and went down in the water. A marine with a soaked rifle and or cartridge box would be virtually useless.

"Spread out! Move forward and stay low!"

Hunched over as low as he could, Jeff rushed up the sandy beach with his rifle at the ready. To his left and his right his men moved along with him. Bullets cracked through the air and past them as they did so. They moved forward nonetheless. Case had learned that if you led from the front, your men usually followed you.

They started to pass bloody bodies clad in blue and red. Many of them were already dead. Others would be soon. A few were screaming at the top of their lungs. Jeff didn't speak French, but he didn't have to in order to know that they were crying out in pain. They sounded like damned souls. The farther up the beach they moved, the more intense the enemy fire became, and the more dead and wounded Frenchmen they passed. Just ahead several Frenchmen were lying on the ground in a prone position and firing towards trench lines to the south. Just in front of them was a large stretch of black entanglement that he recognized as barbed wire. Several French Marines had been caught up in it while trying to get across. Most of them were now dead. Their lifeless bodies hung limply from the entangling wife. They reminded Jeff of flies stuck on glue paper. Letting out a filth laden curse, he hit the beach just in front of the barbed wire. He looked to his left and right. Most of the men of his section were still with him. Jeff grabbed his entrenching tool and started to make sand and dirt fly. They were at the point where the beach started to give way to regular dry ground. Case hastily made a pile of sandy earth in front of him. His men followed suit. Their hurried efforts didn't offer much protection, but it was better than nothing.

Case worked the bolt on his Richmond and looked for a target. Ahead of his position the enemy had dug a trench line. A khaki clad soldier popped up just long enough to squeeze off a shot. Case aimed at the spot where he'd seen the muzzle flash. Sure enough the hapless enemy soldier popped up again in that same place.

Bang! Case's rifle barked. The enemy soldiers head exploded into a spray of red mist. He then worked the bolt on his rifle again. Several more Confederate marines soon arrived on the scene and dug in alongside Case and his men. Jeff was surprised to see that one of them was Captain Fordice.

"What's the holdup, Sergeant?"

In lieu of asking the officer if he was a blind idiot, Jeff answered what should have been the obvious.

"It's this blasted wire, sir! If we try to get through it we'll get hung up and they'll cut us down like dogs!"

"Then we'll just have to go around it!" The Captain rolled over and addressed Lieutenant Fudge who was on his other side. He shouted so as to be heard over the rifle fire. "You and Sergeant Case take your platoon, fall back a couple of dozen yards and then head east! We'll stay here, give you covering fire and see if we can't cut through this wire! We've got to flank these bastards! Wait for my order! I'm gonna see if I can get the French to help you."

Fordice looked around and then crawled twenty yards to the west to where a blue uniformed officer in a fancy gold embroidered red kepi was huddled down in front of the barbed wire along with several French troops. A minute or so later about two platoons worth of French marines fell back towards the south. Fordice then made his way back like a worm on its belly.

"Get going!"

Jeff and Fudge led the men back the way that had come. At first they crawled but after a few yards they got up and ran hutched over. One marine caught a bullet in the buttock. He went down screaming bloody murder. Another caught one in the back of the knee. He screamed even worse. They turned east just about the same time that they met up with their French counterparts. Bullets continued to rip through the air. Another Confederate marine and three more

Frenchies went down before they finally reached the end of the wire. By the time they had gotten in position to begin the flanking attack, enemy fire had slackened to almost nothing.

Either the Spanish and their flunkies didn't extend their trenches this far east, or they don't have the numbers to man the line out this far. Either way we're about to hit em hard!

Case cried to his men.

"Alright boys, fix bayonets!" He drew his own notched blade and affixed it to the end of his bayonet. The Frenchmen were also preparing for close quarters fighting. Whereas the Confederates used shorter sword type bayonets the French used longer spear-like ones. The French weapons had greater reach. The Confederate ones—especially the ones that had been notched by their owners—did greater damage.

A moment later a French Lieutenant cried out "Charger!"

The Confederates let loose with a Rebel Yell. The Frenchmen sounded their own cri de guerre. "Pour Le France! Pour le'empereur!" Confederates in gray and French in blue charged forward together, the southern cross and the tricolour fluttering side by side.

After a hundred yards, gun fire erupted in front of them. The defenders had dug an auxiliary trench to protect their flank, but the pathetic number of muzzle flashes showed they didn't have near enough men to hold the line. A few of the attackers went down but the vast majority surged on. There was no barbed wire protecting the auxiliary trench. Case leapt down into it and fired his rifle at a khaki clad Legionnaire. The shot exploded into his chest and he fell dead to the bottom of the trench. Case worked the bolt on his rifle, stepped over the corpse, and proceeded cautiously down the trench. The other defenders of the auxiliary trench had already been dispatched by other French and Confederate marines. A couple of Frenchmen were in front of Jeff as all three of them approached the place where the auxiliary trench intersected with the main trench. One of the French marines caught a bullet in the face just after he rounded the corner. His companion charged around the corner himself but was impaled in the gut by the bayoneted rifle of a large khaki clad negro. Case took aim and fired. His rifle cracked but the bullet missed its mark. He worked the bolt of his rifle, but before he could fire the negro lunged at him with his bayonet. Jeff leapt to the left just barely avoiding the negro's blade. Instinctively he brought up the butt of his rifle and smashed it into the black soldiers face busting his nose. Jeff then came about with a ferocious cry and with all of his strength brought his notched bayonet up through the man's lower jaw and into his skull. The negro dropped his weapon and momentarily brought his hands up to the blade but a half second later his body lost all strength and fell back to the ground. The negroes eyes were wide open but still. Jeff then gruesomely rung out the bayonet while simultaneously keeping his booted foot on his chest. When the bayonet came out, it brought with it large chunks of flesh, muscle, bone and bloody gray brain matter, leaving a massive, gaping, gory wound worse than any rifle bullet could have inflicted. Jeff pressed on. He rounded the corner and fired his rifle. He worked the bolt and fired again. Suddenly something hit him in the leg, just above the knee. Suddenly the limb didn't want to work. He was confused for about a full five seconds and then all at once fiery pain radiated outward from the spot on his leg and throughout his whole body. He fell forward and hit the trench bottom hard. Slowly and painfully he rolled over onto his back so that he wasn't face down in the mud. Blue sky loomed above him. All at once he let out a screaming cry not unlike that of a wounded animal. He tried to force himself to sit up but found he didn't have the strength. He reached down to feel the wound. It was literally spraying blood with each beat of his heart. He wanted to try to apply pressure but once again he found he didn't have the strength. He felt suddenly cold. He just barely noticed as several French men in blue and red and Confederates in gray and blue made their way past him. His thoughts turned to Ellie and the child in her belly—his child. All at once he started to cry. Time stretched out into what seemed a painful eternity. His eyelids became heavy as stones. He felt a strange tingling sensation. Sudden realization came upon him that strong hands were upon him. A fresh surge of adrenaline let him know he wasn't dead yet. He was cognizant of his surrounding enough to know that someone had pulled him up and leaned him against the trench wall. His belt was suddenly pulled off of him and wrapped around his leg just above the wound.

The belt was suddenly pulled tight. Pain unlike anything he'd ever known shot throughout his entire body. Reflexively he clenched his jaw so tightly that it might have cracked his teeth. The pain never let off, but somehow someway he adapted to the new level. His vision was blurry but he finally made out the man trying to save his life. A blue uniformed Frenchman with a white armband and a red cross was busily dressing his wound now that he'd applied the makeshift tourniquet. Unnatural terror filled Jeff but at the moment he had no strength at all. The Frenchman said something in his incomprehensible native language. Jeff heard it as though across a great distance. The man then held up a canteen. Jeff's fear slackened. The Frenchman brought the canteen to Jeff's lips and gave him water. A few moments later he was laid back down and then it seemed as though he were lifted off the ground. The sky once again dominated his view. He became vaguely aware that he was being carried on a stretcher before finally losing consciousness.

When he next awoke he was still starring at the sky. In the distance he could hear the distinct sound of rifle and cannon fire. The other noises around him were a strange sonic collage of waves crashing against the shore and the tortured pain filled cries of wounded men. The bizarre mixture of peaceful and nightmarish sounds sent fresh waves of despair through his soul. He turned his head to the side. He was laid out on the beach along with many other wounded marines. A short while later a Confederate medic came and gave him another drink of water. He was soon asleep again. He kept moving in and out of consciousness.

The next thing he realized was that he was in a rocking boat. The sky, now grayer, still dominated his view. Off in the distance he could still hear the sounds of the raging battle.

The next time he awoke it was because of fresh waves of pain emanating from his leg. Someone was prodding the wound. Adrenaline flooded his system. He tried to get up, to flee but found that he was strapped down.

"Take it easy buddy, we're just…"

Jeff started screaming in rage and terror. His body shook and convulsed as he fought against the restraints. With the uncommon strength made possible only by the fight or flight instinct that all humans have, Jeff ripped free from the restraints with his right hand and desperately started trying to pull himself free from the other.

"Give me a hand, Joe! This guy's gone nuts!"

In a moment several pairs of strong hands grabbed hold of him.

"Calm down partner, it's gonna be okay!"

An eruption of curses, swears and blasphemies erupted from Jeff's mouth like the pyroclastic flow of a volcano.

"My leg! You're not gonna cut off my leg!"

Jeff let loose with a war cry that sounded not unlike the scream of a madman. He was completely irrational and driven only by the compulsion to escape. It took four men to hold him down while a fifth man re-restrained Jeff's right arm—this time much tighter than before. When the men released their grips Jeff was still straining madly against the restraints.

"This guys gonna give himself a heart attack or an aneurism! Joe get the ether!" The orderly grabbed a green bottle and poured liquid onto a cloth. He then put the cloth over Jeff's face. He struggled and screamed like a drowning man for a few more seconds then all at once he fell unconscious. The orderly pulled away the cloth. Even knocked out, Jeff's body twitched and quivered.

The surgeon took a deep breath.

"Alright, let's get that bullet out and his leg stitched up."

LVII

"They're getting through the wire, Major!" cried Captain Dominic Malcom as he fired his Enfield.

"I can see that, Malcom!" replied Pershing. He raised his own rifle and took aim at a Frenchman. The Enfield barked and the blue and red clad marine went down clutching at his chest.

"Nice of the Frogs to make themselves such nice targets," said Malcom. As if to drive home the point he took aim at a red kepi a few yards to the south and pulled the trigger. The head of the Frenchman wearing the kepi explode like a melon.

Pershing fired his last shot and then rapidly started to refill the weapons magazine with bullets from his leather ammo pouch. Not far away the attacking force had somehow opened a gap in the barbed wire. Several French and Confederate marines were trying to surge through. A few yards to the left of Pershing a Maxim machine gun started chattering. Several enemy marines in both gray-blue and blue-red were cut down.

"Don't forget you English wore red for ages."

"Don't remind me!" said Malcom as he worked the bolt on his rifle and fired again. "At least we finally learned our lesson."

Off to the left the Maxim fell suddenly silent. Pershing turned and saw the two man crew desperately pouring water from a canteen into the chamber around the barrel.

"I don't think we'll be able to hold them for much longer!" cried Malcom. As if to underscore his words fresh gun fire erupted to the east. "We've been flanked!"

Pershing wasted no time.

"We've done all the damage we can here! Runner!" A lanky, khaki uniformed soldier with very little gear came running up. "Get to General Whitmore! Tell him our lines have been breached! We'll do our best to get to the fall back point!" The soldier saluted and then ran westward. " Pershing then turned to the bugler.

"Sound retreat!"

The soldier brought the bugle to his lips and the somber marshal notes sounded across the battlefield. While his men started to pull out of the trenches and withdraw to the southwest, Pershing worked the bolt on his rifle and stood his ground. He wouldn't fall back until his men did. He fired at the oncoming enemy marines then turned to Malcom.

"Get out of here, Dominic!"

Malcom ignored him and fired his rifle.

"I do beg your pardon, sir, but shove it up your arse!"

The two men continued to fire at the oncoming French and Confederates. Finally, at the last possible moment, they began to withdraw together. At first they backed their way out of the trenches, continuing to work the bolts on their rifles and fire. Finally they turned tail and ran. Bullets from the oncoming enemy chased after them. Pershing heard several bullets crack past his head and felt one tug at his coat sleeve as they cut their deadly swath through the air. He and Malcom were at the tail end of the retreating force of Legionnaires. Up ahead the majority of his force had taken up position at the one fall back position between the beach and the one bridge that led into San Juan along with another detachment of Legionnaires led by Whitmore himself. The old man was on horseback which made him a terribly exposed target. Even though bullets continued to rip through the air, somehow none of them struck the eccentric old millionaire. Maybe none of the French or Confederates had the stomach to shoot such an obviously exposed man. Maybe he was protected by a magical aura. Whatever it was, Whitmore sat there, pointing at the oncoming French and Confederate marines with a drawn saber, like a statue out of some past war. The commander of the Spanish Foreign Legion cried to his men.

"Hold them back men! Drive these French tyrants and these Rebel traitors back into the sea!" The men of the Legion let out a cry just as Pershing and Malcom took up their positions near the front of the new line. This time they had no trenches to hide in. Like the oncoming enemy they were out in the open.

Like most of the troops around him, Pershing went prone and opened fire. When they'd first hit the beaches, the French and Confederates had come ashore in great numbers. They'd lost a lot of men driving the Legion out of their trenches. The beach to the northeast was absolutely littered with bloody corpses clad in gray-blue and blue-red. Though there weren't near as many French and Confederates as there had been, they still far outnumbered the thin khaki line that stood in their way. Pershing worked the bolt on his Enfield and fired at the oncoming enemy marines. Beside him, Malcom likewise blazed away at them. Rebel Yells and cri de guerres, sounded from the throats of the enemy soldiers as they surged forward, ready to slaughter the remnants of Whitmore's Legion. Pershing drew his sword-bayonet, affixed it to the end of his rifle, and readied himself to leap to his feet for the bloody man to man climax.

Suddenly new sounds reached his ears. Off to the east fresh gunfire erupted along with a new battle crie: "Viva Espana! Viva Leopoldo!" Fresh Spanish troops, clad in Prussian blue, with spike topped helmets and armed with Mauser rifles, pitched into the French-Confederate flank with a fury. The once seemingly unstoppable enemy attack ground suddenly to a halt. In a matter of minutes the French and Confederate marines went from relentless charge to headlong retreat. The emboldened Legionnaires and their newly arrived reinforcements charged after them.

Pershing leapt to his feet and quickly made his way back over the ground he'd given up. The French and Confederates ran for their lives. The tide had turned. The hunters had become the hunted. The blue and gray clad marines reached the trench works and tried to make a stand, but the Legionnaires and Spanish regulars were right on their heels. Pershing leapt back into the trenches he'd abandoned on a short while earlier, and startled a hapless Frenchman. The blue and red clad marine tried to raise his Lebel but Pershing shot him in the face before he could fire. Another enemy soldier, this one a Confederate, was desperately trying to climb out of the other side of the trench. Pershing aimed his Enfield at the fleeing Rebel and pulled the trigger at almost point blank range. The rifle clicked harmlessly. Pershing had fired his last round. Rather than let the gray and dark blue clad marine escape, Pershing stabbed him in the back with his bayonet. The enemy soldier collapsed to the bottom of the trench as Pershing rung the bayonet loose. Blood dripped down the blade. Pershing then proceeded to climb out of the trench. The tattered remnants of the enemy force were now retreating across the beach and towards the shore and their boats. The Legionnaires and Spaniards charged after them again. Outnumbered, exhausted, low on ammunition, and with their backs against the sea, the remaining French and Confederates dropped their weapons and threw their hands into the air in surrender.

"We did it, Pershing!" cried Joseph Whitmore from his horse. "We showed those blasted Rebels and their French dogs that they can't bestride this world like a colossus! We've shown them this hemisphere is not there's for the taking! More importantly this will show the people back home that our enemies aren't invincible!" He turned to look around the beach that was absolutely littered with the bloody corpses of French and Confederate Marines and blasphemed almost reverently. No...they were far from invincible. "At last we can hold our heads high again...I tell you I've waited over twenty-five years for this day!"

"Congratulations, sir," said Pershing.

Whitmore nodded.

"To all of us, Pershing...to all of us. Mark my words this is only the beginning. Now begins the time that we get back everything that's ours that those blasted Rebels took from us!"

As the prisoners were led away, Legionnaires and Spaniards up and down the beach held aloft rifles, hats, and gold and red Spanish flags. They screamed and cheered. They hurled their cries of victory at the French and Confederate ships still sitting off shore. Out on the sea to the west a naval battle was raging between the Spanish, French, and Confederate navies. The sound of the guns sounded like an approaching storm. As Pershing stared at those ships his thoughts went to the armada of US and British warships that had yet to arrive but would at any time. Neither France nor the Confederacy would be seizing Puerto Rico, not now. But he still wondered if just offshore, another bigger war was about to start.

LXIII

The surgical tent was bustling with activity as Joshua Winslow finished bandaging the mutilated leg of a wounded Legionnaire. Outside, the fierce bark of rifle fire and the thunderous booms of artillery, gave the impression of an approaching storm. The fierce fighting was less than a mile away and it was getting closer.

Joshua made a last check of the tourniquet that was keeping the man from bleeding to death and then made his way toward his next patient. Across the tent, Dr. Rollins was desperately trying to stem the bleeding on another patient who'd taken a nasty hit in the shoulder.

"Miss Harper! I need more arterial clamps! Dr. Winslow! Your assistance please!"

"Coming, Doctor!" chorused Joshua and Jennifer simultaneously. Strictly speaking Joshua wasn't a doctor yet, he was a senior surgical student. Nonetheless he now had more actual surgical experience than many of his instructors back in Chicago. In dealing with the gruesome casualties back on Cuba and now on Puerto Rico, Joshua had saved hundreds of lives. He'd proven himself a capable surgeon. Dr. Rollins recognized that fact.

Joshua took up position beside the head surgeon and hurriedly began helping him to tie off arteries. Their hands worked skillfully side by side. They were so soaked and stained with blood an observer wouldn't have been able to distinguish which belonged to a white man and which to a black. An outsider that saw their bloody surgical leather aprons might have thought that they were butchers. A moment later nurse Harper brought a handful of extra surgical clamps which were intended to temporarily stem the bleeding in a wound as gruesome as the one in this soldiers shoulder.

Joshua noted that she wasn't wearing the ring she'd so excitedly shown the entire surgical staff that morning.

A cry suddenly came from outside the tent.

"We've got more wounded!"

"They're coming in faster than we can deal with them!" said Rollins in a frustrated tone of voice. The head surgeon looked around for his other assistant surgeon Dr. Wesley. The British surgeon was in the midst of an amputation.

"I've got this, Joshua. I need you to go outside and triage the new arrivals."

For a moment Joshua felt as if his heart had stopped, but he rallied quickly.

"Yes, sir." There were times when being a surgeon on a battle field felt dangerously close to playing God. There'd been moments where he'd had to make a split second decisions as to who to treat. He'd learned very quickly the ugly truth that he couldn't help everyone. He couldn't be more than one place at one time no matter how desperately he was needed. Now he had to go outside and divide the wounded into those needing immediate care, those who needed care but not as badly as the first group, and those beyond help.

God, please help me!

The scene outside the tent reminded Joshua of hell itself. Nearly a hundred wounded men were strewn about the ground on stretchers. Moans and cries of agony came from most of them. Several of them had already been triaged by Dr. Wesley but there was a large group of new arrivals close to the road.

The sound of rifle fire was now exceedingly close. Trying to tune it out, Joshua focused on his task. There were nearly two dozen men waiting to be triaged. Battling down his emotions and hardening his heart to everything but medical truth, Joshua went to work. Just about everyone who was gut shot or had a sucking chest wound went into the hopeless category. At Joshua's command they were taken away by black orderlies, given morphine injections, and made as comfortable as possible while they awaited the end. Those few with chest wounds or gut wounds that he thought had the slightest hope went straight to the front of the line along with anyone with a head wound or heavily mutilated limbs. Men with lesser wounds like bullet grazes or even single hits to an arm or a leg where the bleeding seemed to be under control and the bone didn't appear shattered went into the middle tier of men who needed care but would have to wait.

Suddenly fresh bursts of rifle fire came from the south. Several Legionnaires in khaki were fleeing north. On their heels was a company of blue and red uniformed French Marines. Joshua stood his ground as nearly thirty enemy soldiers bared down on the surgical camp. The lead Frenchman aimed his bayoneted rifle at Joshua and barked something in French. By way of reply the young negro surgeon jerked his thumb towards the large white flag with a red cross that flew from the front of the surgical tent. The Frenchman's eyes went wide for a moment but he quickly lowered his rifle and ordered his men to do the same. He shouted loudly in French to someone further to the rear. A moment later two French soldiers came forward carrying one of their wounded comrades on a makeshift stretcher. The first Frenchman pleaded with Joshua in his incomprehensible language and he beckoned him desperately to come forward. Joshua reflected that had these been white soldiers from the USA or CSA they would have been much more hesitant to allow a negro to work on one of their wounded comrades, but from all he'd seen the white men of Europe were, in most cases, slightly more enlightened.

Joshua went forward and kneeled over the wounded Frenchman to examine him. From all the gold braid on his dark blue coat Joshua deduced that the man was an officer, possibly even a high ranking officer. The man's head was wrapped tightly in a makeshift bandage. Joshua pulled it back slightly so that he could see the wound. Joshua winced. It didn't look good. A bullet had struck the man's skull indirectly, just above the left temple. The last time he'd seen a wound like this he'd been on the front lines and not back at the field hospital.

Technically speaking I'm on the front lines right now even though I'm at the field hospital!

From his cursory inspection, Joshua didn't hold much hope for the man. The bullet had struck the man's skull at an odd angle and miraculously been deflected. Unfortunately, however, he showed all the signs of internal bleeding on the brain from the force of the impact.

The man was unconscious. Joshua opened his eyes and checked his pupils. The one on the side of the wound was fixed and unresponsive to the daylight. His breathing was labored, even though there was no obvious damage to the lungs or respiratory system. Sighing, Joshua picked up the man's wrist. He had a pulse—not as strong as it should have been—but for the present not yet near death.

I have to try.

He called for the orderlies and instructed them to take the wounded French officer directly to the surgical tent. The other Frenchmen gave him a half dozen *mercis* and then trudged back towards the battle.

Joshua made his way rapidly back towards the tent. A few of the wounded men sitting outside gave him murderous looks for sending in an enemy officer. Joshua paid them no heed. He was a surgeon, not a soldier. His job was to heal not to kill. His duty was to all men, regardless of what color their uniform was.

Once the orderlies had set the wounded Frenchman on his surgical table, Joshua carefully peeled away the make shift bandages so he could examine the wound closely. He confirmed that the skull had not been penetrated by the bullet impact. As far as Joshua could tell from his limited examination the man's brain was under pressure from an epidermal hematoma. If Joshua was to save his life, he had no choice but to do what many of his instructors had said never to do. He had to open the man's skull to release the blood and the excess pressure.

The London medical journals he'd read on board the Capricorn had said that British doctors had developed a special diamond tipped drill for the procedure. The instrument was supposed to bore a simple hole in the skull while doing minimum damage to the surrounding cranial bone. Utmost care had to be taken by the operating surgeon not to damage the brain on the other side.

The instrument at Joshua's disposal was decidedly cruder. American medical science always seemed to be a step behind Europe. The drill Joshua pulled from the surgical tools lacked a diamond tip. Joshua hoped the crude metal drill bit didn't do more harm than good.

He's going to die one way or the other. This is the only way. God please help us...

An orderly helped Joshua position the Frenchman's head and then secure it and the rest of his body tightly to the surgical table with tight leather straps. Joshua shaved off the blood matted hair around the impact site. Joshua positioned the hand cranked surgical drill over the patients head, about an inch above the temple. Joshua took a deep breath and started to drill. He held the drill steady with his right hand while he cranked with the left. He bored a small hole through the skull about a centimeter in diameter being as careful as possible not to push the drill into the brain itself. There was a moderate eruption of blood and fluid as the brain cavity was opened and the pressure was released. Joshua released the strap holding the Frenchman's head and then turned it to the side. Exactly how much to let it bleed was something that had been debated in the journals. Joshua erred on what he thought to be the side of caution and took a conservative approach.

Better too little than too much.

Joshua then rapidly began to bandage to wound. It would have to be kept meticulously clean, even more so than an ordinary wound. If a limb got infected it was bad but an infected limb could be cut off. If this Frenchman got an infection...

After wrapping the man's head so tightly in bandages that it resembled that of an Egyptian mummy, Joshua had the orderlies carry him away. Ideally he would have liked to sit and observe the patient. Unfortunately on a battle field he had no such liberty. Only time would tell if the operation had been a success, or merely delayed the inevitable.

The gunfire had moved off to the west and south, but all of a sudden it came back with a fury. One of the less critically wounded soldiers poked his head into the surgical tent.

"They're falling back! We're driving them back!"

The surgeons and nurses paid little attention. They had their hands far too full to worry about who was winning the battle. Newly wounded men began to arrive outside.

Joshua soon found himself dealing with a particularly difficult amputation. A young Spaniard in a Prussian blue uniform had been brought in with a wounded arm. The limb had been hit by three different bullets—all within a few inches of each other. One of the bullets had completely shattered the bone. The mangled and mutilated arm was beyond saving, but the young Spaniard didn't see it that way. Joshua needed the help of three orderlies to strap the terrified young soldier down. He was shouting frantically in Spanish. Was he cursing them? Begging them not to amputate?

Calling for his mother? Joshua wasn't sure. Fighting back tears he grabbed a bottle of chloroform, poured it into a cloth and then placed it over the boy's nose and mouth. The wounded and terrified soldier started to panic even more. No matter what the journals said, he'd seen that chloroform didn't work as fast as was commonly reported. It took several minutes of holding it over the patient's face and forcing them to breathe the overpowering fumes before they would finally fall into unconsciousness. Joshua consoled himself that at least then they would be spared the horrors that patients undergoing surgery had had to endure in decades past when they'd often been given nothing but a shot of whiskey and a piece of leather to bare down on lest they bite off their own tongues in pain.

When the young Spaniard was finally unconscious, Joshua turned to Jennifer Harper who handed him the surgical saw. Joshua positioned the blade over the ruined arm, just below the tourniquet and started to saw through the mangled flesh and bone.

Suddenly the ground seemed to shake. Loud explosions resounded outside. First one, then another than another—each one closer and louder than the last. The French and Confederates might have been driven back to the sea, but the big guns on their ships off shore were punishing the victors with everything that they had. All at once the world seemed to explode. Joshua felt himself lifted up into the air and then slammed down hard on the ground. Smoke and dirt filled the air obscuring his view. In the aftermath of the thunderous explosion fresh cries of pain and agony arose. For the poor wounded men in and around the hospital tent, hell had just gotten a little bit worse.

Joshua staggered to his feet. He was no longer standing in a tent. The tent wall to the south was still half standing. The rest of the tent had been ripped to shreds by the explosion and its shrapnel. The young man he'd been operating on only a moment before no longer needed his services. Off to his left he saw Dr. Wesley sprawled on the ground, a wad of bandages still clasped in his cold lifeless hand. Joshua tried to take a step. His foot hit something on the ground. Joshua looked down to see the lifeless body of Jennifer Harper spread across the ground. The front of her body had been splayed open by hot flying shrapnel. Strangely enough, she had a look of perfect peace upon her face. He doubted that she'd felt any pain. She never knew what hit her. Joshua's thoughts went to Major Pershing. After an engagement of less than one day, his beloved fiancée was dead. The thought was enough to bring tears to his eyes, but unfortunately he had no time for such a thing. Another deafening explosion nearby let everyone know that the bombardment was far from over. Joshua through himself flat to the ground along with all the other survivors and prayed that he wouldn't meet the same fate as so many others.

LIX

"What's going on?" demanded Roger Connery of the Spanish naval orderly in the sickbay of the Spanish battleship *Leopold.* The Spaniard let loose with a stream of incomprehensible Spanish. Roger Connery cursed. The ship's engines had fired up and the hull was vibrating—which meant they were underway. Anxious and harried Spanish voices had sounded from the speaking tubes more than once.

The Spanish had evacuated him and the other wounded soldiers from Santiago on the *Leopold* and other Spanish warships. When they'd reached San Juan Puerto Rico there hadn't been room in the port city's hospitals to accommodate all the wounded. The *Leopold* had the most extensive medical facilities of any ship in the Spanish navy. They had therefore used it as a makeshift hospital ship. Connery had been one of the "lucky" ones that got to be quartered on the *Leopold.*

In Santiago, Connery had thought that the hospital ward was crowded. Now he knew better. On the *Leopold* the wounded were crammed into the sickbay like sardines in a can, but to Connery that was not the worst of it. Back in Santiago he'd been cared for English speaking doctors and had had the simple comfort of female nurses. Connery had not lain eyes on Jennifer Harper nor any other woman since the *Leopold* had arrived in San Juan several days earlier. By comparison the Spanish naval orderlies provided substandard care. There were too many wounded men and not enough orderlies to care for them. The Spaniards certainly lacked bedside manner. But worst of all…

Morphine! I need Morphine! He wanted to rebuke himself for his own thoughts. He was thinking like a drug addict.

No, I'm thinking like a man with broken ribs and a bullet shattered shoulder… Connery was in intense and constant pain and the Spanish, damn them, were doing almost nothing.

I'd almost rather be cared for by that nigger, then these dagos! Despite everything, Connery had endured it, not that he'd been given much choice. Then the shelling had started. It had gone on for the better part of a day. No one had bothered to tell the men confined in sickbay what was going on, though it wasn't hard to deduce that San Juan was under attack. Still, despite the pain, and despite the lack of either courtesy or common sense from their caretakers, Connery had remained calm, but no more.

"English, you worthless dago!" roared Connery. "English! Find someone who speaks English to tell us what is going on!" He cursed and swore, and shouted and threatened violence. He turned the air blue with profanities and demands but in the end it did no good. The orderlies simply withdrew from the sickbay as was their habit when their foreign patients annoyed them. A short while later, a group of Spanish sailors hurried through the corridor outside talking excitedly. The vibration of the deck and hull increased as the ship seemed to pick up speed.

"You don't think we're going into battle do you?" asked the man across from Connery. "Surely they'd get us off first, wouldn't they?"

In lieu of telling his fellow ward what an idiot he was, Connery focused his rage upon the Spaniards themselves.

"Don't forget who we're dealing with here," he said disdainfully.

Suddenly the entire ship shook and reverberated with the thunderous noise of the *Leopold's* main guns firing.

"There's your answer," replied Connery bitterly.

"They can't do this!" declared the man. A second volley from the battleship's guns declared that they not only could, they darn well had. Whether filled with wounded soldiers or no, the Spaniards could not afford to hold back a vessel like the *Leopold* as a hospital ship nor had they bothered to evacuate those men before sending the ship into battle.

"If this ship sinks we're dead!" said the man in bed across Connery, his voice trembling and laden with fear. Connery didn't think the man a coward. He was missing his right leg, and his wound was far from healed up. If the new battle went badly and the *Leopold* went down he'd most certainly die. If he was lucky he'd simply drown. Connery had always heard that was the most peaceful way to go. He didn't believe it. As far as he was concerned there was no peaceful way to go. But the other possibilities if the *Leopold* was struck by the shells of another battleship that they would either be blown to Kingdom Come, or burn to death. Since neither of those appealed to Connery either and since he still had all his limbs he forced himself to get up out of the bed.

Immense pain shot through his body from his side and from his shoulder. For a moment he fell back to the bed, but he barred his teeth and forced himself back to his feet.

"What are you doing?"

"I'm not staying here." *If I have to die, I'm taking some of these bastards with me!* Connery looked around the sickbay for something he could use as a weapon. He found what he wanted when he spotted a rack on the far wall with surgical scalpels and other surgical tools. His fellow patients stared at him in confusion. He didn't care.

One way or another they'll be dead soon enough. After taking the scalpel with the largest blade, Connery stumbled into the corridor outside the sickbay. Thankfully he didn't see any of the orderlies. If they'd caught him out of bed they would certainly try to force him back to it. He'd have given them a nasty surprise if they had. A couple of times every minute, the ship resounded with the thunderous booms of the main guns firing. The roar was deafening. As he made his way down the corridor a nearby explosion announced that someone was shooting back at the Spaniards. Half a dozen yards down the corridor, Connery came upon the ship's laundry bay. He winced in pain as he pushed open the wooden double doors. With the ship in the midst of a battle and everyone at general quarters, the ships laundry facility was deserted. Connery set about searching for a uniform. He could have had a common sailor's uniform instantly—there were plenty of those lying around. Connery swore when he couldn't find an officer's uniform. It was as much in pain as it was frustration. Finally, he spotted a large curtain hung on the far side of the room. Connery hauled it back to reveal an entire rack of officer's uniforms. He grabbed a coat with gold braid and the trousers that went with it and put them on over his Johnny Gown. He found socks, but no shoes, nor did he find an officers cap. With no shoes or cover, he knew he looked slightly odd but he was certain he'd draw less attention then if he were wandering the ship in nothing but the Johnny Gown. He was reasonably certain the gold stripes on his sleeve would keep the average sailor from asking too many questions but if not…

He placed the surgical scalpel into the front uniform pocket carefully and then made his way back into corridor. In one sense, battleships were much easier to blow up than freighters. He reflected that blowing up the CSS Mississippi in Havana Harbor had been much easier than blowing up the Capricorn. On the later he'd had to improvise. He'd have to improvise here as well, but if he could get to the powder magazine, he'd cause an explosion just as spectacular as the one he'd caused on his own country's warship. But first he'd have to find one of the powder magazines. Before he did that, he wanted a better idea of what was going on.

He made his way towards a gangway and started to climb towards the upper decks. With each rung he felt as though a dozen knives were stabbing him in the side. Still he forced himself on. At one point the pain threatened to drop him, but then he emerged onto the upper deck and the fresh sea air sent waves of fresh energy through him. He'd been cooped up below decks in the stench filled sickbay so long he'd forgotten what fresh air felt like.

Boom! The *Leopold's* four 7.9 inch guns fired. The sound of the blast nearly blew out Connery's eardrums and he instinctively brought up his hands to cover his ears. Fresh pain roared through his shoulder as he did so. Dazed from the blast, Connery searched the sea for the Spanish battleship's target. The shells exploded into the sea, not far from a gray battleship that was about five hundred yards away. Connery had no binoculars, but even at that distance he could clearly make out the Confederate Battle Flag fluttering at the ship's bow and the Blood Stained Banner flying at the stern though he could not make out her name. The Confederate warship responded to the *Leopold* in kind. Her twelve inch guns boomed. The shells shrieked overhead and exploded into the sea just behind the Spanish flagship. The Leopold fired again. This time one of her shells exploded into the side of the CS battleship, leaving a gruesome fiery wound in her upper hull well above the waterline. Once more the Confederate vessels weapons roared in reply. This time they found their mark. The *Leopold* shook violently as the twelve inch Confederate shells slammed into her. One exploded into her superstructure sending fiery shrapnel in all directions. A Spanish sailor not far from Connery wound up with an errant chunk of metal stuck in the side of his neck. The wounded sailor panicked and hastily pulled out the metal fragment. A fountain of blood instantly sprouted from his neck and sprayed the armored siding behind him red. Another nearby sailor rushed to help his wounded comrade. He never made it.

Suddenly to Connery the whole world seemed to explode. This time the sound of the blast did rupture his eardrums. For the briefest instant all he saw was fiery red. The flames roasted his flesh and for a moment that seemed like an eternity a new hellish pain surged through his body. The force of the explosion through him away from the ship like a rag doll. He hit sea with tremendous force. Whereas a moment before everything had been fiery red, now all was a watery darkness. Connery felt himself sinking as though a great claw were dragging him down into the black abyss. He tried to struggle, to somehow fight his way to the surface but the pains from his shoulder, his ribs and his new burns were overwhelming and he had no strength left. As his last breath forced its way out of his lungs and cold merciless sea water took its place, Connery felt his heart stop, and then he never felt anything in this world again...

LX

The crew of the *CSS Texas* let out wolf like howls of victory as the powder magazine of the Spanish battleship they'd hit exploded. The enemy warship went up in a spectacular fireball that reminded Captain Blake Ramsey of the tragic end of the late battleship *Mississippi* and he was suddenly filled with the sensation that his dead comrades had been avenged. He stared grimly at the burning hulk of the Spanish flagship. Spanish sailors, many of them on fire had been thrown from their ruined ship by the massive explosion. Many that hadn't but who were desperate to escape the flames, also leapt into the sea. The *Leopold* was flooding rapidly. The explosion had not only ripped open her hull, it had broken her back. The Spanish vessel still hadn't struck her colors, but when Ramsey considered how engulfed she was in flames and how rapidly she was going down, he doubted the enemy would be able to. He lowered his binoculars.

"Cease fire! Bring us about to course 350, maintain speed!" The *Leopold* had been dealt with, but the rest of the Spanish fleet that had dared come out of San Juan to challenge the French and Confederate armada still needed to be dealt with.

"I still can't believe they came out to fight us!" said Ray Brisk excitedly. "Combined with the French we've got them outnumbered more than two to one! They've got to know the Yankees and Brits are on the way. Why not wait it out in the harbor under the protection of all those forts and guns until they get here?"

"I imagine it's because they gave us such a bloody nose on the beaches."

Brisk half nodded and half cocked his head to the side in annoyance. A bloody nose was—if anything—an understatement. The Spanish had completely repelled the French and Confederate landings. They had literally driven them back into the sea.

"They think because they beat us on land that they can whip us on sea too?"

Ramsey nodded.

"They're Spaniards, Ray. Once you get their dander up, you can't hold em back! Funny thing is if they hadn't come out to fight we'd probably be withdrawing now! Our landing forces have been devastated. But if they want to give us the chance to sink their fleet before we go, I'm happy to oblige them."

"If you ask me that makes them fools," said Brisk.

Raising an eyebrow in irony, Ramsey reached into his pocket, pulled out a gold coin, and held it up. Robert E. Lee's stern visage stared back at him. Ramsey reflected that the Confederacy's greatest hero had a few traits in common with the Spaniards though he doubted his first officer would have called Marse Rob a fool. Ramsey recalled that once, right after taking command of Confederate forces, Lee had won a stunning series of victories in Virginia over a course of seven days during the War of Confederate Independence. Often overlooked, however, was that on the final day of that otherwise glorious campaign Lee had ordered his men to assault Malvern Hill. It was a formidable position, and had been massively fortified by Union artillery. Lee had ordered assault after assault and one after another they had been beaten back. Like the Spanish fleet they were presently blowing out of the water, Lee had allowed his previous victories to make him momentarily reckless. Having watched the disastrous landings and knowing that US and British warships were on their way, Ramsey feared the entire Confederate States may have allowed themselves to become reckless.

We aren't ready to fight the Yankees or the Brits!

Far off to their port the guns of the French battleship *Andre Massena* thundered. Admiral Fournet's flagship was after prey of its own. Ramsey watched flame belch from her twelve inch guns as the French warship sent explosive shells raining down on another Spanish vessel. The Spanish cruiser responded in kind. The shell found its mark. As it exploded into the hull of the *Andre Massena* Ramsey winced. Just a short while earlier, the *Texas* herself had taken a hit. The Spanish shell had actually penetrated her hull. Ramsey thanked God it hadn't hit the boilers or one of the powder magazines and that his men had contained the fire, otherwise the *Texas* could easily have suffered the same fate as the late *CSS Mississippi*. But the Texas had been hit by the guns of the *Leopold.* The Spanish flagships main armament had been just slightly more than half the size of the *Texas* and the *Andre Massena*. The *Leopold's* guns had been just big enough to penetrate the *Texas'* armor but nonetheless Ramsey's ship had sent the pride of the Spanish navy to the bottom. The other ships of the Spanish fleet had weapons even smaller than those of the late *Leopold*. Ramsey nodded in satisfaction when he saw that though the Spanish cruiser had scored a hit on the French battleship, its armor had not been pierced. Ramsey was starting to agree with Brisk. The Spanish naval commanders were fools. Not only were they going into battle outnumbered, they were also going out gunned.

Suddenly, the telephone connecting the bridge with the crow's nest rang. Ramsey made his way to it, picked up the ear piece, brought it to his ear, and then shouted into the wall mounted receiver.

"Bridge!"

"Sir! Lots of smoke on the horizon! Bearing 010!"

"Understood! Keep a sharp eye! Let me know the moment you identify them!"

"Aye sir!"

"What is it, Captain?"

"Unless I'm mistaken, Mr. Brisk, our guests are about to arrive. Helm! Come right twenty degrees! Make your new course 000!"

"Aye aye, sir!" said the large burly sailor manning the large spoked wheel as he began to turn it to the right. "Now heading due north, sir."

Ramsey turned to Brisk.

"Ray, get to the signal mast and warn Admiral Fournet on board the *Andre Messina*, let him know we've spotted smoke to the north."

"Aye, sir, but I think he knows." Brisk pointed towards the French Flag ship. "They're turning north too, and unless I miss my guess, they're picking up speed." Ramsey brought up his binoculars. The French battleship was indeed putting out fresh black smoke from her stacks.

"We'd better put on more speed as well. Tell the boiler room to lay on more steam!"

"Are we going to fight the Yankees and the Brits, sir?"

"I told you, Ray, Richmond's orders are that we support our allies." He looked suddenly over at the *Andre Messina*. "I'm sorry to say that it's up to the French. Go ahead and signal Fournet. Ask him 'Fight or Withdraw?' Get going. I'll handle the boiler room." Ray nodded. The message was short and sweet. Hopefully it wouldn't take long for the French to translate it. It would also allow them the simplicity of a one word reply.

Ray made his way out of the bridge and ran along the side of the Texas' superstructure. He climbed a gangway up to battleship's uppermost. The signal mast was located just behind the forward crow's nest. At Brisk's order the signalmen began to prepare the flags. He hoped the French lookouts were paying attention. He'd heard the British navy had begun to use signal lamps to flash messages in Morse code as opposed to the use of signal flags. He found himself wishing the Confederacy had followed suit. It would have been quicker and more likely to be spotted. Sometimes time was of the essence. At the moment, it could mean the difference between peace, and the outbreak of world war.

A few moments later, fifteen small flags went up the signal mast. Brisk then made his way rapidly back to the bridge.

"Signal flags raised, Captain!"

Ramsey nodded. The Captain was looking dead ahead and nervously smoking a cigar.

"The lookouts called while you were gone. They've identified the approaching ships. We're facing eight battleships—four flying the Union Jack and three flying Old Stripy."

Old Stripy, together with Old Ugly and the Stars and Streaks were common derogatory terms used by the people of the Confederate States to describe the flag of the Union. A few older people in the CSA still held a certain amount of reverence for the old flag, even though they no longer owed it any allegiance. Ramsey, however, had been in diapers when the Confederacy freed itself from the tyranny of the north. To him and millions of younger people in the CSA the US flag represented nothing but a hostile foreign power that had twice tried and twice failed to conquer his home.

And now we're about to hand them another excuse to try again...

Ramsey knew there were a few hotheads in the CSA who themselves wanted nothing more than a chance to go at the Yankees like their fathers had before them. As far as he was concerned they were fools.

Ramsey spun his gaze about to look at the *Andre Messina*. Admiral Fournet had still not replied to his inquiry for instructions. He found himself most uncomfortably contemplating the fact that the United States and Great Britain made much more efficient allies with each other than did the CSA and France.

At least they speak the same language!

Up ahead, the smoke billows that had been on the horizon had transformed themselves into the forward silhouettes of warships. Behind them, more smoke was on the horizon. The US and British battleships undoubtedly had other warships in their wake.

"Orders, sir?" asked Brisk. "We'll be in firing range in a matter of minutes."

Ramsey took a long drag on his cigar and let out a cloud of smoke.

"Maintain, course. Tell the gunners to bring the guns to bear on approaching ships but hold their fire unless I give the order!"

Ramsey's heart was pounding with anticipation. He shifted his cigar to the corner of his mouth and chewed on it nervously. The US ships ahead were the equivalent of his own and those of the French. The British ships, however, were both larger and more powerful. They had guns bigger than any of those in the Confederate or French fleet. As far as Ramsey could tell, they were already in range of the British weaponry. Ramsey knew the orders that President Stone had given him. He wondered what instructions, if any, that Napoleon IV had given to Admiral Fournet. He shifted his gaze back over to the French flagship. If the Emperor had ordered him to fight, would the commander of the French fleet obey under the present circumstances? The landings had been defeated. No matter how much the French wanted Puerto Rico, they wouldn't be taking it, not with the present expedition. And the approaching armada had the combined French and Confederate fleet both outnumbered and outgunned.

Ramsey turned his attention back to the approaching warships. The US and British ships loomed menacingly ahead. He could make out their flags though his binoculars. Ramsey new that the most devastating war his country or the world had ever faced was bearing down on them all like a giant colossus. The question was who would be the first to shoot?

"Captain!" cried Commander Brisk pointing at the *Andre Messina*. Ramsey stared at her with his binoculars. The French battleship had replied with a single word: "WITHDRAW." Even as Ramsey read the signal flags the French warship had begun to turn away to the east along with the rest of the French fleet.

"Hard about!" cried Ramsey. "Make your course 270 get us out of here!"

The French and Confederate fleets parted for the approaching Union and British warships like the red sea before Moses. Ramsey let out a long sigh of relief then lit himself a cigar. The world wasn't going to war. At least not that day…

LXI

Even though he was a civilian, and even though he disagreed with what was happening, Cole Allens and his wife stood at respectful attention in the main courtyard of the La Fortaleza. French and Confederate troops had been driven from the island. On the sea their fleet had gone nose to nose with that of the United States and Britain—and backed down. Cole found himself dwelling on just how close they had come to the outbreak of an intercontinental war and he silently cursed the politicians for bringing them so close to the brink. But Cleveland's gamble had paid off. The French and Confederates had blinked first.

Three large groups of soldiers stood in formation in the vast courtyard of the Spanish castle. The soldiers on the right wore US Army blue. Those on the left wore the different shades of Spanish blue. Between them was a group of Whitmore's khaki uniformed Legionnaires. Two military bands were also present, one Spanish and the other American.

Cole watched as General Daniel Webster Flagler, of the United States Army and General Weyler, approached the massive flag pole that stood at the center of the courtyard together. The US army band struck up the Spanish national anthem. As the martial notes of the Marcha Real sounded throughout the castle the soldiers snapped to attention and the few civilians present removed their hats. General Flagler and General Weyler brought up their arms in crisp military salutes. All eyes focused on Spain's Red and Gold la Rojigualda as it billowed above in all its glory in the air above the fortress for the last time. As the anthem played, Cole watched tears flow down the faces of many of the Spaniards present. The music ended and a squad of resplendently uniformed Spaniards came forward. The honor guard lowered the flag and then reverently folded it. For the first time in four-hundred years, the banner of Spain no longer flew over the island.

As soon as the Spanish color guard had withdrawn its US counterpart hurried forward and unfolded the Stars and Stripes with equal reverence. As Old Glory rose above the La Fortaleza, the Spanish army band began to play the Star Spangled Banner. Once again the Generals brought their arms up in salute. A few moments later the music stopped, the ceremony was complete and for better or for worse, Puerto Rico had become a territory of the United States of America. Without delay one of Weyler's Colonels shouted commands at the Spanish troops who as one did an about face and then column by column began to march out of the castle.

Cole wondered what they were thinking. They had fought so bravely to hold onto the island and now their government had sold it out from under them.

The small crowd of civilian and foreign observers began to break up. Cole turned to his wife.

"Well Mrs. Allens are you ready to go home?"

"I don't know," she said half seriously as he took her arm and they began to walk out of the castle together. "Now that Puerto Rico is part of the United States I was thinking we might move here permanently. It's so nice to have a nice warm beach to go to without having to leave the country." Then suddenly she had another thought. "I wonder when they'll add another star to the flag? Thirty-one stars would look interesting."

Cole laughed.

"I'm sure it will be a few years before Puerto Rico gets to be a state."

She smiled.

"Well until then let's go home. I don't think I've ever missed Louisville as much as I do now. Just promise me that we're not going home via the CSA."

Cole shook his head.

"Mr. Whitmore and his people are setting sail for New York tomorrow. We've been invited along. We should be home in a week."

They walked arm and arm through the streets of San Juan. Cole couldn't decide if the people were excited or anxious.

Probably a little of both. From what he'd seen of Puerto Rico he was fairly certain that US rule would be good for the island, at least economically. When they returned to the Hotel San Juan', they found Churchill and Barnes waiting for them.

"We wanted to tell you goodbye, Mr. Allens," said Reginald Barnes.

"Then both of you are leaving?" asked Cole.

"I'm afraid so," said Churchill. "Reggie here has been ordered to India and I've been posted to London."

"Surely the two of you can dine with us this evening," said Helen.

"I'm afraid not dear lady," replied Churchill. "Our ship leaves tonight, and we have much to do."

"It's been a pleasure knowing the two of you," said Cole sincerely.

"And you as well, Mr. Allens. I do hope you'll correspond with us." He handed Cole an envelope containing their contact information.

"I'll see to it that he does," said Helen.

After shaking Cole's hand in turn and kissing Helen's, the two young British officers made their final farewells and headed back out into the streets of San Juan.

"Those boys are going to be something one day," said Cole. Helen nodded. Cole continued. "Especially Winston. I don't know what it is. But something about him just screams that he's destined to do great things."

"Oh really," said Helen in amused tones. "So now you're a fortune teller?"

"No, but I do consider myself an excellent judge of character."

With that she couldn't argue.

"Well I have news for you Mr. Allens," she said, once again taking his hands in hers. "I'm going to tell your fortune. You are…" She paused, looked up into his eyes, and spoke softly.

"You are going to be a most wonderful father…" For a moment, Cole looked absolutely dumfounded as the reality of what she'd said sunk in. Slowly but surely a smile made its way across his face.

"You're…you're…you're…"

"*We're* going to have a baby."

For a moment she thought he was going to faint, but then all at once he took her in his arms and kissed her right there in the hotel lobby. A few people guffawed but only a few. Cole had seen that Spaniards were a far more passionate and romantic people than the prudes back in the USA. In any event, at that particular moment, Cole didn't care. He literally held the two things he cared most for in the world in his arms.

LXII

Nathan Audrey awoke to the smell of eggs and bacon cooking in a skillet. In the corner of the small cabin he'd commandeered as his quarters, Barbara Mayes was standing over a cast iron wood burning stove, busily preparing them breakfast.

"Good morning," she said with a smile.

"Good morning," he replied. If there was any awkwardness in his voice it was drowned out by a yawn and a loud cry that was half pain, half pleasure as he stretched his arms and legs. They'd had a good long romantic walk the night before. His instincts hadn't been wrong and he hadn't misread her signals. Once he'd returned them in kind she'd opened up quite readily about how she felt about him. When he'd pointed out that she'd only known him a short while she'd had a reply.

"And in that short time, look at all you've done for me," she replied. In her eyes he was her rescuer, defender and avenger. Audrey and his men had rescued her from the Mormons and hung the men that had burned her town. Audrey supposed that lay at the heart of her attraction to him. Women valued security. But he also knew she was a lonely widow that longed for the comfort of a man. She'd told him in greater detail about how her late husband had died just a few years earlier.

Audrey had opened up to her as well—about everything. If they were indeed going to spend their few remaining years together she deserved to know who he really was and what he'd done. By the light of the moon she'd listened as he told her of the horrible atrocities he'd witnessed under Custer twenty-seven years earlier, how the ruthless commander had tried to force him to kill an innocent Indian woman, and how, in a moment hysterical rage, he'd murdered Custer instead, and then shot his way out of his own camp. He told her how he'd been on the run in the west as a wanted murderer and how he'd made his way south into Mexico and joined up with the French Foreign Legion. He told her about the war of 1869 and how he'd been the only survivor of the Legion's last desperate stand at Fort Moultier. He'd told her how the secession of California had given him a new place to call home and how he'd served first as a bounty hunter, and then as a lawman for North America's latest nation state. Finally he told her how Goldwyn had recognized him and offered him a place in the army. In short he'd lived a long hard, adventurous, and above all lonely life.

When he'd finally finished telling her his story he half expected her to turn and walk away. Instead she stared at him with increased reverence and awe. She had reached up and caressed his rough weathered face. He'd taken her soft hand in his own and kissed it. A moment later they'd taken each other in their arms and brought their lips together in passion. When he'd next tried to speak she'd simply brought her finger to his lips to hush him. Her hand tightened around his own and she'd led him quietly back to the cabin. They were done talking for the evening, at least with words. Alone together in the stillness of the night, they loved one another in the most intimate way a man and woman could. In his long lonely life, Audrey had been with only a few women. They had been like ships passing in the night. But that night, he'd experienced a love and a passion he never had before.

The early morning sunlight was leaking through the closed curtains in the window of the small one room cabin. Barbara had laid out his clothes on the foot of the bed. He rose from the bed, feeling a lifetime younger and dressed while she divided up the eggs and bacon onto two plates. He'd always wondered what it would be like to have a normal life—to have a wife and a home. For the first time ever, he had an idea what it was like. For a man who'd spent his entire life alone, Audrey felt as if he were in heaven.

"I hope you're hungry," she said as he sat at the small wooden table. She placed the plates then took a seat across from him. He took hold of her hand and found himself fumbling for words.

"I know we kind of got the cart before the horse last night, but I wanted you to know…that is I wanted to ask…will you…would you…" He took a deep breath. "Would you do me the honor of being my wife?"

By way of reply she kissed his hand tenderly.

"I think you know the answer to that."

Suddenly, the sound of gunfire reached their ears. A few moments later the bell in the tower of the town's one small church started to ring the alarm. With great regret Audrey leapt to his feet and quickly put on his woolen green coat and his hat. He turned to see Barbara holding up his belt with its holstered pistol. He quickly put it on but before he rushed out the door he took her in his arms and kissed her fiercely, passionately and deeply.

"Be careful!" she said. "I love you."

"I love you," he replied. The words sounded strange to him coming from his lips. But both hearing them and saying them, and above all knowing that they were true was comforting in a way he'd never known before.

Audrey ran to the small stable behind the cabin and retrieved his horse. Because he knew this moment could come he'd kept the cavalry mount saddled. He climbed up on his horse, and then used a flick of the reins and the pressure of his legs to get it going. The gunfire was coming from the hills just north of town. Audrey didn't ride to the top of the hill. He had no desire to present himself as the perfect target for a sniper. Instead he dismounted halfway up the southern slope, handed off the horse to an orderly, and climbed the rest of the way on foot after retrieving his binoculars from the saddlebag.

Lieutenant Jergins was already there. Audrey was pleased to see the young officer and his men had been alert and ready.

"Good morning, Colonel! Sorry about the rude wake up but I'm afraid we've got some unwelcome guests."

"I can see that!" replied Audrey. Down below a squadron a blue uniformed Mormon Cavalry were regrouping after having been bloodily repulsed.

"They tried to crest the hill and we jumped them good!" said Jergins.

Audrey nodded and raised his binoculars. A few bloody blue clad Mormon troopers had been shot from the saddle. Their bloody corpses were lying still on the hill's northern slope. Audrey surveyed the remaining enemy cavalry, wondering if they'd be foolish enough to try again. They were not. Instead they turned north and headed back the way they had come."

Audrey pulled out a cigar and lit it.

"Well it won't be long now. Spread the word. The enemy could be here in force in less than an hour. I want every able bodied man ready to meet them!"

Jergins saluted then took his leave to carry out his orders.

Less than an hour later, the Mormon cavalrymen returned, this time at the head of a large column of infantry. The Beehive Banner fluttered proudly above them. The Mormon army wasn't quite as large as Audrey had expected, but it was still plenty large enough to overrun Pine City and its defenders.

Unless, everything goes according to plan. He took a drag on a fresh cigar. He knew how likely that was. One of the first things they'd taught him at West Point, decades earlier was that plans seldom survived contact with the enemy. He half expected them to begin an immediate flanking attack around to the east. If they did, then the 'surprises' he and his men had prepared would take out a lot of them, but he doubted that they alone would be enough to turn back the entire Mormon force.

All at once, the Mormon force came to a halt. Two riders—one of them carrying a white flag—broke off from the main group and began to approach the hill.

"Hold your fire!" cried Audrey and his command was then echoed by others up and down the line. Audrey immediately called for his horse. He quickly mounted and rode downhill to intercept the Mormons half-way. He didn't want them reaching the top of the hill and using the parley to get a look at the town and its defenses. The Mormon rider carrying the white flag reined in and allowed his companion to ride forward the rest of the way to meet with Audrey at the base of the hill. The Mormon officer brought his mount to a halt and then raised his hand in salute. Hesitantly, Audrey returned it. For a brief second, the Mormon eyed Audrey's cigar with almost contemptuous disapproval but then went ahead with his message.

"Good morning Colonel, I am Captain Richard W. Young, of the Army of Deseret. I will be brief and to the point. My superiors have instructed me to inform you that this entire territory has been granted to the Mormon people by Almighty God, and we will not rest until it has been purged of the gentile dogs that have defiled it for so long."

Part of Audrey wanted to laugh in his face. The other part warned him that religious fanatics were the most dangerous of the breed. He wondered absently what the Byzantines and the Sassanids had thought when Mohammed and his fanatical followers had come riding out of the desert crying about Allah and Holy War. They'd underestimated the upstart Arabians and their Prophet, and as a result Mohamed's fanatical religion had ended up stretching from Spain in the west to Persia in the east and beyond. Audrey chose his words with care.

"Captain, these people are citizens of the Republic of California. They were here first. They built this town with their own sweat and blood, and I and my men are duty bound to protect them."

The Mormon officer pointed his finger at Audrey as though it were an artillery piece.

"Then you hear my words, gentile! You, your men, and the other unbelievers have three choices." He reached into his uniform pocket and pulled out a small leather bound copy of the book of Mormon and held it out.

"First, you may open your eyes and see the light of the Prophet Joseph Smith, and accept the one, true faith. Pray to God and He will give you a burning in your heart and soul that what the Prophet says is true." The fire in the Mormon's eyes left no doubt as to the sincerity of his own faith. He then turned that fiery gaze back onto Audrey. "Your second choice is for you and your men to stack your arms and your flags and march with your heathen townspeople back to California with your heads bowed low."

"And my third option?"

Asked Audrey.

"Be purged with fire and sword."

In his mind, Audrey was making a cold calculation. An enemy as fanatically proud as the one he was facing could be easily angered and provoked. If he pulled it off just right, their anger and their pride just might blind them to sound strategy and cause them to act hastily.

"I'll take option four," he said suddenly, "and send you and the rest of your miserable fanatics to join Joseph Smith and Brigham Young in hell."

The fire of fanaticism that had so radiated the Mormon's eyes had been joined by the fire of murder. For a moment Audrey thought the man might actually reach for his gun. If he did he'd be dead before he had his weapon from his holster. Audrey might have gotten older but he knew, not without modesty, that there were few men faster on the draw than himself. He hadn't survived for over twenty years as a bounty hunter and a lawman by being slow.

The Mormon was so angry that he literally shook with rage. He said nothing else but whipped his horses head back around and then set spurs to the beast. Audrey quickly hastened back to his own defensive line. He had poked the proverbial bear and it wouldn't be long before it attacked.

"Well Colonel?" asked Jergins when he'd returned.

Audrey never had a chance to answer. Down below trumpets and drums started to sound and the Mormon Infantry began to move into a loose formation like a giant skirmish line.

"Are they coming straight at us?" asked Jergins, his voice radiating surprise.

"It certainly looks that way," said Audrey as he reached into his saddle bag and pulled out the stock of his custom sharpshooter rifle. Next he pulled out the barrel and attached it to the stock. Then he pulled out the scope and mounted it. He then adjusted the sight, chambered a round of ammunition and made his way back to the makeshift fieldworks his men had constructed atop the hill. He looked over at his one battery of artillery that his men had positioned at the center of the crest.

"Tell Sergeant Jones and his men to hold their fire until I give the word! If they haven't seen that we've got cannons up here I don't want them to know yet." If the Mormons had their dander up enough to attack his entrenched position atop the hill, he didn't want to give them an excuse to change their mind and try a flanking maneuver.

A minute or so later and it began. The Mormon Infantry began to march forward. At Audrey's command the Californian riflemen opened fire. The soldiers of Deseret had bolt and lever action rifles of their own and they returned the fire of the Californian soldiers and townsfolk in kind. To Audrey's chagrin, the Mormons sent a lot more bullets at he and his men then they sent back at the Mormons. This was partly because the Mormons had them outnumbered. But it was also because just under half the Mormons were armed with their own brand new native manufactured 1895 Browning Lever Action Rifles. The Mormon gunsmith John M. Browning was known across the North American continent and beyond as one of the greatest gun designers of all time. His small company had the backing of the Mormon government, and kept many of his most brilliant designs to themselves. Audrey was thankful that the small Mormon nation had such a limited industrial capability. The bolt-action Krag Jorgensen rifles his own green clad men carried were good weapons, but the Mormon BLARs put them to shame. The Winchesters carried by most of the townsfolk worked on the same principle, as the Mormon weapons, but with their smaller ammunition, difficult loading, and propensity to jam had more in common with the old henry rifles from the First War of Rebellion than they did with the sleek modern weapons being carried by the blue uniformed Mormon soldiers.

Audrey raised the scope of his sharpshooter to his eye and took aim at one of the advancing Mormons. Audrey fired and the man from Deseret went down with a bullet hole in his forehead. Audrey then worked the bolt on his rifle and searched for his next target.

The Mormons advanced relentlessly up the hill, but even though they had the defenders both outnumbered and outgunned, they were still terribly exposed. Several Mormons were cut down by bullets but those behind them kept advancing up the rocky slope, working their levers, and firing as they did so.

Once it was clear that the Mormons were fully committed to the attack, Audrey shouted at the top of his lungs over the gun fire at Sergeant Jones.

"Sergeant Jones! Fire at will!"

"Which one's will?" asked one of the townsfolk incredulously. A moment later the two cannons fired. The artillerymen had loaded them with grape-shot which had in essence transformed them into giant shotguns. Two lethal sprays of lead balls ripped into the oncoming Mormons. Still the survivors pressed on. Sergeant Jones and his men worked feverishly to reload the artillery.

"Pour on the fire, boys!" cried Audrey. The riflemen atop the hill redoubled their efforts to gun down their oncoming foes. Not far from Audrey a green uniformed soldier caught a bullet in the face. Down the line, two of the townsfolk were wounded and screaming. One was shouting enough profanities to turn the air blue, the other might have been screaming for his mother, but his cry was so tormented and pain filled it was hard to tell.

Boom! Boom! The cannons spoke again. Once again the advancing Mormons were hit with a merciless hail of small metal projectiles. This time arms and legs and head went flying from the force of the blasts. The Mormon's flinched back and then their advance collapsed completely into a retreat. The Californian defenders atop the hill let out cheers of victory. Audrey gravely raised his field glasses to his eyes.

"We haven't won yet," he said to Jergins. "Not even close. Tell the men to get ready. We've got to be prepared for either a second wave or to redeploy to face a flanking attack. My money's on the second."

Sure enough the Mormons quickly reformed for a flanking attack. But instead of moving towards the east as expected, they started to move around to the west. That suited Audrey just fine. The Mormons had played right into his hand by impulsively attacking the hill with a full frontal assault. If the defenders managed to repel them on the western flank as well, then the next attack on the eastern flank would serve as the coup de grace.

We might just pull this off!

Audrey redeployed to the western side of the town with his men, leaving behind a token force to hold the hill just in case the enemy had a change of heart. After quickly making his way down the southern slope of the hill, Audrey made his way between the general store and the bank to one of the makeshift parapets he and his men had constructed from old barrels and a few pieces of split rail fence. Because the buildings on Pine City's west side had been so close together and because a deep dry creek bed ran down that side of the city, the western flank of the town had been easily fortified, and offered an advantageous position from which to defend. For those reasons Audrey hadn't really expected the enemy to attack there. Nonetheless, one hundred yards westward, Mormon infantry began to form up for an attack in three separate waves. A moment later they were once again advancing, still in the giant skirmish line formation that they had used before. Audrey and his men blazed away at them. The Mormons returned the fire in kind. Several bullets cracked past Audrey's head, or slammed into the wooden bits of barrels and split rail fencing that the defenders had used to build their fortifications. A few feet away one of the Mormon bullets hit a green clad soldier in the throat. The Californian fell, vainly trying to stem the spraying fountain of blood that was erupting out of his neck with his hand.

Despite the torrent of led being thrown at them the advancing Mormon line held its cohesion—until it reached the edge of the dry river bed. The first wave of Mormon infantry hesitated for a moment but then with great discipline and no small amount of courage descended into the river bed. Once there they were terribly exposed to Californian fire. More and more of the advancing Mormons wet the dry river bed with their life's blood. Those who weren't hit continued to advance but found themselves unable to effectively fire at the well-entrenched defenders on the other side. As the blue uniformed Deseretans neared the western side of the river bed they found themselves staring down—or rather up at—rifle barrels that would soon be shooting at them at point blank range. At that point, the second attack ground to a halt. The Mormons were brave—fanatical even—but not stupid. They began an orderly withdrawal back across the river bed and didn't turn their backs on the Californians till they had climbed back up the western bank. Audrey took aim at one of the Mormon soldiers as he proceeded to climb out of the river bank but stopped at the last moment. In the heat of battle or not he couldn't bring himself to shoot a man in the back. Audrey then noticed that several enemy troops had made certain to retrieve the BLARs and ammo packs from their wounded comrades. He did take aim at them and cut them down like ducks in a pond. If the Californians managed to hold the town, he wanted those rifles. They wouldn't be worth much in and of themselves but if California could reverse engineer Browning's design it would put Audrey's country on an equal footing with Deseret when it came to fire arms—at least temporarily. Looking at the large number of Mormons lying in the riverbed—many of whom were still writhing in pain—Audrey half expected the Mormon's to ask for a temporary truce to retrieve the wounded. But there were no white flags forth coming. Instead the Mormon force shifted again back the way it had come. Audrey and his men shifted with them back to the top of the hill, though Audrey made certain to dispatch a couple of troopers to retrieve the Mormon lever action rifles. As he expected, the Mormons didn't stop to renew their attack on the hills but kept moving around them so that they could hit the town from the east. The Californians redeployed one last time and prepared for what—for better or for worse—would be the last stand of the battle.

Audrey took up his position at the center of the line, in the large gap between the hotel and the saloon. Compared to his previous position on the west side, he felt horribly exposed. As he waited for the enemy, Audrey reached into his uniform coat for another cigar but then thought better of it. Not far away the four barrel bombs he'd ordered constructed sat inconspicuously against the side of the hotel and of the saloon—two on one side and two on the other. The fuses all connected to one point behind the makeshift barricade. Audrey had given himself the dangerous assignment of lighting it. As the Mormons made the final preparations for their assault, Audrey worked furiously to reload his sharpshooter rifle. He then took a moment to look around. He noticed that his young Lieutenant was nowhere to be seen.

"Where's Jergin?"

"I'm sorry Colonel," said one of the Sergeants, "But he got hit as we pulled away from the west side. They took him to the town Doc along with the rest of the wounded but it didn't look good." Audrey felt a sudden tightness come over his chest. He knew he was getting old. He'd long since reached the point when he was certain there were fewer days ahead than behind, but Jergins like so many of his soldiers was young with his entire life ahead of him. The thought that the boy might be dead both weighed down upon him and at the same time reminded him how blessed he was to still be alive himself after such a danger filled life. He pulled out his small silver crucifix and kissed it, made the sign of the cross, and silently sent a quick but fervent prayer heavenward for his wounded aide de camp. He then worked the bolt on his rifle, perched it on the wooden barricade, and waited for the enemy to attack. He wasn't long in waiting.

The Mormons let loose with a fierce war cry. They'd spilled a lot of blood in the previous two attacks but far from being disheartened, they were ready for both victory and vengeance. They surged across the open ground east of the town and blazed away with their rifles as they made the charge. The defenders fired at them, both from behind the barricades and from the tops of the buildings. Up above and to the left, one of the townsfolk atop the hotel caught a bullet in the chest. He fell from the roof top, one hand clutched to his bloody chest the other still grasping his Winchester. He hit the dirt with a thud and did not rise again.

As Audrey predicted the Mormon advance began to concentrate towards the large gap between the hotel and the saloon. This was partly because Audrey had designed it to appear like the weakest point in the line and because the riflemen on the roof tops had been positioned to channel the enemy into it with their rifle fire. The plan appeared to be working. Even so, Audrey still didn't give the order to fall back. He didn't want to give the enemy the slightest hint that they were walking into a trap. The Mormons continued to advance. Several more Californians both on the ground and on the rooftops went down clutching bloody wounds. The forward most Mormons began to converge on the gap. Audrey readied the fuse.

"Go!" he cried. His fellow defenders began to flee with great urgency. Audrey struck a match and lit the fuse just as the first Mormons reached the forward part of the gap. Over sixty or not, Audrey moved with a speed that would have done justice for a road runner. His plan was to leave the barricade and run around the east side of the hotel and then as far north as he could, before the explosives went off, using the buildings as a shield.

Suddenly a bullet slammed into the back side of us upper right arm just as he made it around the corner of the hotel. The hot lead bit into his flesh and tore away a large chunk of skin and muscle. The impact sent torturous waves of pain throughout his body and sent him reeling so that he crashed face first into the dirt. A great number of Mormons had entered the gap—in fact the first ones were just entering the town proper—when the explosives went off. Simultaneously the four barrel bombs exploded as did the extra dynamite buried in the ground. The effect was as if four large artillery shells had exploded amongst a great throng of men at pointblank range. Dozens of enemy soldiers were literally blown to pieces by the blasts and by the fierce bits of shrapnel that shot out in all directions. The buildings themselves suffered enormous damage. Audrey was showered with glass from the busted windows of the hotel, and though most of the nails and other nasty metal bits that had been used for shrapnel had been blocked by the hotel, a large amount of deadly wooden shrapnel was blown into the town proper by the concussive force of the detonations. Lying as he was, face down in the dirt, Audrey was spared the worse of this, though a few small errant pieces of glass and wood did bite into his flesh to add to the torment of the wound in his arm.

For a brief moment, Audrey thought that he was either dead or dying. The world seemed to be spinning, and the world seemed to have gone mostly dark and quiet. He could still hear the sound of rifle fire and men screaming but it seemed as though it were a great distance away.

Suddenly he started coughing and his eyes started to burn. He wasn't dying—at least not yet—there was just so much smoke and dust in the air he was having trouble seeing. All at once a new pain added itself to the others. His ears were ringing loudly. He feared the monstrous noise of the explosions might have caused his eardrums to burst. Summoning reserves of strength he hadn't known he possessed, he started to stagger to his feet. He suddenly felt a strong hand on his good arm, trying to help him up. He didn't make it to his feet but he did make it to his knees. He turned and saw…

"Barbara!"

"You're wounded!" she cried terrified. "We've got to get you to the doctor!"

"There's no time!" Unbeknownst to himself he was practically shouting. "Just tie me a bandage around it tightly so I don't bleed to death."

Barbara started to rip a large strip of cloth from her skirt.

"Look out!" Audrey cried suddenly and despite intense pain drew his army revolver with his right hand. Behind her he had spotted a Mormon soldier. Audrey was a half second away from blowing the man's head off when he realized that he was unarmed. As the air started to clear and he got a better look at him, he was surprised the Mormon was even on his feet. His uniform was tatters. His body was covered in wounds and burns. His left arm was missing. He seemed to move without direction, simply stammering to and fro, unaware of his surroundings and in total shock. A moment later the man toppled over like a tumbleweed. His body lay face down in the dirt, the only sign of life an occasional twitch.

Forcing herself to turn away from the poor soul, Barbara proceeded to tie a makeshift bandage around her beloved's arm and then helped him to his feet.

"Get back under cover!" he ordered her.

"But you're hurt! You don't have to fight anymore!"

"I said get back under cover! If the Mormons take this town you and the other women will suffer a fate worse than death. I can't, I won't let that happen!"

Hesitantly she obeyed. Audrey surveyed the ground looking for his sharpshooter rifle. He spotted it but he didn't risk trying to pick it up. He knew if he fell he might not get back up, and Barbara—though she had obeyed him—was undoubtedly watching from one of the western buildings and would not hesitate to come back out if she thought he needed her. He sighed heavily. With his wounded and bandaged arm he wouldn't be able to use it properly any way. Adrenaline alone had allowed him to draw his revolver a few moments earlier. Now he transferred the seven shooter to his left hand. It was his off-hand but he figured he could hit the broadside of a barn or a Mormon if he got close enough.

Slowly but steadily Audrey made his way back towards the gap along with several other Californians. A

413

strong metallic smell reached his nostrils as though he were entering a butcher's shop or a slaughtering house. An enormous number of mangled men and pieces of men lay strewn about the pure carnage that had once been the gap between the hotel and the saloon. It wasn't possible to get an accurate count of how many of the attackers had been killed, but Audrey had no doubt it was a large number. As he looked east he saw that the shaken survivors of the attack had withdrawn back to the Mormon lines and were regrouping with the remnants of the Deseretan cavalry. He also saw, to his dismay, that they had another entire formation of men that had been kept in reserve and that were ready to attack.

He sighed heavily. His dismay almost caused him to lose the mastery he had over the pain of his wounds. He winced, but remained on his feet.

"It's just like Fort Moultier all over again," said Audrey in a voice like ashes. A few feet away from him the sheriff raised a confused eyebrow but Audrey had no time to explain. The Mormons were moving forward again. Audrey perched himself behind what remained of the barricade and took aim with his pistol. The sheriff worked the lever on his Winchester and fired a round. Up and down the eastern perimeter of the town other defenders did likewise. Audrey feared it was futile but he had no intention of surrendering. The Mormons had already proven their fanaticism in how they'd treated the town of Rattlesnake Cove, and after the vicious manner in which the defenders had slaughtered so many of their comrades, Audrey doubted the men of the Deseret would be inclined to accept a surrender.

The advancing Mormons let loose with a fresh war cry and blazed away with their BLARs and other rifles sending a hail of lead at the besieged Californians. Bullets cracked past Audrey's head and slammed into the wood barricade. He paid them no heed, but blazed away with his revolver until it was empty.

Suddenly, fresh waves of torment shot through Audrey as a bullet slammed into his shoulder. He collapsed against the railing as fresh bursts of blood made their way out of the new wound. He dropped his pistol and brought up his hand to his shoulder to try and stem the bleeding. Then, all of a sudden, he heard a new sound over that of the guns and cries of the wounded. It was the sharp martial notes of a military bugle. From the hills to the north east an entire company of green uniformed Californian cavalry came charging down the slopes and towards the rear of the Mormon attack. Audrey could just make out the white and red Bear Flag fluttering at their vanguard.

It's about time, Goldwyn... Relief flooded his soul...and the strength left his body. He slid down to the ground. He felt his heart beating irregularly and he felt suddenly cold. His eyes focused upon the serpentine Californian flag fluttering over the unfinished court house and his thoughts went to Barbara.

In a way, I've made her a widow twice...It just wasn't meant to be. Audrey's life flashed before him. His eyes became heavy. The sounds of the battle grew distant and the light faded until at last all was silent and all was dark.

LXIII

Cole and Helen Allens found New York City breathtaking as they stared down Broadway from the street side along with thousands of other spectators. Men wearing bowlers and women with plumed hats lined the streets as far as the eye could see. They stood on the curbs, on the entry steps and in the windows of the many buildings. True to its name, the brick paved avenue was broad, and ran between two rows of seemingly endless brick buildings, ranging in height from five to twelve stories. Though normally packed with horses, carriages, wagons, and trolleys, the street had been completely cleared for the victory parade of Whitmore's Spanish Foreign Legion. Despite the mercenary group's name, (and the fact that nearly half of them were British and Canadians) the buildings along the parade route were draped with red, white, and blue bunting. Old Glory flew from street-side poles, from buildings, and from the outstretched hands of thousands of the cheering onlookers. Cole couldn't remember the last time he'd seen such a fervent display but as he looked at the joyous faces of his countrymen and listened to the thundering sound of their cheering voices he was torn as never before. He loathed the idea of war, but even he could not deny the sense of national consciousness and sense of pride that had been held back for so long and was now bursting forth like a raging river through a broken dam. For a quarter century the United States had lived under the shadow and the shame of its two defeats in 1863 and 1869. Now, all at once, Whitmore and his upstart Legion had proven that the once seemingly invincible Confederacy and its allies could be defeated. When combined with the news that Britain and the United States had entered into a new alliance against their common foes it was like a flame of victory being touched to the gunpowder of long hoped for redemption. The resulting explosion of patriotism and jubilation revealed that at heart the people of the United States desired to regain their rightful place in the sun, and a deep seeded belief that in order for that to happen, there had to be a day of reckoning with their long estranged brethren to the south. Across the nation newspapers were extolling the triumph of Whitmore's mercenaries and many politicians were rushing to do likewise, and to fervently avow their approval of the new alliance with Britain and all that it entailed.

"The entire country seems intoxicated!" said Cole.

"They're happy," replied Helen. She put a comforting hand on her husband's arm. "And you can't blame them. America has gained new territory for the first time in forever, we have a strong new ally, the Confederates and French have been shown they can't just do whatever they want, and it was all made possible because Americans fought and won."

When Cole turned to face her, Helen feared she might have angered him, then she saw that his face held grief not wrath. He placed his hand on her belly in which the child created by their love for one another grew.

It's all too likely to end in war...a war far larger and worse than any ever before fought. How long? Five years? Ten? Twenty? His hand tightened slightly on her belly. He'd already lost so much to war. *Will our children have to deal with the consequences of the course we have charted?*

Suddenly the cheers of the crowds grew louder until they were almost deafening and Cole and his wife returned their attention to Broadway. The martial notes of a military band suddenly reached Cole's ears and grew louder by the minute. Cole recognized the tune as the old Battle Hymn of the Republic. It wasn't long before Cole spotted Whitmore, dressed in a brand new uniform and riding atop a white horse. Some militaries of the world had a rank even higher than General. Whitmore's new uniform would have made any Field Marshal in Europe proud. The coat was a deep blue, with buttons and epaulets of pure gold. He wore two sashes—a red white and blue one across his chest and a red and gold one around his waist. The Spanish government had showered him with medals and ribbons. At his side he wore a sword sent to him by Queen Victoria herself. In a nod to the British he wore on his head a large ornate pith helmet encrusted with a golden eagle and topped by a spike. Like a returning hero of the ancient Roman Empire, the eccentric millionaire made his way down Broadway in triumph to the cheers and accolades of thousands of his countrymen. Cole noted without irony that Whitmore had no one to whisper in his ear "thou art mortal." Just behind Whitmore to his left and right rode two of his most decorated Legionnaires. These were also dressed in new uniforms though they were of the standard khaki the Legion had worn in the field. Cole recognized one of the men as John Pershing, one of a handful of young American officers that had resigned their commissions in the US Army to join Whitmore in what many had considered a fool's errand but was now being regarded as a Holy Crusade. Cole had no doubt that the young officer would soon be welcomed back into US Army and that he would subsequently enjoy a meteoric rise through the ranks in the years ahead. Pershing and his men had played a large part in keeping the French and Confederates from seizing Puerto Rico. If most of the papers in the USA were to be believed Pershing and his men had done it single handedly. The papers had taken to calling him "Black Jack" because of his fierceness in battle and the fact that most of the troops under his command had been negroes.

Cole put his arm around his wife. On the voyage from Puerto Rico to New York, Cole had learned that Pershing's fiancé who'd been serving as a nurse in Whitmore's Legion, had been killed by one of the last artillery barrages of the battle for the island. Cole had tactfully sought an interview with him through intermediaries but the young officer had spent the entirety of the voyage secluded in his cabin consumed with grief. Cole saw no grief on his face now, only a cold, hard, stern, glare. Pershing rode through the throng as though oblivious to their existence.

Behind Whitmore and his escorts, came a color guard holding aloft the Stars and Strips flanked on one side by the Union Jack and the other by the La Rojigualda. Behind the colors came the band and behind them rank after rank of mercenary soldiers. To Cole's surprise the lead unit was Pershing's negro troops. He wondered if that might stifle the zeal of the crowds. Slavery might have been over three decades gone, but racism was still just as alive in the North as it was in the South. But the newspapers had also been filled with accounts of the negro uprisings in the CSA and of the Confederacy's ruthless and merciless response. To Cole's surprise the cheers increased. He wondered how many people remembered that negroes had also fought under the Southern Cross in the recently ended conflict.

Far more than had served in Whitmore's Legion, that's for sure. Cole wondered how the recent uprisings would affect the CSAs fledgling abolitionist movement and affect the way it treated its growing number of free negroes. *Not in a good way*, was the obvious answer.

When the parade finally ended and the crowds began to disperse, Cole took tight hold of his wife's arm and the two of them started to carefully make their way through the throngs. After walking a quarter mile down Broadway, Cole suddenly spotted a large number of beaten and bloodied men being loaded into a horse drawn police paddy wagon. Piled up on the curb were several red flags and a few crudely made signs one of which read "No War!" Instantly his reporter's instincts kicked in. He started towards the policemen but his wife brought him up short.

"Darling have you forgotten we have a train to catch?"

Cole pulled out his pocket watch and scowled. He sighed.

Three hours later they were on a west bound train. In the seat across from him, Helen slept. Not for the first time he envied her ability to do so. Cole contented himself by watching the passing fields, greenery, and towns and by reading various newspapers. He didn't do the latter for long. He found most of the stories unwelcome and most of the editorials wholly unpalatable. He read one article that extoled the peace and stability that would be insured by the new Anglo-American alliance. He read another article on the ceasefire between the Republic of California and the Mormon Nation of Deseret. Though overshadowed by other events in the world, the conflict between the two small far western nations had been both brief and bloody. Representatives from Sacramento and Salt Lake City would be meeting in Vancouver in a month to supposedly draw up a treaty but by all appearances the Californians had come out of the war on top and stood to gain much of the disputed Nevada territory.

Next he read on article that made the wild assertion that the construction of the United States' new capital city of Franklin was now on schedule and that the Federal government would soon be able to take up residence. Washington had gone almost completely unused during the past twenty five years. The War of 1869 in general, and Confederate artillery on Arlington Heights in particular, had demonstrated in no uncertain terms the impossible position of a country having its capital city located directly on the border of a hostile foreign nation. In the years since the US government had mostly relocated to New York and Philadelphia. Another article dealt with reactions to the new Anglo-American alliance amongst British subjects. Cole's thoughts went suddenly to his British friends. Absently he wondered if Winston Churchill and Reginald Barnes had arrived safely back in London.

At last Cole put aside the papers and pulled out his writing pad and pencil and worked on an editorial he planned on publishing in the Gazette as soon as he returned to Covington.

Both the Democratic Party and the United States are at a crossroads. By all appearances President Cleveland, aided by Joseph Whitmore and his admittedly brave volunteers, and by political War Hawks (many of whom have been masquerading as men of peace and cool headed reason and have now, like wolves in sheep's clothing, shown their true selves) has steered our nation down a course that must inevitably bring us into a head to head confrontation with both the Confederacy and the French Empire. The world is now a powder keg. It requires only a spark to cause on explosion. Most of the civilized world is now divided into one of two great alliance systems. Many politicians and political commentators have expressed the view that this is somehow a good thing, and that somehow the impending threat of a war so great it would spell mutual annihilation, will somehow deter the great powers from viewing war as a viable option in settling international disputes. All I have to say in response is that those who fail to learn from history are doomed to repeat it. In the decades leading up to the First War of Rebellion many people foresaw the secession of the southern states and the bloody civil war that it would precipitate and yet many people said "It will never happen!" "It would be too terrible! Our leaders will never let it get that far!" "There are too many cool heads in Washington for such a thing to happen!" Well we know now how it turned out. The politicians couldn't settle their differences and as a result America was torn apart by the two most violent wars it had ever experienced before or since. Shall we now stand idly by and allow the same thing to happen on a global scale? At this point the Hawks will cry, "The alternative is worse! The alternative is to yield to our enemies!" This is not the case at all. By all means let us have a strong army and navy! Let us protect what is ours! Doves are in favor "armed neutrality" that is of speaking softly while carrying a big stick and not involving ourselves in other people's concerns. We must heed the advice of our national forefathers and avoid entangling alliances! Make no mistake. Most of the British do not care for our country, they merely seek to use us as a weapon against their own historical foe.

The Hawks would next raise the argument, hostile nations like the CSA and France must be contained! The Doves reply if we see to our own defenses they will not come after us. Bully's inevitably pick on those smaller than themselves. We cannot be the world's policeman. Let bullish nations expand and then let them collapse under the weight of their own Empires. Having been in Cuba in person I can testify that the Confederate States have acquired what will become a great albatross for their neck. Cuba will be a burden to the CSA just as it was for the Spanish before them. France is in a similar position having recently added the Philippines and various other territories to their already vast holdings around the world. When added to the pressures of maintaining puppet regimes in Mexico and Central America it is easy to see how the Confederacy's and France's resources will be taxed to the limit.

For better or for worse our present government has charted its course. The beauty of our democracy, however, is that with a single election we may, as a nation, chart a new course. Peace Democrats must not be swayed by recent events. Many of our countrymen are overcome with emotion right now to be sure, but I continue to believe that the people of this great nation are led first and foremost by reason! Let us hold the courage of our conviction, continue to point out and remind our countrymen of the horrors of war and advocate a national policy that will both insure the security, integrity, and prosperity of our country while at the same time sparing it from the awful consequences of an Intercontinental War. In order to do this effectively I fear that the informal divide that has so long divided the Democratic Party must be made official. "But that will strengthen the Republicans!" In the first place I would point out that after losing both the First and Second Wars of Rebellion the Republicans are unlikely to ever hold high political office again, even if the Democrats fractured into ten parties. In the second place, I would point out that the War Hawk Democrats have in essence become Republicans in everything but name. Let us not fail to notice that many of the politicians who have suddenly broken out the war drums like a dogs new spring fleas have ties to big industries that stand to earn a fortune if a war breaks out. How convenient this new alliance system must be for them. They supply the weapons and equipment while our brave sons provide the blood!

This discussion naturally leads into other areas that we as a nation must address. We condemn the Southerners for holding slaves to this day and rightfully so, but our own nation is desperately in need of fair labor laws for from the other direction of the spectrum is another enemy—the Red Enemy—Socialism! Sweat Shops must be abolished! Child Labor must be highly regulated! Safe working conditions must be insured! A fair living must be made available to every American lest we drive people into the arms of the Red Radicals! Reform is needed!

Cole stopped suddenly. For one thing after filling three pages of his pad with writing he needed to sharpen his pencil, for another he felt that he'd hit upon a small gold mine with that word Reform. Almost of itself the name *Reform Party* formed in his mind. He bent back over his pad and began to write with a fury, this time even more intensely than before.

LXIV

Jethro Winslow wiped sweat from his dark skinned brow, heaved his hoe over his shoulder and then started out of the fields and back towards his Nebraska farm house. His hired hand Obadiah took that as the signal that the work day had come to an end and likewise trudged behind Jethro towards the house. It was a little early, but the next day was a big day.

"Yous really think we gone git it done in two days?"

"We're going to try," replied Jethro. "But this I know, one way or another we're going to hold services on Sunday morning. We'll get enough done for that."

"Dat be real funny if de roof ain't done and it rain."

Jethro gave Obadiah a brief but cold stare. The field hand joked about virtually everything and he had a bad habit of raining on his parades.

"If the Lord sends rain we shall be thankful." Jethro doubted it would rain Sunday but nonetheless he made a mental note that when they started construction on the new church house the following day to give priority to the roof. Sometimes Obadiah's foolishness had its uses.

For years Jethro and his small family had had no choice but to worship at home. There were precious few Baptist churches in their part of Nebraska and none of them cared to allow a family of non-whites to worship with them. Then six months earlier the Underground Railroad had brought him a family of four from Texas. Jethro and his family had been a part of the secret network for twenty years but that was the first time that any escaped slaves from the CSA had actually made it to him. The closest parts of the CSA to Nebraska were Missouri to the east and the Indian Territory of Oklahoma to the south. Any slaves escaping Missouri headed north and or east. The Oklahoma Indian Territory, as its name implied, was almost completely inhabited by American Indians. The five so-called civilized tribes had sided with the secessionists during the Wars of Rebellion. As a reward the victorious Confederate States had granted them the status of being a self-governed territory within the CSA. They'd granted the Indians in the New Mexico and Arizona territories a similar status though those didn't quite have the same amount of leeway as the tribes in Oklahoma.

It was a rare thing for negroes in Confederate Texas to escape north through Oklahoma and into the USA. Those who tried to do so virtually never succeeded in getting past the Indians and through their territory. The Confederate authorities paid handsome bounties for captured runaways so the Indians were perfectly willing to catch them and hand them over. But somehow Washington, Roberta, and their two small children had managed to pull it off. After escaping the south Austin rancher that owned them, they had somehow snuck aboard a train carrying cattle north. For the Confederate state of Texas, the beef export industry was one of its greatest sources of income. Washington and his family had ridden the train out of Texas, through Oklahoma and across the international border into Kansas and then on to Nebraska where they'd linked up with Jethro. Jethro was only supposed to give them shelter and rest and then speed them on their way. But he'd found having them around far too pleasant and had convinced them to remain in Nebraska. There was a slight risk, involved with that. The small number of negroes native to the USA were required to possess paperwork that proved they were native to the US and not "foreign negroes" from the CSA. The USA only had a handful of blacks and it didn't want anymore. But Jethro knew from experience that it was an imperfect system. Each state handled the paper work and registrations differently.

Some, like Kentucky, Missouri, and Maryland kept scrupulous track of all negroes within their boundaries. They'd been forced to give up slavery after the First War of Rebellion and if they couldn't have blacks as slaves they didn't want them at all. Other US states had so few negroes they didn't bother with it at all. Nebraska was one of those states. In the twenty five years that he'd lived outside Nebraska he'd never once been required to produce paperwork proving he was a US native. In Joshua's opinion they were safer staying in Nebraska than trying to make it all the way to Canada. To his delight they had agreed. He'd even given them a small plot of land and planned on buying them more in the future. In the meantime, he'd led Washington and Roberta to receive Jesus Christ as their Lord and Savior. Having two new believers necessitated two baptisms and in order to have proper baptisms it required a real gospel church. With no Baptist church to attend, Jethro had long entertained the notion of starting one. He'd finally written his former pastor—the now eighty-five year old Brother Thompson in Pennsylvania requesting a letter of authorization from the church he pastored to start a new congregation south of Lancaster. The letter had arrived less than a week earlier. The small new church would require a building to meet in. Jethro had purchased the lumber and it had arrived. The next morning they would start work at dawn. Jethro had set aside all day Friday and Saturday to build the small house of worship. The morning after that, the fledgling congregation would hold its first services.

If only Joshua could be here to see it. Thinking of his son brought tears to his eyes. He fought hard to keep them down. Every week he'd gone into Lancaster to get all the news he could about the war. After Whitmore's Legion had left the US, Jethro and his wife had gone months without a letter from their son. No matter how Jethro worried, he'd had to remain strong for Lilia. He'd persistently reminded her that in Cuba the Legion would be cut off from contact with the US. In reality he'd been trying to reassure his wife as well as himself. The things he'd read in the papers were not good. One of the ship's carrying the Legion had sunk before reaching Cuba (Jethro had intentionally not mentioned that to Lilia). He'd read that the Legion had been involved in heavy fighting in Cuba. The only accounts Jethro had been able to read had come from a Union war correspondent traveling with the Confederate army in Cuba. Later the news had broken that the Legion had left Cuba and gone to Puerto Rico where it had taken part in the heavy fighting for that island. It was only after news of that, that they had finally received a telegram from Joshua informing them that he was alive and well and that the Legion would be returning to the United States soon. In the three weeks since then they had heard nothing more. But Jethro and Lilia were overjoyed even so. They were confident that if God had kept their son from harm during the preceding months of war and carnage, He would eventually bring him home to them safe and sound. Jethro only feared how seeing such death and destruction might have changed his son. Of itself his hand went up to the scar on the back of his head where a spent bullet had struck him in the heat of battle and by God's grace had failed to kill him.

Lord, please bring him home! Please let him be okay!

As they neared the farmhouse, Jethro suddenly caught sight of a horse drawn wagon making its way down the road, leaving a trail of dust behind it. He watched it absently. His farm was on the extreme outskirts of Lancaster and it was rare for anyone else to be out that far. He expected it to go past the entrance to his property but was surprised to see it turn down the main drive.

Who could it...?

A sudden flame of hope ignited in his heart. The carriage drew nearer. Jethro recognized the driver as a negro teamster he'd met occasionally in his trips to Lancaster. But it was the passenger he was interested in. Next to the driver, sat Joshua dressed in a khaki military uniform. Jethro had long since ceased to be a young man, nonetheless for that moment both the years and the long day of farm work he'd just endured melted away as nothing.

"Lilia! Lilia come quick! Our boy's home!" He let out at full speed to meet the approaching wagon. Lilia came flying out of the farm house just in time to see her son leap from the wagon into Jethro's waiting arms. She wasted no time in hiking her skirts and running up the drive herself.

Joshua was released from his father's embrace only to be engulfed by his mother's who also proceeded to smother him with kisses. When at last the hugging, and kissing, and crying had ended, Jethro asked, "Why didn't you tell us you were coming home!"

"I did, father, that is I sent a telegram when we got into New York. Since you weren't waiting for me at the station in Lancaster I assumed it never arrived. But Forbes here was happy to give me a ride."

Joshua turned to Forbes, thanked him, shook his hand profusely, and made sure to invite him back for Sunday morning. About that time Obadiah came up and stared in awe at Joshua's uniform and the medals that covered his chest.

"Some things nev'a change. Yous is still one fancy nigga!" The field hand then threw his arms around Joshua in a brotherly embrace. "But it good to have you back in one piece!"

After saying goodbyes with Forbes, Joshua walked arm in arm with his parents back towards the farm house while Obadiah carried his duffle bag and his hand bag.

"What's this I heard about church services Sunday?"

Jethro beamed even brighter and filled his son in on all that had happened since he'd gone off to war.

Once in the house, Joshua went upstairs to his old room, removed his uniform and put on some of his old farm clothes. After so long the cotton shirt and overalls felt strange. He made his way back downstairs and joined his father and Obadiah at the table, where Jethro offered up a long prayer of thanksgiving not only for the food but also for Joshua's safe return.

"If we'd known you'd be here I would have prepared a very special meal!" said Lilia has she plopped an enormous helping of corn hash with little bits of beef on her son's plate.

"This is a very special meal, momma," he said almost reverently.

"So what was it like?" asked Obadiah before taking a big bite out of a hunk of cornbread.

Joshua took on a blank empty expression and Jethro recognized on his face the look of a man who'd seen horrors unimaginable and who was searching in vain for a way to describe it. Jethro had seen things over twenty five years earlier that had haunted him all the years since. Now his son had likewise seen the awful barbarism that man was capable of wreaking upon his fellow man. For a moment father and son locked eyes silently and Joshua knew his father understood. Hesitantly he answered Obadiah's question as best he could.

"It was bad. A lot of people got hurt and killed, and not all of them were soldiers." His mind flashed back to the nurse Jennifer Harper. In his mind he saw her broken form on the ground. He remembered how a few hours later Major John Pershing had arrived, learned of her death, and utterly collapsed into tears and grief before her body. "I'm glad it's over. And I hope I never see such carnage again. If everyone could see the suffering, and the pain, and the grief, and the death of a battle and its aftermath then, hopefully, there would be no more war."

"Amen…" whispered Jethro.

That night, after Lilia had gone to bed and Jethro had ordered Obadiah to turn in for the evening as well, father and son sat up in the living room in front of a crackling fire, smoking their pipes, and talking at length about things that only they could understand. Jethro told his son about things he'd seen during the Second War of Rebellion and Joshua described for his father the horrors he'd seen working as a surgeon and the torment and guilt he felt over spur of the moment medical decisions of life and death that he'd been compelled to make.

"You did your best son, and before God that is all you could do. I thank Him that you at least were there to help and to heal, and for that, no father could feel more pride than do I." The one thing Jethro did ask his son about were the Confederate negroes.

"Yes, sir. They fought for the Confederacy, and they fought bravely. The few that I had occasion to talk to stated that they were fighting for their freedom. Whether the Confederacy intends to keep its promise to them I don't know."

Jethro shrugged his shoulders. The US papers had talked at length about the severe reprisals the Confederacy had exacted on all the negroes in regions where the slaves had risen up in rebellion. Even if the Confederate government had originally intended to honor its word and free the negroes that had taken up arms on its behalf, he wondered if the defeated uprisings hadn't changed their minds.

Only time will tell…

As the clock struck ten, the two Winslow men turned in as well. They had a busy and exciting day before them. The civilian clothes might have seemed unfamiliar to Joshua at first (though his body had quickly and gratefully become accustomed again) but after months of sleeping on an army cot, his old bed made him feel as though he were sleeping on a cloud.

The entire family rose before dawn. It was still dark when Jethro, Joshua, and Obadiah walked to the corner of the family property where the new church house was to be built. There Joshua met Washington for the first time. The four men wasted no time. The moment that dawn cracked and they could see, they set to work with a fury. Jethro, Obadiah, and Washington had already set posts in the ground to serve as a foundation. Now the four of them hand sawed two by six inch planks to the proper length to use as base boards which they nailed to the posts. Then they cut and nailed floor joists and laid down planks for the flooring. By eleven in the morning a small twelve by thirty foot platform had been constructed. Despite the cool air they were all drenched in sweat but they didn't slow down.

Next they laid out and constructed the walls. The bottom plate boards went down first, then they nailed in the studs and top plate boards. At one-thirty they started to cut the roof joists and nail them into place. By four the full skeleton of the structure had been finished. They spent the last three hours cutting weather-treated roof boards and nailing them into place. Obadiah cut them, Jethro handed them up, and Joshua and Washington nailed them into place. By the end of the day they were exhausted but in a strange way Joshua felt refreshed. After all he'd been through, the joy of building a church house seemed almost like food for his soul.

As they had the day before, they again rose at the crack of dawn. They spent the first half of Saturday cutting and nailing on the siding. Then Joshua and Jethro build the front steps while Obadiah and Washington whitewashed the entire structure. Finally they put in the four small windows and a pair of double doors at the front. When they'd finished they stared in triumph at the small white one room cabin that would serve as their new churches house of worship. There were lots of little details that would be finished in the coming weeks, (Jethro hadn't yet decided on whether to top the roof with a small cross or with a small steeple, and the interior walls would need paneling) but the structure itself was finished. The last thing they did before going home for supper was to go to the barn and load up the small pieces of furniture that Jethro had built by hand. In the previous months he'd build a pulpit, a small table carved with the words "Do this in Remembrance of Me" and six small straight back wooden pews. It took three short trips with the horse and wagon but by late afternoon all was ready for their first service.

They went to bed early on Saturday night and rose late by farm standards. They all dressed in their finest clothes. Joshua had plenty to choose from because of the fine wardrobe his father had purchased for him to wear at medical school. In the preceding months Lilia had taught Roberta to sew and together they had sewn one pair of nice clothes for everyone else. White cotton button up collared shirts for the men and Roberta's little boy and blue dresses for themselves and Roberta's little girl.

As they headed out of the farm house Joshua was pleased to see Forbes coming up the road with his wagon. He'd brought his pregnant wife and her mother. He smiled.

If this keeps up we'll have to build a bigger church house.

At eleven in the morning the small congregation crowded into the tiny church house and completely filled the four pews that Jethro had built. He resolved to build more as soon as possible. They had no pastor, Jethro would have to serve in the interim. He'd been leading his household in prayer, worship, and Bible study for over twenty five years so it came naturally. He took his place behind the pulpit and called on Joshua to deliver a prayer. He then led them in the singing of the old negro spiritual "Were you there when they crucified my Lord?" and of the hymn "Amazing Grace."

Afterwards Jethro stared in awe at the small flock. His Indian wife, stood out as did his son Joshua by virtue of his height and mixed heritage. The other eight members of the congregation had skin as black as midnight.

Jethro took a deep breath and opened his worn leather Bible, read from the Gospel of Mark and talked of Christ's crucifixion, death and resurrection. He then turned to the third chapter of John's gospel and from it proclaimed loudly the need of all mankind to believe on Jesus and be born again, and of Christ's love for all people of all races. Finally he turned to the story of Jesus and John the Baptist and urged his hearers who hadn't done so to believe on Christ and to be baptized.

Joshua smiled. His father had been teaching him out of the Bible his entire life, but this was the first time Jethro had ever preached a sermon. He did it well. The old cavalryman ended his discourse with warnings about the fires of hell and promises of eternal life in heaven for the faithful. They closed with prayer and the hymn "Amazing Grace." Afterwards they left the church house and went down to the creek where Jethro baptized Washington and Roberta, though not their children who were as yet too young to understand the meaning and the commitment. Afterwards Jethro was approached by Forbes, his wife, and her mother. After leading them in a prayer by which they accepted Jesus into their hearts, he made arrangements that they should all three be baptized the next Sunday.

Joshua smiled again, and reflected what a blessing it was to actually have a church, even if it was small. When he'd been saved as a child, his family had had to take a train trip down to Wichita KS to find a Baptist church that would give him scriptural baptism. That same church had baptized Obadiah a few year later.

The entire group crowded into the Winslow's farm house where they feasted on roast beef and vegetables. Joshua spent the rest of the afternoon reclining in the living room, smoking his pipe and reading the Bible. For the first time since leaving Puerto Rico he felt at peace.

The next day the telegram he'd sent from New York finally arrived and the entire family had a good laugh. But there was also another telegram and it was addressed to him and upon inspection he saw that it was from the US War Department. He took it upstairs and opened it in private.

From: Lt. Colonel Evan Hitchens, US Army Medical Corps,

To: Mr. Joshua Winslow,

I have been instructed by my superiors, on the recommendation of one Lt. Colonel John Pershing, to offer you now, or in the future when you have completed your formal training at the Chicago school of medicine, a position as a surgeon in the US Army Medical Corps with the entry rank of Major. We look for your prompt response.

Joshua was stunned. His first impulse was to throw the telegram away but then he hesitated. Ever since starting medical school he'd wondered exactly where he'd serve as a surgeon. Regardless of his grades he knew that most whites would not want to be touched by a negro doctor. He feared he'd be forced to mete out a living by starting a private practice in some US city with a large enough negro population to give him a large enough customer base to survive. He'd never dreamed he could be offered entry into the army's surgical division.

And at the rank of Major...

He let out a sigh. His father had served in the United States army. It would be an honor to follow in his footsteps. He'd already seen the reality of war, and though he never wanted to see it again, he was not so naïve to believe there wouldn't be more in the future. In fact he was sadly certain of it. Letting out another sigh, he took the telegram downstairs to show to his father and to seek both his counsel and his wisdom.

LXV

"The Lord is my shepherd, I shall not want..." The Methodist minister dressed in black somberly read the shepherd's psalm.

Lt. Colonel John Pershing heard the words of the minister as he stared at the flower covered wooden casket that would soon be lowered into the ground, but he derived no comfort from them. Joseph Whitmore had paid for Jennifer Harper's body to be sent to Keokuk Iowa for burial. As the casket was lowered into the ground, Pershing felt…nothing. He'd done his grieving. Jennifer was the only woman he'd ever loved. When she died, part of Pershing had died as well. It was as if his heart and part of his soul was being buried with her and all that was left was a cold, pitiless, and merciless soldier, and an intense hatred of his enemies. He stood, as rigid as a statue in his new blue US army uniform, now with silver oak leaves on his shoulder straps. He'd been welcomed back into the US Army with open arms and had been promoted two steps in rank. He now had far more combat experience than any other officer of his generation.

The minister finished the psalm and began to pray. Though the clergymen spoke of heaven, Pershing's thoughts were on hell, and on sending as many Confederates and Frenchman there as possible. Jennifer had been the one light in his life, the one chance that he would turn from his vengeance and live his life. But now like his father and siblings, she had joined the list of loved ones that his enemies had robbed him of. The grave diggers started to shovel dirt into the grave, a sound that to most people was the most final in the world. Not to Pershing.

I swear to you, when I've driven the Rebels from Missouri, and its soil is soaked with the blood of our enemies, I will rebury you there.

He felt a slight tug at his arm. His half-sister Loraine had been holding onto him by the arm trying to comfort him. Along with his brother in law Richard Paddock, Pershing and his sister were the only three mourners at the small funeral. Paddock discreetly paid the minister, then made his way back over to his wife and Pershing.

"Shall we go?"

Pershing took one last look at the grave and then allowed his sister to pull him away. They climbed into a waiting landau where Paddock took up position in the driver's seat, flicked the reins and got the horses moving. They passed the iron gates of the cemetery and made their way into downtown Keokuk. Despite the somberness of the funeral, it was a beautiful day, and uncommonly warm. Lorain tried to brighten her brother's mood.

"Shall we get an early lunch at the waterfront?"

Pershing said nothing. His only reply was an indifferent shrug. Lorain tapped her husband on the shoulder. "Take us to that nice Jean's Café." Paddock nodded. Half way there, he tried his own luck at breaking Pershing's melancholy. If his brother in law didn't want to talk about lunch maybe he'd like to talk shop.

"Have you finished that report for the War Department that Colonel Jensen asked you for?"

Pershing nodded. He'd been instructed to write a list of recommendations for reforms in the US army based on his experiences in Cuba and Puerto Rico.

"I'll hand it in to him first thing in the morning."

"Mind letting your old brother in law in on what it says?"

"Some things that some of the higher ups won't like," said Pershing flatly. Paddock was about to pry for more details but Pershing went on of his own accord.

"I've asked that every American from the Legion be offered positions in the army."

Paddock nodded. That made sense. Their experience would prove useful—if they could make the leap from being mercenaries to being soldiers in the US Army.

"Does that include your negroes?"

Pershing's face darkened suddenly. The papers called him "Black Jack" in an effort to make him sound more heroic and fearsome. That didn't bother him. But unbeknownst to most of the reading public the nickname's origin was that several of the other officers of Whitmore's Legion had called him "Nigger Jack" because he'd commanded black troops. The name had followed him back to the US Army. Jealous officers back at Fort Halleck were already calling him Nigger Jack behind his back.

"It most certainly includes them," said Pershing. "They are the bravest men I've ever led."

"Well I don't think the higher ups will have a problem with that."

Pershing nodded. But then he made his second recommendation.

"It's also time that the army stop giving promotions based on seniority and base it on ability and merit."

Paddock nodded agreement. That was something that had plagued the US army for decades. He could see its need, but old traditions died hard. There'd be resistance to that one.

"I've also recommended that we change our uniforms from blue to khaki like the British."

Paddock looked down at his own blue uniform. Once more he felt his brother in law was tampering with sacred tradition. The Army had worn blue since the days of George Washington.

But John's right. Times have changed. In the days of black powder muskets brightly colored uniforms had been necessary in order to see and identify others on the battle field through clouds of smoke. With the advent of smokeless powder that was no longer necessary and with the shift from massed battle formations to a looser model geared towards high fire power and mobility or to trench warfare it made a lot more sense to try to blend in the with the terrain. British khaki would be much better suited for that. He wondered absently how much resistance there had been in the British army to giving up red.

"Anything else?"

Pershing went on and on about modernizing the artillery (particularly to Prussian models), standardizing the rifles and ammunition of the infantry, developing better machine guns, landmines, barbed wire, training for trench warfare and a whole host of other things. The army had asked for his recommendations and he intended to give them without sugar coating anything and without holding anything back.

Paddock let out a long sigh. If the War Department adopted half of what Pershing was recommending the army would become vastly different than it was. He felt as if the last vestiges of class and style were being purged from the army and replaced by the cold hard pragmatism of the industrial age.

They arrived at the waterfront. Lunch was short and silent. Afterwards, Pershing declined to ride with his sister and brother in law back to their home, choosing instead to spend some time alone by walking along the waterfront where he and Jennifer had tread together what seemed like a lifetime earlier. Pershing stared south across the Des Moines River and into Confederate Missouri. His sharp eyes glared at the Confederate fort that stood on the other side of the river. He glanced at the artillery positions on his own side—empty at the moment—but in time of war would be equipped and manned. In his mind he saw massive artillery pieces blasting the enemy side of the river and machine guns chewing up the banks. He pictured assault forces fording the river and marching south, driving the Rebels that he so hated back in a deadly slaughter. With every fiber of his being he knew the day of his vengeance would come. As far as he was concerned the sooner the better. He couldn't wait for it to begin.

LXVI

All was dark and cold. The whole universe seemed nothing but endless, frigid shadow. Then suddenly—light. At first he was unaware of what it was.

Where am I? Am I dead?

Suddenly the faintest noise was added to the sliver of light. He felt suddenly warm. He sensed a pleasant aroma like that of cooking food. Presently the light grew brighter…the darkness became a blurry vision. The noise coalesced into a voice and Nathan Audrey slowly realized that he was very much alive.

"Uhhaag…" he moaned and stirred in the bed.

"Nathan!" came the now familiar feminine voice.

Audrey slowly—and painfully—sat up in bed. He tried to move his right arm but found he could not. It was tightly bandaged. He brought his left hand up to his face and rubbed his blurry eyes until they came to focus. When he again looked up he beheld Barbara's smiling face. He recognized the small one room cabin. He brought his free hand up to his aching head.

"I feel like I've been run over by a cattle stampede…" he said hoarsely.

She smiled and held a glass of water up to his lips. He sipped it gratefully. The cool liquid felt good to his dry parched throat.

"Don't kid yourself," she said smiling and then set the glass on the bed stand. "You aren't getting out of marrying me that easily. I've already found out where the nearest Catholic church is."

Audrey suddenly brought his hand up to his chest, feeling for his crucifix. He relaxed when he realized it was still there.

No, He's still not ready for me to bite the dust...

Audrey sat up and rolled his neck, trying to get the crick out of it.

"What's left of me is all yours," he said wryly.

She rushed over to his side, to help him sit up.

"You be careful, there! You've still got to get your strength up. Doc Robins said you lost a lot of blood."

She stepped away momentarily and made her way across the room to the small cast iron wood burning stove where a skillet was sizzling. A few minutes later she returned with a plate of scrambled eggs with bits of salt pork.

Audrey ate like a starving man, wolfing down most of the plate in a couple of minutes. When he choked on one of the last bites Barbara lectured him like a mother hen.

"Nathan Audrey! You're supposed to chew your food not swallow it whole!" She gave him the glass of water to wash it down.

He smiled at her. She shook her head.

"So where are we going to live?" she asked still focused on their pending nuptials.

Audrey wasn't sure how to answer her question. As a life-long loner he'd never settled down anywhere. He'd been as much a drifter as a bounty hunter and lawman over the past twenty-five years. Fortunately, she already had a place in mind.

"Pine City's not so bad," she said. "The folks around here are already calling you the hero of the town."

Audrey sighed.

"I'm no hero."

"Oh yes you are," she said. "You're my hero. That's why I fell in love with you. But beside that, it was only because of you that we were able to hold out long enough for help to arrive."

"What happened with the Mormons?"

"General Goldstein and his men drove them off."

Audrey winced momentarily. His head was sore and thinking back was difficult. He just barely remembered the Californian cavalry charge before he lost consciousness.

"I'm just glad it's over," he said.

Barbara nodded.

"I don't think the Mormons will be back. Not anytime soon anyway. General Goldstein told us that their two main forces have been routed. They've withdrawn from our areas of Nevada and we've liberated a few other areas."

"At least we came out on top."

"For now. In the meantime General Goldwyn has assured me that you have an extended leave of absence. We have all the time in the world for our own...pursuits." She leaned over and kissed him slowly and passionately. He brought his good hand up to caress her hair. He wasn't sure how much longer he had on earth, but he decided that whatever time he had left, he would spend living...

LXVII

The Confederate House on the corner of Capitol Street and Mill Street was Jackson Mississippi's finest hotel. In the Presidential suite, Thomas Jackson sat at a large oak desk with a copy of the Daily Clarion Ledger spread out before him. He stared gloomily down at the headlines.

NEGROE REBELLION CRUSHED! FOREIGN POWERS RESPONSIBLE FOR ARMING NIGGERS! PRESIDENT STONE PROMISES SWIFT ACTION! THOUSANDS OF NEGROE INSURRECTIONISTS KILLED! MORE IN HIDING!

Jackson shook his large leonine head at the last two. The revolting slaves in and around Natchez had indeed been defeated and killed, but so had thousands of others who'd had nothing to do with the insurrection. Jackson had tried to restrain the military forces. Even though he had no official authority, he'd used every bit of influence being a former General and President had given him. He'd had some success—but not near enough. The white citizenry of southern Mississippi along with thousands of compatriots from neighboring Louisiana had formed dozens of paramilitary militias and were bent on killing any free negro they could lay hands on. Tens of thousands of blacks had been hung or shot outright. Jackson would never forget the sight of hundreds of negroes hanging from telegraph polls as far as the eye could see during his ride from Natchez to Jackson.

God forgive us…

While Jackson harbored no doubts that God would forgive the Confederacy if only they would recognize their error and turn from it, he had great doubts that the white people of the Confederacy would ever forgive negroes for the late rebellion. Never mind that it was only a relatively small number of insurrectionists and that the majority had had nothing to do with it. Never mind that it had obviously been instigated, funded, and supplied by foreign abolitionists. Never mind that the rebelling negroes came from the cruelest of the plantations. Never mind that a great many negro slaves had sided with and even defended their owners. The fact of the matter was that black men had dared to take up arms against their rightful white masters and for that, there was no forgiveness. For that, all would bear the guilt. The newspapers weren't making things any better. They reported all the gory and horrid details of the insurrection. Tales of burning plantations and negroes raping defenseless white women filled the pages, but somehow the other details didn't seem to warrant space in the paper.

Jackson sighed. For the moment, he had no doubt that his emancipation plan had been mortally shot in the heart. It would take years—decades—to recover if ever.

One thing is for sure. I certainly will not live to see it fulfilled. He sighed again and hung his head. Then, taking a deep breath, he raised it high again. *Which matters not at all. Moses did not live to enter the Promised Land. Israel went in all the same.*

"Are you all right, sir?"

"Yes, Sandie, I'm fine."

"It's nearly 1 O'clock, sir."

"I know. I shall not keep the vultures and wild dogs waiting." By vultures he meant the swarm of reporters waiting to ambush him down stairs as soon as he showed himself. By wild dogs he meant the Mississippi Legislature that had subpoenaed him to appear before them to give testimony about all he knew and saw both before and during the late insurrection.

"It's outrageous, sir."

Jackson nodded.

"They know I had nothing to do with it, but they cannot resist the opportunity to grind my face in the mud and all the more tear down our cause."

"We should have taken the first train to Richmond. Virginia would never acquiesce to another state extraditing you and no one would dare try to apprehend you." He spoke as if he'd happily shoot the first man that tried. The former Confederate President didn't think him wrong. The sovereign state of Virginia would never have allowed Mississippi to extradite such a favored son as the great Stonewall. The State's Rights philosophy that had helped give birth to the Confederacy was a great hindrance in such matters, even when the subject was less important than the former Confederate President. Confederate courts were all but dilatory in such matters. The Confederate constitution stated that CS justices were to serve during "good behavior." In the US that basically meant for life or until they chose to retire. In the Confederacy "good behavior" had basically been reinterpreted to mean "at the pleasure of state legislatures." Judges that went against the wills of the state government where they served often found themselves out of a job. Even the Confederate Supreme Court had been set up in such a way that there was one justice for each state plus a chief. While each justice was appointed by the President and confirmed by the Senate, all but the chief justice could be recalled by the legislature of the state they represented. Had Jackson left Mississippi, Mississippi could never had compelled his return. But Jackson shook his head.

"Shall I run like a guilty fugitive? Shall I give them yet more fiery shells to lob at us and at our cause? No, Sandie. Besides, I have never run a day in my life, and I will not give these people the satisfaction of seeing my back. Besides, there may yet be planters in Mississippi and elsewhere that may yet be interested in my plan."

Pendleton's thoughts went to Lester Jones—shot dead by his own slave—and though he didn't dare disagree with Jackson for fear of hurting the old man's feelings, he thought the elderly President was being far too optimistic considering the circumstances. But then Jackson went on.

"After all, a man who has emancipated his slaves doesn't have to worry about his negroes rising up, burning his home and murdering his family. Self-preservation can be just as good a motivator as profit. When you combine the two…"

Pendleton smiled wryly.

"I must say sir, you have an uncanny ability to see the silver lining."

Jackson inclined his head and then pulled his pocket watch and checked it against the clock on the mantle. He then rose to his feet, put on his coat, grabbed his hat and cane and headed for the door.

"It is still a little early, sir. Shall I call the coach anyhow?"

"No, the Capitol is not far, just down the street. I shall walk—and see if I can't send these reporters fleeing with their tails between their legs as I did McDowell at Manassas."

Most inconspicuously, Pendleton moved to follow Jackson out of the room and escort him down the stairs. The former President took the steps carefully one at a time, but he kept himself steady with his own hand on the bannister. As he knew they would be, a group of reporters were waiting for him in the lobby like a pack of jackals.

"Mr. President, what do you think the state Legislature wants with you?"

"Did your proposals for emancipation help fuel this revolt?"

"Do you feel you might face criminal charges?"

Jackson met the questions with the same calm resolution that had given him his famous nickname.

"I have no idea what light the austere legislators of this state think I can shed on this recent tragedy. Nonetheless,

I am perfectly willing to give them my counsel. Whether they choose to follow it is up to them."

Jackson made his way out of the hotel and proceeded down the sidewalk of Capitol Street. The flock of reporters stayed with him wielding pencils and notebooks like swords and bayonets. Sandie Pendleton followed behind them all, ready to come to Jackson's aid if the need arose.

"Then you deny that your reckless policies had anything to do with this nigger uprising?"

"My policies helped insure our victory in the recent war. I presume you gentlemen have read about the successes our negro troops enjoyed in Cuba? But if you are referring to my policy proposals, which have not as yet been approved, then I fail to see how offering negroes freedom could entice them to rise up so violently. I suggest you look elsewhere for the culprit, like in the cruel and inhumane treatment many negroes suffer that I once tried to remedy."

"So sir, you are claiming that it is a mere coincidence that the niggers in Natchez rose up at the same time you were there fostering your emancipation views?"

"Once again, I fail to see how my proposals for the compensated emancipation of the negro could possibly entice him to rise up. I will also remind you, that not all of the negro slaves in the region did rise up. There were many who remained loyal to their masters, and I am sad to say that many such innocent negroes in this state have been unjustly punished by overzealous and vindictive bands masquerading under the guise of militas and in fragrant violation of any civilized spirit of law and order."

"You speak as if you think niggers deserve the protection of the law."

"Everyone deserves the protection of the law," replied Jackson. There were audible gasps and growls from the reporters whose writing increased to a fevered pitch. Jackson had no doubt they would twist what he said.

Nothing new. Papers had been doing that to him for years. In a way it helped instead of hurt his credibility. Like his Divine Master, the accusations leveled against Jackson often contradicted one another. But at least one of the

441

reporters asked a pointed question of clarification instead of assuming the worst and going with it.

"So you are for giving negroes equal rights with white men?"

Jackson shook his head.

"I am for affording them protection from gross injustice. From mistreatment. From cruel and unusual punishment. Things I made perfectly clear during my time as President and have not ceased to advocate since. The black man can never be equal in authority to the white man…" *At least not in this day and age…* "…but as the masters we have an obligation from God to care for those we call our servants. The black man cannot totally care for himself, therefore we must—as adults over children—care for them properly. If anyone deserves the blame for this recent tragedy it is the harsh brutal masters whose mistreatment of their slaves sowed the seeds of discord long before this insurrection occurred. I will note once again, whether you care to admit it or not that on several plantations the negroes remained loyal. If you would care to investigate the matter you would find that those who treated their slaves kindly did not face the rebellion that those who mistreated their slaves faced. You gentlemen may ignore that if you will. You may be certain that other papers across the Confederacy will not."

"Mr. President what do you know about this nigger abolitionist from up north,… Du Bois? Had you ever heard of him before he helped lead this insurrection?"

"Before the insurrection I had never heard of him. I have since read that in addition to being a militant abolitionist he also has ties to red revolutionaries in both the US and the British Empire."

"Is it true he's being held in Libby Prison in Richmond? What do you think will happen to him and will Richmond return him to Mississippi to stand trial?"

"I'm afraid gentlemen I'm not in a position to answer any of those questions, they would be better put to President Stone."

At that point they approached the place where Capitol Street met State Street. The three story Mississippi State House with its copper dome stood across from them. Three flags flew atop the structure, the Blood Stained Banner, the

Magnolia Flag, and the Bonnie Blue flag. The latter was the banner Mississippians had raised after hauling down the hated Stars and Strips in the aftermath of the ordinance of secession. A delegation of Legislators were already waiting for him at the entrance. Jackson knew he was about to walk into the lion's den. A gray uniformed policeman stepped into the street to halt the traffic of horses and carriages so that Jackson and his unwanted entourage could cross. As he ascended the front steps of the capitol one of the reporters shouted one last question at him.

"Mr. President do you still think that it is in the best interests of the Confederacy to end slavery?"

Without hesitation Jackson answered.

"I do. No matter what angle you look at it from, whether political, economic, or moral, the gradual compensated emancipation of the negro, will improve our standing in the world, increase our ability to defend ourselves, add to the prosperity of our great nation, and may I add, bring the smile of a loving and benevolent God on our land."

"What about from the angle of a white man's pride?" asked another reporter in a hostile tone. "Even if all that stuff you said is true, there's plenty of us that think we ought to keep the niggers in chains as a matter of principle."

By way of answer, Thomas Jackson quoted the Bible.

"Pride goeth before destruction, and an hearty spirit before a fall." With that, Jackson turned and walked into the capitol to fight his next battle.

LXVIII

Jeff Case stepped off the train in Biloxi with a heavy limp. Though still a young man in his twenties he used a cane to steady himself, and would likely continue to for the rest of his life.

It could be worse... he thought. *They could have cut it off...* A surgeon had taken his father's arm during the War of 1869. Case had grown up hearing his father curse them all and given him good reason to avoid them his entire life. He'd feared they do the same to his leg. They hadn't. They'd removed the bullet and sewed him up. They hadn't completely repaired it though. It hurt like a firebrand with every step he took.

Thinking of his father caused his heart to sink. He'd had letters from both of his parents asking when he would finally come home to Norfolk. Sadly, he knew he probably never would. When his parents learned why they would never want anything to do with him again.

It had taken a lot longer for Jeff to get to Biloxi then he'd ever intended. He'd spent a month recuperating in a Confederate Army hospital in Havana and then another month cooling his heels in Mobile awaiting his discharge orders and just as importantly his Cuban land grant. As part of the treaty between the Confederacy and its new commonwealth, Cuba had been required to offer small land grants to every Confederate soldier that had served in the 'liberation' of Cuba from the Spanish. Word was it was actually a scheme to keep Confederate negroes who had earned their freedom by serving in the Confederate Army from returning to the CSA proper. Of course the politicians couldn't get away with giving something like that to negro veterans without offering better to whites. Case also had a land grant, and word was it was twice as big as what a negro got, though still not very large—seven acres. Case wondered what he'd do with it.

Live on it, with my child and the woman I love.

Cuba's unique political situation also afforded Case a unique opportunity. One of the reasons the CSA had made the island a commonwealth instead of annexing it outright was because there were so many free negroes and mulattos on the island. Whites, had been intermixing with natives and slaves for so long that an enormous percentage of the population had some sort of mixed heritage. Making Cuba a commonwealth allowed the Confederacy to keep such a population from becoming a part of its territory proper. It also kept Cuba's marriage laws intact and outside the Confederacy's national ban on interracial marriage. Jeff sighed. He wouldn't go to prison, but he would still pay a price.

As he made his way through the streets of Biloxi his uniform (he still hadn't obtained civilian clothes), his Purple Heart, his Southern Cross and most of all his limp earned him the admiration and accolades of virtually everyone he passed. Men tipped their hats or shook his hand. Women and girls curtsied. Young boys came to attention and saluted him. Biloxi was a patriotic city. Even though the war had officially been over for a month an unusually large number of Blood Stained Banners and Confederate Battle Flags continued to fly. City Hall was still decked out in white and red patriotic bunting.

"God bless you!"

"Well done young man!"

When one older gentleman shook his hand he pressed something cold and hard into it before walking away. Case opened his hand to see John C. Calhoun's fierce countenance staring up at him from a large gold coin. As he pocketed the twenty-dollar gold piece, he found himself wondering how these people would treat him if they'd known he'd fathered a child with a mulatto girl and planned on marrying her.

No, I don't have to wonder... I know.

He made his way out of the city, and along the beach towards the spot where Ellie kept her clothing stand. Sure enough, it was standing right where it always had. A moment later he spotted Ellie herself busily packing up her stand for the day and stowing it and the merchandise onto a cart that was hitched to a horse. Ahead in the western horizon the sun was getting low. Ellie was so busy packing up her small business for the day that she failed to notice him as he approached. That suited Jeff just fine. He wanted her surprised, and it gave him a moment to admire her beauty, a beauty that in spite of everything he'd ever been taught and raised with, had struck to the deepest depths of his heart and soul. To Jeff she had the face of an angel. Her long hair was like black silk. Her lightly colored skin was the precise color of cream and coffee.

"Excuse me mam but would you happen to have any hats?"

Like lightning she turned to face him. The look of joy and surprise on her face was worth the world to him.

"Jeff! Baby!" she cried and all but leapt into his waiting arms. He let his cane fall so that he could catch her. Fresh pain shot down his wounded leg but the pleasure of holding her again at last masked it. Their lips came together in a deep passionate kiss. Neither of them wanted to let go, neither of them wanted it to end. Jeff's leg had other plans. It collapsed under him and his butt hit the sand hard.

"Oh baby! Are you okay?" she said kneeling to help him.

"I am now, darlin'. I am now." He took hold of his cane and let her help him back to his feet. It was only then that he noticed.

She's thin...could...

His thoughts got no farther, for the sudden sound of a baby's cry reached his ears. Ellie smiled.

"Come on Jeff," let me introduce you to your son."

With his heart pounding, Jeff watched as she stooped down behind the stand and came back up with a teeny tiny baby swaddled in blanket. She carried him over to Jeff, and pulled back the blanket so he could have a look at him. To Jeff's astonishment he was of an even lighter complexion than his mother. His hair was still jet black, but unless he changed dramatically as he aged Case was fairly certain he'd be able to pass for a full white. In the world in which they lived that would be a blessing.

"He was an impatient boy," she said smiling. "Just like his father. He came a month early."

"He's so tiny...what's his name?" asked Jeff transfixed upon his boy.

She smiled.

"Jeff after you. Reuel after my father."

Jeff caressed his son's face lightly with his finger and the babe reached out and clasped it with his small hand. Now Ellie smiled.

"Here you hold him while I finish packing up!"

Jeff set aside his cane and hesitantly accepted the baby, holding him as he would a fragile piece of crystal.

"Relax baby it's just a baby."

A short while later, the small family made their way back to Ellie's cabin as the sun set below the horizon. Wounded leg or not Jeff insisted on stabling the horse and securing the wagon while Ellie took the baby inside. At last he climbed the steps of the front porch and pushed his way through the front door. The sun had now fully set and the small one room cabin was lit only by a small kerosene lamp.

Ellie had put little Jeff to bed in a small crib in the corner. She turned to face Jeff and raised her finger to her mouth and made a slight *shush* sound. Without a word she walked to the bed, pulled back covers, and turned to face him. His heart pounded and his body trembled. They'd been parted from each other for over eight months. For all that time he'd thought about her every day and every night.

She slowly and calmly bore herself to him letting her dress and undergarments fall to the floor. He gazed transfixed upon her feminine beauty. She extinguished the lamp then made her way to him in the darkness. She took his cane and put it aside. He took her in his arms and they kissed passionately and deeply. She slowly helped him out of his uniform and to the bed where they took one another fiercely—making love in a storm of romantic passion. Later as he lay there in the stillness of the night, the woman he loved in his arms, and her face buried in his chest, Jeff's thoughts went to the future. He had the funds to get his small family to Cuba. Once there he and Ellie could finally get married. Even though he'd been discharged he would receive a small stipend from the Confederate government for the rest of his life because of his disabled leg. He thought about his parents. He'd begun to compose a letter telling them everything. He planned on finishing it and posting it in the morning. He doubted he'd ever hear from them again. Most of all he thought about the baby sleeping quietly and peacefully only a few feet away. Little Jeff was oblivious to the world and its troubles and Jeff envied his son's innocence. He feared that all too soon the child would learn just how cruel and unfair the world could be. And yet Jeff felt that there was hope. For the first time with official sanction, blacks and whites had fought together for the Confederacy. Jeff knew that he owed his life to black soldiers who'd helped storm the beaches of Havana and to those who helped assault the bloody slopes of Kettle Hill. He held out hope that with all the Confederacy's problems one day blacks and whites would be able to live together in both peace and equality. He knew it wouldn't be easy and he knew it wouldn't be quick. He hoped nonetheless. He even dared to hope, that one day, his parents might forgive him, and more than that open their hearts to Ellie and to little Jeff, who was, whether they accepted it or not, their own flesh and blood.

Jeff kissed Ellie tenderly on the head, held her tightly to himself and slowly drifted into the most peaceful sleep he'd ever known.

THE END

We hope you have enjoyed reading Reaping the Whirlwind. The author welcomes comments and feedback. Check out www.billybennettbooks.wordpress.com for information on alternate history, science fiction, and upcoming novels. Billy Bennett's next book in this series will be called: Flags and Glory and will pick up the story in 1914, when the entire world goes to war.

17488261R00247

Printed in Great Britain
by Amazon